"Hide — Run — Hide!"

"Men here—killing us—killing us—" The squadron of Lanthian soldiers, clad in the green and gold of the Ducal Guards, displayed little interest in their inhuman victims, as they advanced toward Terrs.

He waited for them, the sword that he still carried uplifted in readiness. His expression was icy and merciless, and once again Verran thought, *Fal Grizhni*.

Sparing a glance for the white bodies littering the floor of the cave, he inquired, with deadly calm, "Are you still so anxious for me to learn the ways of humanity, Mother?"

The Sorcerer's Heir

လလလလ

Praise for *The Sorcerer's Lady*:

"An energetic tale told with great verve and dash."

—Meredith Ann Pierce,
author of *The Darkangel*

"Heart-gripping . . . refreshing . . . masterful!"

—Marvin Kaye,
author of *Ghosts of Night and Morning*

Ace books by Paula Volsky

THE LUCK OF RELIAN KRU
THE SORCERER'S LADY
THE SORCERER'S HEIR

THE SORCERER'S HEIR

PAULA VOLSKY

ACE BOOKS, NEW YORK

This book is an Ace original edition,
and has never been previously published.

THE SORCERER'S HEIR

An Ace Book / published by arrangement with
the author

PRINTING HISTORY
Ace edition / June 1988

ISBN: 0-441-77231-5

Ace Books are published by The Berkley Publishing Group,
200 Madison Avenue, New York, New York 10016.
The name "ACE" and the "A" logo
are trademarks belonging to Charter Communications, Inc.

PRINTED IN THE UNITED STATES OF AMERICA

10 9 8 7 6 5 4 3 2 1

Prologue

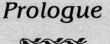

"Shall I meet my father tonight, Mother?"

"Terrs, your father is dead. You know that," Lady Verran replied.

"How can you be sure he's dead?"

"Only death could have kept him from joining us here."

"Can't I meet him anyway?"

"No. Try to understand. When someone's dead, then he's gone forever. That's what death means. You can't meet a dead person."

"Why can't I?" the little boy demanded. *"Everyone else does."*

Verran sighed. There were times when her son seemed scarcely human, and this was one of them. But was it any wonder? His seven years of life had been spent entirely underground among the Vardruls of the Nazara Sin. To the child, those odd white creatures represented the norm, and already he viewed himself as a misfit. She did not want to add to his unhappiness, but there were certain lessons he needed to learn. When she spoke, her voice was gentle. "Terrs, you're a human being. You're like the Vardruls and yet unlike. There are things they have that you don't have. You can't know the Ancestors as the Vardruls do."

"Yes I can. I can do anything I want if I try hard enough," the boy replied, and at that moment the resemblance to his father, the great savant Terrs Fal Grizhni, was uncanny.

"Listen, child—" Verran attempted diplomacy. "You should be proud you're a human being. There are lots of things that you can do that the Vardruls can't." Terrs looked skeptical and she continued. "For example, you can go Surface in daylight without damaging your eyes. You can endure low temperatures without lapsing into Cold Stupor—"

"I don't care about that, Mother! I just want to know my
Ancestors like everyone else!" Despite his vehemence the boy
spoke in subdued tones, for he had been enjoined to quiet at
the start of the excursion. "I *will* know my Ancestors, and feel
the—clan-warmth." *Clan-warmth* was a Lanthian approximation of the Vardrul term describing the powerful surge of affection, understanding and oneness that passed at a touch between
kinsmen.

"Terrs, look around you," Verran directed.

Terrs looked. He and his regrettably human mother, together
with their hybrid servant Nyd, marched in the midst of a sizable
party of Vardruls. The creatures moved in comparative silence.
Their musical conversation was muted, their personal luminosity low. They walked along a stone passageway that marked the
outermost limit of the Gravulan Extension of the caverns of
Nazara Sin. Caution was necessary, for the Gravula Wasteland
lay above them, and the Gravula was the domain of Man. Here
at the frontier of the Vardrul realm the rock-light failed. The
only source of illumination was the lambent flesh of the Vardruls
themselves. To Terrs, this luminosity was a comfortable and
familiar sight. To Verran, the spectacle remained eternally unsettling. The Vardruls were heavily fortified against the cold.
Ordinarily the heat and humidity of their caverns permitted
them the comfort of nudity. In this forsaken corridor, however,
even the great heating system created by the Cognition of Terrs
Fal Grizhni could not maintain an adequately high temperature.
The angular forms of the Vardruls were swathed in heavy
wraps. The nearly fleshless faces, with their huge, expressive
eyes, glowed beneath deep hoods. Such protection was essential, for even a minor loss of bodily heat could precipitate the
comatose state known as Cold Stupor, sometimes called "the
Little Death."

The Vardruls pushed forward eagerly. Perilous and unpleasant though the Gravulan Extension was, it provided sole subterranean access to the Granite Sages, those mysterious monoliths
that had brooded over the Wasteland since the beginning of
time. The Sages marked the traditional site of the ritual Knowledge of Ancestors.

"Tell me what you see," Verran requested.

Terrs had not yet mastered the art of description. "I see the
Extension," he replied uncertainly. "And I see—I see—" He
hesitated, then lapsed into singing Vardrul speech.

"Speak Lanthian," Verran interrupted with a hint of sharpness.

"I can't. The words aren't there."

"Yes they are, if you look for them. Speak as a human, Terrs—as your father spoke."

"I see," the boy floundered unhappily, "the—father—leader—uh, first one of the Zmadrc-group-that-is-one-and—and-all-are-bound-to-one-another."

"The Patriarch of the Zmadrc clan," Verran translated, with a glance at the Vardrul in question.

"He's leading us to the Granite Sages for the Knowledge of Ancestors. And his hiir—I mean, the way he shines—tells us that this place and the place up above are—are—" Human speech failed him again. *"Ruu Gravulani zmd fu krakweii Lahnziumi ni Ftva'ardhtruli fu—"*

"That the atmosphere of this place is more suitable to the humans of Lanthi Ume than to Vardruls." Seven years of life underground had given Verran a fair command of the Vardrul language.

"No, Mother, that's not all of it. He's telling us more, and you're not saying it all," Terrs objected.

"I'm saying enough." Verran controlled her frustration with difficulty.

The column stopped to rest and the Vardruls lowered themselves to reclining positions almost simultaneously. Verran, Nyd and Terrs were left standing. Terrs took a hopeful step toward the Zmadrc Patriarch.

"Wait, we're not finished," Verran remarked, and the boy paused reluctantly. She seated herself and patted the ground beside her. "Sit with me."

His face froze. "I'm not comfortable that way." The Vardruls never sat.

"All right, lie down then." He obeyed and lay regarding his mother with a wary expression that grieved her. For a moment she considered releasing him to join his friends. *No, he needs to learn.* "Look at the Vardruls, Terrs. See their glowing flesh, their great eyes, their boneless fingers. Now look at yourself and look at me." Terrs looked away. "Tell me what you see," she commanded. He did not speak, and she was forced to answer for him. "You see creatures with opaque skin, bony fingers, relatively small eyes. Creatures who cannot know their Ancestors. Hardly creatures of the light who need fresh air, wind and rain, the sea, and green growing things. Moonlight, stars, and sunshine—*sunshine,* Terrs!" Verran's feelings were running away with her and that wouldn't help the boy. "You see human beings. Not Vardruls. Humans."

Terrs perceived his mother's agitation and it upset him. Part of what she said was incomprehensible, but he understood enough to feel pain. Tears sprang to his eyes. "I don't want to be human. We're ugly!" the child observed, his voice still pitched low despite the intensity of his feelings. "Our faces are squashy. Our skin looks like dead people! We're the only ugly ones here, and I hate it—" He searched for human words to express the inferiority of beings incapable of knowing the Ancestors, failed to find them, and lapsed again into the Vardrul tongue. An emphatic tremolo combined with a rise in pitch communicated his misery in traditional Vardrul style. Had he possessed hiir, it would have been low and erratic.

Terrs now expressed himself in staccato melodic outbursts, too swift for his mother to follow. The tears spilled from his black eyes, adding to his discomfiture—for Vardruls did not cry. The boy turned away, and Verran stretched forth a hand to detain him. Her words had worsened matters and she wished to make amends.

"Don't cry, Terrs. Someday we'll leave this place, return to our own kind, and you'll never feel lonely again—"

He twisted away from her. "I won't leave. This is my place and I won't go. *And I'm not crying!"*

"I understand how you feel—"

"No you don't. Half the time you don't even know what I'm saying, so how could you understand how I feel? You don't really know what anyone's saying."

"Don't talk to me that way. I won't stand for it."

"I'm sorry."

"Terrs—"

The boy jumped to his feet. "I'm going to talk to my friends now." Before moving, he deliberately composed himself. The tears vanished and his face cleared. Even at the age of seven, his self-control was remarkable.

Like his father, Verran thought. *So much like his father.* Before she could utter another word he was off, threading his way through the recumbent ranks of Vardruls to the side of the Zmadrc Patriarch's only surviving female child, who lay among her kinsmen. The memory of her thirteen dead sisters was honored and preserved in the youngster's title of Zmadrc Fourteen. Just ten Great Vens old, sweet-voiced and vital, she was Terrs's favorite companion.

Verran watched uneasily as her son settled himself beside the Zmadrc clanmembers. He seemed so much at home among them, so much happier than he ever appeared in her company! As she looked on, the great black bat that rode the shoulder of the Zmadrc Lesser Patriarch hopped down to perch on Terrs' head briefly before taking to the air. Terrs joined in the laughter of his companions. It was not human laughter. The fluting, rhythmic trills sang weirdly through the passageway and Verran shivered.

"He sounds just like one of them," she observed aloud, and Nyd, who sat beside her, croaked in agreement. In the years following his flight from Lanthi Ume, Nyd had changed but little. His eyes and fangs were as sharp, his strength as formidable as ever. Verran couldn't guess the hybrid's natural lifespan, but his obvious vigor was reassuring. Nyd was the only companion of her Surface days. When he was gone, there would be nobody who shared her memories of Lanthi Ume and of Terrs Fal Grizhni. There would only be the dim, hot caves; the kind but alien Vardruls; and a boy who seemed less human with each passing day.

"I don't like to see him growing up here," she told Nyd. The hybrid could not follow all her thoughts, but it didn't matter—she knew he sympathized. "It was all right when he was a baby, but now he's getting older and he has no idea what it is to live as a human being. Oh, the Vardruls are kind, gentle, wonderfully generous. They saved our lives, they gave us a home, and I'll always be grateful. But we weren't meant to live out our entire lives underground. This isn't what Lord Grizhni would have wanted for his son." Nyd croaked mournfully at the sound of his creator's name. "And it certainly isn't what *I* want. At this rate he'll grow up to become—I don't know what."

She turned to encounter the gaze of the Zmadrc Lesser Patriarch. He caught her eye, and the triple ridges of muscle ringing his great eyes writhed at her. Clearly a message of some sort was intended, but Verran could not read it. She was familiar with most ordinary Vardrul expressions, but alien facial subtleties eluded her understanding.

The Vardrul leader rose and his kinsmen did likewise. The quiet trek resumed, not to be interrupted again.

Eventually the Extension angled sharply Surfacewards, a sure sign that the tunnel exit was nigh. The rocky walls were cold and bare. No sign here of rock-light, edible fungi, carvings, shadow-sculptures, or the many-colored vegetative slime species that lent such Vardrulesque beauty to the inhabited excavations. There was little to see, but Verran's excitement mounted quickly. In just another few moments she would be Surface again for the first time in—how long? A year? At least a Great Ven-and-a-half, she thought, and suddenly felt like crying. For the thousandth time, she considered the possibility of taking Terrs and Nyd, departing the caves and seeking safety elsewhere. *We can never return to Lanthi Ume, that's certain. Perhaps we could go to my mother's kin in Gard Lammis?* And stay with them—until her whereabouts were discovered by agents of the Duke of Lanthi Ume. For the Duke would not give up searching, she was convinced. Povon Dil Shonnet would never rest easy as long as he had reason to suspect that the widow and child of Fal Grizhni still lived. *He'd kill Terrs without a second thought if he got the chance. Whatever the cost, Terrs is safest right here.*

The Vardrul column halted. A few paces ahead the corridor ended in a wall of solid rock, or so it appeared. Having traveled this route in the past, Verran knew better.

The Zmadrc Patriarch applied tentacular fingers to half a dozen unmarked pressure points. The stone swung aside, revealing a flight of stairs which The Zmadrc climbed alone. The stairs led up to a chamber concealed within the greatest of the Granite Sages—the immense monolith known as the Master. This chamber served as a Vardrul observation post. The removal of various stone plugs permitted surveillance of the surrounding Gravula Wasteland. Now the Zmadrc Patriarch checked for the presence of human predators.

A very soft rumble overhead and a breath of fresh air informed Verran that the hidden portal in the Master's northern face had opened. The Zmadrc's voice lifted, crescendoed, died away. The Vardruls ascended in single file, passed through the belly of the Master and out onto open Surface.

Fresh air! Verran's lungs expanded and her spirits soared. Fresh, cold breezes; wide open space, stars overhead; and a full moon—a huge autumn moon whose light bathed all the desolate landscape in silver. Deserted and inhospitable the Wasteland was—too barren of soil, too jagged and flinty to support so much as a modest farmstead. But to Verran, the empty hills possessed a beauty that the most gorgeous fungoid-crystal gardens of the Vardruls could not hope to equal. The

wind was swift and cold to the point of discomfort, but it
breathed freedom. The habitual oppression of which she was
barely conscious receded as if carried off on the breezes. *Even
in this place, it feels right,* she thought. *It's Surface. Home.*
Beside her, Nyd hissed and his nostrils flared to catch remembered scents.

In the shadow of the monoliths glided the Vardruls, hooded
heads bowed and faces luminous as the Deadly Radiance fungus
that flourished in the innermost caverns. In silence the clanmembers ranged themselves about the perimeter of the stone circle.
The slight agitation of their loose garments bore testimony to
their mild distress. The Vardruls were shivering. It was cold
on Surface—painfully cold to those accustomed to a Cogni-
tively-maintained tropical clime, and a frightening environment
for beings subject to Cold Stupor.

Verran, Terrs and Nyd stood well apart from the others.
They could not take part in the ritual Knowledge of Ancestors.
It was only as a gesture of respect to Fal Grizhni that Grizhni's
widow and son had been invited to attend. Terrs had been
reluctant to come until he learned that The Zmadrc and Fourteen
would be there. Now the boy watched his friends longingly.

"Look, Terrs," Verran replied, pointing upwards. "You've
never seen a full moon before. And look over there at that
cluster of stars—that's the Lion constellation. Isn't it beautiful?"

"They're pretty," the boy agreed indifferently. "The ceiling
must be awfully high."

"Ceiling?" She smiled. "We're Surface, son. There *is* no
ceiling here."

"Then what's the moon attached to? And the stars?"

"They're not attached to anything, as far as I know."

"Then why don't they fall down?"

"That's a difficult question, actually. Things don't always
fall down, not everywhere. Your father could have told you—"

"There *must* be a ceiling, Mother. Every place has a ceiling.
If there's no ceiling, then where's the top?" She didn't answer,
and Terrs folded his arms. "I believe in the sky-ceiling. Even
though we can't see it, I know it must be there."

The Vardruls had deployed themselves. Motionless in their
dark wraps, they were nearly invisible save for the lucent faces
shining in the shadow of the Sages. The Zmadrc Lesser Patriarch
advanced to the center of the circle, mounted a large rock and
took his place between the two stone columns that crowned
the flat summit. The Zmadrc's ruu—the expression described

a Vardrul's state of self-knowledge and serenity, together with his relationship to kinsmen, to the environment and to the Ancestors—was in its most harmonic phase, and therefore he had been granted leadership of the expedition. His responsibilities included recitation of the traditional Preamble to Knowledge. The Knowledge of Ancestors, like all Vardrul ceremonies, was very simple and the Patriarch's remarks were brief. Translated into human speech, with unfamiliar concepts excised or modified, they would have run approximately:

"Once more we Vardruls tread the Surface, our original home. Once more we assemble at the Granite Sages, product of our Ancestors' art and oneness. We come to this hallowed place in darkness and in stealth, for we may not move freely over Surface as in times gone by. The land we once occupied is now ruled by Men. Humans build their cities upon the ruins of our cities, and the death-pools of our Ancestors are dry. In order to escape destruction, our Ancestors sought refuge underground, and there we flourished. Thus our beautiful caverns are at once the preservation and the prison of our race. There are those among us whose serenity is marred by hatred of usurping Man, and this hatred poisons our oneness. Let us abjure such disharmony, for it is not only injurious, but superfluous. It is prophesied that a great ruler will arise among us, and he will lead the Vardruls back to the Surface. We shall know when the time has come, for the skies will proclaim our ascendancy and the Surface will ready itself for our coming. All the forces of Nature will extend a welcome, Man will flee before us, we shall resume our rightful place, and the world will be restored to normalcy at last. Such is the prediction and such is the promise of our Ancestors. The Ancestors are with us now and always. Their wisdom sustains us and makes us one. Beloved kinsmen, let us know the Ancestors."

Thank-you, Zmadrc R'dsvyllsch, Verran thought resentfully. *You confirm my son's dislike of his own kind.* She glanced down at Terrs. The boy watched the proceedings with an unreadable expression inherited from his father.

Preternatural silence reigned as each Vardrul began the internal journey backward in time, farther and farther back along the chain of familial memory inherent in blood, bone and nerve. It was the Vardrul gift to direct vision inward and to follow this chain from generation to generation, but the talent varied according to the individual. The very young, or the merely unfortunate, knew only the Ancestors of the most recent generations. But a Patriarch like The Zmadrc, in a favorable state of ruu, could see as far as the primitive Ancestors who skulked through the corridors of the Nazara Sin, as wild and timid as the native bats. And sometimes, although it could have been fancy, The Zmadrc believed he traveled all the way back to the creators of the Granite Sages to greet shining figures who walked without fear beneath the starry skies.

Verran forgot her resentment and her misgivings as she watched. The Vardruls concentrated devotedly. Their faces were blank, with ocular bands relaxed. It was in the fluctuations of hiir that the intensity of effort revealed itself. At first the creatures flickered like draft-stricken candles. Then, as the Ancestors were encountered and known, the flickering gradually ceased. The collective hiir leaped and, one by one, the Vardrul faces lightened to extraordinary brilliance. A slight sound beside her caused Verran to look down at her son. Terrs was breathing very fast and his face was no longer unreadable. He gazed upon the Vardrul circle with an expression of undisguised yearning. Verran placed a consoling hand upon his shoulder, but the boy did not seem to notice.

The Vardruls had all attained knowledge and now they shone like a ring of fire in the night. The circle of statue-still, darkshrouded figures with lambent faces—the ancient monoliths, the full moon overhead—presented a rare spectacle, and Verran realized that she and Terrs might be the only human beings ever to behold it. Her attention was diverted by a quivering beneath the hand that still rested on her son's shoulder. She looked down and as she turned to him, Terrs bolted. She was too startled to restrain him.

Terrs hurled himself straight forward, full into the circle of the Vardruls. If he expected a response to his intrusion he was disappointed, for the clanmembers were unconscious of his presence. The Knowledge of Ancestors continued, untroubled by so much as a flickering of hiir. Terrs gazed around him wide-eyed, as if abashed by the effrontery of his own action.

"Terrs, come back here. *Now*." Verran hissed. Her son did not move. "I said come back here—*this instant!*"

Terrs ignored her. For a moment longer he hesitated in obvious confusion, then dashed to the foot of the great rock atop which the Zmadrc Lesser Patriarch towered like the phosphorescent image of a god. "Zmadrc R'dsvyllsch, help me know my Ancestors," the boy pleaded in his high, childish voice. "Help me know my father, the Fal Grizhni Patriach. I'm a Vardrul too!"

His pleas went unanswered and Terrs turned blindly from the rock. "I'll prove it, then. I'll know my father. I *can* do it!" The child took a deep breath and strove unsuccessfully to compose himself. He managed to calm his ragged breath, but his hands shook with excitement and nervous tension. Terrs assumed an erect stance in conscious imitation of those around him. His black eyes squeezed shut and he concentrated with all the power of his young mind. His small fists clenched, his face contorted and the sweat started out on his brow. The will of Grizhni's son was precociously strong, but hardly sufficient to overcome the limitations of human physiology. For grim minutes his struggle continued until the first tears oozed from the corners of his eyes. His concentration faltered, and he fought furiously to regain it. Terrs gritted his teeth and his whole body stiffened with effort, but the Ancestors maintained their silence. Presently his head began to ache, and his concentration broke disastrously. He recognized his defeat, and the uncontrollable tears slid down his cheeks, adding to his humiliation.

Verran, who had watched in painful pity, turned to Nyd. "Perhaps he'll be able to understand now. Take him out of there, Nyd." The hybrid bounded forward.

But Terrs was not finished. "All right, I can't do it alone yet," the child muttered. "I still need help." He cast his eyes around the glowing circle, then turned once more to face The Zmadrc, and cried out at the top of his lungs, "Zmadrc R'dsvyllsch!" His voice, astonishingly loud, bounced back and forth among the monoliths and echoed out over the empty hillocks of the Gravula Wasteland. The Vardruls did not hear it. Again he lifted his voice and again he went unnoticed. Thwarted desire and intense excitement had paralyzed the child's judgment. To the horror of his watching mother, Terrs launched a sudden assault on the great rock, clambered up to the flat top and ran to The Zmadrc's side. "Show me how to know the Ancestors," he begged, demanded.

"Terrs, stop it! *Get out of there!*" Verran commanded ineffectually. It was doubtful that he even heard her.

"I know I can do it if only you show me!" Terrs argued, and went so far in his abandon as to jog the Vardrul's arm urgently.

The Zmadrc's hiir altered and his face dimmed. For a moment, awareness seemed to invade his pale eyes, and the ocular bands contracted. Then his hiir flared like a torch as he strove with all his mental power to reestablish the tenuous, imperilled connection with the Ancestor. But the distraught human child was impossible to ignore and The Zmadrc's efforts failed. Gradually the brilliance faded from his flesh and normal expression returned to his eyes. The tie was roughly broken and Ancestral Knowledge lost. In shocked silence The Zmadrc stared down at Terrs.

The distraction of their Patriarch affected most members of the Zmadrc clan, and many Vardrul faces reflected an ominous flicker that signalled the weakening of the Ancestral bond. In several cases the failure of concentration was critical, and contact with the Ancestors was broken. The distressed Zmadrc kinsmen warbled softly among themselves.

All at once Terrs realized what he had done. His clamor ceased and he froze, staring open-mouthed up at The Zmadrc. His face suffused with a flush of deepest shame and guilt. Even in the moonlight the darkening of his cheeks was obvious and it flitted through the mind of his watching mother that Terrs had finally approximated an alteration in hiir. "I'm sorry." The boy offered his wretched apology in a whisper and then spoke up in a shaky voice intended to reach all the clanmembers he had offended. He lifted his chin. "I didn't mean to ruin it. Zmadrc R'dsvyllsch, I'm sorry."

Verran didn't catch the Patriarch's reply, which was soft and low. Nor could she quite interpret his expression as he bent to her son, but she recognized it as a look he often wore when addressing his own children. Terrs undulated his fingers in the Vardrul gesture of assent and climbed down slowly to surrender himself to Nyd, who waited at the foot of the rock. The boy took the hybrid's paw and together they walked from the circle. Terrs' head was bowed and his eyes were fixed on the ground, but he must have felt the Vardrul stares pressing upon him with an almost tangible force. As her son drew near, Verran saw that he was still crying. He had lost the fight to contain his tears, but his lips were tightly compressed and not a sound escaped him.

Her glance shifted to the Vardrul circle. Most of the participants had remained unconscious of the incident. Of the Zmadrc clan, many had already resumed Knowledge of Ancestors and their faces were once again radiant. But the Zmadrc Lesser Patriarch seemed to find it difficult to collect his faculties and so did his daughter Fourteen, who still gazed after Terrs.

Her son stood before her, his head drooping. "I'm not going

to punish you, Terrs," she told him evenly, "because I don't think there would be any point to it. The way you're feeling now is punishment enough. You understand what you've done, don't you?"

"Yes." He nodded, black eyes fixed on the ground.

"Do I have your promise that you will never, *never* do anything like this again?"

"Yes."

"And do you see now that you aren't a Vardrul, can never *be* a Vardrul?"

"No."

"What?"

"No, Mother." He raised his head at last to meet her eyes and she saw his pain and humiliation, but behind them there was steel. "I'll find a way to join and someday I'll know my Ancestors and they'll be my clan. I'm going to keep on trying."

"Child, you're not making any sense. Can't you see—"

"Mother," the boy interrupted, "what's Cognition?"

The question took her by surprise. "Why—Cognition is the power over objects and events employed by the savants of the Select of Lanthi Ume."

"My father was a savant of the Select."

"The greatest that ever was, Terrs."

"And the Men killed him."

She was silent. In recent years, fearing to poison the mind of her son, she had ceased her outcry against the murderers of Fal Grizhni. But it appeared that some damage had already been done.

"It was his writing that you brought from the city and used to teach me to read, wasn't it?"

Verran nodded uneasily. She now perceived the direction of his questions and didn't like it.

"Is there Cognition in my father's books?"

"Yes."

"Then I'll learn it and I'll use Cognition to let me know my Ancestors."

"You can't learn it." Verran spoke very calmly. "It's much too difficult, and—dangerous. In any event, there's no one here to help you with it and you can't learn it alone."

"I can. I will. You'll see." The boy was no longer crying. His face had hardened and he looked remarkably unchildlike. "I'm not giving up, Mother. I promise I'll never give up."

Chapter One

❧❧❧❧❧

They had blockaded the Sandivell Canal, and now *Sublimity* was trapped. The great venerise wallowed like a downed bird, pennants and silken sails a-droop. Her master, the Duke Povon Dil Shonnet, gazed out over the water and beheld a horde of angry citizens. This time his subjects had outdone themselves. A fleet of rafts, barges, dombuli, and sendilli clogged the mouth of the Sandivell. The small crafts swarmed with citizens, all of them attired in deepest black, their faces concealed behind death's-head masks. Similarly clad citizens—hundreds of them—lined the docks and moorings. Although the sun had not yet set, they carried lighted lanterns and candles. Deathly silence brooded over all. The Lanthians were nothing if not imaginative.

The Duke Povon nibbled a handful of sugared nuts and eyed his people without affection. "What do they want of me?" he demanded. "My blood? My life?"

The questions were essentially rhetorical, for he had little confidence in his companions' ability to provide intelligent reply. One did not, for example, expect much insight on the part of Lord Beskot Kor Malifon. Not that Beskot wasn't a good fellow—his fetes, his pageants, his masked balls, were miracles of artistry and extravagance. He dressed to perfection, his mansion was splendid, and his latest venerise, *Golden Exaltation*, was nonpareil. The moonlit launching of *Golden Exaltation* two years previously had been a memorable occasion, complete with fireworks, musicians attired as grotesque shackled water-goblins, and a banquet for two hundred guests. Beskot's then-current mistress, a matched brace of Rhelish

13

funambulists, undraped and gilded to adorn the festivities, had
posed and cavorted upon the bowsprit. The spectacle had scan-
dalized half the city, and simultaneously introduced a short-
lived fad for rope-dancers among the more imitative rakes of
the court. Yes, Beskot Kor Malifon certainly possessed great
flair, tremendous style. But insight—no.

Then there was the Keldhaam Gnuxia, equally unpromising
as a source of counsel. Gnuxia, daughter to the Keldhar of
Gard Lammis, was an overwhelming virgin of some forty years.
Tall, erect, massive and brawny, grizzled of hair and grim of
jaw, she loomed like a monolith upon the parquet deck of
Sublimity. Beneath straight bold brows, her dark eyes beamed
ineffable disdain. Contempt broadened her fleshy nostrils and
curled her wide lips. Povon regarded the burly figure, the
determined stance, the amazonian biceps, the coarse, capable
hands, and he sighed. Some months earlier, when payment of
one of the largest of the many promissory notes held by the
Keldhar of Gard Lammis had fallen due, the Duke found himself
in more than ordinarily embarrassed circumstances. In order
to avoid inconveniencing his "esteemed cousin of Lanthi Ume,"
the Keldhar offered at that time to cancel the debt, provided
that the widowed Lanthian ruler take to his bosom the Keldhaam
Gnuxia, sans dowry and preferably sans delay. "For it is such
a union of two soft and loving hearts that paradoxically serves
to forge a bond of steel between our city-states—a bond that
shall never be severed, come famine, pestilence, or strife," the
Keldhar had written with characteristic grandiloquence. It was
a sentiment open to a variety of interpretations, yet the Keldhar's
offer seemed to provide immediate relief and Povon found it
expedient to accept. His sense of deliverance evaporated at first
sight of his huge and graying betrothed. Upon closer acquaint-
ance the Kildhaam Gnuxia had revealed a domineering character
and a bitter tongue. Povon now viewed the prospect of marriage
with reluctance amounting to revulsion. Many and ingenious
were the stratagems whereby he had postoned the inevitable.
There was no escape, however, and the passing days bore him
toward the altar as inexorably as the tumbril carries the prisoner
to his death.

The remaining guest was perhaps the least promising of them
all. Lord Sneever Dil Shonnet, sole son to the Duke, stood at
his father's elbow—too close, in Povon's opinion. One never
knew which of Sneever's innumerable maladies might prove

contagious. Sneever had spent his entire life in a state of continual dyspepsia. Owing to multifarious allergies, his nose was perpetually runny, and his phlegmy bark of a cough was chronic. Duke Povon loathed the sound of that cough. Sneever was undersize, scrawny, rickety, and ramshackle. The blue veins crawled like worms across the backs of his hands, and at the age of twenty-seven, he was losing his hair. His complexion was pallid and his great protuberant blue eyes were always filled with fear or something worse. A tentative, too-frequent smile—a twitching eyelid—a countertenor voice—and an anxiously ingratiating manner completed the picture of a most unpromising heir apparent. Thus it came as a surprise when Sneever answered his father.

"They want bread, your Grace."

"Can't they go out and work for it like decent men?"

"They claim that wages are low and unemployment is rife. They cite the recent increases in the price of food and fuel. They are hungry and cold, your Grace."

"And must they blame me for that?" the Duke complained. "Why don't they take their grievances to the greedy merchants that are responsible?"

"They look to their ruler for help in times of distress, your Grace."

"You are naive, boy. You should stick to your amusements, if you have any, and leave politics to those who understand the game. Those pampered malingerers out there don't seek assistance. They desire a scapegoat and they have selected me, their Duke, to serve that purpose. Shall the Duke of Lanthi Ume perish, a sacrifice upon the altar of his subjects' greed? Oh, these are degenerate days!"

"Degenerate indeed, Betrothed." The Keldhaam Gnuxia's tone and expression transformed what might have been an endearment into a term of opprobrium. "Degenerate days, degenerate populace, degenerate city. Degenerate and chaotic. Let me assure you it is not so in Gard Lammis. In Gard Lammis the populace, being properly governed, knows its duty. In Gard Lammis the mob is not permitted to run wild. My father, his Splendor the Keldhar, would not suffer it. The Keldhar of Gard Lammis is accorded at all times the deference that his rank and his person merit. Thus it is with a born ruler."

Father and son, although acutely dissimilar, bestowed identical glances of dislike upon the Keldhaam Gnuxia.

Before them the theatrics continued, as citizens aboard a centrally located raft produced the effigy of a human corpse. The long figure was shrouded in a black pall and weighted at the ankles with an iron chain and a cannonball. Around the neck hung a placard inscribed, THE HONOR OF LANTHI UME. Amid much ceremony, the effigy was heaved overboard to sink in the Sandivell Canal. Oddly enough, the silence remained unbroken. The black-draped Lanthians were mute behind their skeletal masks, and the effect was unnerving.

The Duke's plump face flushed and he drummed his ring-laden fingers upon the deck railing. "They go too far," his Grace muttered. "If only Kronil and his Guardsmen were here!"

"Why are they not here?" Gnuxia demanded, and folded her muscular arms. "The Guardsmen of the Keldhar attend upon his Splendor at all times. Such is their devotion to their lord. Have your Lanthians forgotten the concept of personal loyalty? Did they ever know it at all?"

A second effigy appeared. This time the figure was short and plump. Its placard read THE DUKE'S HONOR. The effigy hit the water with a splash, and Duke Povon began to chew his varnished nails. "Murderers," he whispered. "Savages. What do you want? Will you be satisfied with nothing less than my life?"

"You are afraid." Gnuxia's contempt waxed visibly. "The ruler of all Lanthi Ume and you are afraid. Why do you not whip these curs home to their kennel?"

"You do not comprehend these matters, Keldhaam."

"I comprehend them perfectly. Am I a daughter of Gard Lammis for nothing? It is your own understanding that is faulty. Ah, his Splendor knew not what he did in consigning me to Lanthi Ume!"

"Woman, have you no inkling of diplomacy?" the Duke demanded.

"Ha! Diplomacy I understand—cowardice, never. And I pray that our union may never be cursed with offspring. Betrothed, lest you sire a race of cravens similar to yourself and to—*that*.'' She jerked a contemptuous thumb at Sneever, without bothering to turn her head. Sneever flushed deeply and his eyelid twitched.

"Should Fortune in her charity bestow fertility upon a bride whose years merit nothing less than veneration, I shall consider myself blessed," the Duke murmured, and Gnuxia glared at him.

A few yards away the black-swathed citizens conferred. Povon watched uneasily. "They do not trouble to disguise their intentions—they foment revolution," he opined. "Those madmen will tear this city apart. Is there nothing to be done? Is there no help to be had?"

A grunt of disgust escaped the Keldhaam Gnuxia, but Beskot Kor Malifon spoke up with praiseworthy solicitude. "Perhaps I can help, your Grace." Another surprise. Duke Povon turned to him eagerly. "I'm carrying a quantity of Sny's Ambrosia," Beskot explained. "An exquisite essence—exquisite. Almost as perfect, in its own way, as the Moon Dream of Uhanna, although perhaps deriving some intensity at the expense of subtlety. Does your Grace know the Ambrosia?"

Povon shook his head.

"Sny's Ambrosia will banish doubts, strengthen the spirit, and fire the heart with courage. I'm told the formula was discovered among the personal effects of—let me see, who was it? Used to be famous. I never can remember the names of those savant fellows. Half of them aren't even well born, and who can pronounce with dignity the names of the Commons? They all sound like pigs grunting. Oh, yes, I recall, of course—it was Saxas Gless Vallage. Nothing wrong with *that* name. An old and noble family, gentlemen all. Your Grace recalls Saxas Gless Vallage?"

"Of course I remember my friend Saxas," the Duke replied feelingly. "He presented me with this venerise *Sublimity,* and his essences were marvelous. A pity he's not here now—his Cognition would have served us well at a time like this. If there were any justice in the world, Saxas would have assumed leadership of the Select, for he was a loyal friend to his Duke. The same cannot be said of that contentious upstart Preeminence Jinzin Farni. But even Farni's preferable to his predecessor." The Duke paused to shudder briefly, unwilling to contemplate, much less pronounce, the name of his great long-dead enemy, Preeminence Terrs Fal Grizhni. "I should like to sample your Sny's Ambrosia at once. As your Duke I am oppressed with burdens heavier than any mortal man should be called upon to bear, and I must have solace."

"Artificial solace to foster artificial courage." The Keldhaam Gnuxia turned her back on him. The others strove to ignore her.

"My privilege, your Grace." Beskot dug into his pocket and withdrew a metal box and a tiny spoon, which he proffered to the eager Duke. "Use it sparingly."

Povon snapped open the lid of the box, which contained a thick greenish unction with an iridescent sheen. He dipped in, removed a heaping spoonful, and swallowed. "Odd flavor, but not unpleasant." He dipped his spoon again and took a second swallow.

"One taste should be sufficient," Beskot advised, but it was unclear whether the Duke heard him.

"Whatever happened to the Cognizant Saxas Gless Vallage?" Sneever Dil Shonnet inquired curiously. "Is he dead?"

"Loony as a rutting Swamp-Splatter these seventeen years. They've got him chained to the wall in a freezing damp cellar at Vallage House. Sub canal. I think his family keeps hoping he'll take a chill and die, but his constitution defies their efforts. Poor fellow. Tragic." The Duke frowned absently. "I don't feel anything yet. How long does it take? I shouldn't have to wait." He took a third swallow of Sny's Ambrosia.

"What was the cause of his affliction?"

Povon shrugged. "Who can say? In any case, this isn't the moment to discuss it. Our lives are in danger. Look." He pointed with a shaking hand.

A small flotilla of sendilli had detached iteself from the main fleet and now bore down upon *Sublimity*. The commoners seated in the boats appeared reassuringly civilized. They had set aside their masks. One of them signaled with a blue flag.

"Why are they waving rags at us?" Beskot Kor Malifon inquired.

"They desire a parley," Sneever explained.

"Does a ruler parley with animals?" demanded Gnuxia. "It is not so in Gard Lammis."

"Nor is it so in Lanthi Ume, Keldhaam." The outcome might have been far different had the Duke ingested less Ambrosia. Povon's expression changed as the drug took him. His pupils dilated and his eyes caught fire. Turning to the helmsman, he rapped out orders with sudden, uncharacteristic decisiveness. "Essence of power." It was this command that authorized full use of the Cognitive features furnished the venerise by her creator, Saxas Gless Vallage. "To the Lureis, at top speed! Take her through!"

His companions exchanged glances of amazement.

"But the citizens, your Grace, are—"

"Take her through! Top speed! Top speed!"

The helmsman shrugged philosophically. The Duke's commands were obeyed. *Sublimity* gave a hitch and lifted herself partially out of the canal. She bounded forward at incredible speed and, skimming lightly over the surface of the water, rushed like a tidal wave upon the small boats and rafts that blocked her path. After a moment's disbelieving hesitation, most attempted to clear the way. The delegates in the sendilli plied their oars wildly, and *Sublimity* missed them by a hair. Shouts and cries of execration arose on all sides. Duke Povon ignored them. He stood poised at the bow of the boat like a chubby figurehead, with jaw outthrust and pupils so vastly expanded that the normally pale blue eyes appeared black.

Sublimity swept down on the blockade, and the dombuli fled before her. A few enraged spectators on the shore hurled rocks, to little effect. By the time the speeding venerise reached the mouth of the Sandivell, the water was almost clear. Only a few of the slower-moving rafts remained to bar the way. Duke Povon did not hesitate. "There," he commanded, pointing at a gap too small to admit the passage of a sendillis, much less of *Sublimity*. "Helmsman, let us fly!" He threw back his head and laughed in exhilaration.

Sublimity leaped forward. The raftsmen saw her coming, and most of them wisely threw themselves overboard to swim for the wharves. But those burdened with poor reflexes suffered. The reinforced keel of *Sublimity* struck the nearest raft, which cracked like a toy. Timbers split and snapped, Lanthian bodies flew through the air, and screams arose from water and from shore. Some of the raftsmen were dazed by the shock, unable to swim, and these unfortunates swiftly sank.

"They will learn with whom they deal," Povon declared, and his betrothed eyed him with unwonted interest.

Sublimity sliced a path through a cluster of doomed sendilli, bounced an inflated float aside, rammed one last barge and sank it. Then the water before her was clear of obstacles and the venerise whipped freely along Sandivell Canal, with green sails spread and golden rigging winking in the sunlight. Around her rose the polychrome towers, domes, and palaces of Lanthi Ume. The city was as glorious a sight as ever, despite the poverty and increasing despair of her citizens. Only the refuse polluting the once-spotless canals, and the crumbling masonry of a few of the glittering bridges, bore obvious testimony to the growing demoralization of great Lanthi Ume. It was doubtful, however, that Duke Povon ever paused to consider such disagreeable matters. It was doubtful that Duke Povon ever

paused to consider anything at all, for his personal diversions
were taxing. Deep thoughts rarely, if ever, troubled the ducal
mind, and the ducal conscience was wholly nonexistent. It was
therefore with some surprise that Beskot Kor Malifon observed
a frown of trouble cloud his ruler's brow. Following the Duke's
gaze he beheld a great heap of scorched stone, charred timber,
and twisted metal. *Sublimity* had reached the junction of the
Sandivell and Lureis canals. The blackened ruins were all that
remained of Grizhni Palace, and they had lain there undisturbed
for seventeen years. It was assumed that the bones of the Ducal
Guardsmen who had died in the great conflagration still lay
beneath the rubble. But no one knew for sure, for no one had
ever attempted to exhume them. If the bones of the Guardsmen rested there, then with them lay the bones of Terrs Fal
Grizhni himself, who had died along with his enemies. And
surely the spirt of the greatest savant the Select had ever produced lingered beside the mortal remains. Even the relatives
of the slain Guardsmen dared not risk disturbing the bones of
Fal Grizhni. Even the thieves of the city, who might well have
discovered remnants of the silver that once sheathed the palace
dome, left the spot alone.

Povon shrugged uneasily and turned his back on the ruins.
Sublimity flashed by the remains of Grizhni Palace, veered
slightly, and entered the Lureis Canal. Past the parks and palaces
she sped; past the fashionable Prendivet Saunter, lately become
the favorite haunt of a growing population of pickpockets; and
past the Skrevulis Fountains, known to local wags as the
Scrofulous Fountains, owing to the assortment of beggars wont
to congregate upon the premises. Povon shook his head in
disapproval. It was high time that he drafted an ordinance
banning mendicants from the Skrevulis Fountains, perhaps from
the banks of the Lureis itself. Their presence blighted an otherwise splendid area.

Sublimity anchored in the shadow of the ponderous Ducal
Palace. One of her boats carried the Duke and his guests to
the gilded moorings. Povon glanced around him. The Lureis
appeared tranquil. His disgruntled subjects would not presume
to follow him as far as the palace—at least, not today. Povon's
dilated eyes beamed triumph. His short-lived satisfaction was
marred by the delivery of a message from the helmsman an-
nouncing the death of one of the condemned felons whose life
forces powered the venerise.

"Install a replacement, then," the Duke snapped, and took

a couple of additional swallows of Sny's Ambrosia to soothe his chafed nerves. Annoyance ebbed, and the world itself receded. Roseate fog softened the city skyline. Sweet fragrance blotted out the summertime stench of the filth-laden canals. Contentment flooded every vein. The sensation was delightful, and Povon paused to savor it. Through the haze he noted his companions observing him with respective curiosity, contempt, and concern.

"Beware the Ambrosia, your Grace," Beskot Kor Malifon warned. "A marvelous creation, to be sure, but ambitious of sovereignty. Like a woman, the most perfect of slaves, but given license, the cruelest of tyrants."

"I've no patience with your foolery, you porridge-brained popinjay," the Keldhaam Gnuxia declared.

Povon giggled. "My fair betrothed is right, Beskot. You malign the Ambrosia. I will not give ear to slander, and therefore you must leave me. All of you. Leave me." He turned on his heel and stumbled toward the palace. Beskot and Sneever seemed disposed to obey, but the Keldhaam Gnuxia was not so easily dismissed. Three long strides brought her level with her wavering intended. A hand descended upon the Duke's shoulder.

"The Guardsmen—do you not intend to call them out?" Gnuxia demanded.

"No need, Keldhaam," Povon replied in a slightly slurred voice.

"No need? No need? Are you stupid? Unruly subjects have defied and threatened you. Do you not intend to assert your authority?"

"Not now. I am much fatigued. We shall discuss the matter at another time." The Duke took a hopeful step toward the palace.

"No. Now. We'll discuss it *now*." Her voice rose and the Duke winced. "As your future consort, it is my duty to point out the deficiencies of your policies, and to correct your errors where I can. The situation as it now stands demands your prompt and forceful response. You've dealt too gently with your disorderly Lanthian Commons, but that must end. *I say it must end*. Where is your pride, Betrothed? Where is your strength, your manhood? Do you understand me? Answer. I insist that you answer."

The voice battered at Povon's head. The pastel haze lost something of its charm. Distressed, he snapped open the metal casket and once again dipped into Sny's Ambrosia.

"Put that away. Do not touch it again. You will scramble the few brains you possess, and I will not have it. I am not minded to tolerate this Lanthian depravity," Gnuxia declared.

It was impossible to ignore her, and Povon gave up trying. Out of the corner of his eye he saw Beskot and the wretched Sneever looking on in fascination. He lifted his chin. "I will not be deprived of my solace. As Duke, I am oppressed with every sort of care, and I am entitled to all comfort I can find." He raised the spoon to his lips.

Gnuxia struck the implement from his hand. Undeterred, Povon sank a finger into the gooey mass of Ambrosia, withdrew a gob, and sucked blissfully.

"*That's disgusting! Disgusting!* I won't have it! Stop that at once! Do you hear me?" Povon apeared deaf. Goaded beyond endurance, Gnuxia cuffed him sharply, and the spectators gasped. Startled by the sudden pain, Povon dropped the metal casket. Sny's Ambrosia hit the moorings, skidded over the edge, and into the Lureis Canal.

A cry of sorrow escaped the Duke, and he turned on his betrothed in a woozy fury. "Take care, Keldhaam. You go too far, and you are not beyond punishment. It lies within my power to govern an unruly woman."

"Pish, it hardly lies within your power to govern yourself. You stand in need less of a consort than of a keeper. But this is the role that Fate and his Splendor the Keldhar have chosen to assign me, and it is my duty to perform without discredit." She drew herself to her full height and stared down into his eyes. "As for your feeble threats, Betrothed, I scorn them. You would not dare to lift a hand against a daughter of Gard Lammis. A daughter of Gard Lammis does not permit herself to be used thus by a Lanthian. I defy you to attempt it. I defy you to face the wrath of my father, his Splendor the Keldhar, who will surely protect his own."

The fight went out of Duke Povon. With a hopeless shake of the head, he stumbled toward the palace. Her voice stopped him in his tracks.

"Wait. Our discussion is not concluded. Much remains to be settled. I will accompany you."

"You can hardly accompany me to my own apartment. Keld-haam."

"Nothing lies beyond the power of a woman of spirit. Betrothed. I say I will go. Six of my women shall attend to safeguard my honor."

"It wouldn't take nearly that many," the Duke muttered, and resumed his wobbling progress. Presently he reached his private suite and sought the sybaritic sanctuary of his bedchamber, where even the redoubtable Gnuxia and her warlike women dared not follow. Povon threw himself down upon satin cushions. His stomach churned and the room spun. He closed his eyes and sleep claimed him at once.

Sleep did not bring peace.

Povon dreamed. In the dream, he wandered among the ruins of Grizhni Palace, which lay black and smoking beneath a flame-colored sky. Around him rose a wilderness of charred rubble. The proud towers had toppled, the palace and its lord were fallen at last. This scene of desolation marked the Duke's triumph. But true happiness eluded him, as always. It was unfair. Even in sleep, he resented the injustice. Did contentment inevitably escape the great? Must he ever pay for the so-called gifts of birth, fortune, and intellect? Was there no end to victimization?

The ruins were oppressive, and Povon desired escape. Above all things he longed for the comfort and luxury of his beloved *Sublimity,* which lay at anchor on the Lureis Canal, but a short distance off to the right. Or was it the left? The Duke realized that he had lost his way. As he gazed about in confusion, the darkened stones that had lain at rest for seventeen years began to move. Slowly at first, and then with increasing speed, the ruined walls rebuilt themselves, rising higher and higher, arching overhead to block out the light of the fiery sky. Duke Povon found himself imprisoned. Stalactites dripped from the dungeon's ceiling, stalagmites rose from the floor, and reddish slime coated the walls. The atmosphere was tropically warm and humid. There were no windows and no door. In vain Povon pounded the walls and screamed for help. His exertions served only to attract the attention of a hideous companion.

Out of the shadows stepped a being such as Povon had never imagined. Tall and angular it was, with luminous white flesh, tentacular fingers, and huge inexpressibly alien eyes. For all its grisly appearance, however, the being did not seem violently inclined. It bestowed one brief, inscrutable glance upon the cowering Duke, its flesh brightened noticeably, then it turned its attention to a pile of rocks that lay in the middle of

the room. One by one, the creature rolled the stones aside,
until nothing remained but a heap of small loose rubble.

The rubble was quivering. Povon watched in dread, and
scarcely noted the silent discorporation of the white creature.
Gravel rattled, dust drifted, and a bloodstained human hand
dug its way to the surface. A black-clad arm followed. Povon
cast his eyes about the dungeon. There was nowhere to run,
nowhere to hide. He flattened himself against the wall. Before
him, a second arm slowly emerged. Then, amid much agitation
of stone and mortar, a tall figure rose from the grave.

And Povon beheld once more the pallid, rigid features of
his former nemesis, Preeminence Terrs Fal Grizhni. Grizhni—
alive again, albeit marked with the blood of a hundred wounds.
Grizhni—with his white, contemptuous face and his dreadful
eyes in which the dire knowledge glittered like frozen murder.
Fal Grizhni advanced.

Povon strove to cry out, but no sound escaped him. His
limbs were leaden, and he could not stir. He could only watch
in petrified fear as his foe approached, black-swathed arms
uplifting, white hands extended like talons, lips writhing to
shape inaudible Cognitive syllables . . .

Povon's terror found expression in a wild shriek, a shriek
that woke him. His screams continued for several seconds after
his eyes opened. The clamor was audible to the Keldhaam
Gnuxia, her women, and an assortment of household servants.
A couple of the domestics ran to the aid of their howling master.
They discovered the Duke sitting bolt upright among the satin
cushions, his eyes wide and bulging in a purple visage, his
hair soaked with sweat. It was with some difficulty that they
managed to calm him.

Awareness returned at last, leaving the Duke shaken, trembling, and somewhat ashamed of his recent panic. Assurances
of discretion on the part of the servants restored much of his
equanimity. Lanthi Ume would not hear of the ghastly episode
which was, after all, unlikely to recur. Never again, he promised
himself, would he pollute the ducal body with Sny's Ambrosia.
Never again would he experience another such appalling nightmare.

In this, the Duke soon found himself mistaken. The Ambrosia
was seen no more, but the dreams returned again and again to
fill his nights with horror.

Chapter Two

❧❧❧❧

Verran regarded the fungoid-crystal garden critically. "They're going to hate this," she observed.

Nyd tapped his talons upon the stone floor.

"Oh, yes. They'll find it most amazingly ugly. However, I don't care," she added without conviction.

Yet by human standards, the garden was beautiful—a great, kaleidoscopically intricate arrangement of black and green crystals interspersed with sapphire slime, laid out in polygonal beds whose regularity echoed the symmetry of the crystalline components. Tending her garden was one of Verran's chief occupations, and over the course of many Great Vens she had watched it grow from a meager patch of green crystals—chosen for their color reminiscent of Surface vegetation—to a glittering expanse that covered three-quarters of the floor of a sizable excavation. But the balanced formality so pleasing to the eyes of Lady Verran was alien to the Vardruls, whose gardens meandered with an irregularity similar to that of the caverns themselves. They demonstrated no outright disapproval—indeed, the Vardrul language possessed no notes exactly expressive of the human concept of disapproval—but their unobtrusive avoidance of the defaced excavation revealed their sense of profound disharmony. Verran felt it keenly, but the garden was one of the few sources of satisfaction in her life, and she could not bring herself to give it up.

"Think I should add some red accents at the outer vertices?" she inquired. Having little feeling for such matters, Nyd grunted noncommittally. It was clear that the hybrid, while anxious to please, couldn't have cared less about the fungoid-crystal gar-

den. Nyd's indifference was hardly surprising, but depressing
nonetheless, for it underscored the general futility of his lady's
activities. Even in Verran's own eyes, her varied diversions
appeared pathetically inconsequential. There was the garden,
her stone-carvings, and her weaving. There was her journal—
she still made regular entries, most of which lacked substance.
What was there to write about, after all? Her waking hours
were uniformly uneventful. A few times in the past she had
composed songs, rhymes, and stories for Terrs. It had seemed
important once that her son learn of Lanthi Ume and the world
of men. But attempts to chronicle Surface memories had
plunged her into black depression, and she had long since
abandoned such efforts. As for the songs and poems—once he
was past infancy, Terrs had shown no fondness for such things.
He far preferred Vardrul atonality, designed to counter the
harmony of Vardrul conversation, to simple Lanthian melody;
and the rhymes meant little to childish ears attuned to the
subtleties of Vardrul speech. So much for her writings.

What else was there? Well, there were the language lessons,
which arguably possessed some significance—or had done in
the past. For many Great Vens Verran had worked to increase
her command of the Vardrul tongue, and to some extent her
efforts had been successful. She could communicate effectively
with her inhuman hosts. She could with difficulty chant the
tongue-twisting syllables, make herself understood, and understand in turn the words of the Vardruls, most of the time. The
words—that was all. The words, but not the attitudes, the
reactions, or the emotions. That the Vardruls possessed feelings, and deep ones at that, Verran did not doubt, but she was
utterly at a loss to comprehend them. Vardrul reactions were
eternally mystifying. The impossible facial expressions, the
infinitely subtle variations in vocal pitch, the fluctuations of
hiir—these manifestations defied human analogy. Verran would
never understand them, and had long since accepted her own
limitations. Conversely, the Vardruls displayed no great affinity
for human speech. Verran had volunteered to tutor her hosts
in Lanthian, and the offer had been accepted. A period of
instruction had followed, and a few of the most persistent
among the younger cave-dwellers had more or less mastered
the rudiments of Lanthian syntax. One such accomplished scholar
was Terrs's friend, Zmadrc Fourteen—undoubtedly an intelligent and diligent youngster. But Vardrul attendance had fallen

off swiftly. Even Fourteen's interest had lapsed in time, and the lessons had ceased for want of students.

And what have you done since then that matters half a dakkle to anyone? she wondered.

I've been a good mother to Terrs. By all standards, that matters.

Does it really? Terrs is grown. He doesn't need a mother now, if indeed he ever did. And what's more—the thought came unbidden—*he doesn't want one.*

Not true. Not true at all. He knows I've cared for him and loved him all his life. That must mean something.

You love him, so he must love you, is that it? Think again. He's never really forgiven you for being human.

"This is getting ridiculous." Verran spoke aloud, and Nyd shot her a questioning glance out of his yellow eyes. "And it's unhealthy. I'm not going to think this way."

Are you not? Think you can control your own thoughts, you wretched woman? Go ahead and try it. I wish you the best of luck.

I can. I will. Verran's hands clenched in her lap. "Nyd," she said deliberately, "I've decided to add the red accents. What's more, I'm going to enlarge the entire garden. I'll have to plan out the pattern and color scheme, and it's going to require my full attention—"

No it won't. You could do it in your sleep. You don't distract yourself that easily. Better try harder.

"Also, I think I'm going to begin compiling a Lanthian/Vardrul dictionary. Such a thing might be useful."

To whom? The Vardruls don't read—or write either, unless you count those picture-things.

True, but someday human beings might use it.

Really? How? When?

I don't know. But it could happen, and I hope it does.

A cruel hope. If Man and Vardrul face one another, these gentle Vardruls will be annihilated. You know that.

I know nothing of the kind. It doesn't have to be true.

"If the Vardruls could speak to humans," she continued grimly, "then perhaps it would reduce their mutual fear. White Demons of the Caverns indeed! Now let's see—the only way to render the Vardrul language in writing would involve a combination of letters and musical notes. I could do that, but it still wouldn't convey the sense of the fluctuating hiir. Should

I invent a set of symbols representing degrees of luminosity, or would that be getting too complicated? What do you think, Nyd?"

Nyd had no opinion to offer on the subject.

"It will be an absorbing project. Terrs can be a great help, since he understands them so much better than I do. We can work on it together, perhaps it will bring us closer together—"

You're clutching at straws.

"I should have thought of this years ago."

Yes, but how many years? How many years have you spent underground? It's so hard to keep track down here—it's been so long, and lately so featureless. It must be twenty-four—no, twenty-five Great Vens, which works out to about seventeen years.

"Seventeen years!" she whispered, and something in the tone of her voice caused Nyd to whine anxiously. "Lord Grizhni dead these seventeen years. And Terrs is seventeen—the same age I was when I came to this place."

Which makes you thirty-four now. A middle-aged woman.

Odd, I don't feel middle-aged. I wonder how I look? I haven't really seen myself in all this time. The Vardrul caverns were devoid of mirrors, as the Vardruls themselves were devoid of personal vanity. Their aesthetic sense was well developed, and by human standards almost incomprehensible. While greatly appreciating the beauty of their own race, they attached little significance to minor physical differences among its individual members. To a Vardrul, all other Vardruls maintaining a favorable state of ruu appeared equally beautiful. Thus, no need of mirrors. Verran had glimpsed her reflection from time to time in the pools of tepid water that dotted the caverns, but such wavering images were unenlightening at best. Now she glanced down at herself. Her body, clad in its simple gray robe of hand-woven fiber, was slender and lithe as ever. The robe—or rather, the fact that she wore anything at all—was in that environment somewhat unusual. Owing to the warmth and humidity of their caves, the Vardruls habitually eschewed clothing. Fibrous coverings were more than superfluous, for they not only blocked acute dermal sensors, but also camouflaged variations in hiir, thus inhibiting a basic means of communication. But Verran could not bring herself to go naked. It was not simply a question of conventional modesty. Nudity, she had discovered to her discomfort, greatly accentuated the differences between herself and her hosts. On the few occasions, Great Vens earlier, that she had ventured to appear sans robe, she had found herself the object of unwelcome academic attention. Despite their innate courtesy, the Vardruls could not forbear studying the opaque human body so disturbingly like and unlike their own. Their regard had been analytical and utterly insupportable. Verran's instinctive reaction had been confirmed by the judgment of such notables as the Zmadrc and Lbavbsch Patriarchs, who had cited her own emotional turmoil, rather than the fact of her physical anomaly, as the source of disharmony. Terrs, though only a small child at the time, had stated the matter more succinctly. "We're freaks, Mother," he had observed. "Two ugly freaks. I want to hide." Since then Verran had always gone clothed, and Terrs did likewise, to this day.

Gray hair, yet? She took a strand of her own hair and examined it closely. Still long, still glossy, still the color of wild honey. Perhaps a little darker now, for the golden streaks once bleached by the sun had long since vanished. If any gray threads mingled there, they were invisible in the subdued rock-light.

And her face? She touched her cheek, her forehead, her temple. The flesh felt soft and smooth as ever. But still—"Thirty-four!" she said aloud, and Nyd croaked responsively. Verran studied the hybrid, who had not managed to escape the punishing hand of time. There could be no doubt about it—Nyd was old now, quite old. The wiry hair on his face and limbs was grizzled. His step had lost much of its elasticity, and his fangs had yellowed. But he remained active and alert as yet; and still the most devoted companion she had ever known.

"Don't die on me, my dear." She spoke in a consciously casual tone that the hybrid could not possibly interpret. "I don't think I could stand that."

But you'll have to stand it one day, perhaps not long from now. Sooner or later he'll be gone, and then what? Barring accident or disease, you've still a long life ahead of you—perhaps decades. Come, how do you plan to spend the next forty years or so?

I don't want another forty years in this place!

Unfortunate, because you've probably got them. Possibly more, as you come of long-lived stock. Remember Grandmother

*Deesquil, still strolling the Prendivet Saunter at age ninety-six?
Think of the decades to come, spent underground among the
Vardruls.*

I don't think I can manage it. I don't think I can. Verran
noted an odd constriction in her throat. Her breathing quickened. The sensation arising within her was one of panic.

I want the sunlight. Fresh air. Other people. Human beings.

*Calm yourself. It's not that bad down here. It's really not
that bad at all.*

I'm suffocating!

After seventeen years, you ought to be accustomed to it.

I'm not accustomed. It's getting worse.

Calm. Calm. Calm.

*I want other people to care about, and people to care about
me. Not like Terrs.* The thought intruded itself mercilessly.
He's more Vardrul than human anyway.

*No he isn't, he'd just like to be. What he is is his father all
over again. Stay calm.*

*I can't stay in this place for much longer. I'll go mad. I
don't care how comfortable and safe it is, how kind and gentle
the Vardruls are, how lucky I am to be alive at all. This place
is not for human beings. I can't stand a whole lifetime of it, I
can't stand it. I'd rather die now and end the misery, the
emptiness.*

Feeling tremendously sorry for yourself, aren't you?

What if I am? she thought resentfully. *It's not a crime.*

*No crime, just cowardice. Where's your breeding? You were
Fal Grizhni's lady. Act like it. Control yourself.*

"I will control myself." She turned to meet Nyd's yellow
gaze. Evidently the play of expressions over her face had troubled the hybrid, whose facial hair bristled uneasily. "It's all
right, Nyd. I'm fine."

Nyd croaked in sympathy.

"Don't worry. No need. Now we were talking about that
dictionary, weren't we?"

Nyd evinced little interest. Verran could not blame him. She
found it difficult herself to work up much enthusiasm for the
dictionary project.

It will help to pass the time.

"I wonder if it would be best to list the phrases alphabetically,
or according to musical pitch?"

Nyd patently did not comprehend the matter.

And why should he? What does it have to do with him—he's neither Man nor Vardrul. He may well be the last of his kind. Chances are his nestmates were all slaughtered when the Ducal Guards stormed Grizhni Palace seventeen years ago. Nyd is very likely the last surviving Grizhni hybrid, poor creature. And you thought you were lonely! He has far more cause.

"Nyd," she heard herself inquire, "do you remember our Surface days? Do you ever think of Lanthi Ume, Grizhni Palace, and Lord Grizhni?" She hated herself for asking. Ordinarily she did not permit herself to dwell on the past, the recollection of which contrasted too painfully with her present circumstances. But now she had fallen into the most insidious of mental traps, and worse, she had dragged Nyd in as well. It was unfair, downright cruel, to remind the hybrid of his vanished happiness, but the words had slipped out almost involuntarily.

A croak of grief escaped Nyd, and remorse stabbed Verran. "No, I'm sorry, don't think about it—"

But he would think about it now, and it was entirely her fault. He'd remember and he'd be miserable, unless she could find some way of distracting him. "Come, I've an idea," Verran suggested with tolerably convincing enthusiasm. "Let's go find Terrs. I haven't seen him since f'tvarjrii—" It was one of the few Vardrul expressions that had found its way into her ordinary conversation. The Vardruls, in tune with one another and with their environment, tended to awaken from sleep almost simultaneously. Periods of rest were measured in terms of Colorations; that is, the amount of time taken by a certain species of native slime to progress through its very regular cycle of transformation from red, to purple, to black. A small Ven comprised three Colorations. The passage of two hundred forty Small Vens amounted to a Great Ven, as measured by the liquid collected in the calibrated vessel placed beneath the Bleeding Stalactite. The relation of Vens to the alternations of light and darkness by which Surface-dwellers measured out their lives was unclear and probably inconsistent. The Vardrul term denoting the communal awakening that followed a period of rest of approximately one Coloration's duration was *f'tvarjrii*. Verran was wont to awaken from sleep at f'tvarjrii; so much harmony she had managed to achieve. Of late, however, she had taken to frequent napping. She wisely chose not to analyze the reasons for this. Had she done so, she would have been forced to acknowledge a desire to extend her periods of unconsciousness.

"He's likely to be reading," she continued, "and when he does that, he forgets to eat. Shall we go find Terrs?"

A dismal whine answered her.

"He's probably dizzy with hunger by now and doesn't even notice it. You know how he is. You don't want to let Terrs make himself sick, do you?" This plea appeared effective. Nyd hissed and his talons rattled vehemently. "Right. Come, my dear."

Together they traversed the rock-lit passages and excavations, long since grown as familiar as the corridors of vanished Grizhni Palace. At least this particular portion of the maze was familiar. No one, not even the Vardruls themselves, knew the caverns in their entirety. The system, which honeycombed the rock underlying the island of Dalyon, was unimaginably huge and convoluted—greater by far than most Surface-dwelling humans ever dreamed. The corridors were endless, the chambers numberless. This natural complexity had been enhanced by the engineering efforts of the inhabitants, who had enlarged and extended existing passageways, tunneled new corridors as appropriate and convenient, excavated new rooms as required. The artificial elaborations were fairly recent. For many generations—in fact, since the time of their original flight from Surface—the Vardruls had been confined to that relatively small section of the caverns wherein natural hot springs maintained the high temperatures essential to Vardrul activity. It was only the installation of Terrs Fal Grizhni's great Cognitively created heating system, some thirty-five years earlier, that had warmed the stony halls and opened up the entire network of tunnels to the Vardrul population. Now the creatures ranged freely through their subterranean domain. As their settlements expanded, their numbers and their confidence increased from Ven to Ven. Increasing strength and freedom, however, had not altered the timorous, retiring, and essentially gentle character of the Vardruls; nor had their concept of harmony of mind and of nature been affected as yet.

Verran observed with the acuity of vision that she consciously strove to maintain in the face of time, familiarity, and depressed spirits. Her surroundings were undoubtedly beautiful, in the alien Vardrul fashion. All around her diffuse rock-light played on and through the phalanxes of polished, translucent stalactites and stalagmites; on carven columns and on draperies of stone whose natural formation imitated the folds of fabric and the texture of lace; on crystalline growths whose purity of form and color put Surface flowers to shame; on rich curtains of vegetative slime; on dark bubbling pools ringed with snowy fungi; and on friezes of shadow-sculpture illustrating great events of the past. The Vardruls treasured these friezes more for the sake of their artistic merit than for their historical significance. Beings capable of knowing the Ancestors felt little real need of written or pictorial records. To Verran, the shadow-sculptures were in the main incomprehensible, for much of their meaning and all of their continuity was conveyed by means of certain hieroglyphs that the Vardruls seemed willing but unable to explain. Apparently, complete understanding depended on familiarity with the physical and emotional sensations associated with voluntary alteration of hiir. Moreover the sculptures themselves, with their seemingly senseless conventions of representation and their apparent lack of compositional balance, were distinctly unsettling to Lanthian sensibilities. Only one frieze had ever held the attention of Lady Verran, for it depicted the creation of Terrs Fal Grizhni's Cognitively fired heating system, and the scene was entirely recognizable. There was the power source itself, enclosed in a sealed box topped with four glinting hemispheres—an astonishingly small device in view of the vastness of the space that its influence rendered habitable; compact, self-contained, and designed to operate forever, if left undisturbed. And there was Fal Grizhni as he had been at that time—perceptibly younger than the savant that Lady Verran had married. The unknown artist had caught Grizhni's likeness well, from long, lean form, to elongated hands, to the bony structure of the face. Only the eyes were wrong, for the artist could not resist adding a hint of the Vardrul ocular musculature. But it was a good portrait nonetheless, and during her first two Great Vens of residence, Verran had been drawn to the frieze as if dragged there by invisible gaolers. Many and miserable were the Colorations that she had spent transfixed by her lost husband's image. At last her instinct of self-preservation had dictated an end to self-torture, and she had taken to avoiding the spot.

However, she was approaching it now.

The room in which Terrs could usually be found was called by a Vardrul term that translated quite directly to the human expression *Stronghold*. It was a very ancient place—that is, a small chamber of natural formation, unexcavated and undecorated, situated beneath the hills of the Nazara Sin in the oldest inhabited area of the caverns. The Stronghold formed a cul-de-sac at the end of a very narrow, twisting passageway. Access was fairly difficult, hence the title, which was nonetheless a misnomer by human standards. No solid portal guarded the entrance. Such things as gates, grates, bars, and locks were unknown in the Vardrul world. The curtains that veiled the entries of certain chambers had been hung to furnish privacy rather than protection. Vulnerability notwithstanding, the Stronghold was the repository in which the most treasured artifacts of the Vardruls were held. Among these artifacts rested the near-sacred relics of the Fal Grizhni Patriarch—the folio volume, parchment scroll, notebook, and plaque of gold that Verran and Nyd had carried during their flight from Lanthi Ume so many years ago. These isolated specimens of human writing had been used by Verran to teach her son to read, and since that time she'd had ample cause to regret her action. The information contained in his father's records had kindled the ambition of young Terrs, who had set himself the goal of mastering Cognition. For fifteen Great Vens, Grizhni's son had studied and striven. Frequent failure only served to strengthen his determination, and now he practiced incessantly. He had practically taken up residence in the Stronghold, and sometimes Verran did not see him for Small Vens on end. Her sympathy for his disappointments was balanced by an abiding fear of his success.

Along the wall to her left ran the frieze. Although she had not beheld it in Great Vens, the details remained etched indelibly in her mind. So clearly could she envision the scene that it was really not necessary to look. But partly out of curiosity and partly to gauge the accuracy of her own recollections, Verran turned her head to gaze once more upon her husband's bas-relief image in tones of black and gray. There he stood, the great Fal Grizhni, and she braced herself to withstand the inevitable stab of pain. It did not come, and she paused to analyze. Sadness, yes. Regret. The persistent ache of loss and longing. But the original fierce grief had subsided, and remaining sensations were comparatively dulled. *Strange,* she thought. *It's all beginning to seem unreal, like a dream, a warm dream. Another few Great Vens down here, and I'll begin to wonder if it ever really happened. It will be the existence of this sculpture, rather than the strength of my memory, that will confirm the reality of the past.* "And it will be wrong, because his eyes weren't like that," she concluded aloud.

Beside her Nyd hissed questioningly. Unaccustomed to the interpretation of visual symbols, his primitive mind had never recognized the connection between the monochromatic representation upon the wall of the cave and the long-dead Preeminence Fal Grizhni. He did not comprehend his lady's interest in shadow-sculptures.

"Nothing." Verran reassured him. "Let's go find Terrs."

They walked on, past Vardruls who accorded them the courteous, respectful, somewhat impersonal salutations reserved for the unalterably inharmonious. These well-intentioned greetings had depressed Verran ever since she had learned to recognize certain nuances of pitch. She returned them with what good grace she could muster, and quickened her pace. Nyd hopped and puffed to keep up. Soon they entered a twisting passage so narrow that they could not walk abreast; squeezed through a bottleneck so tight that the spikes of Nyd's ruff tapped the walls; passed under a curtain of fiber and into the Stronghold.

Terrs was there, reclining upon a slant and so absorbed in his studies that he failed to note her entrance. She took the opportunity to observe him, and was struck as always by the youth's ever-increasing resemblance to his father. There was the same tall, lean frame; the same coloring; the same strong, chiseled features; and above all, the same large, intensely dark eyes. The shape of the long fingers, the set of the shoulders, the sharp angle of the jaw line—all these were Grizhni's. But there were differences as well. Terrs still lacked a couple of inches of his father's height. He had not yet reached his full weight, and his figure was slim to the point of weediness. Where Fal Grizhni's carriage had been erect and rigid, his stance arrogant, his stride purposeful, young Terrs's movements and gestures possessed the fluid grace of the Vardruls. His facial features, while similar to those of Grizhni, were used very differently. The lifelong emulation of Vardrul forms had left its mark about the eyes and lips.

Unlike his father, the youth was clean-shaven. Only the frantic pleas of his mother had prevented him from plucking out his brows and eyelashes, and shaving the black locks from his head in imitation of his Vardrul companions' utter hairlessness. Verran's genuine distress had moved him. Even more influential, however, had been her reminder that the thick hair helped to camouflage the characteristically human outline of his skull. Given the choice between what he regarded as equally grotesque deformities, Terrs had elected for once to please his mother.

Nyd croaked a greeting and Terrs lifted his head. Verran observed with surprise that his face was slightly flushed. Color rarely touched those pale features never exposed to sunlight. His eyes were unwontedly bright, almost glittering, and at once she feared illness. Terrs had been sickly as a child, growing up underground and subsisting on a diet that sustained life but was never designed for humans. He had contracted all manner of exotic ailments to which the Vardrul youngsters were apparently immune. In latter Great Vens his health had improved, but his mother still worried. "Are you all right?" she inquired anxiously. "You look feverish." She extended a hand to touch his forehead, which proved cool and dry.

Her surprise increased to see him smiling as he rose from the slant. It was a more natural smile now than in the past, for Terrs had abandoned his early efforts to match the Vardrul facial expressions. Many Colorations of effort had at length taught him the impossibility of compensating for his own lack of certain essential ocular muscles. When he smiled now it was as a human, but he did so very infrequently. His habitually impassive expression masked a wintry gloom that his mother was powerless to alleviate.

"I'm well. You needn't worry, Mother. You either, Nyd. I'm very well indeed." He spoke perfect, unaccented Lanthian, but Vardrul influence revealed itself in the unusual rhythm and musicality of his speech. The effect was indefinably alien.

"Nyd and I were afraid you might be starving yourself to death in here," she replied, smiling in turn. "We thought we'd walk in on a skeleton. But I must admit, you're looking lively and happy."

"It shows, then?"

"What does? Has something happened?"

"Yes, something has happened at last. What is the best thing you can think of, Mother?"

It would involve leaving this place, she thought, but knew that could hardly be what her son had in mind. There could only be one, unwelcome, explanation for his unusual satisfaction. "This must have something to do with your studies. You've made progress, you feel you're approaching Cognition?"

"Approaching? I first achieved Cognition two Great Vens ago. I've been using it in small ways ever since."

Verran blinked. "I don't think you quite understand what I'm talking about. You've never seen it done, and—"

"Don't patronize me, Mother." Terrs owned all the natural impatience of any Surface-dwelling adolescent. "After fifteen Great Vens of study, do you think I don't know what Cognition is?"

His father's son in more than appearance. "I know you've read a great deal."

"You don't believe me. I'll prove it, then."

"That isn't necessary. Of course I believe you—"

"Watch." Terrs withdrew a small, colorless octahedral crystal from the pocket of his robe.

"What's that?"

"A Cognitive aid. It will help me to focus."

"Where did you get something like that?"

"Out of Zmadrc R'dsvyllsch's garden. It's ordinary crystal, there's nothing special about it. Any number of small objects might have served equally well. It's how I use it that's important. Now, watch." Terrs fixed an intent stare upon the crystal. He uttered soft words, and after a moment the crystal glowed. Verran repressed an exclamation. A hiss of recognition sizzled out of Nyd. Terrs, wholly absorbed in his work, ignored them both. He continued to speak in a voice almost inaudible, and presently a patch of incandescent red mist appeared out of nowhere to float in the air before him. The turbulent vapor thickened swiftly and condensed to form a three-dimensional character of flame-colored light.

Verran had seen something like it once before, many years earlier. "It's writing, isn't it?" she asked in wonder.

"Yes," Terrs replied. "In the Cognitive language invented by the Fal Grizhni Patriarch for the Select of Lanthi Ume, it means 'Greetings.' If I knew more, if I had more strength, then I could send it anywhere I wanted it to go. As it is, I cannot send it beyond this chamber. But that will change, in time."

Verran looked from the glowing symbol to her son's face. His eyes, alive as never before, were fixed upon his handiwork.

"Now do you see?" he asked softly.

I see only too well. Why must you do this? Beside her Nyd

croaked, and she could feel the intensity of his excitement. Her own mind was dark with misgivings. As she watched, the fiery symbol faded. When it was gone, she turned to Terrs and asked, "Why did you never tell me of this before? Something so important? You've been doing it for two Great Vens and you never even mentioned it?"

He took his time in answering. "I often thought of telling you. But you would have disapproved and complained, you'd have tried to persuade me to stop. I didn't want to hear it."

Is that the way he sees me? But after a moment's reflection, she had to concede his point. "Perhaps there's something in what you say. I might have tried to stop you, because I've always had a fear of Cognition. It's an art so unnatural—"

"No it isn't," Terrs interrupted forcefully. "You wouldn't say that if you only understood what Cognition really is. Nothing could be more natural. It's just a question of comprehension of various forces, total comprehension—"

"So your father claimed."

"Of course. So would any savant."

"But it couldn't save your father, and it was useless when he needed it most. He was certain—so very certain—that his powers would protect him from anything. He relied upon them absolutely, and in the end they failed him. That above all is why I fear and distrust Cognition."

"Only because you don't understand it," Terrs insisted. "As for my father, you cannot state with any certainty that a critical failure of his Cognitive powers resulted in his death. You cannot know that because you were not there to see it. To begin with, we have no absolute proof that he is dead at all."

"He is dead these seventeen years. Of that you may be certain."

Terrs looked down into her set face, hesitated an instant, then continued, "Very well, let us assume that he is dead. You are probably correct. But there is no evidence to support your contention that his death was linked to Cognitive failure. Even the strongest Cognition can break under sufficiently violent attack. Moreover, the power of even the greatest savant can exhaust itself temporarily, but that does not constitute failure. It is possible that the Grizhni Patriarch expended the greater portion of his Cognitive energies upon some significant project just prior to his death, thus leaving himself depleted and unusually vulnerable to his enemies. Would you grant that is possible?"

"It's possible, but there's no way of knowing." *Even his speech patterns remind me of Lord Grizhni.*

"Exactly my point. There's no way of knowing, no real evidence. Thus your distrust of Cognition cannot be rationally justified."

"Not to a boy who knows so little of the habits and needs of humanity."

"That, again? To my mind, I know more than enough. It is not an attractive species."

"Oh, how like your father you are! But at least he had experience, he'd observed mankind at first hand, and knew what he was talking about."

"As I do not, you would say. Well, we've argued that point many times. Let's not get into another quarrel. I won't say anything more about humanity, since it offends you. I'll only repeat that you are wrong about Cognition."

"You truly love it, don't you?"

"It's what I want to do, Mother. It's what I'm going to keep on doing. There's no point in trying to fight me." His expression was as chill and unyielding as his father's had ever been.

I daresay there isn't. That will is granite. Aloud, she replied, "I don't intend to fight you. Believe it or not, it's not my ambition in life to thwart you at every turn. But there's something I want to tell you, something you don't seem to realize. Don't look so suspicious. I only want to say how very proud of you I am."

"Proud?" His face relaxed slightly, but the eyes were still wary.

"Yes, proud of you for what you've done. I never believed you'd actually achieve Cognition. In view of your father's abilities, it's not surprising that you'd have been born with talent of your own. But learning how to use it down here in this place, all alone, with no savant to explain things, no texts or references other than Lord Grizhni's few records to guide you—it's an extraordinary accomplishment, and I admire you for it more than I can say."

His eyes and voice thawed. "Thank you, Mother. I didn't expect you to feel that way. But you give me too much credit. It wasn't as difficult as you imagine, for the Fal Grizhni Patriarch provided commentary so clear that no reader could fail to understand. And it's all so balanced, so interconnected, so—inevitable, once you see it properly."

"To you, since you have the mind for it. What you showed us just now—that writing in the air—was extraordinary."

"But that's a trifle, that's nothing," Terrs informed her. "I've been doing that for the past Great Ven and a half. It's scarcely worth mentioning. No, what has finally happened after all this time is that my Cognition has effected—how shall I put it—an important change."

"You mean, there's more?" She hoped she sounded congratulatory. Perfectly genuine pride in her son's accomplishments could not banish instinctive dread.

"Yes, much more." Excitement invaded his voice, despite his efforts to maintain Vardrulesque tranquility. "Mother, I've taken a great step forward. For the first time, I've seen tangible proof of my progress. So often I've doubted, so often I've feared that I'd never reach my goal. But now at last I know I will succeed."

"Succeed at what? What goal?"

"Harmony. Knowledge of my Ancestors."

"What are you talking about? I don't understand you."

"I know it must be hard to believe. It must seem incredible that a human could expect so much. But, Mother, I am going to do it. I grow closer with each passing Small Ven. When you see the level I've reached, you'll understand and believe."

"Terrs—this Knowledge of Ancestors ritual. I know you've always wanted it, but surely you realize by now that it's meant for the Vardruls alone. What does it take to convince you that we humans aren't equipped for it by nature?"

"By nature—there you've hit upon it. We are naturally inferior, but nature is subject to modification by Cognition."

"Modification? What modification?" Her sense of dread intensified to the point of discomfort. "What have you done?"

"I'll show you." Intent upon his new success, Terrs failed to note his mother's uneasiness. Reaching into his pocket, he withdrew another eight-sided crystal, almost identical to the first. "This hasn't become easy yet. It may take a little time. Be patient."

"What are you doing? Please wait. I'd like to discuss this. Terrs, *what are you doing?*"

He did not answer. His open hands were extended before him, with a crystal resting in the palm of each. His head was bowed, his eyes closed, and he whispered melodically. He spoke at length, and nothing happened. It appeared that the demonstration was a failure, but Terrs showed no sign of anxiety or even awareness. He whispered on and presently, when his mother was on the verge of urging him to stop, the twin crystals began to glow. Nyd hissed sharply, then held his peace. Long ago, as an infant in Grizhni Palace, he had been trained to maintain silence during the act of Cognition. Seventeen years had passed since the hybrid had found himself in the presence of a savant, but he had never forgotten the early lesson.

The rhythmic whispering continued and as the light of the crystals waxed in strength, the rock-light of the Stronghold waned. Verran started, but said nothing. A chill touched the tropical air. She could feel the gooseflesh tingle along her arms. Darker it grew, dim as Surface twilight, until nothing but the palest hint of luminescence shone from the stone walls, floor, and ceiling. In that subdued light, the three living figures, human and hybrid, were barely visible in outline. The details of form, feature, and clothing faded into obscurity. Only the two crystals blazed with pure, hard light that illuminated a process of Cognitive transformation.

Terrs's hands were changing. The outlines softened and rippled. The fingers lengthened hideously. The bones melted, the joints and fingernails vanished, the index and middle fingers had been replaced by a set of strong, flexible tentacles. But even that was not the worst of it. As Lady Verran watched in sick dismay, the hands of her son began to glow. Simultaneously the twin crystals dimmed, as if their radiance fed the human flesh. Human? Verran forced herself to observe closely. The rock-light came up, affording her a clear view. Terrs's tentacles were smoothly featureless and somewhat moist. The skin was perfectly white. By no stretch of the imagination was this flesh human. Disgust almost blotted out her sense of horror.

Terrs dropped the crystals in his pocket, lifted his lucent hands, and rippled the tentacles in delight. A rare smile of triumph lighted his face as he turned to his audience. "There. Look quickly, because it won't last long. I haven't yet learned temporal mastery—that is, how to fix the effect. But there is the proof of my progress."

"What have you done to yourself?" Verran's tone was shrill. She took a deep breath and paused a moment to compose herself. When she spoke again, her voice was under control. "This condition is temporary?"

"Unfortunately so." Terrs looked at her and his smile faded. "What's wrong, Mother? You seem upset. Are you afraid I'll harm myself? There's nothing to worry about. It's quite safe."

"Safe? You stand before me horribly altered—your beautiful hands *deformed*—and you claim that it's *safe?* You don't know what you're saying. I wish I'd never shown you Lord Grizhni's writings!"

"They are my birthright. I had the right to see them."

"Yes, but I should have waited until you were old enough and responsible enough to use them wisely!"

"Yet it was only a few moments ago that you congratulated me on my accomplishments. You claimed to be proud of me, and I believed that you meant it—believed that you might even be willing to consider my point of view. I should have known better," Terrs returned, bitterness audible despite his carefully self-contained manner.

"I meant what I said. But I never dreamed you'd use your new Cognition to disfigure yourself—"

"Disfigure? Are you blind? This is the first Small Ven in all my life that it hasn't sickened me to look at my own hands. Can't you understand that? Can't you be happy for me? Can't you forget your prejudices for once?"

"Prejudice has nothing to do with it. Terrs, if you could only see yourself now—a human boy with the hands of a Vardrul! It's so utterly wrong, such an unnatural joining! You're turning yourself into a—a kind of monster."

"I've been a monster all my life, and now at last I have a chance of achieving normalcy. Do you grudge me that? You may cherish your own human deformities if you choose, but don't expect me to do the same."

Verran stifled a bitter reply. She looked at her son, perceived the pain behind his icy facade and recalled his lifelong unhappiness. Suddenly her anger and revulsion became much easier to manage, and she was able to answer with mildness. "Terrs, a minute ago you attributed my distrust of Cognition to simple ignorance, and I admitted the possibility. Now can't you do the same? Your dislike and distrust of your own kind are likewise based on ignorance. Won't you reserve judgment until you've had a chance to meet and know mankind?"

"The opportunity is unlikely to arise."

"It could," she suggested cautiously. "You could meet other humans, if we left these caves. It need only be for a little while," she added, seeing his face change.

"No. It is out of the question."

"Not even if I ask it of you as a favor?"

"If you must go, Mother, then go. I know you would like to. But don't expect to drag me along with you. I won't consider it."

"Why not?" she challenged. "Afraid, son? Afraid of the light? Or just afraid you might find you've been wrong?"

"Neither. Not afraid, merely uninterested. I've been Surface, more than once. I found it cold, empty, and desolate."

"You saw only the Gravula Wasteland! That wasn't a fair test."

"Moreover," Terrs continued inexorably, "I am not so ignorant of humanity as you suppose. Vardrul history tells me much of mankind, most of it distasteful."

"The Vardruls are hardly qualified to judge the matter. They've been cut off from humanity for hundreds, or perhaps thousands, of years. They are of a different species, and cannot be expected to understand us. In any case, they have no written records—their history consists of ancient tales and legends, which hardly merit much credence."

"There again your bigotry speaks. You accept only one form of evidence, one method of preserving information. You automatically reject all others as invalid."

"And you prefer to rely on the ancient recollections of an alien race, rather than on direct observation. Given the chance to see the world for yourself, you would rather content yourself with Vardrul fables. Which of us is the more truly narrow-minded?"

"Have I not observed humanity at first hand? I have watched myself and I have watched you. I've studied two perfectly good specimens of mankind, and I have witnessed ugliness, physical and moral inferiority, and profound, unutterable disharmony. For twenty-five Great Vens I have seen it, and that is long enough. I need hardly venture Surface to confirm my observations."

"Terrs, your standards of judgment are absolutely warped!"

"I think not. In any event, they are *my* standards, Mother. You will not succeed in forcing your own upon me."

"Forcing? Why must you always speak in terms of conflict? Is there any need for that?"

"Not if you'd accept the fact that I don't think as you think, or feel as you feel."

"I do accept that."

"Really? Then don't try to hold me back, Mother. Don't try to lock me in a cage."

"My dear, I'm trying to let you out of one. I wish you'd understand that I love you and want only what's best for you. And do please stop glaring as if I were your enemy."

The appeal apparently moved him somewhat. Terrs half smiled, shook his head, and refrained from reply. Placing a hand lightly upon her shoulder, he stooped to plant a conciliatory kiss upon her cheek. She could not repress a shudder at the touch of the tentacles now glowing in place of her son's human fingers.

Terrs felt the reaction, shifted his dark gaze to the transformed members, and observed almost inaudibly, "I do not feel the clan-warmth." As he watched, the luminescence began to fade from his flesh. His lips tightened in disappointment. Perhaps emotional agitation had weakened the force of his fledgling Cognition, or perhaps the effect was simply more transitory than he had anticipated. In any event, the light dwindled, the tentacles lost their flexibility, the fingers reshaped themselves, and in another moment the youth's hands had resumed their original form.

Verran breathed an unconscious sigh of relief. Terrs heard it. His brows drew together and he remarked deliberately, "Next time, it will last longer."

"Do you plan to alter your hands permanently?" She spoke with detachment. Any other tone would simply have aroused his hostility.

"The term *permanent* means little. Once I've mastered the Cogniton, I shall have the power to change, and change back again as I will. The choice will then be mine."

"But you refuse to open your mind to the knowledge that might enable you to make a balanced decision. Your view is one-sided. Terrs, don't you see—"

"Mother, we shall start to quarrel again, and neither of us wants that. It is my concern alone, and I will deal with it. But you must accept the fact that my life is here in these caverns. Sooner or later, I will achieve harmony, both for myself and my sons."

"Sons? You want children?" She repressed a smile. Terrs was little more than a child himself, or so it seemed to his mother. Still, his remark provided her with fresh ammunition. "Of course you'll have a son someday. You must carry on the Fal Grizhni name, for that is surely what Lord Grizhni would have wished. But it means leaving these caverns. You must go Surface to find yourself a wife. There's none for you down here."

"Quite the contrary. I have good reason to hope that Zmadrc R'dsvyllsch will soon consent to my entrance into his clan as brother/consort to his daughter Zmadrc Fourteen."

For a moment astonishment paralyzed her tongue, and then she answered without thinking. "That—is—the—most ridiculous—thing—I've—ever heard!"

"Ridiculous, Mother?" Terrs inquired with all his father's frigid hauteur.

"Impossible!"

"Is it?"

"Yes, impossible! You're joking, aren't you?" She saw that he was not joking. "What difference does it make if the Zmadrc Patriarch consents to accept you? You can't be brother/consort to a Vardrul female!"

"I can and I will."

"Not if I have anything to say about it."

"You do not. No disrespect intended, Mother, but I am grown and I will do as I please."

"You are not grown. You are still a boy. And this present perverted scheme of yours proves your immaturity. Your adolescent urges are driving you mad, and there's not a human girl in sight. That is why you must visit Surface, and soon. You need it desperately."

"Not so desperately as you, I suspect. But that is beside the point. I remain here to enter the Zmadrc clan."

"Terrs, I question your sanity. If nothing else, think of the sons you just said you want. Turning your hands white and wriggly doesn't make you a Vardrul, and doesn't mean that a

Vardrul sister/consort can bear your offspring."

"Not yet, but that will change. The Fal Grizhni Patriarch's records contain the secret of hybridization. Hybridization resulted in Nyd's creation. The same procedure will effect my own union with Zmadrc Fourteen and my harmony with all the clan. It is only a matter of time, Mother—and not very much time at that."

Verran had no answer. After a moment, Terrs turned and quietly exited the Stronghold, leaving his mother in a state of near stupefaction.

Chapter Three

Duke Povon woke up screaming—of late a commonplace occurrence. It was, in fact, the fourteenth consecutive night
wherein fearful dreams had troubled the ducal repose. It was
always the same nightmare—the inescapable cavern-dungeon;
the spectral appearance of the luminous white being; and, at
last, the reanimation of a ghastly, vengeful Terrs Fal Grizhni.
Familiarity failed to breed contempt—each visitation was more
terrifying than the last. The Duke reared up in bed to cast a
panicky glance around him. He sat in his own chamber, its
ponderous furnishings illumined by the small night light kept
burning at his order in recent weeks. The familiar surroundings
did not reassure Povon—could not still the hammering of his
heart or the trembling of his limbs. A more efficacious remedy
was required.

The Duke dragged himself from bed and stumbled across
the room to the gold-crusted chest that stood in the corner. The
top drawer yielded a jeweled flask full of the Moon Dream of
Uhanna—sweetest and loveliest of essences, and the Duke's
particular favorite. Povon ingested a generous quantity and was
soon rewarded. His pulse slowed and his hands steadied. A
rainbow nimbus wreathed the night light and the air turned
candy-sweet around him. Terror receded, and within moments
the ducal heart was once again serene. The newfound serenity,
however, was not unmixed with caution. The Duke recollected
the recent outcry doubtless overheard by his attendants, who
would promptly relay the news to the Keldhaam Gnuxia. They
were in her employ, at least some of them. During the term of
her residence Gnuxia had established an extensive intelligence

network, and few events transpiring within the confines of the
Ducal.Palace escaped her notice. Her spies included a number
of the Duke's personal attendants, and her encroachments were
impossible to contain. When Povon discovered and dismissed
the offending parties, Gnuxia simply suborned and/or intimi-
dated the replacements. Given the scarcity of competent servants, is was easier to live with the informers. Thus the Keldhaam was privy to the most intimate details of her betrothed's
activities, and generally managed to turn her knowledge to
good account in terms of meddling and bullying.

She would appear in his bedchamber very shortly, Povon
realized. She would receive the news of his latest demoralization, she would demand admittance, and none of the servants
would dare to bar her path. Then she would be upon him with
her nostrums and her remedies, her pills, potions, unguents,
charms, leeches, and assorted torments. She would regulate
his diet, forbid him the use of essences and alcohol, demand
an account of the frequency of his bowel movements. She
would remain at his side day and night, and nothing he could
say or do would induce her to depart. Each passing moment
brought her nearer, and the prospect was horrendous. The Moon
Dream slowed Povon's mental processes to a crawl. It took
him a minute or two to think of fleeing his apartment. He would
seek sanctuary elsewhere in the palace, and she would never
find him.

With some difficulty the Duke donned his dressing gown
and found his way to the door. His progress was unsteady and
his intentions were nebulous. Flight—escape—concealment—
such were the desires uppermost in his clouded mind, but the
proper method of achieving them was unclear. Povon wandered
from bedchamber to tiring chamber to receiving chamber to
antechamber. At length he passed through the great gilded
double doors and out of his private suite. The pillared corridor
that stretched before him was deserted. So far, so good. The
Duke pressed on along the hallway, down the marble staircase
with its balustrade of miniature caryatids, and along the Gallery
of the Rose, whose walls were lined with silver trellises whereon
the perfectly sculpted vermeil blossoms clustered. He tottered
beneath an alabaster archway and into the vast state Audience
chamber.

Povon paused to catch his breath. Panting, he leaned against the wall. Before him lay a glittering desert of polished marble tile. In the distance rose a dais surmounted by the jeweled ducal throne. A robed figure occupied the throne. The figure sat erect and straight-spined. Its pantomimic gestures were self-consciously regal.

Povon squinted in disbelief, amazed to find an alien posterior desecrating the cushion reserved for ducal use alone. He blinked, and his vision cleared somewhat. Discerning details of the usurper's face and meager figure, he recognized his son. Lord Sneever—the wretched, puling Sneever—dared to seat himself upon the throne of state. Wrath invigorated the Duke. Pushing himself off from the wall, he staggered toward the throne. Drawing near, he noted Sneever's ermine collar and purloined coronet. A sour, half-sober smile bent his lips.

Sneever heard the footfalls on marble, turned and beheld his father. His pale face darkened to carmine. His eyes widened and bulged. His hands tightened on the arms of the throne, and he froze into scared-rabbit stillness. Only the violent twitching of his right eyelid betrayed the presence of life.

The Duke paused swaying at the foot of the dais. "What have we here?" he inquired in apparent wonder. "What do I find upon my throne?"

Sneever's lips quivered, but no sound emerged.

"I see before me a starveling figure tricked out in robe and ducal coronet," the Duke continued thoughtfully. "It does not move or speak. Is it a tailor's dummy? Is it a scarecrow in need of new stuffing? Surely it cannot be a living man?"

"Your Grace—" Sneever attempted.

"It moves. It speaks. I must assume it lives. Who, then, can it be? Is it a traitor masquerading as Duke? Surely not, for the imposture is woefully obvious. Those narrow, girlish shoulders were not made to bear the burden of stately robes. That scrawny chicken neck would bend beneath the weight of a coronet. This is at best the caricature of a duke. There is no deception involved, for it is not meant to be taken seriously."

"Your Grace—Father—allow me to explain," Sneever appealed. His fingers scrabbled at the clasp of his robe.

"No—do not unfasten it. Stay where you are," the Duke commanded as his son attempted to rise from the throne. "It is a rare and delicious sight that I wish to observe at length and, insofar as possible, commit to memory."

Sneever sank back upon the cushion. Only his great blue eyes roved hopelessly around the Audience chamber in search of rescue or escape.

"Now what can it mean?" the Duke mused. No question but he was enjoying himself. "This stick figure decked in my ducal regalia—this quaint mockery-upon-a-throne—what *can* it all mean? Caricature? Travesty? Ah, I have it now!" He snapped his fingers. "It is a joke, after all! I see before me a play-actor, a clown from the Shonnet Theatre, come to entertain the court with his japes and lampoons! But how delightful! Come, my good fellow, can you sing for us? Have you comical rhymes to recite? Perhaps some verses of a stinging political satire? For satire, they say, is the physic that purges the body politic of its complacency, and that is surely your intent? Is it not?"

No answer was forthcoming. Sneever squirmed, fidgeted, and longingly eyed the nearest exit.

"What, no reply? You are something troubled, good clown? Ah, I understand. What profit to perform before an audience of one? You desire spectators, many spectators, whose laughter, whistles, and catcalls will waken your artistry and spur you on to extraordinary heights of comical invention. Applause will nourish your wit, for such is the nature of the true buffoon. You shall have your desire." The Duke lurched forward.

"Father, what are you doing?" cried Sneever.

"An audience, clown. I summon you an audience."

"No—wait—listen to me please—I don't want an audience—"

"Modesty does not suit a buffoon." Mounting the dias, the Duke reached forward and repeatedly pressed an ivory stud set into the arm of the throne. When he had completed the short sequence, music chimed softly in every room of the palace. This device, Cognitive invention of the lamented Saxas Gless Vallage, enabled the Duke to summon servants, slaves, Guardsmen, and courtiers to him as he chose. He had just used it to call every member of his household staff. A few moments later they began to file into the Audience chamber, singly and in small groups. Many of them were yawning and bleary-eyed with sleep, but all were dutifully prompt in their response. With them came a few of the late-gaming courtiers, drawn by curiosity from their cards and dice.

Sneever watched the crowd collect around the throne. The familiar faces were filled with curiosity and speculation. He could not sustain the pressure of their eyes. His own gaze dropped. He looked down at his hands and saw that they were trembling.

"My good friends and subjects"—the slurring of Povon's voice did not preclude a burlesque gravity of manner—"no doubt you are wondering why I summoned you here tonight. A rare and precious treat awaits us. We have in our midst a refugee from the theatre—a clown come to ply his trade at court. This enterprising jester—whose costume and appearance argue an acute sense of the ridiculous—will serve as the mirror wherein we shall view our own frailties and follies. The sheer absurdity of his ducal impersonation will surely provide moral instruction no less than hilarity. And thus, in anticipation of the most delectable entertainment, I step aside to leave our visitor master of the stage. My friends, let us give him our hands in welcome."

The Duke clapped his hands vigorously. Several of the servants and courtiers followed suit. A light, somewhat uncertain pattering of applause arose and swiftly died. Expectant silence reigned.

Sneever regarded his audience. The color drained from his cheeks. His right eyelid writhed like a severed snake. For the first time in his life, his left eyelid did likewise. The two lids twitched in violent asynchronism, and the effect was bizarre.

"Good—very good," the Duke approved. "A truly spectacular introduction, the effect of which might perhaps be heightened by a muscial accompaniment. Excellent. Now, what is to follow?"

Sneever squirmed in silence.

"Come, will you not sing to us? Let me entreat you."

A thin, involuntary gurgling escaped the Duke's son.

"Interesting rendition, but I cannot hear the lyrics. Speak up sir. Speak up." He turned to his subjects. "My friends, our visitor is shy. Let us encourage him."

"Sing, Sneever—sing!" The cry arose from a few of the more obsequious throats present. Most of the spectators maintained noncommittal silence.

"Sing!"

Light applause, a little laughter in which the Duke joined, and one daring, jeering whistle.

Sneever's shoulders sagged beneath the velvet robe. His eyes filled with water. He bit his lip bloody, but the tears would not be suppressed. They overflowed and coursed their way down his cheeks. A confused muttering ran through the ranks of the spectators, many of whom seemed disposed to sympathy.

"Better and better!" Genuine pleasure sharpened the Duke's blurry voice. "For laughter is but a breath away from tears, and a touch of pathos lends savor to the finest comedy. We have among us a master of his craft, a very prince—or rather, duke—of clowns." Povon laughed, and several courtiers desirous of his favor joined in. Sneever's tears flowed faster. He attempted surreptitiously to wipe his nose on his velvet sleeve. His effort did not go unnoticed, and the laughter intensified.

"Our clown seems disinclined to vocalization," the Duke remarked. "Perhaps he'd be so good as to favor us with a dance?"

"Dance, Sneever!" the shout arose.

Sneever scrunched down in his seat in an unsuccessful effort to achieve invisibility.

"Up on your hind legs, sir," urged the Duke. "Arise!"

"Dance, Sneever!" More voices joined in.

Eager hands reached forward to pluck Lord Sneever from the throne. In vain the young man resisted. He stood upon the dais, pitifully exposed to the eyes of all.

"The Marquirvian Prance, clown," the Duke suggested helpfully. "One of my favorites."

"Prance it, Sneever!"

Sneever was motionless save for the twitching of his eyelids. He studied his feet with an air of incomprehension. The cries around him grew more insistent. Someone began to whistle the Macquirvian War Hymn in prance-time. Hands clapped and feet stamped. Some of the spectators remained aloof while others, caught up in the spirit of things, hooted their enthusiasm. Sneever's body was clammy with sweat. The faces around him wavered, swam, and merged. He was swaying, on the verge of collapse, when a strong voice that cut through the surrounding clamor caught his attention and preserved his consciousness.

"What an uproar in the Ducal Audience chamber! Fine respect!"

Sneever's giddiness receded. Dashing the tears from his eyes, he sought out the new arrival. Framed in the distant doorway, the Keldhaam Gnuxia loomed like a goddess of war. Her arms were folded, her black brows drawn sharply together. A vast gown of quilted fabric increased her already-formidable bulk.

A complete hush fell over the room. The Keldhaam strode forward. Behind her trailed a quartet of her most muscular female attendants. The rapping of the women's heels upon the marble floor was reminiscent of the measured tread of booted Guardsmen. Duke Povon cringed at the sound.

Gnuxia arrived at the edge of the audience, which parted before her. Advancing to the foot of the dais, she paused to confront her betrothed. "What is the meaning of this mummery? Explain at once."

"A bit of impromptu merriment," Duke Povon returned with tolerable firmness, "with which the Keldhaam need not concern herself."

"Need not concern myself? Ah, were it only so, what a fortunate woman I should be! For I ask nothing better than to live as consort to a ruler of strength and intelligence, capable of governing his realm without benefit of my supervision. Such is the happy fate of my mother, wed to his Splendor the Keldhar. Alas that my mother's daughter is not similarly blessed! His Splendor has consigned me to Lanthi Ume, no doubt in the hope that my sound judgment may serve to strengthen a decadent ally. As the Keldhar desires, so it must be. So it *shall* be. Therefore, to the limited extent possible, I strive to uphold your public dignity, and the even more perishable dignity of your imbecilic son."

"Madam—" Sneever attempted miserably.

"Silence, sir," she instructed. "Spare us your inanities. Have you not affronted us sufficiently as it is? Remove that coronet at once and come down off that dais. Are you not ashamed to be seen thus? I should think you would be ashamed. *I* could not bear to make myself an object of public ridicule—I would rather die. It seems you have no pride—but then, you are Lanthian and your blood is half canal water. Well, sir? Will you remove that coronet, or is further persuasion required?"

Sneever hastily pulled the circlet from his head.

"I will take that," Gnuxia announced.

He hesitated, and she snapped her fingers imperatively. "Come, sir, is your hand as slow as your wits? Restore what you have stolen, and then you may retire. Do you not wish to retire? *I* should hide my face for very shame. I should not emerge from my apartment without a vizard."

No one present dared to comment.

Sneever relinquished the object of controversy, but did not

move from the dais. He was shaking all over. Perhaps his legs were too weak to carry him from the Audience chamber, or perhaps he wished to listen to the ensuing conversation.

"I will safeguard this coronet, that no additional indignity may be visited upon it by son or father. In the name of his Splendor the Keldhar, I hold it in trust." Having possessed herself of the coronet, Gnuxia lost all interest in Sneever, and turned her attention upon the wobbling Duke. "Your eyes are more than ordinarily glazed," she observed. "Your pupils are dilated, your face is pale, and I suspect the worst."

"The Keldhaam's fears are unwarranted," the Duke returned uncomfortably. He shifted his weight, and his blue eyes roamed. At that moment, the slight family resemblance between Povon and his son was unusually apparent.

"You were heard to cry out in your sleep," Gnuxia continued relentlessly. "I know this to be true, and it is useless to deny it. You are afflicted with evil dreams and visions—a sure sign that your system is burdened with impurities, heavy humors, varied blood-predators, melancholic chill, and perhaps the Invisible Poacher. It is hardly surprising, in view of the poisonous muck with which you persist in abusing your body. But all that is about to change. *I say it is about to change.* You will be cleansed, Betrothed—of that you may be sure. Purgation will prove your salvation."

"Keldhaam, it is hardly the time or place—"

"That is correct," Gnuxia interrupted her intended. "Your Lanthian servants are loose-tongued and untrustworthy. It is unsafe to speak before them. How differently we live in Gard Lammis! No matter. When I am Duchess, be assured the situation will improve. Until that time, discretion is the rule. We will continue this discussion in the privacy of your suite. There is certain information I require. My women will attend to safeguard my honor. Come, Betrothed."

The Duke gazed up into the remorseless eyes of his feminine captors. Seeing there no hint of mercy, he wordlessly accompanied them from the Audience chamber. His head was bowed, his expression resigned.

Following the departure of their ruler, the remaining courtiers and servants loitered aimlessly for a time. Their covert glances of pity and contempt skewered Sneever. A low hum of conversation, punctuated by the occasional suppressed snicker, filled the air. The Duke's son appeared oblivious. He sat on the edge of the dais, spindly legs drawn up, chin resting on bent knees. His gaze was fixed on the floor before him, and his hands still trembled visibly. He was silent, and no one cared to address him directly. The prospect of additional entertainment appeared dim, and the spectators began drifting toward the various exits. Soon the great Audience chamber was empty, and only then did Sneever raise his head. His blue gaze swept the deserted room, still extravagantly lit with the glow of five hundred candles. It lighted on the archway through which his father had exited, and stayed there. Sneever's eyes gleamed oddly. Fanged and scaly creatures sported in the pale depths. It was a highly uncharacteristic expression, and its meaning was anyone's guess.

Events of the night festered in the minds of the Duke and his heir. Povon and Lord Sneever both brooded. Their conclusions were dissimilar, but resulted in simultaneous surreptitious nocturnal excursions. Shortly after sunset the next evening, two dombuli embarked from the ducal moorings within an hour of one another. Each dombulis was unmarked, anonymous, inconspicuous. Each bore one or two cloaked and hatted passengers. Each headed by a circuitous route for the meanest section of the city. The two sets of passengers were mutually unaware.

The first of the dombuli navigated a knotted tangle of narrow back waterways. Here the buildings were close-set and tumbledown. The piers still teemed with humanity, despite the lateness of the hour. The crowd was volatile, boisterous, and garrulous—in short, typically Lanthian. Conversation, music, and the scent of fish and onions frying in cheap oil filled the air. One of the occupants of the dombulis applied a pomander to his nose.

The boat passed on beyond the region of voices and music, and into the ancient Straightwater Canal, whose banks were lined with decrepit warehouses, shuttered booths, decaying tenements. It was dark upon the Straightwater. Few of the surrounding buildings showed any light, for the inhabitants of this ancient, noissome slum known as the Destula were wont to pad their shutters with rags, which served a twofold purpose—conservation of heat in the winter, and camouflage of human presence. In that neighborhood, particularly at night, such camouflage was often deemed advisable. While most shutters were equipped with peepholes, surveillance by the myriad

cutpurses and cutthroats of the Destula was customarily unobtrusive.

The dombulis bumped Destula Pier and the passengers de-
barked. The heavily armed dombulman was left behind to guard
the boat, a responsibility the fellow accepted with obvious
reluctance. The two passengers, carrying lanterns, proceeded
along the embankment as far as the Bridge of Spiteful Cats,
which they did not attempt to approach. Such caution was
justified, for the feral cats of the bridge brooked no invasion
of their domain. A singularly harsh winter, five years earlier—a
time of widespread famine—had verified beyond all question
the legend of the cats' anthropophagous tendencies. The gnawed
remains of no fewer than three unwary mendicants had been
discovered in the wynd behind the abandoned warehouse a
short distance from the bridge. Following the third such incident, certain zealots within the city demanded the extermination
of the offending strays. Civic traditionalists opposed the suggestion, citing the historic significance of the old bridge and its
feline squatters. For months the controversy raged in taverns,
market squares, and hired dombuli all over Lanthi Ume. In the
end, popular interest waned and the Spiteful Cats continued
their reign unmolested. Inbred and distinctive, identifiable by
their violet eyes and inordinate ferocity, the creatures now
prowled their realm in ever-increasing numbers and arrogance.

Carefully skirting the bridge, the passengers from the dombulis continued along the edge of the Straightwater for a time
before turning left into an alley whose entrance was marked
with a carven salamander. A few more paces and a couple of
more turns brought them into a black cul-de-sac with atmosphere so pestilential that the shorter of the two men choked
on it.

"Phew!" gasped Duke Povon, and reapplied the pomander.
"Vile! This cannot be the place, Beskot. We have taken the
wrong path."

"This is the place, I warrant your Grace," replied Lord Beskot
Kor Malifon, his customary resplendence almost extinguished
beneath a cloak and a wide-brimmed hat. "Here we shall find
him, let me perish."

"Why was I not informed? Why was I led to venture forth
unfortified?" the Duke complained. "I've not the slightest whiff
of an essence about me. I should have been informed. I should
never have let you talk me into this. In any event, I do not

believe it—no Cognizance of the Select would kennel himself in such a sewer."

"He is a Cognizance no longer. The self-styled Sapient Nulliad is an Expulsion."

"A what?"

"An Expulsion," Beskot repeated. "A savant expelled from the Select in the distant past."

"How distant?"

"Oh, let's say forty years or so, your Grace."

"Then we are speaking of a senile incompetent."

"By no means. He was—and still is, by all accounts—one of the greatest of all savants. His mind is sharp and his Cognitive powers awesome."

"If he's as great as all that, then why did they kick him out of the Select in the first place?"

"Insubordination, your Grace. Nobody can confirm the story, but 'tis said that a very great savant in the days of Preeminence Lekkel Dri Vannivo—that was Fal Grizhni's predecessor, if I remember my schooling—that a senior member of the Council of the Select defied the code of his order and deliberately contravened the Cognition of his Preeminence. For this infraction he was ordered to appear before the Council. Rather than submit to such indignity, the savant abandoned the Select, dropped the title of Cognizance to which he no longer held legal claim, changed his name, and, in the spirit of ironical parody, withdrew to the Destula to set himself up as the Sapient Nulliad. The wisdom of a great savant is thus made available as never before to the general populace."

"The general populace—I do not care for that, it implies mediocre abilities," observed the Duke. "If this Expulsion possesses talent, why does he not devote himself to the welfare of those in a position to advance his fortunes? Why would he choose to live *here*?"

"Ah, your Grace, who can account for the vagaries of these savant fellows? Perhaps this Sapient Nulliad is prone to ostentatious egalitarianism. Perhaps he hopes to astound the world with his eccentricities. Perhaps he intends to affront the Select. It is my personal opinion—and I fancy myself no mean connoisseur of such matters—that Nulliad's gesture, while lacking in that offhand negligence so essential to faultless style, nonetheless displays evidence of a certain idiosyncratic insolence not unworthy of note."

"Insolence—there you have hit upon it, Beskot. Insolence. The fellow will not deign to present himself at court when summoned. He sends word that the Duke must come to *him*. And I, with no true friend to serve me or to safeguard my interests, find myself reduced to such a state of desperation that I accept his conditions. I, the reigning Duke of Lanthi Ume! Here—in this awful place at night, afoot like a peasant, my sensibilities outraged, and not an essence or even a soothing draught to be had! How has it come to this? You talked me into it, it's your fault."

"The dreams, your Grace. The nightmares," Beskot reminded his lord. "The Sapient Nulliad is counted a master among the interpreters of dreams. He will perhaps bring insight and comfort to your Grace."

"He had better," the Duke brooded. "He had better. If the fellow's a charlatan, I'll have him publicly flogged. I'll have him stripped naked and set adrift on the Lureis for a couple of days, I swear I will!"

"And would his Grace inflict so great an eyesore upon the city? Oh, fie!"

"And be accounted a civic benefactor when the eyesore is carried out to sea."

The Duke's pearl of political wisdom received less than the attention it deserved. The unguarded aristocratic accents had caught the attention of a number of the Destula's most formidable residents. Now a band of them stood athwart Duke Povon's path—five stout, muscular young hooligans armed with luewood sticks made of truncated sendillis oars. Orange lantern light fell upon five pocked visages and five identically courteous smiles. The smiles failed to inspire confidence, their courtesy notwithstanding. The young men shared the peculiar distinction of coal-black teeth—an effect achieved by means of repeated applications of a preparation manufactured for use as a boot blacking. One of the hooligans—whose compact, powerful build suggested unusual strength and agility—stepped forward to address the Duke with an air of respectful solicitude. "Lost your way, sir?"

Povon and Beskot were silent.

"Wandered off from your companions—eh, sir? Took the wrong turning, got confused, and can't find your way back?"

No answer. Povon glanced back over his shoulder to note four more black-teethed young men closing in from behind.

"A dangerous place for two fine gentlemen to wander alone at night." The hooligan shook his head in regret. "I couldn't begin to tell you some of the terrible things that happen here at night. I just couldn't begin to. That's why I never stir a step without my friends here—yes, the ones behind you are my friends, too, sir. It's for protection, you see. A word to the wise, gentlemen."

Povon and Beskot exchanged alarmed glances.

"It's a good idea to carry a weapon in a place like the Destula," the hooligan continued helpfully. "Another word to the wise. Me, I'm never abroad without my trusty stick here. Very useful." Grinning darkly, he dealt the wall beside him a cracking wallop so loud that Povon jumped at the sound of it. "You see?"

Duke Povon found his voice at last. It came out thin and high. *"Do you know who I AM?"*

"A most significant personage, sire, if I may judge by that uncommonly fine ring upon your finger. I could judge better if I could see it plainer. Might I take a closer look?"

"Let us pass, fellow!"

"Of course. Anything you say, sir. Anything you say, to be sure. But might I not make a suggestion? You two gentlemen require protection. My friends and I can furnish it. Our price is high, but our service is excellent. Not a single customer has ever complained."

"We do no require protection, fellow!"

"Oh, but you do, sir. Take my word for it." The hooligans advanced, still smiling.

Beskot Kor Malifon spoke up in desperation. "We enjoy the protection of the Sapient Nulliad."

The name stopped them in their tracks. The black smiles vanished.

"Nulliad awaits our arrival," Beskot continued. "Doubtless he wonders at our delay. Perhaps you could direct us to his residence."

Povon's brows arched. Beskot displayed hitherto-unsuspected presence of mind.

The hooligans conferred in low tones. The name *Nulliad*, pronounced in accents of dread, was audible. At last the leader answered grudgingly, "He lives there." He indicated a decrepit tenement close at hand. The visitors rendered somewhat tremulous thanks and the young men departed muttering.

The Sapient Nulliad lived on the top floor of a five-story building. Never before had Duke Povon been forced to climb so high under his own power. Upon reaching the head of the second flight of stairs, the Duke was flushed and breathing hard. At the top of the third, he stopped to rest, but did not pause there long. The landing was dirty, dim, and roach-infested. Povon stifled his disgust and struggled on. Beskot trailed miserably behind. Both men were gasping by the time they reached the top.

Grime coated the walls of the landing. The armor plating of ancient paint had alligatored, and the cracks were black with filth. Gnawed bones, fish heads, fruit peels, and lumps of petrified porridge littered the floor. But the Sapient Nulliad's door was scrubbed spotlessly clean. A line of light showed under the door. Beskot knocked and a dry old voice bade them enter.

The Sapient Nulliad had succeeded in holding the forces of chaos at bay. His chambers, austere and sparsely furnished, were devoid of pollution. The carpets were threadbare but clean, the furnishing shabby but spotless. The dustless books were arranged in perfect order. The charts, diagrams, maps, and graphs tacked to the wall were spaced at exactly regular intervals. A number of Cognitive instruments displayed upon a shelf were aligned with mathematical precision. Nulliad himself was similarly precise. The old Expulsion's black robe—the robe of a savant of the Select, but minus the double-headed dragon insignia—was starched and pressed to the verge of rigidity. His hands were scrupulously tended, the nails squared off at the tips. His long gray hair hung in a web of interwoven plaits— a style hardly seen in Lanthi Ume for fifty years or more. His complexion was waxen, his stance inflexible, his gestures studied. The sole aspect of his person denoting freedom from restraint lay in the lines of his face. The furrows that snaked across the high forehead, bracketing the thin lips and etching the skin around the eyes, bespoke a variety of characteristic expressions ranging from the tragic to the manic. Such animation, if it existed, was not freely displayed. Nulliad's present expression was remote. The arch of his nostrils, the droop of heavy lids over eyes like a basilisk's, and the elevation of his chin radiated omniscience.

"Your Grace." Nulliad spoke without deference. "Nulliad consents to admit you. You may seat yourself. No, not there.

That is not the proper place for you. Be so good as to seat yourself *here,* but do not move the chair. It is now properly positioned. You—" the Expulsion addressed Beskot Kor Malifon, "may take either of the remaining chairs. On no account is either of you to rise and wander aimlessly about the chamber."

"Why not, Sapience?" Beskot inquired incautiously. "Would we interfere with your—what d'you call it—Cogniton?"

"Random motion is not acceptable," replied the Expulsion. "The forces of disorder must be countered, and in this effort Nulliad requires your cooperation. Do not seek further explanation."

"I am not accustomed to restriction. The Sapience forgets himself." Povon pursed his lips in displeasure.

"The Duke of Lanthi Ume seeks the counsel of Nulliad. If his Grace desires success in his endeavors, surely it behooves him to heed the wisdom he has come so far to find."

"Far indeed, and what is my reward? Impertinence. Intolerable presumption. Let me remind you, Master Nulliad, that the savants of the Select are wont to present themselves at court upon my summons. There are no exceptions to this rule."

"The Sapient Nulliad has outgrown the Select. He has gone on to other, far greater, projects. Here, in this dreadful welter of filth and corruption known as the Destula, Nulliad wages lonely battle against the demons of chaos, disorder, unreason. Here in the privacy of his poor lodgings, he creates a tiny realm of order, regularity, symmetry. Without, all is madness. Within these walls a well-regulated intellect labors to encompass the Great Design of Being. That it is a repeating pattern, Nulliad does not doubt. All is rigorously ordered."

The Duke refused to be put off. "Preeminence Jinzin Farni himself comes to court when I summon him."

"Then why has your Grace not done so in this instance?" Nulliad permitted himself the hint of a wintry smile.

"Bah, this is a matter beyond the abilities of the Select," replied the Duke. "And therefore I have come to Nulliad, who spurned the Select. All savants have their particular areas of expertise, or so I am told. Saxas Gless Vallage concocted the most divine essences. Bome Booru studied the flight of demons. That swine Grizhni was forever inflicting outrages upon the atmosphere. But it is the Sapient Nulliad alone who specializes in—"

"—Dreams," Beskot Kor Malifon completed his master's

thought. " 'Tis said that Nulliad reads dreams as clerks read High Strellian, let me perish!"

"Dreams," the Duke agreed. He heaved a sigh. "Dreams. And so I have come to verify these rumors, and to test the strength of great Nulliad's friendship for his Duke." He did not mention the possibility of financial recompense. Such an offer would have been deemed an insult to the abilities of the savant.

Nulliad inclined his head. "Nightmares trouble the Duke's repose?"

"Nightmare. Only one, but repeated again and again—" Povon shuddered. "Not even my most potent essences bring me peace. I have begun to fear the night."

"His Grace did well in coming to Nulliad. The frequent recurrence of this vision suggests urgency. It is clear that a message of some significance is intended."

"Message? From whom?" demanded the Duke.

Nulliad's gesture encompassed an entire shelf of books. "If his Grace would care to memorize the contents of the first twenty-nine in this series of volumes, then perhaps his Grace will be nearly ready to approach the problem." Povon subsided sulkily. "Suffice it to say the Duke's dream possesses meaning, probably of some more or less prophetic nature. The Cognition of Nulliad will lay bare this meaning."

"Meaning? Cognition?" The Duke rocked nervously in his chair. "I see no need. I came here tonight in search of a savant capable of providing me relief—a potion or a draught to banish evil dreams forever. Or failing that, an essence or inhalation to soothe my spirit. That is all your Duke desires. Meanings are irrelevant."

"There his Grace mistakes the matter. Stop rocking, if you please. You will move that chair out of position. It is only comprehension that will bring true peace to the Duke. It is only knowledge that will lend him the power to act as befits his best interests. For example—there is a strong possibility that the nightmare serves to warn of impending disaster. The benefits of foreknowledge are manifest."

"Perhaps." Duke Povon nibbled a nail. "Yes, perhaps. You have then no inhalations?"

"None. A light Cognitively induced self-revelatory state will serve his Grace far better." Nulliad carefully shifted one of the tables a hairbreadth nearer the window and swept an invisible fleck of dust from the surface.

"Self-revelatory state? You sound like my betrothed. I will tell you my dream. If you are the expert that you claim, you will explain the meaning and propose appropriate protective measures. That will suffice."

"It is not quite as simple as that." The Expulsion's attention shifted briefly to Kor Malifon. "Please do not handle the possessions of Nulliad. Replace that book in its original postion, immediately. There, that is adequate for now. No, your Grace," he continued, "the interpretation of dreams is not the straightforward mechanistic procedure you seem to imagine. Nocturnal visions are rife with curious imagery and symbolism, the meaning of which varies according to the nature and recollections of the individual dreamer. There are no universal symbols, despite claims to the contrary of certain well-intentioned but misguided latter-day quacks. Therefore, no truly specific interpretation may be accomplished without benefit of the insight provided by a Cognitive link. Is the Duke willing to place himself in the hands of Nulliad?"

"How long would this condition last?"

"Only so long as it takes his Grace to relate the dream."

"Will it hurt?"

"Such matters are difficult to predict."

"What if it doesn't work?"

"Then other, somewhat more violent, measures are indicated. It is neither pleasant nor advisable to contemplate them at present. But come, enough of this. Is his Grace ready to proceed?"

The Duke found it expedient to agree. He nodded glumly. His own sense of helplessness was unfamiliar as it was unwelcome, and therefore he turned to his companion. "You brought me here, Beskot. If things go badly, I will hold you personally responsible."

"I? But really, your Grace—"

"The Duke will compose himself," Nulliad commanded. "He will strive to recollect and organize all details of his nightmare."

"I won't have to strive. I couldn't forget 'em if I tried," the Duke muttered.

"Think."

The Duke sat frowning in silence. Beskot Kor Malifon was

similarly speechless. The silence was broken by the sound of a low, indeterminate chant issuing from the lips of the Sapient Nulliad. The syllables marched in measured cadences. Nulliad himself appeared abstracted, empty-eyed. Almost he seemed unaware of his surroundings. Presently a mental expansion signaled achievement of Cognition. The Expulsion approached Duke Povon, who eyed him with misgiving. Laying a double-jointed hand across the Duke's forehead, Nulliad commanded, "Relate the vision in its entirety."

Duke Povon sensed the intrusion of an alien intellect. A fit of trembling shook him and a variety of expressions passed across his features. These expressions were mirrored upon the face of Nulliad. "What have you done to me?" The Duke's voice quavered. "Your Cognition errs. What have you done to my mind?"

"Touched it. The Cognition of Nulliad does not err. Relate the vision."

The Duke gnawed his nether lip. The Sapient Nulliad did likewise. Nulliad's expression was ducally fearful and petulant, altogether not his own.

"Speak."

There followed a detailed description of the Duke's recurrent nightmare—from the ruins of Grizhni Palace, desolate beneath a flame-colored sky; to the humid cavern-dungeon, with its luminous white inhabitant; and at last to the resurrection of the vengeful Terrs Fal Grizhni. Duke Povon spoke in a halting manner. From time to time he paused in his recital to lick his dry lips. Nulliad mirrored the gesture. The narration concluded, and there was silence for a time.

The Sapient Nulliad withdrew his hand and stepped back from his visitor. The Cognitive link was broken. The Duke's alarm subsided, and his breathing steadied. Within moments he had so far regained his equilibrium as to inquire with an air of unconcern, "And has this diversion of Master Nulliad's proved no less profitable than entertaining?"

The Expulsion responded with a question of his own. Something appeared to be puzzling him. "Is Nulliad correct in his assumption that all members of Preeminence Terrs Fal Grizhni's household were put to death seventeen years ago?"

"Correct," Povon responded uncomfortably. The destruction of Grizhni Palace and its inhabitants was an episode on which he did not care to dwell. The act itself engendered not a particle of guilt, but he feared the world's censure.

"Then the House of Grizhni is utterly extinct?"

"To the best of my knowledge."

"There is an inconsistency here. No bastard issue?"

"Ho—not our Grizhni! It is a wonder amounting to a miracle the sanctimonious shard of ice ever managed to impregnate that most unlucky little girl he married. I would suspect that her womb frosted over shortly thereafter. No, no bastards."

"And Lady Grizhni never lived to deliver the child?"

"Presumably not. No, surely not. Impossible."

"Was there not some doubt about that?" Beskot Kor Malifon inquired. He made as if to rise from his chair, encountered the basilisk eyes of his host, and stayed put. "I seem to recall many rumors, much speculation at the time. It was said that Lady Grizhni escaped the massacre. It was said that she'd vowed to avenge her lord. People claimed they'd spotted her, looking pale and tragic, in various unlikely locales. The gossip inspired me to produce one of my most satiric lampoons—*Young Lady Grizhni in the Tavern*. Perhaps your Grace recalls it?"

"Is this correct?" Nulliad demanded of the Duke. "Preeminence Grizhni's wife may have survived to bear a child?"

"Unlikely," returned the Duke, more uncomfortable than ever. "Very unlikely indeed."

"Ah. All uncertainty vanishes. Nulliad may now explain the full significance of his Grace's nightmare."

The Duke suspected that he didn't want to know. His inquiring grunt was halfhearted at best.

"The dream is at once revealing and to a certain extent prophetic."

"Why should I be having such visions now, after all these years?" asked Povon.

"To put it in terms that his Grace will comprehend, the dreams came because it was time." Even Nulliad seemed to recognize the inadequacy of this response, and he added, "Perhaps his Grace recalls some unusual incident associated with the first occurrence of the nightmare?"

Povon shook his head. He did not wish to contemplate, much less discuss, the effects of Sny's Ambrosia.

"Very well, such discussion is fruitless. Let us proceed to the dream itself. The new information concerning the fate of

Lady Grizhni has clarified matters. Allow Nulliad to confirm what his Grace undoubtedly suspects. The widow of Grizhni escaped unharmed. Of this the Duke may be certain."

"I am not worried about Lady Grizhni." Impatience crackled the Duke's voice. "She was only a girl, quite a little charmer at that, and no threat. I'd just as soon have let her live. It is Grizhni himself that concerns me. Surely the nightmare cannot mean—cannot mean that he has returned from the grave?" Povon concluded with difficulty.

"So it does, but only in a metaphorical sense. Do not look so alarmed. Preeminence Grizhni is irrevocably dead. But his lady escaped, evidently gave birth to a son, and it is this latest efflorescence of the Grizhni line that perhaps poses some threat to his Grace."

"There is no 'perhaps' about it," declared the Duke. "If there's a son, he's dangerous. Are you certain of all this?"

"Assuming that no savant's Cognition imposed false prophecy upon his Grace's dreams, then the interpretation of Nulliad is reliable."

"Well then, perhaps the interpretation of Nulliad might extend so far as an explanation of the glowing white monster of the vision."

"Ah. Very interesting. Very interesting. The Sapient Nulliad found no image in the mind of his Grace corresponding to the description of the luminous white being of the dream. It is an utterly alien image. The Sapient Nulliad was forced to fall back upon his extensive knowledge of history, tradition, general Cognition. Thus he concluded that the white being of the dream was a Vardrul." The two visitors looked blank, and Nulliad explained, "Vardruls are those creatures often known to Lanthians as the 'White Demons of the Caverns.' "

"Pooh—a myth," opined Beskot Kor Malifon.

Nulliad deemed the remark unworthy of reply.

"Why would I dream of the White Demons?" demanded Povon.

Nulliad sighed patiently. "Does no explanation suggest itself to his Grace?"

"It is your business to provide the explanations. Even Preeminence Jinzin Farni does as much for his Duke."

"Evidently there is need. Very well. In light of the informative nature of the vision, it becomes obvious that the presence of the Vardrul is intended to suggest a specific locale. His

Grace's description of the abrupt transition from the ruins of Grizhni Palace to what is obviously a cave confirms this interpretation."

"A cave?"

"Surely that cannot surprise his Grace? Surely his Grace has realized by now that Lady Grizhni escaped Lanthi Ume seventeen years ago, sought sanctuary with the Vardruls of the Nazara Sin, and there delivered her son, who presumably throve. Did his Grace actually require the assistance of Nulliad in reaching so obvious a conclusion?"

Povon ignored the insult. "In the dream, Fal Grizhni attacks me. He reached out with those white hands, he means to kill me—" The Duke's voice was shaking. He paused, swallowed, and appealed, "What does it mean?"

"It is to be assumed that the son of Grizhni—now almost a man—is not kindly disposed toward the murderer of his father."

"I did not murder his father! It was Haik Ulf and his Guards. I wasn't even there!"

"Did his Grace not personally authorize the attack upon Grizhni Palace?"

"That's not the same thing!"

"A fine distinction, perhaps viewed in the light of a quibble by young Grizhni."

"Fal Grizhni was a proved traitor to his Duke! He deserved extreme punishment!"

"Abstract concepts of justice may perhaps exceed the reach of young Grizhni's adolescent mind."

"I do not want to hear this! This is not what I came to this place to hear! Beskot, why did you bring me here?" the Duke demanded. Beskot was silent, and Povon's agitation waxed. "What sort of danger does this son of Grizhni represent? Has he sworn to avenge his father? Can you tell me that?"

"It is uncertain whether any formal oath of vengeance has been sworn. The content of the vision suggests young Grizhni's enmity."

"And he plots against his Duke, like his father before him! Tell me, Sapience—does this young traitor possess Cognitive ability?"

"Beyond doubt. However, the extent to which he has learned to use it remains unclear."

"Ah. I see. I begin to understand. A danger exists, a threat to my welfare, and I have been warned. I am given the opportunity to defend myself. Perhaps it was well that I came here after all. Though I should have been fortified." The Duke straightened. "Sapience. Do you mean to tell me that the son of Grizhni lives to this day among the monsters of the Nazara Sin?"

"Such is the import of his Grace's dream. The Sapient Nulliad cannot attest with certainty to the essential accuracy of the information contained therein, but visions of this nature are for the most part reliable."

"That is all I need to know. Grizhni's son lives. Grizhni's son plots my destruction. He dwells in the caverns of the Nazara Sin. My course of action becomes clear. I must take steps to protect myself, whatever steps prove necessary." Povon glanced at Nulliad in search of confirmation, but the Expulsion's face was unreadable. "A military expedition—a surprise raid upon the caverns—destruction of Fal Grizhni's murderous whelp and the traitors who have harbored him all these years—and I shall rest secure."

The Expulsion offered no encouragement.

Povon chose to ignore the other's withering silence. "You have served your Duke well, Sapience Nulliad. Is there any way I may show my appreciation?"

"Yes. Take particular care to avoid disordering the possessions of Nulliad on your way out."

"We shall do so. We leave you to the solitude to which you are superbly suited. Once again, my thanks. Come, Beskot."

Povon and his companion took orderly leave. They made their way back to the Destula Pier without mishap, and there they found their dombulis awaiting them, but no sign of the armed servant. The fellow had disappeared without a trace. Beskot Kor Malifon was forced to man the oars, and proved predictably inexpert. The voyage back to the Ducal Palace was accordingly prolonged. Duke Povon reached home at last. He sought his bedchamber, confident that newfound knowledge had bought him peace at last. Having solved the riddle of the dream, he would now be wholly free of its terror. This proved not to be the case. Povon slept and the nightmare returned, more terrible than ever before. Once more he woke up screaming; and this time resolved to dispatch a contingent of Ducal Guards to the caverns of the Nazara Sin in the morning.

•   •   •

While the Duke conferred with the Sapient Nulliad, another interview took place not far away.

The second vessel to embark that night from the Ducal Moorings also headed for the Destula. The dombulis, bearing an oarsman and a single masked passenger, docked at a dingy little inlet off the Straightwater Canal, a short distance south of the Destula Pier. While the oarsman remained to guard the boat, the passenger disembarked and made his solitary way through alleyway and wynd as far as Grue's Cookshop, identifiable by its sign of the black vulture, intended as an ironic comment upon the abilities of the chef. Grue's Cookshop was closed for the night, but its characteristic aroma of rancid oil and aged fish lingered on. The door was shut and the windows dark. But the windows on the second floor, above the cookshop, were brightly lighted—an anomaly in that neighborhood, suggestive of naive or else uncommonly self-assured inhabitants.

A rickety flight of wooden stairs led up the outside of the building to a second-story entrance. The visitor ascended, paused at the door, took a deep breath, and knocked with a trembling hand.

A masculine voice from within answered. "Who's there?"

"It is the Lord Nobody," the masked man lied. It was in fact the Lord Sneever Dil Shonnet. "I was told you expected me. Have I got it wrong? Didn't you expect me?"

"Perhaps." A scrape as the bolt was drawn. Retreating footsteps within. "Enter, then."

After a moment's hesitation Sneever obeyed, shutting the door behind him. He found himself in a large, very dirty chamber, furnished in peculiarly squalid splendor. It looked like a satirist's version of the Ducal Palace. Gold paint was peeling in sheets off the massive, elaborately carved tables and chairs. The upholstery was filthy, sagging, shredded. The mirrors in their battered gilt frames were dim and cracked. The crystal lusters on the chandeliers were gauzy with cobwebs.

The air of seedy magnificence extended to the two occupants, who sat at the table, the remains of their evening meal spread out before them. One of them was a long-limbed, stout, and brawny man teetering on the verge of middle age. His face was broad and florid, the nose distinctively cleft. His hair, gleaming with pomade, was molded into a tall pompadour. His beard, likewise pomaded, was frizzled and forked. The man's ill-fitting apparel aspired to elegance—his brocade tunic, brave with tarnished lace, was elaborately puffed and slashed. The grayish linen visible through the slashes appeared not to have been changed in several years. Wine stains and grease spots covered the front of the garment. His figured tights were similarly sullied. His shoes, boasting the longest of pointed toes, were new and fashionable. A quantity of jewelry completed the costume. The numerous rings, chains, earrings, knee-sparklers, and beard-beads glittered with colored stones whose glassy sheen shouted counterfeit.

On the opposite side of the table sat a young girl, perhaps twelve or thirteen years of age. She was chalk-skinned, straw-haired, and moon-faced, with a tiny lipless slit of a mouth, a cleft nose, and whitish lashes shading pale eyes as bright and hard as her companion's counterfeit jewels. Her short, thickset body was incongruously clothed in a gown of silk, a woman's gown cut down to fit her. The sleeves were pushed back to display square, powerful-looking hands and muscular forearms. The grease-spotted skirt was hiked up. Evidently she prized freedom of movement above style.

The two at the table did not trouble to rise at the entrance of the visitor. Lounging back in their respective chairs, they eyed him with a lordly condescension that Sneever, despite his high birth, found discomforting.

Sneever stood fidgeting while the silence lengthened. At last he cracked and inquired uneasily, "The bravo Whurm Didnis?"

"I am the Lord Yans Whurm Didnis," the man at the table replied. "Lord Whurm Didnis by right of birth, Bravo Didnis by the cruelty of fate."

Sneever, unfamiliar with any noble family named Didnis, maintained politic silence.

"Beside me sits my beloved daughter and heiress, the Lady Josquinilliu Whurm Didnis," continued the bravo. "Salute our visitor, my darling Josky!"

Josky's pebble-hard eyes flicked Sneever up and down. "Make him take off that mask, my lord," she suggested.

"Ah no, my dear child. We must respect the privacy of our guests. It is in our observance of ordinary forms of courtesy, despite our station, that our breeding reveals itself."

"I want to see his face." The girl's jaw set. "I'll be nervous if I don't see it. Do you want me to be nervous, my lord? Do you want me to get another stomachache, the way I did last time?"

"Sweet child, you know I do not. But our visitor prefers anonymity. Surely it ill-befits our hospitality to insist—"

Josky appeared unaccustomed to contradiction. She scowled and her hard eyes grew harder yet. "I *want* to see his face! If he keeps that mask on, how do we know if we can trust him?"

"And if he takes it off, how shall we know?" Whurm Didnis smiled indulgently. "But my Lady Josquinilliu shall have her desire."

The hard set of Josky's jaw relaxed, and the storm clouds cleared as if by magic. Leaning across the table, she planted a kiss upon her father's cheek.

Whurm Didnis glowed. Turning to Sneever, he remarked, "Well, sir, you have heard. My little princess will not rest until she has seen your face. It is pointless to refuse her—she *will* have her way. I must require you to remove your vizard. Come into the light, where we can see you. You may seat yourself, if you please."

Sneever sat down at the table. His hands rose reluctantly to the ribbons of his vizard. Despite his reluctance, it did not occur to him to disobey the bravo's commands. As it happened, his fears were groundless. Unmasked, he continued unrecognized. The Lady Josky vented a small grunt of satisfied curiosity, and that was all.

"Well, sir, you may state your business." Whurm Didnis spoke as a lord to a tradesman.

Sneever felt his exposed face redden. He was, as usual, incapable of projecting the effortless, quelling superiority that was the appropriate response to the bravo's insolence. Instead, he grew tongue-tied and his eyelid started to jerk. He saw Lady Josky looking on in youthfully frank curiosity, and his embarrassment intensified. At last he summoned the presence of mind to speak. "You are the Whurm Didnis who will, for a price—er—assist in the removal of—of—certain difficulties, which I take to mean implies—"

"I am the bravo Didnis. My services are available to the select few. I am swift, unerring, and no victim escapes me. Are you answered?"

"Surely, sir—" Sneever's discomfort was well-nigh unbear-

able. He cast an anguished glance upon the impassive Lady
Josky. "Surely it is not right to discuss this matter in the presence
of a child—"

Whurm Didnis opened his mouth to reply, but his daughter
forestalled him. "Child yourself." Josky exuded pubescent contempt. "I am his lordship's assistant and apprentice, almost his
right arm. Already I am so proficient that he couldn't do without
me. Isn't that so, Dad? Together we repair the wrecked fortunes
of the noble House of Didnis. His lordship has taught me
everything. Do you think I don't understand poisons? Ask me
a question, any question. You think I'm not strong enough to
twist a garrote? Ha! Would you like to place a wager? Would
you bet your life? You'll see what kind of a child I am, you will."

Whurm Didnis roared with laughter. "Now there's a spirit
for you!" he exclaimed. "There's a brave heart and a noble
mind! What a girl I have! My lady Josky, I am proud of you!"
He turned to Sneever, who listened in mingled fascination and
revulsion. "There you have it. She is privy to my closest affairs.
You may speak freely."

Sneever saw no way out of it. His mouth was dry, but he
managed to speak. "Well, then, my lord Didnis, I have a task
for you—that is, a commission—an endeavor of great significance that I hope you will—"

"Who?" Whurm Didnis squelched his client's ramblings
without compunction.

"I've come to you because you are said to be the best—and—
and no less discreet than skillful—"

"Who?" Didnis repeated.

"It is a matter of no small delicacy, and requires the utmost—"
Sneever broke off as he met the bravo's flinty eyes. "That is
to say, it's—well—it's the Duke," he concluded in a rush. "The
Duke Povon Dil Shonnet."

There was a moment's silence. Sneever experienced a certain
feeble satisfaction in producing at last an impression upon his
hosts. Whurm Didnis had been taken completely by surprise,
there could be no doubt of that. His doubt and consternation
were plain to see. The response of Lady Josky, while dissimilar,
was no less heartfelt than that of her sire. Her pale eyes glowed,
and she murmured in awe, "Oh, suPREME!"

"The Duke himself. That is not an easy target," Whurm
Didnis observed at last.

"Does the bravo Didnis, first among assassins, limit himself to easy targets?" Sneever inquired. The indecision of his host restored much of his shattered confidence. His confusion abated and his eyelid quieted. "Has your competence been overrated, sir? Is the task beyond you?"

"No task exceeds the capacity of the Lord Yans Whurm Didnis," the bravo asserted. "We nobles are bred for courage, and I'm fit for any venture. But the Duke—that requires thought."

"I will pay you thrice your customary fee," Sneever promised recklessly. A certain odd sensation of freedom, almost of exhilaration, was beginning to sweep through him.

"I would expect no less. And yet—to dispatch a man so much in the public eye, and then escape unscathed—it would not be easy. Careful thought and planning, down to the last detail of execution, would be required. It would be a considerable undertaking."

"But a worthwhile endeavor," Sneever replied and continued almost involuntarily, as if a dam had broken inside him. "There is not a man alive more deserving of death than the Duke. He is a monster of cruelty, of selfishness, of evil. He should be dead. And if he suffers—that is only common justice. I want him to suffer. I should like to watch. I should like to watch for hours. I should like to hear him squeal and scream and beg for mercy. And then I should like to see his face when that mercy is denied. That would make me very happy."

"Ah, the vendetta is it?" Whurm Didnis nodded sagely. "I can understand that. But that is no concern of mine, and as yet I remain undecided—"

But Lady Josky was not undecided in the least. "My lord—you're not going to turn him down, are you? He'll go somewhere else, and then *somebody else will get the Duke!*"

"That's true, my princess, but there is much—"

"We're the best, my lord. *We* should do it. Just think of it—the Duke!"

"My lionhearted daughter, you've a noble courage, but—"

"We can take him, Dad. The two of us, together. I know we can. If we don't, someone else will do it and then start putting on airs and bragging that he's better than we are. *And it wouldn't be true!*"

"Dear child, you are somewhat hasty—"

Josky's pale eyes narrowed. She leaned forward in her chair. "I *want* it, Dad. Please say yes. I want it more than *anything!*"

Whurm Didnis could resist no longer. Turning to Sneever he remarked, "I'll need some information concerning the Duke's habits, and the location of his apartment within the palace."

Sneever nodded. "Easily done."

"And I require half my payment in advance."

"Agreed."

"In that case, Lord Nobody, be at ease—the Duke is as good as dead."

Sneever reached under his cloak, ostensibly to search for his purse of gold, but actually to conceal the trembling of his hands. Lady Josquinilliu smiled, and blew her father a kiss.

Chapter Four

When Lady Verran, as the Grizhni Matriarch, received the chain of pebbles that served as notification of the Zmadrc clan's willingness to accept her son as future brother/consort to young Zmadrc Fourteen, her agitation was intense. It was not that it came as a complete surprise, of course. Terrs had made his intentions clear, and she'd certainly had fair warning. But she had never expected events to move so swiftly.

"It's too soon! He's only a boy! He doesn't know his own mind!" Verran exclaimed aloud.

Her hybrid companion croaked. As usual, Nyd responded more to his lady's tone than to her actual words, but Verran imagined she heard more than simple concern in the sound. She considered her own statements, and was forced to concede that Terrs knew his own mind only too well.

"But he doesn't understand what he's doing! Brother/consort to a Vardrul—it's so unnatural, so wrong! He's choosing an alien way of life, he's destroying himself—and *there's nothing I can do to stop him.*"

The thought rankled. It hurt to admit that her son had grown beyond her influence. But she was well aware that no appeal to reason, affection, guilt or sentiment, no argument or plea, would keep Terrs from anything he really wanted. He would go his own way, as his father had.

"There's no point in arguing with Terrs," Verran informed the uncomprehending Nyd. "He won't listen. But maybe the Zmadrc Patriarch will. Perhaps I can persuade him to cancel or at least postpone this acceptance. Then Terrs would have to wait, whether he likes it or not. The longer he waits, the better the chance that he'll come to his senses. Yes, I must talk to The Zmadrc. Try, at least." The prospect was daunting. The proposed conversation would have to be conducted in the Vardrul language, for the Zmadrc Patriarch spoke not a word of Lanthian. Verran's command of the alien tongue was tolerably good—more than sufficient for ordinary purposes. But there were many shadings of pitch and hiir that continued to elude her understanding, and she would never achieve true fluency, much less eloquence. She could not express her thoughts with absolute precision, and even more important, she could not accurately gauge the reactions of her Vardrul listeners. Oh, Zmadrc R'dsvyllsch would listen politely enough. The Zmadrc was always courteous, always kind. But he would stare at her with those vast inhuman eyes, and she would never know what he was really thinking or feeling. Still, she would have to try.

"Come with me, Nyd?" she invited, and the hybrid assented enthusiastically. As they exited her chamber and made their away along the rock-lit corridors, Verran could not help but notice that Nyd was struggling to keep pace with her. He was limping and seemed to be in some pain. "What is it? What's the matter, my dear?"

Nyd croaked impatiently and quickened his pace. Evidently he considered the matter unworthy of attention.

Sore joints, Verran thought. *He's getting old. He's not the only one.* She deliberately slowed her steps, and was rewarded by the sound of Nyd's half-suppressed hiss of relief.

Even walking slowly, it did not take long to reach the great combined fungoid-crystal gardens of the Zmadrc and Lbavbsch clans, where the Zmadrc Patriarch could usually be found during the First Coloration of each Small Ven. It was not necessary to request permission or make an appointment to address The Zmadrc Lesser Patriarch. One could approach him directly, and if he was not otherwise engaged, he would speak. This relative lack of ceremony was one aspect of Vardrul society that Verran actually found preferable to the formal conventions of Lanthi Ume.

Before her straggled the enormous Zmadrc-Lbavbsch gardens, irregular and meandering after the Vardrul fashion. Various members of the two families congregated there, but the subjects of their ordinary discourse remained unknown to Verran. Not that they deliberately excluded her from their conversations—their manners were too good for that. But on past occasions when she had tried to join in, she'd sensed the air of constraint, the faint tension, the never-failing disharmony. After many such uncomfortable attempts, she had finally given up trying.

At the center of the garden bubbled a natural hot spring surrounded by a pale of giant, swordlike crystals. There, where the rock-light was soft, the heat intense, and the humidity almost unbearable by human standards, stood a number of slants, one of them occupied by the Zmadrc Lesser Patriarch, toward whom Verran directed her steps.

The Zmadrc rose at her approach, interlaced his tentacles politely, and warbled the Vardrul greeting reserved for respected guests not regarded as intimates. The acceptance of Terrs by the Zmadrc clan might have entitled Verran to a modified familial greeting, but such would have increased her discomfort; and, presumably, The Zmadrc's as well. Insofar as she was capable of comprehending him at all, Verran appreciated The Zmadrc's tact.

She returned the greeting and, in accordance with Vardrul simplicity of style, stated her purpose at once. There followed a stilted, uneasy conversation, only approximately translatable into human terms.

"Zmadrc R'dsvyllsch, I have received the chain of pebbles, and I am troubled," Verran announced, humming the difficult syllables with care. "I am extremely disharmonious. The prospect of my son's acceptance into the Zmadrc clan alarms me, despite the honor, for the attempt denies nature and denies reality."

The Zmadrc Patriarch considered her remarks. The Grizhni Matriarch's uneasiness was apparent, but her attempted explanation decidedly obscure. "The young Fal Grizhni Terrs is esteemed and accepted for the Grizhni Patriarch's sake." The wavelike contraction of his ocular ridges combined with a correspondingly rhythmic alteration of hiir would have conveyed reassurance to another Vardrul, but the Grizhni Matriarch showed no sign of understanding. "He has formed connections among the Zmadrc members, who admire his resolve"—the Vardrul expression actually used implied prolonged determination in the face of overwhelming difficulties, with the suggestion of a nearly unattainable goal—"to mold the substance of his essential being. We are gratified to accept him."

"Patriarch, you have been a friend to my son all his life,

and he has needed it. I know Terrs has asked this favor of you, and your kindness in granting his request makes me grateful. But Terrs is still very young by Surface reckoning, certainly unready for great decisions. He does not always know what is best for him. What he has asked of you, he does not truly comprehend." How difficult the Vardrul language was! The concept she wished to express was that of immaturity, but the closest she could come to it was a series of notes carrying the connotation of mild foolishness or gullibility, which was far from her meaning.

The Zmadrc evidently misunderstood. "The intellect of the young Fal Grizhni Terrs is powerful, so much so that I stand in—" The word he used might have meant awe, or amazement, or even mild fear. The modifying tremolo failed to clarify matters.

"Yes." Verran spoke more carefully than ever. "He is wise, perhaps even as wise as the Grizhni Patriarch, although not nearly so learned. But that does not mean he cannot make mistakes. He is making one now. Zmadrc R'dsvyllsch, how can my son enter your clan? He is human. He tries to deny this, but he cannot succeed in denying nature." Curse this barrier that imposed such verbal constraint! "He will be a misfit among you, always. He will feel it terribly, and he will be more unhappy than ever. He will bring disharmony to the Zmadrc clan." Did The Zmadrc understand her? Did he agree? As usual, the huge eyes in the luminous face beamed unintelligible messages.

The Grizhni Matriarch was concerned for the state of her son's ruu. Her misgivings apparently extended as far as the welfare of the entire Zmadrc clan. An explanation of the Balance of Hdsjri might have set her mind at rest, but the unfortunate human would never understand it. The Zmadrc might have discoursed at length upon the highly relevant topic of F'tvar'drsch Re, but again, she would not understand him. Despite his wish to comfort the dissonant Matriarch, Zmadrc R'dsvyllsch's options were few, and he could only observe, "We see hope for the young Fal Grizhni Terrs."

Was that all he could say? She stared at him and saw his flesh darken. The Zmadrc's dimming suggested compassion, or pity, or moderate grief, or a combination thereof. Whether for Verran, or for Terrs, or for both, was unclear. Verran persisted. "How could my son be brother/consort to your daughter Fourteen? Surely you do not wish such disharmony upon her?"

The Grizhni Matriarch seemed not to comprehend fully the true nature of disharmony, else she could not have asked so meaningless a question. An explanation, however, would be impossible without reference to the Lvjirri, which she, never having known her Ancestors, had never experienced and would not understand.

Why doesn't he answer? Verran wondered. *Doesn't he care about his child?*

At last The Zmadrc replied, "The young Zmadrc Fourteen, being grown to her full height, has made her own choice, thus demonstrating her belief in her future brother/consort's ultimate achievement of harmony."

"But children, Zmadrc R'dsvyllsch?" Verran forced herself to ask. She hated even to consider the possibility. "What of children?"

"We may hope for them, Grizhni Matriarch."

Is this hypocrisy? No, he means it. But how can he? Aloud she observed, as calmly as possible. "It would be better if there were none." This time Verran was able to interpret The Zmadrc's reaction without difficulty—simple astonishment. The Vardruls, with their limited fertility and their sense of oneness, regarded children as an unqualified blessing. The Zmadrc could scarcely conceive of a differing point of view.

The Zmadrc's flesh flickered erratically. He hummed a single note, high-pitched to the extreme limit of audibility. His companion almost felt it rather than heard it.

"If children come, they will be half human, half Vardrul," Verran continued. That thought was relatively easy to express, but thereafter things grew more difficult. "Long ago, my consort the Grizhni Patriarch told me that Cognition cannot alter a man's basic nature. Thus Terrs may change himself in appearance, may even come to know his Ancestors, yet he will always remain essentially human. If Terrs takes a Vardrul sister/consort, the issue of that union will"—she groped for the right syllables, the right pitch—"carry humanity within them. They will carry humanity from clan to clan, until the nature of Man infuses itself throughout the veins of all the race of Vardruls. Your people will change, Zmadrc R'dsvyllsch. They will be Vardruls no longer."

"I do not understand. The young Fal Grizhni Terrs strives

for oneness, for harmony. If he achieves these things, so good in themselves, how can the outcome be other than good?"

How can I explain? She moistened her lisp and made the attempt. "Patriarch, you do not know human character. There is a savagery, a ferocity, a cruelty in Man that is sometimes very visible, sometimes hidden deep inside—but always there, to some degree. The Vardruls are free of this taint. Your kinsmen/subjects are kind, gentle, peaceable. Best that they remain so. The consequences of change are apt to be harmful, perhaps tragic." The Vardrul vocabulary did not encompass the human concept of tragedy, with its underlying suggestion of self-destruction. Verran's actual phrase was closer to "ultimate grief, final destruction of all hope and happiness."

The Zmadrc digested this advice in silence. His diminution of hiir was pronounced, and his ocular ridges were unwontedly still. His reply, when it came, was incomprehensible. "And yet the ruu of the Zmadrc Ancestors fulfills the conditions of Lvjirri as never before. Did you not know?"

To Verran, it bordered on gibberish. Had he understood her at all? She found it impossible to judge. There was only one crucial point that he *must* be made to understand. "Zmadrc R'dsvyllsch," she implored, "accept Terrs as a kinsman/subject if you must, but I beg you, do not name him brother/consort to Zmadrc Fourteen."

This time she had succeeded in making herself clear, and the Zmadrc Patriarch was able to answer with assurance, "That is the decision of the young Zmadrc Fourteen, who has already conveyed the crystals of assent. Surely the young ones must not be deprived of their just liberties and privileges. Thus the acceptance of Fal Grizhni Terrs by the Zmadrc clan will take place upon the verge of our family death-pool two Small Vens hence. And yet the Grizhni Matriarch need not fear, for the young Fal Grizhni Terrs shall not be brother/consort to my daughter, but only her Future, until he has known his Ancestors, and experienced the clan-warmth. Only then can true consortship exist."

This reply, while less than Verran had hoped for, did offer a certain measure of hope. Terrs was not irrevocably committed until he had known the Ancestors. It would take many more Vens of study and practice before his Cognition would be equal to such a task. With any luck, he would never succeed at all. *He might, of course, succeed a Coloration from now.* In any case, she assured herself, there was still time left—time in which he might come to recognize his own folly. Verran felt her tension ease a little. The situation, while very ominous, was not yet desperate. The Zmadrc Patriarch was speaking again. She would have to pay attention if she hoped to understand him.

"Grizhni Matriarch, we find it difficult indeed to communicate. I do not believe this can ever change."

"I fear you are right, Zmadrc R'dsvyllsch." She managed a faint smile.

The Zmadrc, aware of the general meaning of the majority of human smiles, brightened and contracted his inner ocular ridges. "But there is one thing I wish to say to you, and for this our differences need not stand in the way of understanding. I recognize—as do we all—that the Grizhni Matriarch's life among us has been neither easy nor happy. Isolated from others of your kind, there can be no oneness and no harmony. Without harmony, no contentment. We are powerless to improve matters. Yet it should be recognized that the Grizhni Matriarch is surrounded by friends."

Verran was startled. In seventeen years no Vardrul had ever addressed so personal a remark to her. She found herself touched. The Zmadrc Patriarch, like all Vardruls, was inexpressibly remote and mysterious. She had always resented him a little as a rival for her son's affections. Now she saw his goodness, the generosity capable of bridging the gap between differing species, and regretted her past distrust. Her smile was genuine this time, as she replied, "I thank you, Zmadrc R'dsvyllsch, and I will remember your words. My son is fortunate in his new kinsmen and his new Patriarch."

Two Small Vens later, Verran stood upon the shore of the Zmadrc death-pool to watch her son accepted into the clan as Future to Zmadrc Fourteen. There had been some talk of postponing the ceremony, due to the presence in the hills overhead of a party of Ducal Guardsmen. Such a visitation was uncommon as it was unwelcome. Rarely, if ever, were armed Guardsmen to be glimpsed so far from the city of Lanthi Ume. The Vardruls greeted the intrusion with characteristic timidity. They camouflaged the entrances to their caverns with brush and disappeared within, refusing to venture Surface day or night. How different, Verran reflected, were Vardrul and human reactions! Faced with a similar situation, human beings would have posted sentries, would have sent out scouts and trackers, would have kept the invaders under surveillance at all times. If circumstances seemed to warrant, men would have prepared for an attack. But not the Vardruls, whose instinctive responses tended toward flight and concealment. Humans might have called it cowardice. To Verran, it seemed but the natural softness of creatures hitherto innocent of predatory impulses.

Innocent? Yes, they really are—for now. And if Terrs gets what he wants? Then what?

She didn't want to think about it. Better, far better, to concentrate on the scene before her. Upon the urging of Terrs, the Zmadrc clan had elected to proceeed with the simple ceremony of acceptance, Guardsmen notwithstanding. That ceremony was about to commence, and Verran was to participate.

It was the first time in all her Great Vens of residency that she had actually seen a death-pool, for such places were regarded as the inviolable private retreats of their respective clans. As nearly as Verran could determine, the pools were not literally *owned* in the human sense. Rather, the various families voluntarily respected the sanctity of those locales wherein clan members were able to achieve a specific, intense sense of oneness that superseded even the close unity of the Vardrul race as a whole.

The death-pools were customarily difficult of access, often approachable only by way of tortuous passageways so low that one had to wriggle through them with face all but pressed to the stone floor. Such passages were known by a humorous Vardrul term that translated approximately to "Bellyscrapers." Other pools were guarded by chasms crossed only by the most perilously slender and narrow of natural stone bridges. Had it been so in this case, Verran would never have attempted attendance. There were many areas of the caverns wherein she, unlike the Vardruls born to subterranean life, did not dare to wander. It was but another of the myriad differences that set her apart from her hosts. Terrs, whose determination overcame all obstacles, could navigate the caverns with the confidence of a true native.

Fortunately, the Zmadrc death-pool was easy to reach—uncommonly easy, in fact. The Zmadrcs, already established as a thriving clan at the time of the Vardruls' original flight to the caves of the Nazara Sin, had availed themselves of one of the first pools of appropriate depth to be discovered in the new domain. It lay but a few hundred yards from the Mvjri Dazzle, one of the largest and most conspicuous of the various Surface gateways. Such entrances, particularly the larger ones, were often termed *dazzles* in reference to the visual discomfort experienced by Vardruls venturing too near with eyes unveiled during the daylight hours. The Zmadrc death-pool lay at the end of a broad, straight corridor. The way was undemanding, and moribund clan members were easily transported. The pool had been the site of innumerable expirations, and the atmosphere breathed history. In that hallowed chamber, knowledge of the Ancestors was attained with comparative effortlessness. Exchange of such knowledge was an integral part of the ceremony of acceptance.

The pool was funnel-shaped, with sloping, rock-lit sides. The blood-warm wavelets that lapped the stony bank appeared to glow. Some distance below the surface the light failed, for reasons that had never been investigated. It was assumed that the character of the rock itself must change, but no one could be certain. Whatever the cause, the bottom of the pool was lost in shadow that preserved the privacy of those many Zmadrc sons and daughters who had achieved the ultimate oneness.

Scores of Vardruls stood ranged about half the perimeter of the death-pool. The entire clan was assembled to greet the new Future to Zmadrc Fourteen. Their luminous bodies glowed and flickered rhythmically. The pattern was simple and repetitive, and for once Lady Verran was able to decipher the message of the Ftvyi—the Vardruls extended welcome to their new kinsman Terrs, and to those others of his clan now to be honored as direct Connections to the Zmadrcs. Ordinarily such ceremonies linked entire clans, promoting unity of the race. In this case, Terrs's clan consisted of the Grizhni Matriarch alone, and possibly of Nyd, whose status had never been conclusively determined. Thus, the Grizhni half of the bank was occupied only by two anomalous, conspicuous figures. Verran inclined her head and interlaced her fingers in her best approximation of the Vardrul gesture of courtesy. Young Terrs did likewise, but the boy was not bound by all the anatomical limitations that handicapped his mother. He had transformed his hands for the occasion.

Verran regarded her son with some reluctance. She could hardly bear the sight of his lucent Vardrulesque members, the fingers elongated and sickeningly flexible. How long would it last this time? In the Small Vens that had passed since he first demonstrated his new achievement, he had practiced fanatically. It was only reasonable to assume that his Cognitive competence was increasing.

One of these Colorations he's going to learn to fix the effect permanently, and then his hands will never be human again. And then he'll go on to change his feet, or perhaps his face or his eyes. It will be like watching the progress of an incurable disease. But will it make him happy?

Terrs stood on the Zmadrc side, separated from his mother by the entire width of the pool. *Appropriate,* thought Verran dryly. Attired in his customary simple gray robe, he stood straight and tall, taller than anyone else in the room. What an intelligent, strong face he had, and how proud of him she could be, if only— *If only.* Terrs's tentacles were knotted. His expression was serious, as befit the occasion, but Verran could sense his satisfaction.

Can't you do as he asked, and try to be happy for him? Try? Possibly. Succeed? Doubtful.

Beside Terrs stood Zmadrc Fourteen, also attired in a robe.

Why is she wearing that? Is it part of the ceremony, a tradition? Or is she doing it so that Terrs and I won't be the only ones here covered up? Verran observed Fourteen closely, as if she had never seen the young Vardrul before. *My prospective daughter-in-law. Of sorts. Will it really come to that? No, there's still time—surely they'll change their minds before it's too late!* Fourteen was average in height, far shorter than Terrs. She was slim to the point of emaciation, flexible, graceful, and very sure in her movements, like all her kind. There was nothing that particularly set her apart in appearance from other Vardruls of similar age, with the possible exception of a pair of huge eyes, brighter than the rock-light, alive with intelligence and feeling, unusual in size even by the standards of her great-eyed people. Those eyes were fixed on Terrs. Verran was a little too far away to catch the expression, and probably could not have interpreted it in any case.

Why has that girl—she's not a girl, she's a brfva'ardtruliinjr, but I can't manage that and I'm just going to call her a girl—why has she chosen to accept a human brother/consort? I cannot understand why she would want to. Granted, she's always been close to Terrs, but even so—brother/consort? Is it necessary

*to go to such lengths to prove her regard? I know why Terrs
wants this match, that's clear enough. But why do the Zmadrcs
agree? I don't understand their reasoning. I'll never understand.*

Fourteen was talking to Terrs, flickering and warbling with
the vivacity that had characterized her from earliest childhood.
Verran was too far away to hear the phrases, would probably
have missed half of them anyway, for Fourteen, blessed with
a headful of ideas and a generous measure of youthful enthusiasm, fluted her phrases with twice the speed of the average
Vardrul. Terrs, of course, could understand her very well. He
looked down into her eyes as she spoke, and his expression
reflected none of the wary reserve that his mother knew so
well. Fourteen's ocular ridges undulated, and her hiir rose.

What exactly does that mean? Verran wondered.

Just behind Terrs and Fourteen, the Zmadrc Patriarch stood
atop the low, flat Speaker's Stone. The slight additional elevation directed collective attention to the speaker, but did not
serve to separate him from his clan.

A hush fell over the assembled Zmadrcs. Some mysterious
shared inner voice had informed them that their Patriarch was
about to speak. The Zmadrc's remarks would be minimal,
serving as a brief introduction to the exchange of information
that was the true purpose of the ceremony of acceptance. For
the ceremony was not an empty ritual, and the Connections
established upon this Coloration were based on more than mere
tradition. On the shore of the Zmadrc death-pool, the clan
members would achieve knowledge of the Ancestors. That
knowledge would be passed on to the Grizhni family, thus
effecting a closeness and understanding obtainable by no other
means. It was recognized, of course, that the Grizhni clan's
limitations precluded an equal exchange. But the humans, incapable of knowing their Ancestors, would offer what they
could—the Grizhni Matriarch's description of her own immediate Ancestors of the House of Verras, together with an
account of the life and character of her late consort, the Fal
Grizhni Patriarch. To be sure this hardly equalled knowledge
of Ancestors, but all information related to The Grizhni, whose
conquest of the cold had opened up the caverns, was to be
prized.

"Beloved friends and kinsmen/subjects, we gather here in
the presence of our Ancestors to welcome a new member to

our family," The Zmadrc announced with typical simplicity.

As usual, Lady Verran mentally eliminated untranslatable phrases and concepts. It was almost as if she didn't hear them. This editing accomplished, she was able to follow most Vardrul conversation with fair success.

"Fal Grizhni Terrs enters our clan as Future brother/consort to the young Zmadrc Fourteen. Our family is fortunate indeed to receive the son of the great Fal Grizhni Patriarch."

An appreciative hum arose. Sincere? The Vardruls were not given to hypocrisy, but their melodies might well be governed by simple courtesy. A more reliable indication of their true feelings was provided by the level of their luminosity, which was not at all times under strictly voluntary control. Verran noted that the hiir of the Zmadrcs was uniformly strong and steady. Their pleasure in Terrs's admittance was unfeigned.

"Our acceptance of Fal Grizhni Terrs establishes Connection for all time between the clans of Zmadrc and of Grizhni. In this too is clan Zmadrc honored," The Zmadrc continued.

At this point the ritual response of the speaker for the visiting clan might have been expected, but the very unusual circumstances surrounding this ceremony permitted an alteration in the customary procedure. Zmadrc Fourteen stepped up onto the Speaker's Stone to stand beside her father. Turning to face Lady Verran, she spoke in halting Lanthian. "We extend welcome to the family of Terrs Fal Grizhni. We hope that the Lady Grizhni and the Nyd Grizhni share our happiness in this joining."

Verran was startled. Great Vens earlier she had taught a little Lanthian to some of the children, and Fourteen had been a promising student for a while. But the lessons hadn't lasted long, and she hadn't expected the young Vardrul to remember. She'd forgotten herself how surprisingly human a Vardrul could sometimes sound. Fourteen's voice was sweet and clear and altogether—girlish. Only the intense musicality was subtly alien.

This is a pretty gesture. I wonder if Fourteen thought of it herself? If so, she's got her father's tact. She will need all of it if she really does end up as Terrs's sister/consort. No, I can't think about that now. A response was obviously called for, and Verran answered in her rigidly careful Vardrul notes, "The Grizhni clan is much honored. We extend our thanks and our warmest regards to clan Zmadrc." Not the most effusive of returns, perhaps, but courteous enough, and for the life of her, she couldn't say more. The collective Vardrul attention made her too nervous, too aware of her verbal shortcomings. Beside her, Nyd croaked uneasily. It always disquieted him to hear the inhuman syllables sing from the lips of his lady.

Verran's response, brief though it was, appeared to gratify the Zmadrc audience. Many present brightened, and Terrs bestowed one of his rare smiles upon her. It was Terrs's turn to speak now, and the prospect evidently did not intimidate him in the least. Mounting the Speaker's Stone with confidence, he delivered a brief address in which he proclaimed his allegiance to the Zmadrc clan; reaffirmed his natural and unbreakable ties to clan Grizhni; and expressed his happiness at the prospect of his impending brother/consortship to Zmadrc Fourteen. Terrs spoke clearly and well. He was completely at home with the Vardrul language, and there was no trace of adolescent clumsiness or uncertainty in his manner. Moreover, he spoke with a forceful economy more than a little reminiscent of his father.

He could be a leader, Verran thought. *Or a savant, if he chose. He could be anything he wanted. If only I could get him out of these caves!*

Terrs's remarks concluded, and the boy resumed his place. It was time to proceed with the activity around which the ceremony of acceptance truly centered—the Zmadrc clan's knowledge of Ancestors, and verbal conveyance of that knowledge to the new clan member. Since knowledge of Ancestors was dependent on blood relationship, the Zmadrc Ancestors could only be known by Zmadrc clan members. Individuals possessing ability to know the Ancestors of more than one clan were rare, owing to the Vardrul propensity for inbreeding. Verbal exchanges of knowledge, however, promoted the unity and harmony of the race.

Once more Verran beheld a group knowledge of Ancestors, and her mind jumped to the scene she had witnessed Great Vens earlier, out upon the Gravula Wasteland at the foot of the Granite Sages. Now, as then, the Vardruls before her concentrated fiercely, straining every nerve to direct their awareness back link by link along the tenuous inborn chain, back as far as determination and innate ability could carry them. Their faces were blank, the ocular muscles relaxed. Now, as then, the erratic fluctuations of hiir signaled the intensity of mental effort. Verran recalled her son's look of longing, his desperation as he had watched them upon that long-ago evening. Terrs was older now and in much better command of his emotions. His face was very still, almost masklike, the lips firmly compressed. But even separated from him by the width of the pool, Verran could not miss the intensity in his eyes. *Same as ever,* she thought. *He hasn't changed at all. And he never will, not as long as he insists on remaining down here.* She tried to catch his eye and failed.

The collective hiir was rising. One by one, the Vardrul forms and faces flared as the Ancestors were encountered and known. At no time was hiir so high as in the presence of the Ancestors, and in this stronghold of Zmadrc unity, upon the shore of the death-pool itself, contact was particularly strong. On the previous occasion that Verran had witnessed such a scene, the Vardrul bodies had been swathed in heavy wrappings. Now they were uncovered, and the light of the Zmadrc flesh was extraordinarily brilliant, almost painful to the eyes. The Vardrul tentacles, ordinarily so expressively flexible, were stiff, immobile. The great eyes were open but blind, all vision directed inward. Awareness of present surroundings had fled.

Only three figures in the death-pool chamber remained dark and dull—two human and one hybrid. Only three figures in the chamber remained isolated, excluded, untouched by the ancient currents of thought and emotion. Terrs's expression was less guarded now, Verran noted. His hunger and determination were quite visible.

Zmadrc R'dsvyllsch began to speak. It was not his rank as Patriarch of the clan that granted him precedence, but rather his power to commune with the earliest and most remote of Ancestors, beyond the reach of any of his kinsmen/subjects. He spoke, his voice slow, as if it traveled infinite distances; harsher and far less melodic than usual, as if issuing from the throat of a creature far removed in kind and thought from Vardruls of the present day.

"Zmadrc—Zmadrc—Zmadrc—Nvgr'llnjr of Zmadrc mourns the loss of the sky. Loss—grief—anger. The sky—the stars— the moon—all lost to us, stolen by Men. Fear. Fear of Men, the destroyers. Fear. Grief. Loss. I am the last alive to remember, and I am very ancient. Soon all recollection will belong to the Ancestors alone, and the living, knowing nothing but these caves, will forget the sky. Loss—grief—anger—grief."

There came a pause, and when The Zmadrc resumed, the voice that was not his own grew feebler. "Tired. Grief. Tired. I lie upon the bank of the new death-pool, and the grief is with me yet. The sky is lost, the stars are hidden, but someday we shall reclaim them. Return to the surface, led by a great one, as it is promised. Reclaim the sky, the moon, the stars. Return. Return. Return."

A longer pause, and The Zmadrc's tones altered. He no longer spoke in the voice of Nvgr'linjr of Zmadrc, and his discourse grew far less intelligible. He spoke of the Zmadrc role in the development of the Balance of Hdsjri, and the description was riddled with phrases that Verran could not begin to understand. Despite the wonder of the scene before her, her attention flagged a little, and the near-sacrilegious question popped into her mind, *How do they know that any of this is true? How can they be so certain that the Ancestors are a trustworthy source of information? What if they hear what the Ancestors honestly believed to be true, and what if the Ancestors were mistaken?* But the Vardruls accepted and believed without reservation. Terrs believed too—she could tell by the rapt expression on his face as he listened. Terrs believed every word.

The hybrid Nyd was the single being in the entire room whose attention was unengaged by the knowledge of Ancestors. Thus Nyd was the first to notice the arrival of a group of Vardruls. His hiss of alarm alerted his lady, who turned to look. At once she knew that something was very wrong.

The newcomers were dull, human-dull. The light of their flesh was extinguished, the hiir at the lowest possible ebb. Only one or two still flickered weakly, and the pace of their signaling was frenetic. The diminished hiir and the super-rapid, irregular flickerings conveyed overwhelming negative emotion. One look into the staring eyes of the arrivals served to inform Verran what that emotion was—fear amounting to panic. She had seen frightened Vardruls before, and recognized the signs—the extreme expansion of the concentric sets of ocular ridges, and the filminess of the eyes. Once, Great Vens ago, when the Lesser Matriarch of the R'jnrllsch clan had emerged Surface too lightly covered to sustain the winter chill and had lapsed into Cold Stupor, Verran had seen true fear cloud the eyes of the Matriarch's kinsmen/subjects. But never in all the length of her residency had she witnessed anything approaching the intense terror she now beheld.

They came in running, about a dozen of them, mostly members of the Lbavbsch and F'tryll'jnr clans. Some of them were crying as they ran, and the sound, while subdued, was astonishingly discordant—the Vardrul equivalent of human screams. Their entrance roughly severed the Ancestral connections of a number of Zmadrc clan members. The Zmadrcs, shocked at the abrupt loss of oneness, warbled in astonishment and pained bewilderment. Their bewilderment deepened as the new arrivals hurried to and fro, shaking and prodding their tranced compatriots. The inexplicable assault was successful. Within moments, the Zmadrc clan's hiir dropped. The intense fleshly brilliance faded. The Vardruls dimmed, then began to flicker as contact with the Ancestors was broken. Knowledge gave way to alarm and disharmony. The exclamations of the Zmadrcs added themselves to the screams of the Lbavbschs and F'tryll'jnrs, and for a few moments confusion reigned. It did not take long, however, for the newcomers to make themselves undersood. Their warning was succinct: "Men here—killing us—killing us—"

Men within the caverns? It was almost inconceivable. The Zmadrcs darkened in wonder rather than fear.

"Hide—run—hide!"

Still somewhat stunned by the abrupt loss of Ancestral knowledge, the Zmadrc members were sluggish. Trilling their incomprehension, they awaited the verdict of their Patriarch. But Zmadrc R'dsvyllsch, whose trance had distanced his consciousness by countless generations, remained dazed and speechless.

Verran clutched Nyd's paw. "Quick, we've got to get to Terrs." Together they circled the edge of the pool. Before they reached the oposite shore, human forms appeared in the doorway and came spilling into the Zmadrc death-pool chamber.

It was a squadron of Lanthian soldiers, clad in the green and gold of the Ducal Guards. Most of them were sopping wet, covered with sweat and colorless Vardrul blood. Their drawn swords were dripping with the viscous, transparent fluid. At sight of them the Lbavbschs and F'tryll'jnrs fled screaming. Most of them wisely retreated to the back exit of the chamber—a little-used crevice channeling into the jagged Bellyscrapers of the Hllsreg Net. A few, blind with panic, attempted to break past the humans to reach the main doorway, and these the soldiers instantly cut down. Four F'tryll'jnrs fell almost simultaneously, and their remaining brethren fluted in anguished incredulity as the last vestiges of light faded forever from the dying bodies.

The Guardsmen displayed little interest in their Vardrul victims. It was not to hunt the White Demons that they had come to the Nazara Sin. The leader of the squadron cast a rapid glance around the room. His eye lighted on Terrs, standing among the dumbfounded Zmadrcs, and a single exclamation escaped him, *"There!"*

The soldiers advanced and the Vardruls shrank from their path. Many Zmadrcs, still confused, did not move quickly enough. The Guardsmen slaughtered without compunction, and their way was soon littered with white bodies that twitched and flickered and darkened as they died. Vardrul cries of pain and grief echoed weirdly among the stalactites. Many of the Zmadrcs, apparently half-stupefied with horror, loitered by the corpses of their kinsmen. These unfortunates were swiftly dispatched.

They were closing in quickly on Terrs, but the boy seemed unaware or else indifferent. Together he and Fourteen strove to guide the dazed Zmadrc Patriarch to the crevice at the rear of the chamber. Zmadrc R'dsvyllsch, still disoriented, leaned heavily upon the human shoulder. His proximity to the true object of the Guardsmen's search was likely to cost him his life, but only Verran recognized the deadliness of her son's altruism. Instinct told her why the Guards had come. Her mouth was sticky-dry, but she managed to shout, "Terrs, *get away!* It's you they're after!"

He heard but disbelieved, and would not leave the Zmadrc's side. The Guardsmen heard as well. Quickly locating the source of the Lanthian call, the Commander ordered, "Get the woman!" Three of the soldiers detached themselves from the main group and started for Verran, who quickened her pace—to no avail. Deftly they cut her off from her son and advanced, swords poised to strike. Verran watched in oddly detached disbelief. *They cannot mean to kill me—just like that? So casually?* A quick survey of three remorseless faces and three dripping blades convinced her otherwise, and she thought, *They'll do it. I am going to die.* But not without some effort to save

herself. Verran turned to run, and the Guardsmen fanned out
to intercept her. Simultaneously, Nyd snarled and sprang. At
that instant, the aches, pains, and advancing feebleness of extreme old age were forgotten. Once again he was Nyd, best
and bravest among Fal Grizhni's servants, designated protector
of Fal Grizhni's lady. Renewed purpose lent him fleeting
strength and vitality. The hybrid threw himself upon the nearest
Guard, who staggered beneath the assault. The man's skull and
vitals were protected by helmet and breastplate, but a single
stroke of dagger talons raking along the right arm severed an
artery. Blood fountained in a magnificent arch, and the Guard's
sword clanged on the stone floor. Verran pounced on the
weapon as Nyd turned to the remaining enemies. The wounded
soldier clutched his arm and tottered backward, squealing com-
ically. On the brink of the death-pool he tripped, lost his footing,
and hit the water with a tremendous splash. Instantly the pool
was tinted red with human gore, and the rock-light filtering
through the colored liquid took on a rosy cast. Pink light illumined the struggles of the wounded Guardsman, who
thrashed, kicked, gasped, and gurgled for a time before submit-
ting to his fate and allowing himself to sink beneath the warm
waves to take his improbable place among the Zmadrc Ancestors.

Almost without pause, Nyd leaped for the second
Guardsman, who retreated, unprepared to deal with the hirsute,
flame-eyed demon that now confronted him. Nyd followed,
without a thought to spare for the enemy at his rear. His carelessness would have cost him his life had not Verran perceived the
danger and employed her captured sword. Gritting her teeth,
she dealt two quick, low slashes. The soldier yelled and went
down, the tendons in his lower legs severed. Nyd scarcely
noticed. His remaining enemy thrust and lunged, far overextending himself. The hybrid dodged with all the speed of his
youth and slid within the other's guard to drive his claws into
the unprotected face. Luck or skill directed the blow. The
Guardsmen shrieked and fell back, both eyeballs pierced. The
sword fell from his grasp as he clapped both hands over his face.
Nyd hissed, struck again, and the soldier fell, blood streaming
from his slashed throat.

The way to Terrs was clear. With Fourteen's assistance, the
boy had succeeded in steering Zmadrc R'dsvyllsch about half
the distance to the back exit. The task was becoming easier as

full awareness and coordination returned to The Zmadrc. An entourage of terrified kinsmen/subjects huddled about their Patriarch. Verran saw to her terror that the Guardsmen had reached the edge of the group. The steel blades rose and fell with workmanlike regularity, and where they descended, Vardruls died. At his present speed, Terrs would never reach the exit in time—would never reach it at all.

"Get him out of here," she directed her companion breathlessly. "If he won't come, use force." Nyd croaked and bounded forward. Verran trailed close behind. They reached Terrs's side just as a Guardsman sent his blade plunging into the breast of Zmadrc R'dsvyllsch.

The Zmadrc fell in silence. For a moment he flickered in rapid, irregular pulses, then Fourteen touched him and his hiir soared as the clan-warmth flooded his veins for the last time. His great eyes lifted to Fourteen and her Future, and he hummed in a voice almost too low to be heard, "Escape. Run. Hide." His ocular bands relaxed as consciousness lapsed, and then he darkened as abruptly as a sky from which lightning has fled. Thin, wavering notes signaled the horror of the surrounding kinsmen/subjects at the death of their Patriarch. But those who lingered to mourn would surely follow him. The Zmadrc's murderer lifted his sword. This time the blow was aimed at Terrs.

Verran screamed. It was a purely instinctive reaction, and in this case useful. Terrs looked up, saw his danger, and dodged. The Guardsman's sword whistled by his ear. A tremulous cry of terror escaped Fourteen. Terrs's face was a battleground wherein Vardrul fearful horror warred with human vengeful fury. Humanity prevailed. His hands resumed their natural form. He cast a quick glance around him and his eye lighted on his mother, still carrying the dead Guardsman's reddened sword. Before she knew what he was about, he had wrested the weapon from her grasp. Terrs knew nothing of swordplay, but strength, rage, and youthful reflexes served him well. He lunged, and his steel transfixed the Guardsman's throat. Terrs drew back, and the soldier fell. A second lunge, and a second Guardsman died. But it could not continue—the boy's enemies were too numerous and too disciplined. The Guardsmen drew back, exchanged swift signals, spread out in an expert flanking movement.

"Terrs, *run!*" Verran pleaded. He ignored her, and she turned to Nyd in desperation. "*Make* him go!"

Nyd needed no further urging. Seizing Terrs from behind,
he dragged the boy toward the exit. For a moment Terrs struggled fiercely, and the hybrid was hard pressed to restrain him.
Then the sight of the advancing Guardsmen, together with the
frantic pleas of Verran and Fourteen, restored some measure
of sanity, and Terrs resisted no longer. Nyd cautiously released
his grip. The four of them turned and ran for the exit through
which the last of the panic-stricken Vardruls were disappearing
like white rabbits down a hole. One after another, Fourteen,
Verran, Terrs, and Nyd squeezed through the low opening.
The Guardsmen, arriving a split second later, sensibly hesitated
to follow their quarry into that narrow, unknown passage.

It had been Great Vens since Verran had navigated a Bellyscraper. Loathing the discomfort and constriction of the lowest
tunnels, she ordinarily restricted her wandering to the widest,
most populous corridors of the caverns. Her aversion was not
founded on indolence. Rather, it was the extreme narrowness
of the Bellyscrapers, the inescapable closeness of the rock walls
pressing in on all sides, that outraged some deep and basic
Surface instinct, leaving her prey to nameless apprehension.
On a more practical level, the Bellyscrapers—particularly those
of the Hllsreg Net—honeycombed the rock in patterns of mind-
breaking complexity. It was an easy place in which to get lost,
and even the Vardrul youngsters, with their hereditary affinity
for mazes, occasionally did so. There was no danger of that
now, for Zmadrc Fourteen was leading the way, and Fourteen
knew the Net well. No, the real danger lay behind them, and
as Verran crawled along on hands and knees already sore from
the unaccustomed punishment of the stone floor, she strained
her ears for the sound of pursuit. So far she had heard none.
Perhaps the Guardsmen feared the tunnel—or perhaps they
were cunning and cautious and had somehow managed to follow
in silence. Try as she would, Verran could not suppress the
image of the silvery blades drawing colorless blood, the Vardruls falling, darkening, dying—*How many of them?*—and all
of it so professionally efficient, such vast ruination inflicted in
so short a time—too much to comprehend as yet— *And they
are looking for Terrs, I know it. But why now, after all these
quiet years? What has happened in Lanthi Ume? Why now?*

The ceiling dipped, forcing Verran down on her elbows. Her
progress was clumsy and moderately painful. Zmadrc Fourteen,

quite accustomed to this means of locomotion, advanced nimbly. Already she was drawing well ahead. *I should have had Terrs go before me. I'm probably holding him back.* Behind her she heard a light, repetitive tapping, a sound that chilled her until she identified it as the click of Nyd's spiky ruff against the walls and ceiling of the tunnel. Nyd, with his bulky build and his spikes, had never been created to crawl through subterranean passages. The poor sore-jointed creature was probably suffering acute discomfort, infinitely worse than her own. *Nyd saved our lives back there. How many times has he done that?*

The Bellyscraper widened and the way grew easier. Presently the tunnel ended and they emerged into a small chamber with a ceiling of moderate height from which the stalactites dripped in translucent clusters. Some anonymous artist had been at work there. Several of the stone icicles were covered from base to point with deeply incised carvings. The artist's tools—crude chisels, a mallet, pots of acid and water, brushes, and polishing rags—lay on the floor. Several Vardruls already occupied the chamber. Two Lbavbschs and one F'tryll'jnr, their flesh still dark with terror, huddled against the opposite wall. They glanced briefly at the newcomers, and then their filmy eyes slid away. Apparently their grief and fear precluded conversation. Terrs, however, desired information. He addressed them in the Vardrul tongue, but so basic was the subject matter of the exchange that Verran had not the slightest difficulty in following it. She noted that her son had regained his customary steely self-possession. His manner was composed and surprisingly authoritative.

"Where have the others gone?" asked Terrs. His voice, pitched low, could not have been heard in the surrounding tunnels.

"They have hidden themselves throughout the Hllsreg Net," replied Lbavbsch Eleven. "And some seek safety in the Dri'iz Far Extension. Others spread warning among the clans, that our brethren may fly in time to save themselves."

"Fly? Abandon our homes? No," said Terrs.

Four sets of Vardrul eyes regarded him in astonishment. Fourteen hummed inquisitively. Nyd, understanding nothing of the conversation, paid little heed. Verran understood only too well. *Fal Grizhni,* she thought.

"If we remain, we join the Ancestors," observed F'tryll'jnr Rdsdr, oldest son of the F'tryll'jnr Lesser Patriarch.

"Not if we defend ourselves. We are many. The soldier-men are few," Terrs replied deliberately.

"The men are armed."

"As we must arm ourselves."

"They are violent and terrible beyond imagining."

"It has already been demonstrated that they are not invulnerable."

"We Vardruls are not killers," Fourteen hummed.

"And yet the Vardruls must protect their home, else lose it," Terrs insisted. "Moreover, what of Zmadrc R'dsvyllsch, and all the slain kinsmen? Is nothing owed for them?" It was as close as he could come in the Vardrul language to expressing the concept of vengeance.

Fourteen flickered rapidly at mention of her murdered father's name, and the muscles around her eyes quivered. A slight glow illumined the hitherto lightless flesh of the two Lbavbschs, and F'tryll'jnr Rdsdr's hiir rose noticeably. Terrs's suggestions seemed to be taking root in fertile soil.

He'll incite these gentle creatures to violence with which they aren't equipped to deal, thought Verran. *He'll ruin them, and he'll ruin himself—just like his father.* Aloud she said, "Terrs, there's been enough blood spilled. Stop and think—"

"I am thinking, Mother," he cut her off. "I see that we shall be driven from our home if we do not stop the men now—stop them once and for all, instilling such fear in their hearts that they will never again dare set foot in our caverns."

"That is not the way to stop them. The Vardruls aren't fighters, and ineffective resistance will succeed only in rousing the fury of the Guardsmen."

"Who have thus far exhibited restraint?" Terrs inquired. "In any case, the resistance need not be ineffective. Look at F'tryll'jnr Rdsdr." The Vardrul in question had regained much of his luminescence. The stillness of his features reflected deep cogitation.

Verran's brows drew together, but her reply was forestalled by a warning hiss from Nyd. The hybrid's eyes were fixed upon the tunnel opening. Conversation ceased and all present listened intently. The Vardruls darkened in renewed fear. Human voices were audible close at hand. A number of Ducal Guardsmen who had braved the Hllsreg Net in pursuit of their quarry were drawing nearer by the second. Verran's breath caught, and she cast her eyes around in search of escape. A fissure split the

wall not far away, and three of the four Vardruls were already
edging in that direction. Fourteen hesitated, her eyes fixed on
her Future. But Terrs made no move to join her. In two steps
he reached the tunnel and stationed himself beside the opening,
the sword that he still carried uplifted in readiness. Following
his young master's lead, Nyd crouched on the opposite side.
His facial hair bristled and his lips were drawn back from his
fangs. No longer did he look old.

Terrs's expression was icy and merciless, and once again
Verran thought, *Fal Grizhni.*

A scrape, a scuffle, and a Guardsman emerged from the
Bellyscraper on hands and knees. Before the man was fully
into the chamber, Terrs's sword flashed down and blood
sprayed. The Guard collapsed and died without a sound.

He didn't even hesitate. Verran thought, and in the midst of
all the horror experienced fresh pangs of dismay. *He killed a
man, in cold blood this time, and doesn't show a trace of
emotion. Do I know my son at all? Where did he learn this
savagery?* And the thought came unbidden. *He didn't have to
learn it, it's bred in his blood and bones. He is defending his
home,* she reminded herself. *He's defending everything that
matters to him.* She glanced at Fourteen and saw the young
Vardrul, finger-tentacles rigid, flesh flickering in complex, incomprehensible sequences. F'tryll'jnr Rdsdr, palely luminous,
stared as if mesmerized. The hiir of the two Lbavbschs remained
fearful-low.

At a sign from Terrs Nyd dragged the corpse aside. A moment
later a second Guardsman crawled from the passage, and a
single stroke of the sword dispatched him. As Nyd removed
the body, a vibrating hum escaped F'tryll'jnr Rdsdr.

The third Ducal Guard exhibited cunning. Perhaps some
instinct warned him of danger, or perhaps he had been well
trained. Gathering himself just inside the tunnel entrance, he
shot horizontally into the chamber, and Terrs's descending
blade missed him by a hair. The Guardsman rolled and was
on his feet, sword in hand. Two rapid, almost reflexive thrusts
ended the lives of the two Lavbschs. The Vardruls fell as one,
their light extinguished. Without a moment's pause the
Guardsman lunged at Terrs.

A fourth soldier burst in, sword drawn, to face Nyd's fangs
and claws.

Terrs parried inexpertly, gave ground, parried again. Noting

his opponent's inexperience, the soldier feinted, drew another
clumsy response, and engaged swords. An abrupt twist of the
wrist sent Terrs's blade flying, and the boy stood disarmed.
Verran started for the fallen sword, which lay in the middle of
the room. She saw Fourteen approach as well, but neither could
possibly reach the weapon in time. Nyd, engaged in his own
battle, could not assist.

Terrs retreated before the Guardsman's confident, competent
advance. Another few paces, and his back would touch the wall.

"Run, Terrs!" Verran pleaded, but her son did nothing of
the kind.

"F'tryll'jnr Rdsdr!" he called in a voice that conveyed both
appeal and command. "Help me!"

F'tryll'jnr Rdsdr stood behind the Guardsman. His hiir was
up and his expression unreadable. In his hand he held the mallet
abandoned by the anonymous stone carver. He seemed unsure
what to do with it.

"F'tryll'jnr!" Terrs exclaimed, and the Vardrul's decision
was made. Lifting the mallet, he struck tentatively, and his
blow glanced off the Guardsman's helmet. The soldier spun to
face his new attacker, and Terrs jumped away from the wall.
F'tryll'jnr Rdsdr struck again, much harder this time, and caught
his enemy's right arm just above the elbow. The soldier's face
contorted. His arm hung useless, temporarily paralyzed.
Promptly shifting the weapon to his left hand, he lunged at the
Vardrul. The attack was aborted as Terrs leaped in from the
side to seize the Guardsman's arm. As the soldier sought to
fling the boy aside, the increasingly aggressive hammer blows
of F'tryll'jnr Rdsdr rained down upon his helmet and shoulders.
One such blow grazed his cheekbone, and the Guardsman instinctively jerked aside. In that instant Terrs wrested the sword
away and drove the point into his enemy's throat.

It was over, for the moment. Nyd had finished his opponent,
and four Ducal Guards lay dead upon the stone floor. With
them lay the two murdered Lbavbsch kinsmen. Five survivors
remained to view the carnage with expressions that ranged from
the frozen enmity of Terrs, to the simple triumph of Nyd, to
the weary numbness of Lady Verran, to the filmy-eyed horror
of Zmadrc Fourteen. F'tryll'jnr Rdsdr stood apart from the
others. His flesh brightened and dimmed unaccountably as he
glanced from the human corpses to the mallet in his hand, and
back again. Scarcely could he take his eyes from the mallet.

From time to time a soft thrum of dawning comprehension escaped him, and he stared at the homely instrument as if it were a sight entirely new to his eyes.

The Ducal Guardsmen withdrew from the caverns shortly thereafter. Their quarry, the son of Fal Grizhni, had eluded them for the moment and pursuit seemed unprofitable. Following the initial invasion and attack, the White Demons had faded away, disappeared like the unnatural creatures they were, vanished into the unknowable depths of their hideous subterranean maze. The sweltering corridors were endless and apparently deserted. Exploration yielded no results and the soldiers were eager to depart, for beneath their professional bravado lurked a common concern. Of the timorous Vardruls they had no fear, but the home of the Vardruls was another matter. Men might easily lose themselves in the caverns, lose themselves and never find their way out. One such misfortune had already occurred. A party of four under the command of the formidable Ensign Haenil had vanished into a network of low tunnels hours earlier, and never returned. Haenil and the others were hopelessly lost—or worse. No telling what dangers those passageways concealed. The place was oppressive, indescribably alien, inimical. Following a perfunctory search for missing comrades, the Guardsmen gladly took their leave.

A full Coloration elapsed before the Vardruls dared abandon their hiding places. Singly and in small groups they emerged to view the Guardsmen's handiwork. The broad corridor that ran between the Mvjri Dazzle—the invaders' point of entry— and the Zmadrc death-pool was strewn with corpses, none of them human. A number of the small niches and excavations opening off the corridor also housed the dead of various clans. But the greatest scene of horror lay in the death-pool chamber itself. There the floor was white with bodies. Dozens of them— scores of them—lay piled in heaps around the edge of the pool. Others, cut down in flight, lay scattered about the room. All the Zmadrc kinsmen had been assembled in that place. Three-quarters of them had died there.

The surviving Zmadrcs converged upon the death-pool chamber. With them went Verran, Nyd, Terrs, and Fourteen. It was quiet in the chamber. The Vardruls, clearly stunned at the enormity of the disaster, spoke little. The collective hiir was minimal. The flesh of the living and the flesh of the dead were almost equally lightless. Fourteen was silent. Her eyes were filmed to the point of opacity, and she gripped Terrs's hand tightly.

Terrs led them to the corpse of the Zmadrc Lesser Patriarch. The Zmadrc's eyes were still open. Terrs knelt and shut them gently. Verran was startled to see tears glittering upon the lashes of her customarily impassive son. The boy looked up at her. "Do you still extol the virtures of humanity, Mother?" he inquired, quietly enough. "Still so anxious for me to learn the ways of mankind?"

Verran had no answer. She took a step toward him, her hand extended, met his eyes, and the expression she saw there stopped her in her tracks.

"The species is monstrous," Terrs continued, without raising his voice. "I despise it. I will not be a part of it, Mother. I will not."

Chapter Five

It was early in the evening when the blue-smocked craftsman and his apprentice presented themselves at the back entrance of the Ducal Palace. It was an easy matter to gain admittance to the huge kitchen. The place was thronged with cooks, under-cooks, scullions, servants of all description—many attired in the brilliant liveries of their visiting noble masters—off-duty sentries, tradesmen, and many others. In the midst of the general confusion the entrance of two more fairly prosaic figures went almost unheeded. And yet anyone observing the newcomers closely might have noted certain points of interest. The man—a tall and brawny fellow with a sculpted pompadour and a distinctively cleft nose—carried himself with a freedom and hauteur hardly in keeping with his humble calling. The apprentice—a beardless boy with wisps of fair hair escaping the confinement of a large cap—gazed upon the world through eyes as hard and wise as a parrot's. Between the two of them they carried a great, obviously heavy, wooden chest.

No one questioned the craftsmen's entrance into the kitchen, for tradesmen and menials came and went at all hours of the day and night. Passing from the kitchen and into the realms beyond, however, was not quite so easy. The sentry posted in the corridor outside was wont to discourage unauthorized intrusions. When the two craftsmen headed confidently for the servants' staircase at the end of the hall, the sentry barred their way. "Your business?" the guard demanded.

The craftsmen paused to eye the sentry with unaccountable condescension. The apprentice, in particular, radiated hostile contempt. For a moment it almost seemed that they might not answer. Then the man replied civilly enough, "Yorquo the Master Mason, at your service. I am here with my apprentice to repair the fireplace in the Duke's own chamber."

"What's wrong with it?"

"Earlier in the day a great cloud of black smoke and choking fumes billowed from the chimney out into the chamber. Praise be to all things fortunate, his Grace was not present at the time! One can but suspect a damaged flue, which I have been summoned to inspect and restore as required."

"At this hour?"

"Ah, there is no inconvenience to which I will not gladly subject myself on behalf of his Grace. Yorquo is the Duke's most loyal subject."

"What's in the box?"

"The tools of my profession. Behold." The craftsman threw wide the lid to reveal a collection of harmless articles.

"I was not informed," the guard complained.

"Do they inform you of everything, Master Sentry? Will they inform you of the dire, possibly fatal consequences should the ducal chimney remain unrepaired?"

"Oh, very well," the sentry muttered uneasily. "Pass."

The two visitors expertly maneuvered their heavy box up two flights of the narrow servants' staircase, then they emerged into a black and pink marble hallway lined with enormous mirrors in massive gilt and rock crystal frames. The apprentice surveyed the guady scene appreciatively, and murmured, "Oh, suPREME!"

"This, my darling Josky, is your rightful heritage—that is to say, the glory, the splendor, the grandeur, that surrounds the born aristocrat," observed the disguised bravo Whurm Didnis.

"I can tell. I feel right at home here," replied the Lady Josky. "Don't worry, your lordship, it'll all be ours again, just wait and see. *We* can do it, the two of us. Now, where's the Duke's lodgings?"

"His apartment, Daughter. His apartment. I have Lord Nobody's map right here. Put down the box." She complied, and Didnis rummaged in his pocket to bring forth a crudely sketched diagram, which they scrutinized together. "Straight ahead—right turn—right again—and there we are. Our client Nobody draws a clear map."

"I suppose so." Lady Josky grunted as she took up her end

of the box. The two resumed their advance. "But I'd feel a lot better if we knew more about this Lord Nobody. His real name, for example."

"Sweet child, how would that benefit us?"

"If we knew his name, then we'd be able to find him if we need to, and that would make me feel safer. After all, he still owes us half our fee. What if we do the job and then he never comes back to pay us? We'd look like fools, and everybody would laugh. I'd be so embarrassed, I couldn't hold up my head."

"My princess, you will always be able to carry yourself with pride under all circumstances, for you are a Whurm Didnis and that in itself is enough."

"No it *isn't,* not if we're had by a rabbity little sneak like Lord Nobody."

"My lady Josky—" Whurm Didnis spoke with a touch of paternal sternness. "Such cynicism ill-befits a lady of quality. You must learn to trust in the honor of your peers. After all, Lord Nobody is a gentleman."

"How do we *know* that?"

"Instinct teaches us to recognize our own. Moreover, Lord Nobody's hands are white, soft, and adorned with a ring worth at least one hundred silver shorns. This tells us much."

"Oh, all right. But I still want—"

The dialogue was cut short by the appearance in the corridor of an armed sentry. Didnis and his child immediately lapsed into their masonic roles, and bypassed the obstacle without mishap. Shortly thereafter they arrived at the entrance to the Duke's private suite.

They went in and made their way to the bedchamber, where Lady Josky paused on the threshold to admire the ponderous gilt furnishings, the marble floor, and the vaulted ceiling with its brilliantly colored, voluptuous frescoes.

"Look, Dad." Josky pointed. "Look at that one with the satyr and all those nymphs. How can just one satyr ever expect to—"

"To work, child," Whurm Didnis directed. "Let us attend to our business."

The tremendous bed with its suffocating hangings of green and gold sat atop a low dais. The bravo and his daughter set down their great box at the foot of the platform. Didnis lifted the lid and hurriedly removed the top layer of contents, thus exposing to view a plain leather casket with a neat round hole cut through the cover. Carefully he removed the casket, placed it on the floor, and opened it. Within the container stood a very substantial, lidded iron vessel filled with gunpowder; and an upright candle, surrounded at its base with wadded paper. A twisted fuse twined through the paper led to a tiny touchhole in the side of the iron pot.

"Now, my princess, listen closely as I explain the operation of this excellent device—"

"I already know how it works," Josky informed her father. "I know all about it. We light the candle, shut the box, and shove it under the Duke's bed. Then we get out of here. A few hours later when the Duke's lying here asleep, the candle burns down, sets the paper on fire, and lights the fuse, which sets off the gunpowder. Then—KABOOM!" She spread her hands and vibrated them illustratively. "So much for the Duke."

"True, my clever girl. But you have left out one or two significant points which, for the sake of your education, ought not be overlooked. For one thing, you should know that we do not use just *any* candle. This one is my own creation, specially designed to burn very slowly, thus creating a delay of hours between ignition and explosion. Otherwise, our incendiary device might self-consummate early, long before his Grace retires, and there would be our ingenuity and industry squandered. You see?"

Josky nodded attentively.

"Good. Someday soon, my child, I shall pass on the formula for the candle wax to you, for you are worthy. Now, one more small but essential matter. I speak of the chains with which we secure the lid of the iron pot, that no portion of our device's goodness may be wasted."

"The chains!" Josky evinced dismay. "I forgot. I'm sorry, your lordship!"

"You are young, and we must not expect perfection overnight. Have no fear, Daughter—your natural talent will prevail. And now let us conclude." Whurm Didnis reached into the depths of the wooden box to extract a length of stout chain with which he wrapped the iron pot tightly, securing the ends with a padlock. From the pocket of his smock he brought forth flint, steel, and tinderbox, with which he created a flame to light the candle. This done, he shut the casket with care. Then, very gingerly, he slid the infernal machine in well under the Duke's bed. The heat above the hole in the lid assured him

that the candle was still burning. This done, Didnis rapidly
packed all his paraphernalia back into the wooden box, shut
the lid, and rose to his feet. "Come, my lady Josky, it is time
to depart. Having fulfilled a commission, the bravo vanishes
as silently and swiftly as yesterday's prosperity. Come, my
child."

The two of them hurried from the Duke's apartment and
proceeded unhindered back along the corridors the way they
had come, until they came abreast of an open window and
Josky suddenly stopped. Dropping her end of the wooden box,
she ran to the window and peered down into the lantern-lit
garden below. There she spied a number of figures, some
resplendent in the silks, brocades, and jewels of Lanthian courtiers, others somber in the midnight robes of the Select. Two
figures in particular held her attention. One of them was short,
chubby, and epicene. There she recognized her target, the Duke
Povon Dil shonnet. The other, glum and drooping, was equally
familiar. "Lord Nobody!" exclaimed the Lady Josky. "Look,
Dad—right down there! *It's Lord Nobody!*"

"Lady Josky, come *away* from there!" Whurm Didnis implored. "you will attract attention."

"Now's our chance to find out who he really is!" Lady Josky
did not turn away from the window.

"That does not matter now! We must leave this place at
once! My darling child, if you love me—"

"Of course I love you, but this is *important,* Dad. I want
to know. I *want* to!"

Whurm Didnis suppressed his reply. A sentry was advancing
along the hallway. Lady Josky greeted the guard's appearance
with pleasure. Assuming an expression of wide-eyed admiration, she inquired clearly, "Gad, Master Yorquo, have you ever
seen such splendid folk? Who can they be? I wonder."

Didnis cursed inaudibly.

"Could the Duke himself be down there? I wonder." Josky
speculated naively. "Oh, how I should love to see the Duke!
I could tell the folk at home all about it!"

The sentry paused to view the scene with an indulgent smile.

"It's time to go, lad," Whurm Didnis gritted. *"Now."*

"Oh, bear with the boy, sir," the sentry suggested easily.
"No doubt 'tis all marvelous to his young eyes. Here, lad—"
He stepped to the window and pointed. "You see the gentleman
down there in all that cloth-of-silver, with the great jeweled

chain? Well, that's the Duke Povon himself."

"Oh, gad, what a glorified gentleman! I'll never forget this sight, I won't. And who are the others, Master Sentry? Great nobles, are they?"

"That they are, lad. There you see Lord Beskot Kor Malifon, standing beside his Grace. The lady on the other side—that big strapper there—that's the Duke's betrothed, the Keldhaam Gnuxia. Over there in the blue suit—the elderly man with the tragic look—that's Trel Wate Basef, lord of Castle Io Wesha. And of course, the ones in black are all savants of the Select."

"Is Preeminence Jinzin Farni down there, sir?"

"No, lad. Preeminence Farni is sick, so sick it's thought he'll die. All his magic can't keep him healthy, I guess."

"And who," asked Josky, pointing, "is that one huddled up by himself, away from the others? The scrawny one with the receding chin?"

"Why that's the Duke's only son, the Lord Sneever Dil Shonnet."

"The Duke's *son*?"

"To be sure. He'll be Duke himself, one day. Why, lad, I think he sees you watching him. He's staring right up at you. He doesn't look at all well, does he? I hope he's not about to have one of his attacks."

"Oh, suPREME!"

"Your apprentice seems quite overcome," observed the smiling sentry.

"That he is—with admiration, no doubt," replied Whurm Didnis. "The only remedy is to take him out of here, the sooner the better. Come along, boy. Time to go. *Please*."

Having gained the information she desired, Josky dawdled no longer. Within minutes she and her father arrived at the foot of the servants' staircase. But it was not until they were entirely clear of the palace and skimming over the waters of the Lureis Canal in a rented dombulis that Whurm Didnis ventured to address his daughter. "Sweet child, I know your intentions are good and your coolness is admirable. But courage can be carried to the point of recklessness, and in this case—"

"Oh, that doesn't matter!" Josky interrupted. "Just think what we learned! Lord Nobody is *the Duke's son!* Our fortunes are made, Dad! The Didnis fortunes are restored at last!"

The dombulis sped on, and soon vanished into the night.

• • •

Selectic Preeminence Jinzen Farni, far too ill to attend the Duke's reception, lay abed that evening in his chamber at Farni Mansion. The mansion—actually nothing more than a sprawling, upretentious old house—overlooked the less desirable end of the Channel of Ume in what could only by courtesy still be called a fashionable section of the city. It was said by many that Preeminence Farni's manner of living failed to reflect the dignity of his office. But Farni Mansion, in its comfort and its somewhat battered spaciousness, perfectly reflected the tastes of its owner. There the savant, who had no immediate family, lived with his books, his experiments, and a small group of devoted household servants. The affection of the servants was genuine, and their concern for their ailing master considerable. For some weeks past they had strained their collective powers of invention to find a cure for Jinzin Farni, but the succession of home-brewed remedies, delicate dishes, illicit sacrifices to Ert, and nostrums purchased from the floating merchants had proved ineffective. This being the case, there remained but one possible explanation—Farni's malady was rooted in melancholia. His Preeminence clearly required diversion, good cheer, and the society of his intimates. In the absence of family and close friends, this last was not easily obtained. It was therefore with particular pleasure that the elderly butler greeted the appearance on his master's doorstep of a familiar lean and rangy figure. "Master Ril!" he exclaimed warmly, and opened the door to admit Rillif Har Fennahar, Preeminence Farni's favorite nephew. "Welcome back, sir!"

"Thanks, Drundle. Good to see you again." Fennahar stepped over the threshold into the light. He was a tall man, still young, with sun-streaked brown hair and a naturally fair but deeply tanned complexion against which his intelligent gray eyes stood out in startling contrast. The serious and worried expression in those eyes was belied by the network of smile-lines fanning out from the corners. Har Fennahar had the face of a man who smiles easily and often, but at the moment he looked frankly perturbed. He wore traveling clothes of expensive cut, now sadly battered and at least ten years out of date. His hat was egregiously antique, and he wore not a scrap of jewelry. By no external sign was it evident that here stood the Lord Har Fennahar, master of vast Fennahar House and one of the most considerable of Lanthian fortunes.

"When did you get back, Master Ril?" asked Drundle.

"Only about an hour ago. I found my uncle's letter waiting, together with your note, and I came as fast as I could. How is he, Drundle?"

"Failing, sir. Worse every day. But it's my hope that seeing you might cheer his spirits, and possibly set him on the road to mending. Why don't you go on up, Master Ril? He wanted to see you the moment you arrived."

Fennahar nodded and bounded up the central staircase two steps at a time. When he reached the top, he made his way directly to his uncle's chamber, paused at the door long enough to smooth the worried expression from his face, and knocked. A feeble voice bade him enter. Fennahar walked in to find Preeminence Jinzin Farni sitting up in bed. It was only by conscious effort that the visitor managed to suppress all visible signs of shock at the alteration in his uncle's appearance. Jinzin Farni had always been thickset, barrel-chested, and vigorous, with a broad, blunt-featured, perpetually ruddy face. Now the figure was thin and wasted, the arms scrawny, the hands shrunken to claws. The cheeks and eyes were sunken. Ruddiness had given way to grayish pallor. Only the small, sardonic black eyes remained unchanged, and they lighted up at sight of the younger man. "So you're back at last," observed Farni. "Didn't hurry, I suspect. What was it this time?"

"This time the ruins of Daipool, Uncle."

"More ruins? Haven't had enough of that yet? This was your fourth expedition within two years. When will you stop gadding about, boy? You're master of Fennahar House and you're needed here in Lanthi Ume. It's time for you to settle down, assume your responsibilities and administer your estates properly. If the Fennahar fortunes collapse, it will be the fault of your negligence."

"Oh, stop preaching at me, Uncle Jin. You know as well as I do that my brother Frev can be trusted to manage the properties. What's more, he enjoys it. The work suits him and he does it well, far better than I ever would. The Fennahar fortunes won't suffer by my absence. Most likely they'll benefit. But you already knew that."

"Yes, but I wasn't certain you did." A smile pulled at the corners of Farni's colorless lips. "But really, all joking aside, the question of your obligations can't be so easily dismissed. How old are you now? About forty?"

"Thirty-five."

"Time for you to settle down. Find a wife. Produce heirs. And don't tell me that Frev can take care of it. You carry the title."

"I never wanted it, expected it, or prepared for it. If only poor Stixen hadn't died! As for finding a wife, I haven't the time, Uncle."

"Don't you want a family of your own, Ril? You're not some sort of—ah—misogynist, are you?"

Fennahar stirred a little uncomfortably. "In theory, no. But in fact, I've not met a suitable woman that I like within the past five years."

"You've scarcely been here during the past five years. In any case, liking isn't everything. Several of the great families have healthy daughters of marriageable age. Why not take one and have done? Why make such a fuss over a simple matter?"

"Simple to you, perhaps. You're not being asked to tie yourself for life to some giggling twit of sixteen."

"She won't stay sixteen, no matter how hard she tries. Patience, my boy. Patience."

"I'm too old for these yourng girls, Uncle Jin. I've nothing in common with them. They make me feel old and tired. I've waited too long, and now the daughters of the great Houses seem like children. Sweet children in some cases, but have you ever tried to hold a conversation with any of them?"

"If you find one that's pretty, docile, and fertile, does she have to *talk* as well?"

"In my opinion, yes. I don't fancy lifelong boredom."

"Then take a mistress—or several, if you wish."

"Sounds expensive, and not sufficiently alluring to tempt me from my travels. I should like to head north next, in search of the remains of Prugid's Green Tower. If I can find it, then—"

"Give me patience! Will you never tire of your fallen towers, your broken bits of pottery, your crumbling masonry?"

"Not as long as they continue so informative. Daipool, for example, yielded clear evidence of alien habitation. It is my belief that the city was constructed by intelligent inhuman creatures. If so, then the entire island of Dalyon might have belonged to these creatures before the arrival of Man."

"Theory, boy. Pure hypothesis, and as yet unverifiable. In any case, you needn't have gone junketing to Daipool—or to Undriet, Jobaal, or Great Eivay, for that matter. My Cognition could have shown you all of them."

"It wouldn't have been the same."

"Not the same—better. Think of the time saved. But there, I see by the expression on your face that you won't listen to reason. You always were stubborn as a constipated miskin, Ril."

"Runs in the family, Uncle Jin." Fennahar smiled as he approached and seated himself in a chair at Farni's bedside. "And I trust that family obstinacy in which you share will serve to overcome your malady."

"Ah. No. I think not. A combination of willpower and Cognition has kept my illness at bay for years, but the effects cannot be postponed forever. Such a malady, like a creditor, may be put off for a time, but I believe my debt has fallen due at last."

"You're not giving up, are you?"

"No, but I'm not deluging myself with unrealistic hopes, either. Enough of that—it's a dreary topic, and not the reason I summoned you here tonight."

"Uncle Jin—"

"There's a matter we must discuss and I want to do it now, while I still can. Prepare to listen closely, because this is important."

Perceiving that the savant's disinclination to discuss his illness was genuine, Fennahar nodded dutifully.

"You're going to like this, boy. I want to send you off on one of your expeditions. Ho, that surprised you, didn't it? Now I'll tell you why. To begin with, are you familiar with the events surrounding the death of Preeminence Terrs Fal Grizhni, seventeen years ago?"

"Indifferently so," replied Fennahar. "Fal Grizhni, Preeminence before you, plotted to overthrow the Duke. Somehow the conspiracy was discovered, and Grizhni's arrest was ordered. The Ducal Guardsmen succeeded in storming the Cognitively defended Grizhni Palace, and during the attack, Grizhni himself was killed. The palace burned to the ground, and the charred remains lie undisturbed to this day. Grizhni's coconspirators, if such there were, escaped unscathed. "Fennahar shot a sharp glance at his uncle, whose loyalties had come under public scrutiny seventeen years earlier, but Farni's face was blandly innocent. "And that, as far as I know, was the end of it. There are all sorts of rumors and legends connected to Grizhni's name, of course. Tales of hauntings, vengeance, curses, and whatnot. I place no faith in any of 'em."

"Do you not? Oh, wisest of nephews! Perhaps you should read *that*." Farni indicated a sheaf of yellowed notes that lay on a small stand beside the bed.

Fennahar's brows arched interrogatively.

"That is my own copy of certain secret documents now reposing in the Ducal Archives, and I won't describe the stratagem to which I had to resort in order to obtain them years ago. They are the notes of the scribe present at the official inquest that took place immediately following the destruction of Grizhni Palace. Didn't know there'd been an inquest, did you?"

Fennahar shook his head.

"Most people don't remember. However, Terrs Fal Grizhni was one of our greatest nobles, as well as Preeminent. He was slaughtered without a trial, his entire household died with him, and the palace was razed. Some fainthearted citizens deemed this course a trifle excessive, and our Duke Povon desired to wash his hands in public. Self-purification accomplished, he did his best to suppress the entire affair, but neglected to destroy all records. Thus these notes contain the eyewitness accounts of a number of Ducal Guardsmen actually present at Fal Grizhni's death. Their various versions of the incident are confusing and often contradictory, but they agree on several points. By all accounts, Grizhni resisted arrest, and used his powers to resist. To be more specific, it was said that he filled the sub-canal chamber in which he was discovered with a strange and terrible darkness. The Guardsmen waxed somewhat hysterical on this subject, but I gather that the darkness was unnaturally intense, debilitating, and filled with a distinctive odor."

"What was the purpose of this darkness? Grizhni didn't imagine he could hide from the Guardsmen, did he?"

"Had you known the man, you'd never ask such a question. Terrs Fal Grizhni had a spine of steel and the pride of an emperor. He wouldn't have hidden himself. No, I fear he had something quite different in mind. I'm going dry. Hand me a cup of water, my boy."

Fennahar complied. Farni took a sip and resumed, "When the Duke's Guards entered the cellar room, Fal Grizhni exchanged words with them. Certain prophecies were uttered. Grizhni claimed that the darkness filling the chamber would return one day to cover all the island of Dalyon, starting at the center and spreading outward to the sea. The darkness would be inhabited by creatures—Grizhni's own—who would prey on humanity. It would begin, he told them, when a star shines at noon and a lion gives birth to a dragon."

"Have you any idea what that means, Uncle?" Fennahar was clearly intrigued.

"Any idea? I have several hundred ideas. The possibilities are endless, and that's exactly the problem. But I'm coming to that. The darkness, together with Grizhni's threats, so unnerved the Guards that they panicked and killed him on the spot. And there the story would have ended—but for those prophecies, which have troubled me ever since I learned of them. Troubled? Appalled, rather, since I believe I know what they portend." Farni's voice was growing feebler. He paused to take another swallow of water.

"Are you sure you want to go on with this, Uncle Jin? Hadn't you better rest?"

"Not yet. Listen, Ril"—Farni's manner was uncharacteristically intense—"if my suspicions are justified, then we are in danger, and I mean all of us—not only the citizens of Lanthi Ume, but every human being upon the island of Dalyon. It's obvious from the accounts of the Ducal Guardsmen that Preeminence Grizhni must have achieved and employed the highest possible Cognition in the minutes preceding his death. It's also obvious from Grizhni's own words just what that Cognition entailed. He has inflicted a curse of darkness upon us, and it's equivalent to a sentence of death. No, don't look so skeptical, boy—I'm in earnest. Grizhni's Cognitive darkness was obviously poisonous. If it returns to cover all the land as he promised, then humanity must escape or die. I don't know when it will come, since those hints he dropped about dragons and lions could mean almost anything. But I do know beyond all doubt that Man's days upon this island are numbered."

"You knew him, Uncle. Was he as vindictive as that?"

"Fal Grizhni was a peculiar specimen, Ril. Brilliant, of course—by far the greatest savant that's ever been seen. Extraordinary, unmatched mastery of Cognition. And for the most part, he was well intentioned. In a very impersonal sort of way he was even benevolent, or wished to be. But there was always something inside him—an icy, inflexible, relentless sort of quality—an unforgiving heart—and an absolute inability to deal with other men, to understand or to make himself understood. He was by no means the monster that legend has painted him, but to answer your question—yes, if pushed far enough, he was capable of vast cruelty."

"I don't quite understand. If you've known about this for years, why haven't you done anything about it? You're a great savant, Preeminent of the Select, and one of the most powerful men in this city. If Grizhni has cursed us, can't you break his curse?"

"Perhaps. Perhaps I could, but *only if I knew how he did it*," Farni replied. "You see, despite all appearances to the contrary, Cognition is essentially rational and consistent. In terms of this discussion, what that means is that the appropriate method of breaking a savant's Cognition is entirely dependent on the method whereby that Cognition was originally achieved. Such methods are highly individual and almost infinite in number. Working blindly as it were, I've no chance of undoing Grizhni's work. It would be different, of course, if I had access to his records. He'd have written his procedures down in a notebook or something—all of us do that. But those records are lost."

"Can none of your fellow savants help?"

"No. I'm Preeminent simply because my power of Cognition is greatest in the city—with the possible exception of Nulliad's, and he's a madman. If I can't settle this matter, then neither can any of the others. But you, Nephew, may be just the one to help us all."

Har Fennahar silently awaited enlightenment.

"It's always been my opinion," Farni continued, "that Fal Grizhni managed to save his records, some of them at least. His pride in accomplishment was so great, I don't doubt he'd have found a way. I have a theory about that. You may or may not recall that Grizhni had taken a young wife—"

"Verran," said Fennahar.

"Dris Verras's daughter. Yes, I believe her name was Verran. You've an excellent memory."

"Not really. I knew her years ago when we were both youngsters in Lanthi Ume. She was the prettiest, brightest, and bravest girl I'd ever seen. And she died at age seventeen," Fennahar concluded in a tone of bitterness that caused his uncle to glance at him in surprise.

"Maybe not," replied Farni, and it was Fennahar's turn to be surprised. "No one was ever quite certain what became of Lady Grizhni. She may have died during the attack, but some

people believe she escaped. I'm one of them. I think that Fal
Grizhni conveyed his wife to safety. Her welfare would have
been of particular concern to him at that time, inasmuch as she
was carrying his child. More important, I think he sent some
of his written records with her. There's no proof of that—my
belief is based for the most part upon my assessment of Grizhni's
character."

"You mean to say, if Verran actually escaped, then she could
be alive to this day?"

"Possibly."

"Where?"

"That is the question. My efforts to track her Cognitively
have always failed. Until very recently, I've never had the
slightest clue as to her whereabouts."

"And now?"

"And now," said Jinzin Farni, "I've reason to believe that
she took refuge among the Vardruls of the Nazara Sin."

"What reason?"

"Our Duke's recent behavior is suggestive. I have it on good
authority that he's been troubled with recurring nightmares for
months. Time and again he's been heard to cry out in his sleep
that Fal Grizhni is risen from the grave. He's also babbled of
caves and glowing white monsters. And then, only a couple
of weeks ago, I learned that he dispatched a squadron of Ducal
Guards to the Nazara Sin. The Guards returned, and some of
them were loose-tongued in the taverns. My agents inform me
that the soldiers spoke of a massacre of the White Demons of
the Caverns. One of them also admitted that they'd been under
orders to find and kill a human boy—and they'd failed in that.
They spotted him, but he got away. My pleasure in his Grace's
discomfort is only surpassed by my pleasure in the insight his
visions afford. It would seem that the Duke has discovered the
hiding place of Grizhni's heir, and now seeks to destroy the
lad. Naturally."

"Did they see his mother?" Fennahar demanded. "Is Verran
still alive?"

"I don't know. That's not really the point. What's important
is that Grizhni's son, now living in the caverns, may well hold
his father's Cognitive records. We need them. I want you to
go get them."

"Willingly," replied Fennahar, without the least hesitation.

"That was quick. No arguments, no reservations? Are you

going for the records or for the woman?" Farni inquired dryly.

"Unworthy of reply, Uncle."

"No doubt. How soon can you leave?"

"I can have my gear together in a day or so."

"Excellent. I've maps and a few Cognitive gewgaws for you."

"And I've questions for you. In the first place, assuming I find the Vardruls at all, how am I to communicate? I don't speak their language. What's more, if Lanthian soldiers inflicted a recent massacre, then the creatures are bound to detest all men. They're likely to kill me on sight."

"They're far more likely to hide from you, but let's hope otherwise. Seventeen years ago a delegation of Vardruls visited Lanthi Ume in secret, under the protection of Preeminence Grizhni. I visited the delegates at Grizhni Palace, and tokens of eternal friendship were exchanged at that time. I still have mine. Look inside the velvet pouch in the top drawer of that chest over there."

Fennahar rose, located the pouch, opened it, and withdrew a string of multicolored pebbles.

"Keep that, Ril. When you meet the Vardruls, show it to them. It should mean something. As for the language barrier, that won't apply if you meet up with the boy or his mother."

"Think they're likely to hand the records over to me?"

"You must persuade them. Play on their sense of duty, their consciences, their humanity—whatever's likely to work. If that's impossible, consider theft."

"You're a cynical old scoundrel, Preeminence."

"And proud of it. It's all in a good cause, boy."

"Let's say that I must locate Grizhni's records on my own. What am I looking for and how shall I find it? Those caverns are immense."

"You'll be looking for a set of notebooks, folios, something of the sort. With them will almost surely lie a Cognitive aid of some kind. Even Fal Grizhni required such aids to effect the very highest Cogniton. As for finding it—I've a trifle to help you with that, never fear. A silver wristlet that warms in proximity to Cognitive articles. My own invention, and pretty enough for Kor Malifon's arm. I'm quite proud of it." Pride notwithstanding, a fit of giddiness seized Preeminence Farni. Cold sweat started out on his brow, and he sank back upon the pillows.

"Uncle Jin!" cried Fennahar. "I'll call a physician—"

"Don't bother," Farni whispered. "Useless, and I want no strangers. Come closer, Ril. I'll tell you of the Vardruls, everything I know."

"Don't try to talk, Uncle. It can wait."

"It can't wait. Too important. I must tell you *now*, while I've breath. Don't argue, boy. Closer. Lean down. You hear me? Good."

When the reception ended, a tired Duke Povon betook himself to bed and fell asleep at once. While he slept the dream returned, more terrible than ever. There were the familiar elements—the ruins of Grizhni Palace, charred and smoking beneath a flame-colored sky; the cavernous dungeon, the stalactites and stalagmites; and the dreadful, resurrected Preeminence Terrs Fal Grizhni. But this time there was a difference. This time the dungeon was crowded with those luminously pallid alien creatures identified by the Sapient Nulliad as Vardruls. Even in his sleep Duke Povon remembered, and realized that he faced the White Demons of the Caverns. They were lined up along the walls, clinging to the rock formations, perched atop the blackened heaps of rubble—scores of them, everywhere, as many as the dungeon could hold. They stared at him unwinkingly, and Povon recognized hatred in the huge, uncanny eyes. All around him were those eyes—brilliant, accusing, merciless. The sight was unbearable, and Povon buried his face in his hands. When he lifted his head a moment later, the Demons were perceptibly nearer. Silently, within the space of a heartbeat, they had advanced. He blinked, and they were nearer yet. Blinked again, and they were so close that the veins beneath the translucent skin were visible; so close that they could touch him with their horrible tentacular fingers, if they chose. In the forefront of the Vardrul ranks stood dead Fal Grizhni, dark with the blood of his wounds. Grizhni lifted his black-swathed arms. But even as he reached forward, the savant's face changed. The features sharpened, all facial hair vanished, the flesh whitened and glowed. His face was that of a Vardrul, but the black, unfathomable eyes were Grizhni's still. The savant's icy hand touched Povon's face. The fingers were long and sinuous as snakes. They *were* snakes, the Duke realized, each one tipped with a tiny luminous head armed with needle fangs. They were crawling over his face, hissing as they moved, and he could feel the forked tongues flick his eyes. And then they were growing, lengthening and thickening, their scales chafing his flesh as they slithered down to twine about his throat tightly, tighter yet, chokingly tight . . .

The Duke woke up gasping desperately for air, trembling and terrified as never before. He lay on his back, his mouth wide open, face purple, eyes bulging from their sockets. For a few moments he remained where he was, grateful for the luxury of unobstructed breath. But he could not lie still for long. His entire body was bathed in sweat, and the silk sheets were sticking to him. The feather bed beneath him seemed unaccountably warm, almost smothering. Povon threw the sheets aside, but obtained little relief. There could be but one explanation—fever. He was ill, perhaps dangerously so, with no friend or loved one present to tend to his comfort. As for the servants, they were lazy and callous. He might suffer or even die in solitude, and no one would know or care. He was all alone. The thought of his own loneliness brought tears of grief to Povon's eyes. The tears flowed faster as he contemplated the ingratitude of mankind; the absence of trust, loyalty, and affection on the part of his subjects; the insolence of his enemies; the indifference of his so-called friends; the treachery of his servants; and the contempt of his betrothed. All these burdens were his to bear, and solace there was none. Not a single flask of essence remained within the ducal apartment. The Keldhaam Gnuxia had confiscated them all. Povon sat up in bed. The tears oozed from the corners of his eyes, and a muffled sob escaped him. No comfort to be had, and his need was so very great! Only those born to lonely grandeur could appreciate the intensity of his longings, so far beyond the mundane miseries of the ordinary man! And then the Duke remembered. A bottle of ancient brandy lay concealed in the secret niche behind the tapestry in the alcove at the far end of the room. Gnuxia knew about it, of course—no use trying to hide anything from her. But the Keldhaam's abhorrence of essences did not extend to alcohol, at least not in the same intensity, and therefore the brandy was permitted to remain on the tacit understanding that it would be used in moderation. Any infraction of this unspoken dictum would have resulted in the swift disappearance of Povon's last remaining source of nocturnal consolation.

Still weeping softly, the Duke climbed down from his bed, hurried across the room as quickly as his chubby legs would carry him, ducked into the alcove, and pushed the tapestry

aside. Reaching into the niche, he withdrew the brandy and
eagerly pulled the cork. But the bottle never made it to his
lips. At that moment, a roaring explosion shook the ducal
bedchamber. The great bed upon which his Grace had lain but
seconds earlier was blown to bits. The heavy carved frame
burst asunder, the posts and tester splintered, the mattress dis-
gorged clouds of feathers, and the cushions went flying. A
blast of superheated air slammed the Duke against the back wall
of the alcove. The bottle broke in his hand and the contents
soaked him. Povon squealed and dropped to his knees, arms
up to shield his face and head. For a moment the air was lethal
with whizzing hunks of red-hot iron, bits of shattered glass and
burning wood, none of which entered the alcove. More dangerous yet were the bright clouds of smoldering feathers driven
here and there throughout the chamber. The feathers rained
down everywhere, and where they landed, fires bloomed. A
couple touched the Duke's brandy-dampened nightshirt, and
pale alcoholic flames skittered around the silken hem. Povon
shrieked and collapsed face down upon the floor, rolling from
side to side in a wild effort to extinguish himself. While he
thrashed and screamed, fires licked at the remains of the bed,
at the brocade hangings and padded furnishings. The room
quickly filled with thick gray smoke, and Povon began to choke
on it. His Grace's cries were interspersed with racking coughs.

The homicidal scheme of Yans Whurm Didnis might well
have succeeded but for the diligence of a trio of ducal retainers
stationed in the outer chambers. Momentarily transfixed by the
thunder of the blast, the servants now hastened to the unlocked
bedroom. While one ran for reinforcements, the other two
entered the fiery, smoke-filled chamber in search of their feebly
shrieking master.

Half-stupefied with smoke and terror, the Duke was on the
verge of unconsciousness when his servants found him. His
nightshirt was scorched and smoldering in spots. Seeing this,
the retainers tore the tapestry from the alcove wall, quickly
wrapped their master, and bore the resulting parcel tenderly
from the bedroom.

Assistance arrived, the fires were quickly doused, and the
court physician was summoned. But long before the doctor
appeared, Duke Povon so far roused himself from a daze of
terror as to demand a flask of the Moon Dream of Uhanna.
None was forthcoming—the Keldhaam had forbidden it—and

Povon's teeth began to chatter. His face was the color of lard, and he was trembling violently. Once or twice he attempted to speak, but coherence seemed to have deserted him.

News of the attempt upon the Duke's life traveled quickly through the palace, and the inhabitants, both noble and menial, began to converge upon Povon's apartment. By order of the physician all were excluded, saving only a few personal servants, the Duke's betrothed, and the Duke's son.

Sneever was first to arrive. He came in flushed and panting, still attired in the pea-green velvet suit he had worn to the reception. It was obvious that the young man feared the worst, for his manner was uncontrollably agitated and his great blue eyes beamed terror. The first words out of his mouth as he crossed the ducal threshold were, "His Grace—not dead?" Upon receiving the reassurances of the servants, Sneever blanched—presumably with relief. Speaking seemed difficult for him, and yet he managed to ask, "Who has attempted the Duke's life?"

No one knew.

Sneever was ushered into the presence of his miraculously preserved father, and the reunion was affecting. Father and son seemed equally bereft of speech. Povon still shuddered in the grip of indescribable terror, but there he sat, alive and uninjured. Lord Sneever made an unsuccessful effort to express his joy and relief. A couple of ineffectual croaks escaped him, and then he subsided, overcome with emotion. This display of sensibility produced a strong impression on all who beheld it, and the strength of his lordship's filial devotion was universally admired.

Shortly thereafter the Keldhaam Gnuxia strode into the ducal apartment. Having verified the uninjured state of her betrothed, the Keldhaam's response to the situation was the essence of vengeful practicality. "We must find the assassins and destroy them," she declared. "They must perish in torment, that their deaths may serve as an example to those who dare to plot against the Duke. It is the only way to ensure your safety, Betrothed. I say it is the only way. Do you hear me?"

There was no reply. Povon stared at the floor.

"Have you no spirit? Will you allow yourself to be used thus, without seeking revenge? Will you not lift a hand to defend yourself?" Gnuxia demanded.

Silence. The Duke chewed his lips for a moment, and managed a whisper. "I'm sick. I need the Moon Dream. I need it."

"No. That is forbidden. Such abuse of mind and body is unacceptable to the daughter of his Splendor the Keldhar. I will not tolerate it." Gnuxia folded her arms and scowled down at him. "So much I will permit, however—the physician may prepare you a sleeping-draught—"

"Oh, yes! Yes!"

"Provided—I say *provided* you pronounce the name of the enemy seeking your life." -

Sneever's pulses raced and his intestines seemed to have taken on a life of their own. His face was ghastly, but as usual nobody noticed him.

"Come, Betrothed. Speak. *Now*," the Keldhaam insisted.

Povon closed his eyes, massaged his temples, and thought hard. Only one name suggested itself, but once the idea had taken root, its truth seemed manifest. "Grizhni," muttered the Duke. "Fal Grizhni is my enemy, now and always. He seeks to destroy me, and tonight he almost succeeded. Grizhni."

"Fal Grizhni is long dead." Gnuxia was fast losing patience. "What nonsense is this?"

"Grizhni's son lives. The soldiers saw him in those caves, along with his mother. He is a demon like his father, and he plots my destruction. No doubt his mother assists. It is true. And you are right, Keldhaam—" He opened his eyes and stared up at her. "I must defend myself. I *will* defend myself. Next time my Guardsmen will not fail. I will send them back to the Nazara Sin, and this time my enemies will die. Now may I have that sleeping-draught?"

Chapter Six

"They're going to be back," said Verran. "They didn't get what they were looking for, and those Guardsmen are going to be back."

"Let them come," Terrs replied. "We shall be ready."

Mother and son stood side by side at the mouth of the Mvjri Dazzle. Before them arched the great exit to Surface, and through the opening the thin crescent of a new moon was visible. Cool, fresh night breezes carried the scents of earth and greenery into the cave. Verran inhaled longingly. "Come outside with me for a few minutes," she coaxed, unconsciously employing a unit of temporal measurement that meant little to her son. "There's something we must talk about."

"We cannot use the Mvjri Dazzle," Terrs replied, glad of an excuse to avoid a Surface excursion. "From this Coloration onward, it no longer serves as a Vardrul portal. Henceforth it is a trap intended for our enemies alone."

He spoke with obvious satisfaction, and Verran suppressed a sigh as she regarded the work in progress. For the past several Small Vens the Vardruls had labored at the foot of the dazzle, and now a great, deep pit easily twelve feet in diameter yawned just inside the entrance. The excavation work was complete, and a team of Vardruls under the leadership of F'tryll'jnr Rdsdr applied the finishing touches to the project. A number of wickedly sharpened stalacites had been set upright at the bottom of the pit. F'tryll'jnr Rdsdr and the others were painting the dagger-keen points with a thick almost-gelatinous substance. Verran noticed that the Vardruls took great care to avoid touch-

121

ing the jelly. The explanation was unpleasantly apparent, but she desired confirmation. "Poison?" she inquired with revulsion.

"Yes. A concentrated extract of the Deadly Radiance fungus. Any trespasser falling into the pit will encounter the stalactites. If he escapes death by impalement, then the venom will finish him within hours. He will experience weakness, paralysis, confusion, and delirium before he dies. Personally, I should prefer impalement," Terrs concluded expressionlessly.

"Did you suggest this scheme to the Vardruls?" She knew the answer to that one too.

"Yes, and they were quick to accept it. I was pleasantly surprised."

Verran heard the challenge in her son's voice. "Think I'm going to argue about it, don't you?" she inquired. "Expecting a moral discourse, I suppose? Something touching on the many beauties of peace and forgiveness?"

"And conciliation, Mother." Terrs's lips twitched, a sign that he repressed a smile. "Do not forget conciliation."

"You know well enough that I hate bloodshed. But I realize there are times when it's necessary and justifiable. In defense of your own life and your home, violent measures may be unavoidable. As for this poisoned trap"—Verran indicated the great pit—"it saddens me to see it, but I don't question the necessity—only the efficacy."

"You've suggestions, Mother?" Terrs was clearly pleased at the discovery of an unexpected ally. "The F'tryll'jnrs, R'jnrllschs, and the others have wanted to help, but they only do what I tell them to do. They have no ideas."

"I suspect that may change. For the present this trap of yours is all very well as far as it goes, but it doesn't go far enough. It won't serve to repel an invasion of Guardsmen. It's too small to hold a squadron, and too visible to escape detection."

"Obviously. But it will not be visible by the time I have finished. I shall use Cognition to disguise the opening."

"Cognition? You're that proficient already?" It was not altogether welcome news.

"You'll see for yourself very shortly."

"If you can do that, then why don't you just camouflage the various dazzles? Hide them so that the Guardsmen can never find their way in here again?"

Terrs's dark eyes flickered. "I can't do that yet. I'm not strong enough, I couldn't maintain the illusion. The dazzles must be physically disguised with brush, scrub, and rocks for now, and some of them will be sealed. But this much my Cognition can do—hide the traps that we have built here at Mvjri, at Great Kf'rj, and at the F'jnruu Batgate. Those are the dazzles most likely to be discovered by men, and they will be protected."

"It's not enough," Verran shook her head. "Not enough to stop trained Guardsmen."

"It will hinder, confuse, and demoralize them," Terrs replied. "It will cloud their judgment and shake their confidence. And it is only the first of many obstacles they will meet. I've planned a series of traps and pitfalls to safeguard our caverns—the Grizhni Patriarch's writings have assisted me in this—and eventually all will be constructed. Moreover, I intend to teach my Zmadrc kinsmen and the other clan members to fight in their own defense, and to kill if need be."

"You will teach them? And who will teach you, Terrs? What do you know of warfare, weaponry, and killing?"

"Very little. Only what ordinary sense tells me. I know enough to use the advantages that we possess—that is to say, our superior numbers and our superior knowledge of the caverns. I know that what the Vardrul kinsmen lack in aggressiveness and ferocity must be compensated for with guile and stealth. I know that we need rely on such measures only until such time as my Cognition is strong enough to protect us all from human attack. And I believe that time is not far off."

"As for the Cognition, you may be right—I couldn't say," Verran returned. "In the meantime, you speak as if you imagine yourself some sort of—of a general or something. Terrs, you're only seventeen years—that is, twenty-five Great Vens old. That's mature for a Vardrul, but not for a human."

"You regard me as a child, Mother?"

Verran was silent. As he stood before her now—tall, dangerously purposeful, and iron-willed—there was nothing remotely childish about Terrs. So must his father have looked at a similar age. "No, not a child," she admitted in a low voice. "But lacking a man's experience. What's more, you're not a Vardrul. What makes you so sure they'll be willing to follow a young human's advice?"

"They are already following it. You see it before you now—
they excavate the pit at my behest. They poison the stalactites
upon my suggestion. I have looked for everything human in
me—all the cruelty, cunning, violence—and I have resolved
to place these detestable but useful qualities at the service of
my Vardrul kinsmen. Strange, is it not, that the human barbarities I so despise may prove the salvation of all that I value?"

No, not a child, more's the pity, Verran thought. *It's this
unnatural life he's led. Also—his heritage.* Aloud she replied,
"Innate 'barbarities,' as you put it, aren't enough, Terrs. Nothing can change the fact that you've never been trained to fight.
You've no knowledge, you don't even know how to handle a
sword or any other weapon, and there's no one down here to
teach you. The Ducal Guardsmen are professional soldiers—
well drilled, well disciplined, and highly experienced. You
can't expect to rely on sheer inspiration to defeat them."

"It is my hope to use their experience against them."

"What do you mean?"

"The Guardsmen are accustomed to fighting Surface. Their
knowledge, their expectations, their responses, are based on
their experience of Surface conditions. They know nothing of
our caverns. Ours is a different world, and the Surface tactics—
the only tactics the soldiers know—may prove worse than useless here. We shall play upon their ignorance of these endless
tunnels—we shall mislead and befuddle them—and in the end,
when they are lost and fearful, we shall destroy them."

"Perhaps, but I shouldn't count too heavily on that if I were
you. Those Guardsmen may not be quite the blundering fools
you take them for."

"Then what do you advise, Mother? Shall we try to hide
from them when they come? Shall we live in perpetual fear?
Shall we abandon our home altogether? Or should we simply
allow them to kill us all? Which of these courses do you advo-
cate?"

"None of them, as you well know. But there may be another
way, which is what I wanted to talk to you about. Listen to
me, Terrs," Verran insisted, in tones more commanding than
she had of late seen fit to use with him. "Those Guardsmen
came looking for the two of us. There was no other reason. I
don't know why they've finally come for the son of Fal Grizhni
after all these years. I don't know how they learned we are

here. But I do know that all those slaughtered Vardruls died on our account." She saw his face change minutely, and continued with an effort, "It is true. You know it. You also know that many more of your friends and new kinsmen will die when the Guardsmen return—and again, we'll be the cause. Our presence is deadly to our benefactors—they must realize that by now—but they lack the ruthlessness to expel us. Therefore it's our responsibility to make an end."

"Then you wish to flee the caves, Mother?"

"Unfortunately, that wouldn't be good enough. The Guardsmen wouldn't realize we'd gone. They'd come back here to search, and search again, and the Vardruls would suffer horribly. The soldiers and their master must be persuaded that they've no reason to return, and I know the way to do it. I'm going to give myself up."

For once Terrs was startled out of his customary impassivity. He stared at her in open amazement, shock, and alarm, and for the first time in many Great Vens Verran was reminded of the child he had once been. The youth was momentarily speechless. When he found his tongue, his voice was harsh with dismay. "You must not think of that, Mother! Those men are savages. They would kill you."

"Not necessarily," she replied steadily. "They'd really have no particular reason to kill me. Far more likely that they'd take me back to Lanthi Ume, where I might expect to find some assistance. My family, the House of Verras, was not without influence. In all probability I should not be unduly mistreated." She hoped she sounded convincing.

Terrs was not taken in. "You know better than that, Mother. They already tried to kill you once—you would have died with the Zmadrcs, had it not been for Nyd."

"That was in the heat of battle. Should I return to Lanthi Ume and present myself at the Ducal Palace before the eyes of all the courtiers, it would be a different story. Before so many witnesses the Duke would scarcely dare to order my execution, for fear of universal censure."

"No? He did not hesitate to murder the Grizhni Patriarch," Terrs reminded her. "He would at the very least order your arrest—"

"Well, I can stand that."

"—And then your death. No, Mother. It is unthinkable. In

any event, your sacrifice would serve no purpose. If it is your intention to help the Vardruls, your plan could not succeed. What good would it do to give yourself up if our enemies know that I am still alive and well in the depths of the caverns? You would be destroyed, and then the soldiers would come back for me."

"Not if they think you're dead," Verran returned promptly. "Remember the four Guardsmen who followed us through the Hllsreg Net? I'll say that they caught up with us and killed you."

"The Duke will not believe you."

"I'll weep, mourn, and run distracted. I shall be very convincing," Verran assured him. "The Duke will believe me because I'll be telling him what he very much wants to believe. Thereafter, you and the Vardruls will be left in peace."

Evidently dissatisfied, Terrs studied her closely, performed swift internal calculations, and then answered, "I would not allow you to do it alone, Mother. If you insist on returning to Lanthi Ume, I shall accompany you."

"That's the last thing I'd want!"

"Nonetheless, I will do it. Obviously you cannot prevent me. Is it not simple justice?"

Verran was silent. He had caught her neatly, she saw, and for one angry instant she was almost tempted to call his bluff. Except he was not bluffing—what he said he would do, he would do. The sacrifice of two human lives would save scores or possibly hundreds of innocent Vardruls. On that basis it was a small price to pay. But one of those lives was that of her son—her only child, the sole heir of Fal Grizhni—and she could not forfeit that. Not for all the Vardruls in the universe. It was selfish and unjust, as she was well aware, to place the welfare of her son above that of an entire race of gentle, intelligent beings, but Verran could not help it. And of course, Terrs knew that very well. He was clever enough to gauge her emotions to a nicety and ruthless enough to exploit her maternal affection. Verran's palm itched and she came very near to striking him. When she spoke, her voice shook with rage and frustration. "That's stupid. There's no sense to it. Why sacrifice the two of us, when one's enough to satisfy the Duke of Lanthi Ume?"

"You are right, Mother. I will go to Lanthi Ume alone," Terrs returned deliberately.

"You know that isn't what I meant! You're selfish and childish, Terrs! If you were really concerned about your Vardrul friends, you'd take my suggestion and that would save the lives of all. But you don't really care what's best for them, for all your fine talk. No, you don't want peace. What you *really* want is a chance to play with your traps and pitfalls, your homemade weapons and amateur strategy. All you *really* want is a chance to fight, a chance to prove yourself a great leader and a brilliant tactician. It's pride, nothing but pride. And if the Vardruls—and the human soldiers, by the way—die by the hundreds, well where's the difference? If such slaughter serves to confirm the glory of Terrs Fal Grizhni, Boy General, they will not have died in vain!"

Terrs stared down at her expressionlessly. "If you are truly determined to return to Lanthi Ume, no one can stop you. But if you go, I will accompany you. It is your choice, Mother." She was miserably silent, and he continued, "I am not so self-serving as you imagine. I do not seek glory."

"Be honest."

Uncertainty flickered for a split second in his eyes, and vanished. "You are wrong about me and wrong in your notions of appeasement. You believe that an act of self-sacrifice will placate the Duke and save the Vardruls. In a very immediate sense that may be true, but in the long run it would do more harm than good. Men have invaded our home to discover timorous weaklings. That being the case, they will return to plunder and kill. It does not matter what we give them—your life, my life, the Lightcrystals of J'frnial, it does not signify. It will not be enough, never enough. They will want more, and they will return, for it is natural and inevitable that the strong shall prey upon the weak."

"What do you know of nature and inevitability, when you've never looked beyond these ghastly caves?"

"There is only one way to save ourselves," Terrs continued as if he had not heard her. "And that is to prove to the humans that we have the power and the will to defend ourselves. When they respect us—that is to say, when they fear us—only then shall we truly be left in peace. That is our only real hope."

"You don't know—"

The conversation was interrupted as the Vardruls emerged from the pit, climbing out by way of a rope ladder affixed to a nearby stalagmite. F'tryll'jnr Rdsdr and his cohorts ranged themselves before Terrs to announce the completion of the project. The excavation was finished, the sharpened stone stakes had been set in place and each one smeared with poison. There remained but the Cognition of the Fal Grizhni/Zmadrc Terrs to render the whole invisible.

They're treating Terrs as if he were a Patriarch, Verran thought. *No—worse. As if they were soldiers and he their commanding officer. In a way it's understandable. Young though he is, Terrs is their master in strength, force, and determination. They recognize that in him, and they have need of it now. No Vardrul mind could have conceived this vicious trap they've built, it took a human for that. I wonder if Terrs can actually manage a Cognitive camouflage?*

It seemed she was about to find out. Terrs stepped to the edge of the pit. Reaching into the pocket of his robe, he brought forth the two colorless crystals taken from Zmadrc R'dsvyllsch's garden, and these he held loosely in the palm of his open hand. Bowing his head and closing his eyes, he spoke softly, at inexpert length. But at last the crystals began to glow, and Verran experienced a familiar uneasy thrill. The air around her was charged with an uncanny force that she remembered from long ago. For a moment nothing happened, and her nervous tension increased. Then the ground before her began to change. Subtly at first, so subtly that she questioned the accuracy of her own perceptions, the sharp-cut edges of the excavation wavered and softened. Verran instinctively rubbed her eyes, but there could be no mistake—the stone brink was swimming now, trembling and quivering as if granite had turned to jelly. Then the hole began to shrink, the circular opening slowly contracting like the mouth of a sack whose drawstrings are pulled. Smaller it grew, decreasing steadily, dwindling impossibly to a single dark point. In silence the black point vanished. All that remained to mark the center of the hole was a tiny mound of dust resting upon an apparently solid stone floor. The two crystals darkened. Cognition was complete, and Verran heard her son's tired sigh. Terrs's shoulders slumped and his face was more than ordinarily pale.

The watching Vardruls hummed in quiet wonder, and their flesh dimmed. They stared from the unblemished stone floor to the young savant and back again, with eyes full of unreadable emotion; but Verran thought she detected confusion there, and perhaps a little fear. Finally one of the R'jnrllsch kinsmen picked up a pebble and tossed it. The pebble flew through the air, descended, and disappeared—seemingly swallowed by the floor. An instant later, a tiny clatter was heard as the stone landed among the stalactites at the bottom of the pit. The Vardrul warbling increased in volume and intensity. F'tryll'jnr Rdsdr knelt upon the invisible brink and leaned forward to place his palm flat to the floor. He encountered no resistance, and his hand sank into illusory stone. The Vardrul's hiir plummeted. With a tremulous cry he snatched his hand back, to find the member whole and uninjured. Reassured, he tried again, this time reaching deep into the hole to watch in fascination the slow disappearance of his hand and arm up to the shoulder. Several of the other young Vardruls present pitched pebbles to see them vanish. Excited arpeggios rippled from a dozen glowing throats.

"So. You did it." Verran's anger had faded. She noted with concern her son's look of almost sickly depletion. "Are you all right?"

"I will be when I've rested," he replied. "But I cannot rest yet. There is too much to do. The Grizhni Patriarch's Falling Stones—that is the next one I must learn. That one is more than simple illusion—it will be more difficult. And I must devise weapons for the kinsmen. And the great brown bats must be trained to attack trespassers—" The words gushed forth like matter from a lanced boil.

"Softly, Terrs. Don't think of it now," Verran advised. "You're exhausted."

"I must think of it now. Who knows how soon the soldiers might return? We must be ready. This Coloration, I am resolved to conceal the traps we have built at Great Kf'rj and at the F'jnruu Batgate. It must be done at once."

"You won't help the Vardruls if you destroy your health through overexertion. Even your father had to rest sometimes."

Terrs's reply was forestalled by the emergence of Zmadrc Fourteen from a tributary tunnel. All present turned to stare, for her aspect was extraordinary. Fourteen blazed and darkened like a signal lantern, her hiir alternating swiftly between highest and lowest intensity. Light-dark, light-dark, light-dark. The sequence was mindlessly repetitive, and in the language of

Ftvyi amounted to the mumblings of an idiot. Her great eyes were wide and dull, the ocular ridges perfectly smooth. She appeared dazed, unaware of her surroundings. Her blank gaze swept the corridor unseeingly.

"What's wrong with her?" Verran whispered. "Is she sick?"

"Sick with grief," Terrs replied with unwonted feeling. "Three-quarters of her kinsmen were slaughtered by the Guardsmen, and she cannot bring herself to relinquish oneness. She cannot let them go and therefore, at the expense of her own harmony, she knows the Ancestors for Colorations on end. Prolonged communion with the dead is profoundly bewildering, or so I am told. She wanders the corridors lost and alone, caught between past and present, belonging truly to neither."

"Poor child!" Verran stretched forth a compassionate hand, but Fourteen drifted by blindly. The Vardruls dimmed in her wake. "Can't you help her, Terrs? Can't anyone?"

"No. She must choose for herself between the living and the dead. Should she choose eternal oneness with the Ancestors, that is her privilege."

Verran stared at him in horror. "She's only a child! You're not saying that she might actually—"

Disordant cries of alarm interrupted the question. Fourteen, deaf to all warnings, wandered upon the verge of the invisible pit. Unwilling despite his words to permit his Future eternal oneness, Terrs sprang to her side and drew her gently back from the brink. His touch recalled Fourteen to the present. Her eyes brightened and she gazed upon her companions with recognition. "What disharmony?" she fluted faintly but clearly.

"Danger here," Terrs replied. "A deathtrap for humans, but deadly to Vardruls as well."

"Where?" inquired Fourteen, puzzled.

"Just inside the dazzle. Hidden by the Grizhni Patriarch's art," Terrs explained.

She rippled her tentacles dutifully, but showed little sign of real comprehension. Her customary quickness and vivacity were completely suppressed.

"I don't think she understands you, Terrs," Lady Verran observed. "That hidden pit is a menace to everyone. Something must be done."

"It will be, Mother," he assured her. "We shall erect barriers to block off this end of the corridor. No Vardrul will come to harm here. Only the men sent to kill us will die."

At twilight time a lone human figure roamed the hills of the Nazara Sin. Rillif Har Fennahar was tired, hungry, and frustrated. Following a three-day journey on horseback and on foot across the dreary Gravula Wasteland, he had anticipated little difficulty in finding his way to the fabled caverns. True, the Vardrul inhabitants were wont to conceal all but the largest entrances, but Fennahar was equipped with his uncle's excellent map, which supposedly pinpointed no less than six gateways. Fennahar, however, could find none of them. Or rather he had located one, to discover it solidly plugged with freshly mortared stone. It would have taken several days' effort with a pickaxe or else a major explosion to break through the barrier. The other entrances were impossible to find, chiefly owing to the lack of identifiable landmarks. The hills of the Nazara Sin were barren, monotonous, endlessly repetitive. Jinzin Farni's map relied heavily upon anomalous points of reference—distinctive rock formations, for the most part. But those points of reference had been altered or removed. Fennahar had encountered tumbled piles of broken stone whose jagged faces and sharp new edges spoke volumes. The camouflage of the landmarks was recent and deliberate. The Vardruls' response to the attack upon their home was simple but effective, and the map was now all but useless. Fennahar had searched the hills all day long, searched until his feet were sore and his back ached with the weight of the pack he carried. Now he paused to rest and contemplate his highly uncongenial surroundings. Night was coming on swiftly. Already the sun had sunk from view behind the surrounding hills, and the breezes had turned uncomfortably cold. No sense in continuing the quest in darkness—best to stop while there remained light enough to collect the scrub with which to build a fire. In the morning he would resume, perhaps carrying the search to the eastern range of hills that he had not yet investigated.

Fennahar's hands rose to the straps that held his pack in place and he started to unbuckle, then paused as a shadow in the sky caught his attention. To the east, not far away, arose a great flock of winged creatures, black against the leaden clouds. They ascended by the tens of thousands in a huge,

wavering column, so many that the column sometimes appeared
solid. The soft thunder of their wings filled the air. For a
moment Fennahar stared in simple wonder, which abated as
he identified the phenomenon. At twilight the multitudinous
bats of the caverns ventured forth in search of food. Here was
luck! He need only note the bats' point of egress to find his
own way in.

Fennahar marched swiftly eastward, his eyes fixed on the
dark column that twisted and shifted in the air before him. As
he went the dusk gathered, the world darkened, and the winged
forms above faded into obscurity. It would not be long before
night swallowed them alive. Weariness notwithstanding, Fennahar increased his pace, stumbling over rocks and roots in his
eagerness. For perhaps half an hour he walked. At the end of
that time the bats were invisible and he was relying on memory
alone to guide him to their point of origin. And then he saw
what he was looking for—a faint, soft glow up ahead, a ghostly
smudge of pale light that seemed to float in midair. Against
that background of vague luminosity, the last of the emerging
bats were visible in sinister silhouette. Fennahar hurried toward
the light. Another three minutes of walking brought him to a
sizable hole in the side of a hill. The opening, somewhat disguised with dead branches and tufts of dried grasses, would
have been extremely inconspicuous in the daylight. At night,
however, the light of the rocks leaked through the vegetative
veiling left purposely scanty to admit the nightly sorties of the
bat population. And thus Rillif Har Fennahar found his way to
the dazzle known as the F'jnruu Batgate.

Fennahar paused beside the hole. His expression was dubious
as he watched the last laggard bats emerge to disappear into
darkness, for the prospect of walking alone and armed with
nothing but a hunting knife into the caverns of the Nazara Sin
was far from inviting. He remembered the gruesome legends
of the White Demons of the Caverns, said to batten upon the
flesh of humanity, and uneasiness almost overcame his normally
insatiable curiosity. In vain he recalled his uncle's descriptions
of Vardrul timidity, gentleness, and pacifism. None of these
reassurances banished trepidation. Fennahar dipped into his
pocket to finger the string of multicolored pebbles presented
to Jinzin Farni as a token of eternal Vardrul friendship seventeen
years earlier. He weighed the pebbles and wondered if eternity

could last beyond seventeen years. A flash of heat at his left
wrist broke his reverie and Fennahar glanced down, startled.
The silver wristlet provided by his uncle gleamed faintly in the
soft rock-light. The metal was unwontedly warm, almost hot,
a sure sign that Cognitive influence reigned close at hand. He
took a cautious step toward the hole and the warmth increased
noticeably. Fennahar thought of the Grizhni records and Cognitive aids he had been sent to find, and frowned. Their proximity would account for the warmth of the wristlet, but surely
the Vardruls would not store such priceless articles so near a
gateway to the hostile outside world? Or would they? Perhaps
the Vardruls did not recognize the value of the information
they held? Or were they indifferent? Who could possibly know
what the Vardruls might not think, or feel, or do? The creatures
and their domain were shrouded in mystery, a thought that
proved pure catnip to Har Fennahar. His mind rumbled with
hunger for knowledge. Hesitating no longer, he pushed the
branches aside and slipped through the F'jnruu Batgate.

The moment he stepped through the gateway the temperature
of the silver wristlet mounted, and Fennahar cautiously paused
to reconnoiter. Before him stretched a broad, high-ceilinged
corridor of stone. The walls, floor, and ceiling glowed with
dim rock-light and the resulting flatness, the total lack of
shadow, was disorienting to the newcomer. Fennahar found
himself confused. His perceptions of depth and distance were
distorted, and he hardly knew where to set his foot. The corridor
was largely featureless, with plain walls free of mineral excres-
cences. No offshooting passageways or chambers were visible.
A few small niches near the ceiling showed evidence of bat
habitation, but they were deserted now. The place appeared
empty. There was no sign of life — Vardrul, human, or chiropte-
ran — and the silence was absolute. Fennahar strained his ears
but heard nothing. If they were near, the residents did not
choose to make their presence known, for which he could
hardly blame them. He recalled the words of Jinzin Farni —
They're far more likely to hide from you. — and nodded to
himself. Somehow he would have to convince the Vardruls of
his peaceable intentions. How that might be done when the
creatures refused to reveal themselves was unclear, but he would
find a way. He considered calling out to them, but judged that
the sound of a loud human voice would only arouse their ready

fears. No, he would have to present himself to the inhabitants, reassure them, discover a means of communication—and his pulses quickened at the thought. To the best of his knowledge, no Lanthian outside the membership of the Select had ever conversed with the White Demons. What would it be to encounter creatures intelligent but inhuman? What wonders of alien mind and custom might he not discover—if he could only find them?

Determination restored, Fennahar took an eager step forward, then stopped again as the temperature of the wristlet increased. Why? Where was the source of Cognitive energy? Once again he examined his surroundings. Bare, faintly glowing stone above, below, and before him. At his back, comfortingly accessible, lay the exit. No visible danger here, but something near at hand triggered the Cognitive response of Uncle Jin's silver band. Could it be that the artifacts he sought lay abandoned and forgotten in one of the recesses up above? Did bats nest amid the writings of Preeminence Fal Grizhni? Instinct shouted a warning that Fennahar strove to ignore. Eyes fixed upon the nearest niche, he started forward. At the third step, his foot and leg sank impossibly into what appeared to be the solid stone floor, and he began to fall. Automatically he pulled back and for a moment tottered, body twisting and arms flailing wildly, before plunging over the brink of a concealed trap.

Fennahar fell some twelve feet. A moment before he hit bottom, something grazed his ribcage—something sharp enough to rip through a heavy tunic and the linen shirt beneath to reach his flesh. He felt a keen stinging along his side and then a sudden, violent shock as he landed. He came down on his feet, staggered, and pitched forward, breaking the fall on outstretched hands. For a moment he lay still, breathing hard. When the pounding of his heart had subsided, he sat up slowly to assess damages, which proved surprisingly slight. All bones had providentially escaped breakage. The palms of his hands were scraped raw. Both knees were bleeding, one ankle throbbed, and a long, shallow gash cut across his ribs. There would be bruises, aches, and pains aplenty, but actual damage appeared inconsequential. Thus reassured, Fennahar lifted his eyes to inspect the trap that contained him, and his sense of relief began to fade.

He sat at the bottom of an open pit some twelve feet in depth and twelve in diameter, which gaped the entire width of the corridor. From his vantage point, he had an unobstructed view of the ceiling. Quite unobstructed. Fennahar recalled the apparently unbroken length of stone floor stretching from the entrance into the unknown regions of the cave, and recognized at once the source of the Cognitive influence which even now rendered the silver wristlet almost uncomfortably warm to the touch. The trap had been deliberately disguised by a Cognitive illusion of rudimentary single-directional nature. The question was—whose Cognition? Surely the Vardruls themselves did not aspire to such art—or had they learned to make vicious use of the information left at their disposal? Was this the work of a visiting savant—perhaps of Preeminence Fal Grizhni himself? Or could it be that Lady Grizhni and her son yet survived in this place, and one or both of them had somehow acquired the skill? The son was only a boy, and as for the mother—? Fennahar visualized the young Verran Dris Verras he had known in Lanthi Ume—it was surprising how vividly he remembered every line of her face—and wondered mightily. She'd been sunny-tempered, gay, and spirited then. In the unlikely event that she still survived, however—then how different, how embittered, might she have grown in seventeen years? Bitter enough to engineer this trap, designed to kill rather than capture its victims? For glancing around him, Fennahar saw by how narrow a margin he had escaped immediate death. The floor of the pit bristled with vertically placed, close-set spears of stone. It was only by unlikely good luck that he had fallen in between them to avoid impalement on the cruel points. Presumably it was one of those spears that had gashed his ribs on his way down. Fennahar rose gingerly to his feet and moved to inspect the transplanted stalactites. One of the points nearby was spotted with blood and also bore traces of some odd gelatinous substance that the explorer could not identify. He shrugged and turned his attention to the mouth of the pit, nearly six feet above the top of his head.

Six feet was an absurdly insignificant distance. Unthinkable, even insulting, that such a trifle should stand between the resourceful Rillif Har Fennahar and freedom.

It was too high to jump. In his younger days he had been something of an athlete. Had he been able to run and to work up speed, something might have been done even now, but from a standing position it was hopeless. Fennahar tried nonetheless. Shedding his pack, he jumped like a spring-driven toy and several times his uplifted hands came tantalizingly near the edge of the pit, but in the end he was forced to admit failure. Following this exertion he found himself unwontedly tired. His breathing was ragged and for a few moments he felt slightly dizzy, almost light-headed. The sensation was brief, but Fennahar was puzzled. Perhaps his fall had shaken him more than he'd realized?

He examined the walls of the pit. They were artificially smooth, offering no handholds, and they sloped slightly inward. No possibility at all of climbing out. There was a long coil of rope stowed away in his pack, but nothing above on which to fasten it. For the time being, the rope was useless.

It occurred to Fennahar that the stalactite spears that crowded the floor of the pit might possibly be loose in their mortar bed. Should he succeed in detaching even one of them, it might be used as a tool with which to pry up others. Given an adequate number of the long stone spikes, he could pile up a heap from whose summit it would be possible to reach the edge of the excavation. Alternately, if he could contrive to tie the stalactites very securely, he might construct a kind of climbable pole—the beauty of this plan being that a mere three of the spikes would provide sufficient length.

But that was three too many. Fennahar tested each of the stalactites in turn and found them all immovable. The mortar that held them was new and quite impervious to the point of his knife. Further experimentation would have resulted in the destruction of the blade, and Fennahar soon desisted. Some other stratagem was required, but the explorer found himself singularly slow-witted. Curious lassitude impaired his concentration, and the only course that suggested itself was to shout for help. Shout he did, until the corridor echoed, but the cries drew no assistance. If they were heard at all, they were ignored. When his voice hoarsened and his throat grew raw, Fennahar was silent. The dizziness and breathlessness returned, this time accompanied by intense exhaustion. His forehead and palms were clammy. It struck him as unnatural, but he was too tired and too confused to consider the matter at length. A moment's rest was all he needed, a moment in which to catch his breath and regain his equilibrium. Fennahar sat, leaned his head back against the stone wall, closed his eyes, and instantly fell asleep.

Impossible to judge how much time passed before the pain of a headache woke him. Fennahar opened his eyes with reluctance. Everything around him appeared unchanged, but he himself had altered for the worse. Fog obscured his vision, his extremities were icy, and his limbs seemed weighted with lead. His lungs had forgotten their function, and breathing was a conscious effort. Worse yet—the peculiar confusion, the distraction, the intolerable sense of mental paralysis had increased tenfold, and with it came bitter discouragement. And yet the period of rest had served him to the extent that his mind was now able to generate a new plan, sluggishness notwithstanding.

Fennahar turned to the discarded pack that lay on the floor at his side. Digging through the contents with fingers that felt as thick as cucumbers, he finally located and withdrew the coil of rope. Coil in hand, he stood up with difficulty, using the wall for support. There was no sensation in his feet. He had to look down to make sure they were firmly planted on the ground. His dizziness increased as he rose, and he was forced to rest for a few moments before proceeding. While he rested, a stray thought clamored briefly for attention, then lost itself in the mental mists.

Fennahar lurched to the nearest stalactite, a chest-high spear that stood at the base of the wall. Following half a dozen botched attempts, he managed to tie a clove hitch around the stone. Another tall stalactite rose near the wall some three feet from the first. Or was it six? Or twelve? Fennahar found his perception of distance wildly unstable. The object of his attention seemed to float giddily before him, alterately approaching and receding. Why? And once again a stray thought frisked at the edges of his consciousness, only to flee before he could catch it.

He stumbled three paces to the second stone, stretched the rope taut, and, with infinite difficulty, tied another clove hitch. After that, things were somewhat easier. Back and forth staggered Har Fennahar, winding the rope about the two stalactites again and again in tight layers of figure eights, and finally securing the free end with a triple knot that almost proved too much for him. When he had finished, he paused again to rest. He was gasping for breath and his lungs labored painfully. It seemed impossible to fill them. All sensation had fled his hands, and the cold numbness was creeping up his arms. Abruptly he sat down. His legs had simply given way beneath him.

Fennahar gazed up at his handiwork. He had stretched a taut, sturdy rope sling that formed a kind of precarious platform some four feet above the floor. Assuming that the rope had been properly secured, it was theoretically possible to mount the platform and from that elevation jump high enough to catch the edge of the pit. A fit man with strong arms might then lift himself out of the trap. Fennahar, however, was anything but fit. As for his arms—it was difficult to move them at all, much less use them to perform feats of acrobatics. Nevertheless, he would have to try. The explorer shook his head slowly, in the vain hope of clearing his blurred vision. He was very sick, and there was some reason for it, and there was something he ought to be doing about it—but he could not address those problems now, not with a bewildered, semipetrified mind that longed for nothing but rest.

Slowly he dragged himself to his feet and staggered to the ropes. With vast effort he lifted a hand to press the cords and knots, then leaned his full weight upon them. Why? And he remembered—to test the tension, to verify the security of his construction. No purpose to a sling that would not bear his weight.

The rope coils were tight and unyielding. There was no reason to believe they would not serve their purpose. This established, Fennahar attempted to hoist himself up onto the sling. With deadened legs and arms this task proved impossible. His efforts were brief and few. On the second attempt he lost his balance and fell sprawling. The shock drove the breath from his lungs and some of the mists from his mind. The thought that had for some time loitered upon the fringes of his awareness manifested itself at last. Har Fennahar looked from the jelly-blotched points of the stalactites to the open cut above his ribs, and finally realized he'd been poisoned.

The speed with which his mind cleared was extraordinary. He was deeply alarmed, but knew there was no cause for despair. Among the "Cognitive gewgaws" furnished by Uncle Jin was a universal restorative strong enough to nullify the effect of any known venom. The restorative was contained in a small stoppered vial reposing in his pack. He need only find the vial, ingest the contents, and he would be healthy again; still a prisoner, of course, but that was a matter of far lesser urgency.

Fennahar lay prone. The pack was only a few feet away,

but it took all of his remaining strength to drag himself that short distance. He reached out and his hand dropped like a dead thing upon the canvas bag. Ineffectually he fumbled with the buckle. His fingers, numb and all but immobile, would not serve him, and the explorer felt the beginnings of panic stir in the depths of his brain. He could not afford panic. After pausing a moment to compose himself, he attacked the buckle again and met defeat again. Was it actually possible that he, who had successfully navigated the Straits of Vor and braved all the perils of Jobaal, was about to die because he could not open a canvas pack? Even in the midst of his desperation he could appreciate the irony.

With the last of his failing strength, Fennahar hitched himself forward to apply his teeth to the buckle. A series of careful tugs pulled the end of the strap loose, slid prong from eyelet, and drew the strap entirely free. The cover flap fell back and the bag gaped to reveal its densely packed contents. Fennahar experienced a fresh surge of hopelessness at the sight. Somewhere at the bottom of that mass of belongings lay the restorative that would save his life. In his present condition, how long would it take to find it? And if he did find it, how would he manage to unstopper the flask that his hands wouldn't grasp? No matter. He would deal with that problem when it arose. Grimly he set about the near-impossible task of emptying the pack, one article at a time. The work was exhausting and he was growing perceptibly feebler. His eyesight was failing and if it grew much worse, he would not recognize the flask when he came across it. Given his dire symptoms, the absence of pain was astonishing. His head ached and his lungs burned, but other than that he felt little beyond a profound coldness to which pain would have been preferable.

Deathly illness could not suppress the instinct that warned Har Fennahar he was not alone. The explorer raised his head and beheld, or imagined he beheld, two angular, huge-eyed faces peering down at him over the edge of the pit. To his disordered vision, both white faces appeared to glow. Their eyes, supernaturally brilliant, were filled with inhuman intelligence. Were they real? Hallucinations? Fennahar attempted to speak, tried to tell them that he was a friend, and harmless. But his tongue refused to obey his commands, and nothing coherent emerged from his mouth. He heard his own senseless mumblings and saw the faces above darken at the sound. Dark-

en? Impossible. His eyesight was playing him false. Once
more he strove vainly to speak and then, desperate to communicate, recalled his uncle's gift. Using his lifeless fingers as a
clumsy scoop, Fennahar dipped into his pocket and brought
forth the string of colored pebbles once bestowed upon the
Cognizant Jinzin Farni as a token of eternal friendship, and
this he attempted to present to the view of the spectators above.
The pebbles slipped from his useless grasp, but not before he
saw the faces of the two observers suddenly brighten. For a
moment the light bewildered and dazzled him, and then the
world vanished in comforting darkness.

Chapter Seven

❧❧❧❧

Rillif Har Fennahar woke to find himself on his back with a hideous hirsute countenance bending over him. Fierce tawny eyes blazed into his own from a distance of inches. He flinched and an involuntary gasp escaped him. His ghastly companion hissed at the sound. Its lips curled back to reveal yellowing canines and its talons hovered a hairbreadth from his exposed throat. Fennahar lay lifelessly still and the creature appeared somewhat mollified, but continued to hiss menacingly.

"Stop that, Nyd! Just *stop* that." It was a woman's voice that came from somewhere nearby, but Fennahar didn't dare turn his head to search for the source. Just awakened from deep sleep, bewildered and disoriented, it did not occur to him to wonder at the sound of a human voice speaking in Lanthian.

The creature snarled and flexed its claws.

"No, I mean it. Leave him alone, Nyd. This one isn't like the others."

Nyd croaked doubtfully and drew back with obvious reluctance. Fennahar was now able to take quick stock of his surroundings. He lay on a pallet on the floor of an irregularly shaped chamber, presumably somewhere in the depths of the caves of the Nazara Sin. Beside him rested his closed pack. Muted rock-light illuminated an array of translucent natural columns, elaborately carved and etched; a spectacular fall of stalactites; and a variety of lacelike mineral formations. A curtain of red slime blanketing one of the walls lent the rock-light a pleasant pink cast. Covering most of another wall was a large mosaic composed of bits of colored stone and green crystal, depicting a sunlit forest glade starred with flowers and populated with a collection of wild creatures that included deer, foxes, ornaves, and squirrels. A few feet from him crouched the fanged and hairy creature so manifestly eager to tear his throat open. Farther away stood the speaker, a small, slender, fair-haired woman attired in a simple gray robe. Her face, with its large eyes and delicate features, was entirely familiar to him. There were new, faint shadows both beneath and within the blue eyes. Some of the youthful softness was gone—cheekbones and jaw line were more emphatically delineated now than in the past. Always fair-skinned, she was now excessively pale. Other than that, the greatest alteration lay in her expression—a look of habitual settled unhappiness that had been entirely absent in her girlhood. Nevertheless, she had changed remarkably little.

"Verran," he said. His voice was somewhat weak. he was unwontedly tired, almost drained, but otherwise well. His vision was clear, sensation had returned to his extremities, and the sickness had passed.

She approached and scrutinized him. "Ril?" she inquired uncertainly. "Is it Ril Har Fennahar?"

He nodded. "What happened?"

"Don't you remember? You fell into a trap just inside the F'jnruu Batgate. Thank goodness you avoided impalement, but you cut yourself on a poisoned stake. Your cries were heard, but Terrs—but there was strong insistence that you, as an invading human enemy, must be left to die. However, the Vardruls— that is, the inhabitants of these caves—aren't capable of that. After you'd been down there the better part of a Coloration—I mean, several hours—and they could hear from the sounds you made that you were alive and in pain, they couldn't stand it any longer. So Lbavbsch Hfu and R'jnrllsch Fr'dr went in to investigate. They found you still alive, and they found the symbol of friendship you carried, so they brought you out immediately."

"I remember them. I saw them above, looking down at me—"

"No." Verran shook her head. "They could hear you but they couldn't see you."

"Ah. Of course not. The pit was camouflaged by Cogniton. Somebody's Cognition—"

"They brought you out," Verran interrupted, visibly uneasy at the mention of Cognition, "and administered the antidote to the Deadly Radiance poisoning. By that time though, the poison had had a chance to take hold and it wasn't certain the cure would be effective. Besides, who could know if a Vardrul remedy would work on a human? You've been senseless and delirious by turns for the past three Small Vens, and no one could predict the outcome."

"The past three what?"

"Small Vens. That's nearly three days."

"That long?" With some effort Fennahar lifted a hand to touch the stubble on his chin. What he felt convinced him of the accuracy of her assertion, but the movement elicited a threatening snarl from Nyd. Fennahar froze.

"Nyd, if you don't behave yourself, I am going to be very disappointed."

The hybrid subsided at once.

"Since I'm the only one in this place with experience of ailing humans," Verran continued, "I was the obvious choice to look after you. They brought you here to one of my chambers and when I saw you I thought I recognized you, but wasn't entirely sure. I did what I could to make you comfortable, and hoped for the best. Two Colorations ago, when your fever broke and you fell asleep, I was certain you'd recover. This news brightened the hiir of the Lesser Patriarchs, who'd been miserable with fear that they'd killed one who perhaps came in friendship."

She paused watchfully, and Fennahar realized that she distrusted him—a very understandable reaction, given her circumstances. He smiled as reassuringly as possible. "I did come in friendship."

"For what purpose?" she asked bluntly, no doubt hoping to take advantage of his weakness to catch him off guard.

Fennahar weighed his reply swiftly, and his hesitation was minimal. He decided at once that he dared not confide the true purpose of his visit. Clearly she was suspicious and perhaps a little afraid. Given her history and present situation, she had reason to fear. Out of the question that she would consent to relinquish her late husband's records to him at this point. He would have to win her confidence before broaching the subject. Loathing himself as a hypocrite, Fennahar answered, "I came to explore the caves and to learn the nature of the inhabitants. There is so much to discover." She appeared unconvinced, and he continued, "Do you remember when we were young and we'd go with all our friends to shoot the white water beneath Vayno Bridge?"

She nodded warily.

"I used to resort to all sorts of elaborate stratagems to sit on a thimble-raft alone with you. Once I even went to the extent of paying Drunie Cru Beffel fifty dakkles—my spending money for the month—to give up his place beside you. And being sixteen years old at the time, I plumed myself on my subtlety and was quite certain that you never once guessed what I was about. Do you remember?"

She smiled despite herself. "I remember."

"And while we sat on that raft, I'd tell you of my hopes and ambitions and try to convince myself that you were interested. You were probably bored to distraction, but you were kind enough to conceal it."

"I wasn't bored," Verran told him. "I thought your head was full of dreams, but I certainly wasn't bored. You used to talk about—let me see, what was it? Oh, yes, you talked about traveling—exploring the interior of Dalyon—climbing mountains—visiting ruins—verifying the legends of the Flying Vindual—meeting the Children of the Lost Illusions—finding strange beasts and stranger people—sailing over the sea to Szar or Strell—all sorts of wonderful things that nobody ever actually does. I was sure you'd end up as a gentleman of the ducal court, like everyone else. I loved your stories, but I didn't believe them. How long ago that was, and what happy days they were!" She was smiling, and a trace of color had crept into her white face.

"But you should have believed me, Verran. It turned out to be true. I have traveled and explored strange places, just as I dreamed of as a boy, and it's been everything I hoped for. Now at last I've come to these famous caverns, to learn what I can—and I've come in peace, bearing a Vardrul token of friendship."

"Where did you get those pebbles, Ril?"

From my uncle Jin. You remember the Cognizant Jinzin Farni?"

"Of course. One of Lord Grizhni's great allies."

"He's Preeminent of the Select now."

"Farni succeeded my husband? Good. I was so afraid it would be Gless Vallage."

"Vallage? Hopelessly mad these seventeen years. His mind cracked at the time of—at the time you disappeared. I'm told he's a pathetic spectacle now. As for Uncle Jin—he gave me the token of friendship he'd received directly from the Vardrul delegates to Lanthi Ume. He also provided the maps in that pack there—'' Fennahar gestured and Nyd snarled, gathering himself for a leap.

"Stop that, Nyd! I'm ashamed of you!" Verran chided, and the hybrid's snarls dwindled to penitent whines. "You can't recognize a friend anymore, and that's sad."

Nyd rattled his talons contritely.

"I'll give you a chance to make it up, though. Here—" Verran dug into the pocket of her robe to withdraw a handful of pebbles, from which she carefully selected half a dozen on the basis of color. "Take that to the F'tryll'jnr Lesser Patriarch." She dropped the stones into the hybrid's outstretched paw, then turned to Fennahar. "Are you hungry, Ril?"

He realized for the first time that he was ravenous. "Yes. Very."

"That's a good sign." She turned back to the hybrid and instructed, "Bring our guest something to eat, please. And remember he *is* our guest, Nyd."

The hybrid croaked fervently and departed.

"Please don't think too ill of Nyd," Verran remarked with a trace of apology. "It's not his fault. He's not vicious, he just thinks he's protecting me. With all that's happened recently, he's very nervous. There was an attack by the Ducal Guardsmen and they slaughtered scores of unarmed Vardruls. Since that time, we have all been vigilant." She was watching him very steadily.

"I heard something of an attack," he admitted. No point in pretending total ignorance. She was too clever to believe that.

"Do you know the reason for it?"

He felt himself to be on dangerous ground. The truth could well arouse her fear and anger. Sufficiently persecuted and embittered, might she not choose to sacrifice all of Dalyon to her husband's vengeance—and her own? On the other hand she was possibly testing him with a query whose answer she already knew, in which case an attempted evasion would damage his already tenuous standing. Finally, and most simply persuasive, her life was in danger and she ought to be warned.

He opted for limited honesty. "I'm not in the Duke's confidence. But I believe they were looking for you and your son, Verran. They know you're hiding here."

She nodded. "And you knew it too. You showed no sign of surprise when you woke to find me in this room."

"Quick as ever, I see."

"And you know that I bore a son, who survives. How has all this been discovered?"

"I was told by Uncle Jin. He in turn based his conclusions upon observation of the Duke. It would seem that his Grace has enjoyed prophetic dreams."

"*Dreams?* Do you mean to tell me," Verran asked slowly, "that the attack—all the killings—the pain and fear—happened because of somebody's *dreams?*"

"Yes, and there could be more. You're not safe here any longer, Verran. And your son—even less so. You must think of finding another place." He didn't stop to consider whether the suggestion served his purpose or not. At the moment he was thinking of her safety alone. His genuine concern appeared to affect her, and the wariness began to fade from her eyes. His conscience clamored at the sight.

"I'd like to leave. I'd like to see the sun again," Verran replied, unconscious of the note of pathos in her voice. "But we can't just run away and leave the Vardruls to the mercies of the Ducal Guardsmen. We can't let them die on our account."

"Have you ever considered leaving Dalyon altogether, and then sending a letter to the Duke? His Grace would have to realize that you'd fled beyond his reach."

"That's a very interesting idea, but Terrs would never accept it."

"Your son?"

"Yes. He's convinced that we must repel the Guardsmen by force. He's gained considerable ascendancy over a number of our Vardrul friends, and as of now they support him in this."

Fennahar could not forbear smiling. "But surely your son can't be above seventeen years old. How much weight can the Vardruls attach to the opinions of a mere lad?"

"Mere lad? You don't know Terrs. He's very like his father. He's led an odd life, and his character is most unusual. As for the Vardruls—Terrs is an adult by their reckoning, and I don't think they fully realize how young he is by human standards."

"He's like his father? Then Terrs's Cognition disguised the trap I fell into?"

She looked at him sharply, and he thought he understood her hesitancy. If it got back to the Duke that Preeminence Grizhni's son had learned to utilize inherited Cognitive ability, then his Grace's fear and resultant enmity would increase dangerously. On the other hand, the Duke's enmity was already implacable, the inquirer appeared reasonably trustworthy, and in any even the matter was nearly impossible to conceal. At the same instant that Fennahar reached these conclusions, Verran shurgged and admitted, "Yes. He knows very little."

And how had he learned it? From his father's records, obviously. Uncle Jin had been right. Those records were here, somewhere. For a variety of reasons he longed to deal honestly with Verran—to state the situation plainly and request her assistance. But if she refused, his failure would be absolute and irremediable. With so much at stake, he could not afford the risk.

Her companion's speculative silence appeared unwelcome to Lady Verran. Evidently anxious to divert his thoughts from the subject of her son's Cognition, she inquired, "Can you tell me of Lanthi Ume, Ril? Does it tire you to talk?"

"No. I still enjoy talking to you. That doesn't seem to have changed."

"Then tell me what's been happening in the city. I've heard nothing in all this time, but there's not been a Small Ven gone by that I haven't thought of home. How are my Dris Verras kinsmen? What's become of all our friends—Drunie, Zerril, Naxin, and the others? And Brenn Wate Basef—did he become a great savant, and is he happy? I hope so. What about the city itself? Are the Commons still angry? Did any of the terrible things that Lord Grizhni feared come to pass? Has the Duke emptied the treasury? Are we bankrupt? Is there famine? Did the Keldhar of Gard Lammis or the Duke of Hurba ever attempt an attack?"

She paused for breath. Fennahar regarded her with sympathy—partly for her long incarceration, and partly for her inability to ask the question that was clearly uppermost in her mind. He did not know how to help her. But she required no aid. Verran met his eyes and said evenly, "And I'd like you to tell me everything you can of Lord Grizhni. I know he died long ago. Tell me how it happened."

"As much as I know. Acting upon the orders of their master, the Ducal Guardsmen stormed Grizhni Palace seventeen years ago. I don't know whether you were there at that time or not. Your whereabouts upon that night have always remained a mystery."

"I was in the palace when the attack began. Lord Grizhni sent me away with Nyd, by way of a tunnel. My husband promised to follow."

"But he never had the chance. When the Guardsmen discovered him in a subterranean chamber, they attempted to place him under arrest. Grizhni resisted." Should he tell her of the savant's threats and prophecies? Not yet. "The soldiers panicked and dispatched him on the spot."

"Did he speak to them?"

"I believe some words were exchanged, but not many. Your husband must have died very swiftly, almost instantaneously."

"Then all the time that Nyd and I crossed the Gravula Wasteland—all the time that I wandered the hills of the Nazara Sin—all that time I thought of his face—he was already dead?"

Fennahar said nothing.

"So quickly," Verran murmured. "But no arrest—no trial—no public execution. That was what I most dreaded—that would have been the true horror. I am glad he was spared that."

"He didn't suffer, Verran."

"And so I know at last." She digested the information in silence for a time, during which Fennahar watched her face closely. He saw there a peace and acceptance that encouraged him. She was not bitter. Moreover, her detachment from events of the past afforded him a satisfaction, almost a sense of relief, for which he could hardly account.

Verran looked up to meet the eyes fixed upon her, and smiled slightly. "Don't stare at me like that, Ril. You look as if you expect to see me disintegrate before your eyes. Once I might have, but that was half a lifetime ago."

"Half a lifetime in this place," Fennahar mused, consciously disguising all signs of pity. What a fate for a creature of sunlight!

"It hasn't been all bad, by any means. The Vardruls are kind, and there's been my son. But you haven't answered my questions, Ril." She seemed hungry for distraction. "Won't you tell me what's happened in Lanthi Ume?"

He told her to the best of his ability. He spoke of the Duke Povon's follies, weakness, and mad expenditures. He spoke of the growing influence of the Keldhar of Gard Lammis, and the Duke's betrothal of convenience to the Keldhaam Gnuxia. He spoke of the Selectic opposition to ducal policies, and he touched upon the personal enmity existing between Duke Povon and Preeminence Jinzin Farni. He cited the decline of trade, the growing civic deficit, the ascendancy of foreign interests. He described the corruption of the Duke's favorites, the degeneracy of the Ducal Guardsmen under the slow-witted Commander Kronil, and the profligacy of the peerage. He spoke of the growing misery of the Commons of Lanthi Ume—the hunger, the frustration, the unrest and resentment. He explained Vorg's Rebellion, the Salt Fish Riots, Jeeps's Conspiracy, and the Kwaes-Whetnitz Insurrection. He mentioned the Boot Tax and Worps's Self-Immolation. He even related the rumors he had heard of a recent attempt upon the life of the Duke himself. So engrossing was his topic that he hardly noted the return of Nyd.

Verran hummed a few musical syllables. Fennahar turned to behold the hybrid, who bore a tray of food. Nyd was accompanied by a small group of Vardruls, and Fennahar experienced a thrill of delighted wonder as he took his first clear look at the extraordinary creatures, with their vast, incomprehensibly intelligent eyes; their serpentine fingers; and their lambent, flickering skin. With the Vardruls came a human youth, almost as interesting in his own way as his remarkable companions. The boy—obviously Verran's son Terrs—was tall, straight, and still a little too thin for his height. His pale, chiseled, hawk-nosed face was startlingly similar to that of Preeminence Fal Grizhni, whom Fennahar had glimpsed three or four times years earlier. Terrs's expression was singular—reserved, impassive, the black eyes appraising as they rested upon the invalid—and the entirety invested with an indefinably foreign, alien quality. Wherein the strangeness lay was difficult to judge—it might have had something to do with the look in the eyes, or the set of the lips, or perhaps some peculiarity in the use of the facial muscles. Whatever the reason, the boy's face, while well formed, would have attracted uneasy attention in any human gathering.

Vardruls and human advanced. One of the Vardruls—a tall,

glowing, emaciated being of indeterminate gender despite its nudity—bore Jinzin Farni's string of colored pebbles. With considerable effort, Fennahar raised himself to a sitting position. That was as much as he could do. To stand was as yet impossible. The new arrivals halted before him and the leader spoke. To Fennahar the melodious outpouring was entirely meaningless, as were the accompanying gestures and expressions. The speech, however, was weirdly beautiful as a song of Ert. The explorer listened, entranced; and for the moment meaning seemed irrelevant.

Verran translated. "The F'tryll'jnr Lesser Patriarch, the Lbavbsch Lesser Patriarch, the R'jnrllsch Lesser Patriarch, the new Zmadrc Lesser Matriarch, the F'tlyrlbsch Lesser Patriarch, the young F'tryll'jnr Rdsdr, and the young Fal Grizhni Terrs extend the greetings of their respective clans. The F'tryll'jnr Patriarch apologizes for the misfortune that has befallen you, and requests allowances for the disharmonious measures of self-defense undertaken by the clan members in this time of common peril. He rejoices in the obvious improvement in your health, and trusts that the terrible experience you have undergone has not unduly affected your ruu—er, your state of mind and spirit. He expresses his pleasure in the arrival of a new human friend. You are welcome here."

Guilt. These creatures were friendly and innocent, even following a human attack. They welcomed him, when he had come among them almost as a spy. Fennahar mentally strove to dismiss his own qualms. He was certainly not an enemy, and he meant them no harm. Guilt subsided, but did not vanish. Aloud he replied simply, "I thank you for your kindness. My accident has not harmed me, and I beg you to think no more of it. I am Rillif Har Fennahar, a gentleman of Lanthi Ume, and kinsman to the Cognizant Jinzin Farni who is Selectic successor to Preeminence Terrs Fal Grizhni."

Verran interpreted swiftly, leaving the terms *Cognizant, Selectic,* and *Preeminence* intact in their original Lanthian. Presumably such terms were untranslatable. Fennahar noted the reaction of the Vardruls at the mention of Grizhni's name. Their flesh flickered rhythmically, and low warblings arose. Young Terrs watched attentively, his black eyes unreadable.

"I've come in peace and goodwill," Fennahar continued, with pauses to allow Verran to translate. "I seek to extend my

knowledge of the caves and their inhabitants. It is my hope
that mutual understanding may encourage friendship between
Vardruls and men, and therefore I ask permission to remain
among you for a time."

The Vardruls brightened and hummed. Terrs looked on expressionlessly. It was impossible to guess what any of them
might be thinking. It appeared that Verran's reaction was favorable, which was not surprising. Despite her natural misgivings,
she must be starved for human companionship of any kind,
after seventeen years shut up in this place.

The F'tryll'jnr Lesser Patriarch stepped forward, fluted and
sang eloquently, then returned the string of pebbles to Fennahar
with ceremony. Having done so, he inclined his head and wove
his finger-tentacles into an astonishing knot.

"The F'tryll'jnr's gesture signifies harmony," Verran
explained. "He says you are welcome for your own sake, as
well as that of the Jinzin Farni Patriarch, whose name is still
remembered. He has, for want of specific information, accorded
you the title of Har Fennahar Lesser Patriarch, and he extends
his compliments to all your kinsmen/subjects. As an esteemed
guest, you are encouraged to regard the caverns as your clan-
home. You may wander wherever you please."

Fennahar inclined his head. "I am honored."

"Personally, I'd advise you to keep away from the death-
pools, though. It would be courteous."

"I'll remember."

A musical babble arose as the Vardruls stepped forward one
by one to offer the very individualized salutations characteristic
of their respective clans. One voice spoke in Lanthian. "I greet
you in the name of clan Fal Grizhni, and I add my voice to
the greetings of clan Zmadrc." The voice was surprisingly
resonant and confident. The speaker possessed an adult's self-
assurance, despite his obvious youth.

"I thank you, Lord Grizhni." Out of the corner of his eye,
Fennahar noted Verran's startled expression. Terrs himself
showed no sign of surprise at the unaccustomed form of address.
The boy's face revealed almost nothing. "I thank you all." He
extended his hand. Terrs stared at it blankly.

Verran's face colored deeply. "He means you to shake
hands," she explained in obvious embarrassment. "It's a human
custom, a sign of friendship, or greeting, or accord." She

realized she had spoken in Lanthian, and hurriedly translated her remarks into singing Vardrul speech.

Terrs made no move to take the outstretched hand. His voice was cold as he observed, "No doubt the Fennahar Patriarch will understand that human habits are quite foreign to me."

His companions, however, had no such reservations. The collective hiir rose as each Vardrul bent in turn to shake the human's hand with care and great thoroughness.

Having greeted the newcomer, the Vardruls retired in silence. The humans remained. At a sign from Verran, Nyd placed his tray before Fennahar, and the explorer attacked a meal consisting of thick soup in a two-handled drinking vessel, stewed mushrooms of half a dozen different varieties, blackened Foer's Root, and an unidentifiable but savory amber jelly. He was aware, as he ate, of young Terrs's analytical regard.

Having scrutinized the explorer in silence for some minutes, Terrs spoke at last. "Fennahar Patriarch, the wisest among the Vardruls have accepted your avowal of harmless intent and therefore so must I, for the present."

Fennahar wondered. Where had the boy acquired that rigid formality of speech and that precocious authority? This was an extraordinary personality, even at age seventeen. Aloud he observed mildly, "I'm hardly a Patriarch, Lord Grizhni. Better that you call me Ril—or Fennahar, if you prefer."

Terrs rippled his fingers in an approximation of the Vardrul gesture of assent. Fennahar suppressed all visible signs of surprise.

"In view of the recent human attack upon our caverns," Terrs continued, "you have timed your visit oddly."

"That's discourteous, Terrs," Verran reproved.

"Are we to sacrifice self-preservation to courtesy, Mother?"

"He's got a point, Verran," Fennahar remarked, disguising his uneasiness. "It's a fair question, and I'm willing to answer. I deliberately chose to come at this time because I feared it was the last chance I might have to gain access to the caverns. If the human attacks continue, it's only safe to assume that all entrances will soon be blocked or otherwise fortified. Moreover, I felt it necessary at this time to demonstrate to the Vardruls the good faith of some humans, if there is to be any hope of future friendship between the two races."

"Friendship between the two races? That is a dream. The

thing is impossible," Terrs opined.

"Why so?"

"The nature of humanity is vicious and predatory. This can scarcely be denied. Men know less of friendship than of expediency. They will always prey upon beings less powerful and ruthless than themselves."

"You are as cynical as the Hurbanese moneylender."

"And with good reason. My adopted people were driven from their Surface home by men. That, I grant you, occurred in the distant past. Far more immediate is the persecution and murder of my father, the great Grizhni Patriarch, at the hands of men. More immediate yet is the death of scores of my Zmadrc kinsmen, the slaughter of other clan members, the attempted murder of my mother, and the grief and pain of my Zmadrc Future. These are lessons I have taken to heart."

Fennahar did not answer immediately. At last he conceded, "On the basis of the evidence available to you, your conclusions aren't unreasonable. But that evidence is limited and one-sided. In order to address the issue with any degree of objectivity, you require additional information." He saw Verran smile slightly at this, and guessed that her opinion coincided.

Terrs was thoughtfully silent. This confirmation of his mother's argument by a disinterested third party of obvious intelligence appeared to produce some impression upon him, but he was not about to abandon his position without a struggle. "Information of what sort?"

"You should learn what you can of Men, their works and the lands they inhabit. You should learn of human history, philosophy, art and architecture, languages and literature, mathematics and mechanical contrivance, Cognition—"

"Cognition?" Terrs could not disguise his sudden interest.

"Certainly. You could learn the lore of the greatest savants, if you chose."

"An interesting suggestion, but impractical. My mother and I cannot return to Lanthi Ume."

"No, but there are other cities and other organizations of savants. There are many different places you could go to study Cognition. There's an entire world up there, Terrs—a world of infinite variety. Have you no interest in seeing it?"

The prospect of Cognition exerted a powerful attraction, and for a moment it seemed that the boy was tempted, but his lapse was brief. "There is an entire world down here in our caverns, and it is sufficient to occupy all of my attention," Terrs replied inflexibly.

Fennahar sighed. The discussion was beginning to tire him. His recent illness had drained his energy and in any event, it seemed nearly impossible to produce much impression upon the granite will of Fal Grizhni's son. He saw Verran watching him as if he were her champion in battle, but there was little to gain by continuing the argument—such a course would only serve to strengthen Terrs's resistance. Best to end it, for now. "There is indeed a world down here," he conceded. "But it may perhaps not always remain entirely separated from the world of men above. It's wise to know with whom and what you deal, for your own protection if nothing more. I hope you wouldn't reject knowledge that's immediately available to you?"

"Your descriptions and recollections of Surface?" Terrs appeared indifferent.

"I can do better than that. I've three books there in my pack—"

"Human writings?" Terrs's eyes warmed with genuine interest and pleasure. "Books from the city? I have heard of printed books, but never seen one."

"But you can read?"

"Since I was five Great Vens."

Fennahar leaned over, opened the canvas bag, and withdrew three small volumes, which he handed to Terrs. "Not the best possible choice," he observed with some regret. "But not the worst, I suppose. There's Juffial on the flora and fauna of Dalyon. There's Ches Kilmo's *Ascent of Cognition*. And the last one's particularly good—Vhere Khrennevhere's *The Sea of Ice; Explorations*."

"The sea?" Curiosity seemed to be eroding Terrs's barriers of intense reserve. "Have you ever seen it? Have you actually sailed it?"

"Many times. It's an experience I wouldn't have missed."

"What is it like?"

"More beautiful and varied than I can describe. Read Khrennevhere. He's far more eloquent than I could ever be, but even he can't convey all of it. The sea must be experienced at first hand. It's in the blood of all Lanthians."

"I shall certainly read Khrennevhere, and the others as well. And when I have finished, perhaps you would be willing to discuss the contents?"

"Of course." Fennahar blinked and suppressed a yawn with difficulty. Somnolence threatened to overwhelm him, despite his best efforts.

"Ril, you're exhausted," Verran observed at once. "You need to rest."

The explorer did not deny it.

"Terrs, Nyd, we're leaving now."

Terrs nodded briefly to Fennahar, then followed his mother to the exit. Pausing only to collect the emptied tray, Nyd followed in their wake. Before she passed from the chamber, Verran glanced back over her shoulder to meet the explorer's eyes, smiled and mouthed a silent thank you. Then all three of them were gone.

Fennahar lay back on the pallet, eyes shut, mind filled with images of Verran and her disquietingly eccentric son. He was deeply tired. Despite the turmoil of his thoughts, sleep claimed him almost instantaneously.

Only a few Small Vens elapsed before Lady Verran began to notice a certain peculiarity in the new guest's behavior. At first she thought she was imagining it. After all, Rillif Har Fennahar had come to the Nazara Sin to investigate the caves, and his intense curiosity was entirely appropriate. His recovery from his illness had been swift indeed, owing to a vigorous constitution and probably in part to his native optimism. He had risen from his pallet to commence his explorations within a couple of Colorations of regaining consciousness. Apart from a slight lingering weakness that forced him to pause often to rest, his health seemed unimpaired and his desire for knowledge insatiable. Thus there was no mystery connected to Har Fennahar's long, rambling excursions through the corridors, excavations, and even the Bellyscrapers—or at least there shouldn't have been. But Verran could not rid herself of the notion that something was amiss. Somehow his inquisitiveness seemed at times—excessively finicking. Why, for example, was he so given to poking about the most ordinary holes, crannies, and fissures in the stone walls? And why his air of uneasiness, even embarassment, when anyone noticed him doing it? The only explanation that suggested itself was that he was looking for something, and it occurred to Verran that he might be a spy sent by the Duke of Lanthi Ume to discover the strength and defensive preparations of the White Demons. But that was absurd, really. Following the almost unresisted first attack of the Guardsmen, the Duke and his minions had no reason to believe the Vardruls capable of self-defense at all. There was no need to send spies. Moreover, Rillif Har Fennahar was surely incapable of such duplicity. The boy that Verran had known in Lanthi Ume so many years ago had been notably open and trustworthy. The man appeared little changed, or so she wished to believe.

She wished to believe. Yes, there could be no question of that. She liked him—even more now than in the past—she was drawn to his intelligence and seeming good nature—and she quite decidedly wanted to believe the best of him.

Take care, Verran warned herself. *Naturally you like him. You've been shut up in this place for so many years, and so starved for human companionship that you'd probably like nearly anyone.*

Rillif Har Fennahar is not just anyone.

Quite right. He's a reminder of your happy girlhood, and for that reason doubly appealing. Careful, though. Don't let such things cloud your judgment. Be on your guard.

Against what? Even if his intentions are bad, a lone man doesn't pose any great threat.

No? What if that lone man has been sent by the Duke of Lanthi Ume to assassinate your son—Fal Grizhni's son? The Guardsmen failed in their first attempt. What if the Duke has resorted to subtler measures?

That is ridiculous—ridiculous! I am turning into a fearful, addle-pated old woman. Ril would never be party to such a scheme. Ril is decent and honorable. I know him.

Correction. You knew him—half a lifetime ago. That means nothing now. People change.

True—I have. I've become hard and suspicious, it seems. Well, I've reason. As for Ril, I don't believe for one moment that he'd dream of harming my son. Quite the contrary, he's trying to help Terrs—trying to interest him in Surface life. And Terrs is becoming interested, it's obvious—far more interested than he's ever been in his whole life. He's read those three books and he's beginning to get the idea for the first time that

*all human beings aren't necessarily bad, even if some of them
are. And the possibility of studying more Cognition is fascinat-
ing to him. Ril is such a good influence, he may do what I've
never been able to do—coax Terrs out of these caves and back
to the Surface, even if it's only for a visit. And if Ril can manage
that, then I don't care a dakkle why he's really come here—he'll
have my blessing.*

*Very well. But that doesn't mean that you should just fall
asleep. Whatever your feelings, it won't hurt to keep an eye
on Fennahar.*

Agreed. That much I can do.

Where was he now? Off on one of his endless rambles?
Inspecting the elaborately carved and etched rock formations
in the Jnr'l Chasm? Poring over the shadow-sculpted friezes?
Watching the youngsters communicate in the language of Ftvyi?
She smiled at the thought. There seemed to be no aspect of
Vardrul life and customs in which Rillif Har Fennahar did not
exhibit profound interest. So tactful was he in his investigations,
however, that his curiosity had hitherto proved inoffensive, or
so Verran guessed. As always it was difficult to judge the
responses of the Vardruls, but she believed that the explorer's
presence generated minimal disharmony.

He might not be wandering the caves at all. He might be off
somewhere with Terrs, involved in one of their many long
discussions. No question but that her son enjoyed the explorer's
conversation.

*So do I, almost as much as I used to enjoy Lord Grizhni's.
But it's not a good comparison—Ril is completely different.*

Different, and far more accessible. Nothing remote, icy, or
intimidating about Rillif Har Fennahar, a man capable of inspir-
ing respect unaccompanied by fear.

*And what is he doing right now? Well, why don't I go see?
No harm in that and besides, I'm supposed to be keeping an
eye on him, aren't I?*

Verran rose from her chair—an odd affair of her own construction, made of wooden scraps imported from Surface,
laboriously jointed and pegged together to form a framework,
with woven webbing stretched across the seat and back—the
only chair in all the caverns of the Nazara Sin. Almost she
lifted her voice to summon Nyd, and then thought better of it.
The hybrid was sick again, as he so often was these Small
Vens. At the moment he was curled up by himself in the small

niche across the corridor that he had chosen as his sleeping quarters so long ago. He neither wanted nor accepted assistance at such times. If Verran attempted to approach, he would motion her away with dismal croaks, evidently wanting nothing but solitude. Verran sighed. She had no idea what was wrong with the hybrid beyond advancing age, and no idea what to do for him other than comply with his desire for privacy. He would surely be better in a Coloration or two, however. He always was—so far.

Verran wandered the corridors at a leisurely pace. There was no point in hurrying—Fennahar might be anywhere, and it was perfectly possible that she would not see him until he reappeared at the onset of the Purple Coloration to join in the communal Zmadrc-Lbavbsch meal. Still, she had three or four good ideas where he might be found and in any event, the search would serve to fill her time.

She went first to the Bleeding Stalactite. Fennahar had expressed the desire to observe the calibrated vessels in which the moisture dripping from the stone slowly collected to mark the passage of time, and there was a good chance she might find him there. She did not, however. Nor was her luck any better at Jnr'l Chasm, or K'fdrs Excavation, or the Zmadrc-Lbavbsch gardens. He might, of course, be wriggling around on his belly somewhere in the depths of the Hllsreg Net, but there she did not intend to follow. Still, she hadn't yet checked the Dr'bsch B'sch B'sch J'farl, whose title translated directly into Lanthian as the Cascade Chamber. Named for its remarkable frozen waterfalls of translucent stone, the Cascade Chamber was a spectacle that Har Fennahar did not intend to miss.

He was there. She spotted him through the arching entrance before she reached the chamber, and the peculiarity of his actions was noticeable even at a distance. For a moment she thought he was climbing straight up the wall like an insect. Then she drew nearer and saw that he was pulling himself hand over hand up a rope attached to a hook caught among the stony elaborations near the ceiling.

He's up to something, Verran thought, and was slightly ashamed of her own suspicions. The man's actions might portend nothing more sinister than a closer inspection of the spectacular rock formations up above. And yet—

She approached with a caution almost unnecessary in view

of her quarry's preoccupation. Fennahar, whose ascent was fraught with difficulties, noticed nothing. Verran slipped into the Cascade Chamber, crouched down behind a jut of stone, and watched.

He seemed to be having troubles, probably owing to the effects of his recent illness. She could see the sweat shining on his brow, and recalled that the hot, heavy, moist air of the caverns must be burdensome to unaccustomed lungs. Fennahar paused halfway up, hanging in midair like a discouraged inchworm. After a moment he resumed his efforts, and shortly thereafter reached his goal. Verran noticed for the first time the cluster of three niches, high on the wall of the Cascade Chamber and partially concealed by dripping stalactites. The explorer peered searchingly through the stalactite curtain, then inexplicably stretched his left hand toward the openings.

What's he doing that for? Verran wondered as she watched the rock-light glint on the band of silver that encircled Fennahar's left wrist. *He can't possibly reach in there. He doesn't seem to be trying to, actually. What's he doing, and what's he looking for?*

Whatever he was looking for, he obviously didn't find. Fennahar allowed himself to slide back down the rope. As his feet touched the floor, his head swiveled sharply toward the entrance. Verran flattened herself to the wall and held her breath, but her precautions were unnecessary—his gaze was directed straight past her place of concealment. Evidently some noise in the corridor had caught his attention. Verran could hear it too—swift footsteps, someone approaching in haste. Hurriedly Fennahar twitched the rope free, coiled it, and stowed it away in the pack that accompanied him nearly everywhere. No sooner was the rope out of sight than Lbavbsch Hfu entered the Cascade Chamber at a run.

Hfu's hiir was ominously low and his ocular bands were rigid with concern. "I seek the young Fal Grizhni Terrs," the Vardrul informed Har Fennahar. "Do you know where he may be found?"

Fennahar frowned. He did not understood a single word, but he had caught the name. "Fal Grizhni Terrs?" he repeated. "What is wrong? Has Terrs been hurt?"

Lbavbsch Hfu was similarly at a loss. "Fal Grizhni—where?" he inquired very clearly. Obviously the visiting Fennahar Patriarch recognized the name. "Grizhni? Where? Grizhni?

Grizhni?" The expansion of his outer ridges and descent of vocal pitch signaled the interrogative, but these conventions were unfamiliar to Har Fennahar.

Fennahar shrugged, spread his hands, and shook his head slightly to communicate incomprehension. These gestures were meaningless to Lbavbsch Hfu.

Verran was becoming uncomfortable. She did not enjoy eavesdropping. Moreover, Fennahar and Lbavbsch Hfu obviously required her assistance. It was time to reveal herself, and she could only hope they would not guess she'd been listening to their abortive conversation. Verran rose and stepped around the rock into sight as casually as possible. As it happened, her misgivings were unfounded. Fennahar and Lbavbsch both turned to her eagerly. It did not appear to occur to either that she had not simply entered the Cascade Chamber behind them.

"What is the matter?" Verran inquired in the Vardrul language.

"Grizhni Matriarch, I seek the Fal Grizhni Terrs," Lbavbsch replied, his flesh flickering rapidly and erratically. "There is great danger and grief. The Fal Grizhni's Future, the young Zmadrc Fourteen—"

"She has not joined her Ancestors?" Verran hummed in fear, recalling her son's recent words.

"Not yet, but she stands on the very brink of such a joining. She is—" There followed a spate of syllables and complex facial expressions that Verran could not interpret.

"Slower, Lbavbsch Hfu. I do not understand. Slower."

The Vardrul rippled his tentacles. "In her state of confusion and . . . '' the term that followed was mysterious—"the young Zmadrc Fourteen has wandered Surface without benefit of adequate protection. But a short time ago, two of her kinsmen discovered her out upon the hillside, naked and sunk in a deep Cold Stupor."

Verran caught her breath. Cold Stupor, that dreaded affliction, could result in the madness, idiocy, or death of the victim.

"She has been returned to the warmth of the caverns and the affections of her family, but all attempts to restore her to consciousness have failed," Lbavbsch continued. "It is hoped that the presence of her Future at her side might . . ." there followed an incomprehensible verb—"the ruu of Zmadrc Fourteen."

"My son is often in the Stronghold, trying to master the Falling Stones—"

"He is not there now."

"And of late he spends much time in the Mvjri Corridor, where he trains the great brown bats to perform his bidding."

"Let us search there, Matriarch."

Fennahar, who had listened to this exchange in some bewilderment, now inquired, "What's happened, Verran? Something's wrong."

"It's Zmadrc Fourteen," she explained hurriedly. "A young Vardrul of whom Terrs is particularly—fond—has fallen very ill. Terrs should be with her now, so we're going to find him."

Fennahar nodded without comment, scooped his pack off the floor, and the three of them left the Cascade Chamber together, proceeding as directly as possible to the Mvjri Corridor. Although they advanced at their best speed, it was a long trek that took them through a seemingly endless succession of twisting, branching passageways. Minor flooding in the Gr'fjnr Linkage necessitated a detour and by the time they reached their destination, they found that Terrs had already gone. One of the F'tryll'jnr kinsmen still loitering in the corridor explained that Fal Grizhni Terrs had lately been summoned to the Zmadrc death-pool chamber, where his Future lay in deep Cold Stupor. It was to be hoped that the combined influence of the generations of her Ancestors resting in that spot might affect the ruu of the comatose Zmadrc Fourteen—either to stir her consciousness, or else to draw her gently and by degrees unto the final joining.

Lbavbsch Hfu declined to intrude upon the grief of clan Zmadrc. The Grizhni Matriarch, as an acknowledged Connection, need feel no such hesitancy. And Fennahar? Verran glanced at him in some doubt. He knew nothing of the subtleties of Vardrul attitudes, and he would have little sense of the near-sacred significance of the death-pool chamber. She ought not permit him to come with her, but found she could not bring herself to send him away. The prospect of venturing once more upon the site of the recent massacre to attend the moribund Fourteen was daunting, and Fennahar's presence seemed to lend her unusual comfort.

Is it simply because he's human? Perhaps. No.

She said nothing and Fennahar, innocently unconscious of impropriety, continued at her side during the short walk along the Mvjri Corridor to the Zmadrc death-pool chamber.

Following the Zmadrc obsequies held in the aftermath of the Guardsmen's attack, Verran had not returned to this chamber.

She entered it now with considerable reluctance. Beside her she heard Fennahar catch his breath as he beheld the glowing pool and the massed Vardruls. The Zmadrc family—all that was left of it—had assembled in the presence of their ailing sister. The collective hiir was almost alarmingly low—lower even than custom demanded upon such melancholy occasions. It was clear that the young Fourteen was the object of particular affection among her kinsmen. Moreover, the general air of profound sorrow—obvious even to Verran, who could not usually interpret Vardrul emotions—suggested that the weight of accumulated disaster was beginning to tell on clan Zmadrc.

Fourteen lay upon the verge of the pool at the foot of the Speaker's Stone. Beside her blazed the fire kindled to warm her to wakefulness—an uncertain remedy at best, but the only one the Vardruls knew. At first glance, she appeared dead. She was motionless, her great eyes closed with ocular bands smoothed to the point of invisibility, finger-tentacles straight and rigid, her flesh devoid of light. Only upon closer inspection was the very slight rise and fall of her thin chest discernible. Beside her knelt Terrs, his head bowed in concentration rather than grief. Clearly the youth was attempting a Cognitive cure. His favorite crystals rested in his outstretched palm, and his lips were moving. Success eluded him, however, and the crystals remained lightless as Fourteen's skin.

As Verran drew near, she noted the beads of sweat standing on her son's forehead, his pallor and obvious exhaustion. It was evident that the intensely debilitating Cognitive exertions had continued for some time and Terrs was feeling the effects. Verran's own experience of savants informed her that dogged persistence in the face of failure was very unlikely to succeed. Cognition required a focus and a burst of concentrated mental power—almost a species of inspiration—that a tired, discouraged mind could rarely furnish. Of course Terrs knew that too, and as his mother watched, she perceived his doubt and despondency—distractions that would in themselves tend to block Cognition. The youth finished speaking and paused, his eyes fixed intently upon the face of his Future. The crystals in his hand remained unaltered, and Fourteen's lethal sleep continued undisturbed. Terrs's shoulders sagged and his outstretched hand dropped to his side. For a moment he remained motionless, jaw set, obviously struggling to collect his faculties. Then his spine straightened and he took a deep breath for a new effort.

Before the Cognitive syllables could be uttered, Har Fennahar spoke up. "I believe I can help you."

All present turned to stare at the explorer in surprise. The Vardruls, who did not understand him, flickered and hummed. Verran could feel her face redden. She had never dreamed that her questionable companion would commit so great a solecism.

Terrs looked up, black eyes aglitter with icy anger that faded to mere impatience in the face of Fennahar's obvious sincerity. "Are you then so familiar with Vardrul maladies?" he iquired.

"Not at all."

"Then please do not distract me again from the task at hand. My Cognition is her only hope of life."

"No. She has at her service the Cognition of the current Preeminence of the Select."

Terrs took his meaning at once. "You have brought—"

"A universal remedy devised by Jinzin Farni." Kneeling at Fourteen's side, Fennahar opened his pack. From the welter of its contents he plucked a small vial, which he swiftly unstoppered.

"Wait—isn't that meant for humans?" Verran objected. "How do we know it won't hurt Fourteen?"

"Uncle Jin called it 'universal,' "Fennahar returned. "We can only hope he meant exactly what he said."

"She is dying. My Cognition does not help her," Terrs admitted reluctantly.

Fennahar shot the youth a questioning glance. Terrs nodded almost imperceptibly. Gently lifting Fourteen's head and shoulders, Fennahar poured about half the contents of the vial down her throat. The Vardrul, though unconscious, swallowed convulsively. Fennahar lowered her back to the floor, where she lay motionless.

For long moments nothing happened, and Terrs's face seemed to age visibly. Then as the audience watched in profound silence, Fourteen's hiir began to rise. Very faintly at first, and then with increasing strength, her flesh started to glow. The watching Vardruls fluted aloud in wonder, and Verran felt the tears sting in her own eyes. Even Terrs's customary impassivity deserted him, and his expression reflected almost painful relief.

The light in the death-pool chamber intensified as the collective hiir of the Zmadrc kinsmen climbed. The general luminosity reached its zenith as Fourteen awoke, encountered the gaze of her Future, and hummed clearly, "I dreamed of the Ancestors, and I was with them."

"Not yet," Terrs replied in a low voice. "Rest."

She rippled her tenacles weakly, and sank amost at once into natural lucent slumber. Terrs studied her in silence for a time, then looked up and deliberately met the eyes of Rillif Har Fennahar. After a moment's consideration Grizhni's son extended his arm straight forward at shoulder level, his hand stiff with fingers spread slightly, the thumb perfectly vertical. As Fennahar stared at proffered member in bewilderment, Terrs explained carefully, "I wish to shake hands."

Chapter Eight

❧❧❧❧❧

The windows above Grue's Cookshop were alight, their insolent brilliance proclaiming the confidence of the second-story tenants. As Sneever Dil Shonnet mounted the rickety steps leading up the outside of the building to the private entrance above, he could feel his own carefully nurtured confidence begin to deteriorate. His mouth was dry, his palms wet, and his right eyelid jerked violently. And surely there was no need! He had come to discipline an incompetent hireling, that was all. The bravo Whurm Didnis, having failed miserably in his appointed task, deserved the severest reproof. Whurm Didnis, inefficient and ineffectual, hardly merited the title of "professional." Didnis must offer apology and assurance of immediate improvement, else return the fee that he had accepted under what almost amounted to false pretenses. He wasn't to be let off too easily, either. The bravo should certainly be required to plead and promise at length before Lord Nobody consented to permit him a second chance.

Lord Nobody! Lord Nobody could surely deal with the matter. Sneever's spirits rose at the thought, and he smiled beneath his vizard. The mask that hid his all but chinless face—the broad slouch hat that concealed his thinning hair—the great black cloak that augmented his meager figure—the black leather boots and gauntlets—these exotic accoutrements eradicated his identity, thus freeing him. In the shadow of that delightful anonymity, he was transformed. Lord Nobody was capable of boldness, daring, and audacity to which Sneever Dil Shonnet could never aspire. It was in the guise of Lord Nobody that the Duke's despised and derided heir might realize his truest self—assured, commanding, and utterly fearless. Lord Nobody was a force to be reckoned with. And let the bravo beware!

Sneever reached the top of the stairs and paused to glance down at his gloved hands. They were perfectly steady—not a sign of a tremor. His breathing was even. Only the persistent twitch of his right eyelid gave evidence of lingering nervous tension. Taking a deep breath, he knocked imperatively.

"Who is there?" Didnis's voice from within.

"Your employer. Admit me at once." Sneever spoke in tones considerably deeper and more authoritative than his own. After a moment's silence he heard footsteps, and then the door opened to reveal Yans Whurm Didnis, resplendent in frayed crimson silk, a quantity of gold-colored jewelry, and ersatz ruby beard-beads. Didnis inspected the visitor without enthusiasm. After a moment's deliberation he stepped back from the doorway and Sneever entered the well-remembered apartment, with its tatty gilt furnishings, cracked crystal, and generally seedy grandeur. At the table sat the Lady Josky, carving her initials into the wood with the point of a dagger. She favored the visitor with a long appraising stare as he walked in, then resumed her task. Sneever could not help but note the deftness with which she manipulated the blade. His confidence wavered momentarily, then returned with a rush as he recalled that Lord Nobody was equal to all occasions.

Sneever stalked forward in silence, sat down at the table, and casually poured himself a cup of wine. He drank without haste, and only when he had finished did he deign to address his host. "You have bungled your commission. His Grace lives."

"Having heard no reports to the contrary, I suspected that such was the case," admitted the bravo, without apparent embarrassment.

"I am displeased."

"Alas, this mortal life is rife with disappointment."

"Your levity is misplaced, sir," Sneever folded his arms in unconscious imitation of the Keldhaam Gnuxia. "*I say I am displeased*. You have accepted money and failed to perform. Is this honest? Is this reputable? Is this course worthy of the noble lineage to which you have so loudly laid claim? Is the Didnis pedigree perhaps less flawless than I had been led to suppose?"

"Never, sir!" exclaimed the bravo.

"Then prove it."

"I await the time, the place, the opportunity. Since the evening of the explosion the Duke has not emerged from his palace, whither I dare not venture a second time—"

"Dare not? Dare not?" Sneever permitted himself a restrained snort of derision. His pulses were racing and this time it was with exhilaration rather than fear, for he perceived the other's disadvantage. Yans Whurm Didnis was defending and excusing himself, while Sneever Dil Shonnet for once conducted the attack. Or rather, Lord Nobody conducted it. What an admirable character was his alter ego! "Has Lord Nobody then engaged a coward?"

"By no means. The Lord Whurm Didnis is born of a warrior race. But there is such a thing as just prudence—"

"The term *prudence* scarcely befits your calling, sir. The true bravo is valued for the sake of the two great commodities in which he deals—homicidal expertise and sheer raw courage."

"Which are not worth half a dakkle combined if unaccompanied by the wisdom—caution—judgment—without which the seasoned professional cannot hope to prevail."

"Bah—mealy-mouthed evasions, Didnis, designed to justify your own failure and subsequent inactivity. I am not willing to hear them. You style yourself as first among bravos, and yet your performance would shame the greenest tyro. I expect immediate improvement. If it is not forthcoming, you will be required to return the fee you have accepted, and I shall take my custom elsewhere."

"That will not be necessary," Didnis promised, clearly concerned for his professional reputation. "The Duke has lain sequestered in his palace these past days, beyond the reach of even the most skillful and cunning of assassins. He must shortly emerge, however. The Parnis Regatta commences early next week, and the Duke's attendance traditionally marks the opening of the races. His Grace will be there—along with the Lord Yans Whurm Didnis. That should conclude the business."

"It had better," Lord Nobody returned. "I am willing to give you one more chance, Didnis, but it is the last chance you will have. For your own sake, I advise you to move quickly. And this time, try to get it right."

Whurm Didnis drew himself up with uneasy dignity, his arrogance momentarily quelled. "I know my craft, sir. None better. His Grace need only show his face in public once, and the outcome of our venture is assured. You need not fear on that account."

"I? I do not fear." Lord Nobody's voice carried overtones

of negligent menace. "At worst, I shall merely be forced to engage another tradesman. On the contrary, it is the bravo who proves himself unable to perform his sole function that has reason to fear—for his future livelihood. Take heed, fellow."

It was sheer bliss. But Sneever, almost beside himself with triumph, had overshot his mark at last.

At the last words the Lady Josky, who had maintained uncharacteristic silence throughout the conversation, lifted her head to fix the visitor with a beady-eyed stare. "That's not the proper way to address the Lord Yans Whurm Didnis," the girl observed in an ominously quiet voice.

"My princess, our guest is understandably troubled—" Didnis attempted.

"So what? That's no *excuse*, your lordship! He can't talk to us that way!" Josky turned back to Sneever. "There are a couple of things I want to say to you, but I won't talk while you're wearing that stupid mask. Take it off."

Lord Nobody did not trouble to reply directly. "Didnis," he remarked, "I would advise you to educate this impertinent little wench of yours. I am losing patience."

"And so am I!" Josky flared, her hard eyes dangerously bright. "Are you going to take that mask off, or do I have to get his lordship to take it off for you?"

"My dear child—" Didnis objected.

"I know what I'm doing, Dad!" the girl exclaimed. "You'll see!" Lord Nobody did not stir, and she added, "You may as well chuck the mask. We've already seen what's underneath, Master *Sneever Dil Shonnet!*"

The Duke's son stared at her, aghast. So she *had* discovered his identity the evening of the reception! In that instant Lord Nobody died a quick and violent death. All that remained was the wretched Sneever, feeble and fearful as ever. He felt his face grow hot, and his eyelid convulsed. Almost without volition, his shaking hands rose to the strings of his vizard. The countenance he exposed to the scrutiny of his hosts was beet-red and sheepish. At sight of it, Josky and her sire exchanged significant glances.

"That's better." The Lady Josky nodded grim approval. "Now here's what I want to tell you. In the first place, you are never, *ever* again to address his lordship or me with anything less than the courtesy and respect due our noble rank. Remember, you came to us, not the other way around. You're the one who needs *us,* not we you. So we don't have to take any garbage from you, and what's more, we won't. Just remember that, if you don't want to find youself in all kinds of trouble. You understand me, Master *Sneever*?"

Sneever's head bobbed.

"Then say so."

"I understand you."

"I hope you do, for your own sake. And another thing. That fee you've been complaining about so much—it's not enough. You want us to risk our lives to take the Duke, it's going to cost you."

"Your fee was—was agreed upon at our last meeting," Sneever stammered.

"You took advantage of us," Josky returned unblinkingly. "You played on our ignorance."

"Ignorance of what?"

"The state of your wallet. We didn't know who you were, and we didn't know what you stood to gain by his Grace's death. We just thought it was an ordinary vendetta, so we were willing to help out at cut rates. That's the way it is with us aristocrats—too generous for our own good, we are. Then we find out that you'll be Duke of Lanthi Ume after we do your dad. You've been playing us for fools, but that stops here and now. You're going to pay us twice what we agreed on."

"That's ex—extortion!"

"Oh, come, sir," Whurm Didnis broke in patronizingly. His daughter's aggression and the resulting discomfiture of the visitor had restored the bravo's lordliness in full. Now his gestures were confident and his manner once again condescending. "Reason and justice favor the Lady Josquinilliu. After all, you stand to inherit a great dukedom. When you attain that eminence, surely you will not forget the allies who have helped you along the way?"

"Leastwise not if you're a decent human being, you won't," observed the Lady Josky.

"Surely you will not forget, my friend? Be assured *we* shall not!" the bravo promised.

Sneever, his face still carmine, shrugged sullenly. His eyelid shuddered.

"We shall assume that silence implies assent."

"And we also assume that silence means you'll pay us something on account here and now," remarked the bravo's daughter.

Sneever groped for his wallet. The delay provided him time to order his chaotic thoughts, after a fashion. When he spoke, his voice was shaky. "I'll pay. But you must do what you promised. Soon. You must."

"We shall, my good Lord Nobody," Whurm Didnis promised kindly. "Set your heart at rest. The future Duke may rely upon his friends."

"And vice versa." The Lady Josky linked arms with her father. "Don't forget it."

"Drink." The Keldhaam Gnuxia extended a great goblet brimming with greenish-brown viscous fluid. "All of it."

Duke Povon eyed the substance without favor. "What is it?"

"A remedy to banish your greensickness, Betrothed. A cure for the vapors. Drink it, I say." Her black brows contracted.

The Duke sat up in bed. "I refuse," he announced bravely. "This is not necessary, Keldhaam."

"Is it not? Would that it were so! But you have lain abed this fortnight past and I am forced to conclude that you are ailing, or pusillanimous, or both. The second failing is untreatable. Happily, the first is not. The decoction I now offer will cleanse your blood of the filthy humors responsible for your present languor, feebleness, and idle terrors. Do not shrink from the bodily sufferings this cleansing process entails. The ultimate benefit is worth the cost, or nearly so. Therefore drink, Betrothed. Drink *now*."

"I don't want it!"

Gnuxia's large hand clenched on the stem of the goblet. She did not deign to answer.

"I have suffered greatly in mind and body, Keldhaam," Povon argued earnestly. "The recent attempt upon my life has destroyed my inner serenity and all but shattered my faith in mankind. A period of undisturbed tranquility is essential to the restoration of my mental and emotional well-being. Time is needed to heal my wounded spirit. I require peace, Keldhaam. No medicinal slop. Only peace."

"Bah, you are hardly qualified to judge. Best leave the matter to wiser heads. You have had peace, Betrothed—over two weeks' worth—and it has done you no good. You are as weak, muddled, and fearful now as you were upon the night of the explosion. Perhaps more so. This cordial, which I have prepared with my own hands, will restore you to your former self, such as it was. Take it."

Povon accepted the goblet with reluctance and sniffed the contents suspiciously. The odor was vile. He looked up to find his betrothed's pitiless eyes fixed upon him. No hope of mercy there. Desperation accelerated the Duke's thoughts, and his sole workable means of escape became clear. Setting the cordial aside untasted, he flung off the silken coverlets, swung his short legs over the edge of the high bed, and hopped down to the ground. "The remedy is superfluous. I am restored to health and ready to resume my ducal duties."

"What is the meaning of this?"

"I am still grievously troubled in spirit, Keldhaam, but Lanthi Ume cannot continue leaderless. My people need me."

"Your recovery is sudden."

"True. But my sense of duty will not be denied."

"Duty? Does a Lanthian know the meaning of the term? I place more faith in my remedy than in your sense of duty."

"Your skepticism is as depressing as it is predictable. What will it take to convince you, Keldhaam?"

"More than words. Action. A show of valor, a show of strength. Courage. Decision. Resolution. Astound me, Betrothed. Prove yourself a man."

"Such proof is unnecesary. I am Duke."

"You were Duke. Now you are a prisoner."

"What do you mean?"

"You dare not venture from this chamber. You fear another attempt upon your life. A true ruler would never submit to such indignity. My father, his Splendor the Keldhar, would have hunted down his enemies and destroyed them by now. Even the Duke of Hurba would do as much. But you do nothing. You tremble, you mew yourself up within your chamber, you cower among your feather cushions. Thus you are no Duke, but only a miserable captive. This deficiency I ascribe to melancholy humors and innumerable impurities of the blood. Either a thorough systemic cleansing or else a complete hemal replacement is indicated. We shall attempt first one and then the other, as appropriate."

"No! That is unnecessary! My health is restored and there is nothing wrong with my blood!" Noting her expression of disbelief, he added, "I will prove it to you. You'll have the demonstration you demand. I will find and kill my great foes— Fal Grizhni's son and the young demon's dam. Tomorrow morning my Guardsmen will march on the Nazara Sin. I have delayed long enough. Too long has foolish kindness ruled me,

too long have my enemies exploited my good nature. But no
more! The Guardsmen leave tomorrow. There, Keldhaam. Will
that suffice?"

"For the moment." Slowly she nodded. "Your thoughts are
muddled as ever, and your suspicions are nothing less than
ludicrous. It is apparent to the meanest intelligence that your
enemies reside within this city. I do not doubt that you waste
time, effort, expense, and manpower searching the wilderness.
But at least you *are* searching, and that is a step in the right
direction. It is marginally better than nothing."

Three nights later, the moon shone down on the hills of the
Nazara Sin. So bright were its beams that no artificial illumination was required to light the way of the four figures emerging
from a concealed cavern entrance. Three of the figures were
human, healthy, and vigorous. The fourth was none of these
things.

Lady Verran stepped into the open, and her lungs expanded
hungrily to catch the cool, fresh air. Behind her came Terrs
and Har Fennahar, together supporting the tottering Nyd. It
was only her worry over Nyd's condition that kept Verran from
giving herself entirely over to the pleasure of a rare Surface
excursion. On the other hand, it was for Nyd's benefit that the
expedition had been organized in the first place. The hybrid
was sicker than she had ever seen him, sicker than he had ever
been in all his life. Impossible to guess what was wrong—Nyd
could not speak of his woes, and there was no one in the caverns
with knowledge of hybrid anatomy. In the caverns? There was
probably no one anywhere. Terrs Fal Grizhni had bred the
creatures, he alone had fully understood them, and his knowledge had died along with him. Verran sighed, as she often did
when she contemplated her long-ago life with her late husband.
How much he might have explained to her, had she only possessed the good sense to ask! How many opportunities had she
let slip by, never to return!

She turned to look at Nyd. The hybrid's graying head
drooped, his step was uncertain, and he leaned heavily upon
his human companions. As he stepped into the open air, however, he straightened. He took a deep breath, chest swelling.
Lifting his head, he gazed first at the surrounding hills—a harsh
and barren spectacle by ordinary standards, but obviously beautiful to Nyd—and then up at the moon and stars. The dull eyes
brightened, and a heartfelt croak escaped him.

Verran smiled as she watched. This was indeed the medicine that Nyd needed. Fresh air—sharp breezes—open sky overhead—Surface. If anything could renew his spirits and hasten his recovery, it was the air of Surface. He needed it from time to time. *And so do I,* she thought.

Nyd's nostrils flared, and he snuffled deeply. The scents borne upon the breeze appeared to excite him. He hissed and shook himself free of his attendants, whose support was for the moment unnecessary. With head held high and tolerably steady footsteps, he made his way unaided to the top of the nearest short rise, from whose summit he might more easily read the wind. Verran did not attempt to follow. Best to give him some time to himself—he'd had little enough of that in his lifetime. Accordingly she turned her attention to her human companions, and noted that Rillif Har Fennahar's expression was mildly resigned. That made sense, as Ril took Surface joys so much for granted. The sight of the night sky, barren hills and scrub vegetation left him untouched, as it would once have left her. No, for Ril the true wonder and fascination lay in the caves below.

How long would that last, if he knew he couldn't leave them?

Her gaze shifted to Terrs. The boy was walking to and fro, black regard fixed now upon the ground and grasses, now upon the jeweled sky. His attitude, she decided, was scholarly—objective, observant, detached but attentive. And that was a great step forward. Hitherto Terrs had exhibited no interest whatever in anything that Surface had to offer. It had seemed almost a point of pride with him, in fact, to scorn every aspect of the human domain. Now that seemed to be changing, and there could only be one explanation—Fennahar's influence. Fennahar's conversation and descriptions had awakened the boy's curiosity as Verran had never succeeded in doing, and proof of that lay in Terrs's willingness to participate in this night's expedition. Of course, his genuine fondness for Nyd would have had something to do with that decision, but it was still a great departure. For Great Vens Verran had sought to coax her son Surface, if only for a brief jaunt, and she had always failed. But here he was, above ground at last, and who could say what might follow? He might find he even like it. His sorties might increase in frequency. He might even—Verran allowed herself to dream—he might even in time be persuaded to visit one of the great coastal cities. Not Lanthi Ume, of course, but perhaps Gard Lammis or Rhel.

He might learn to accept his own humanity, and then he could be happy with himself. And Ril is leading him in that direction—assuming that anybody or anything can possibly lead Terrs.

She caught the explorer's eye and smiled. Fennahar's brows rose. He looked both startled and pleased at the warmth of her expression.

Her son now approached. His manner was composed as ever, but Verran thought she detected some hint of uneasiness.

"Fennahar, does this enormous expanse of emptiness not fill you with a sense of desolation?" Terrs glanced briefly up at the stars. "The inconceivable vastness of this space—the absence of walls and visible ceiling—do these not impart a sense of insignificance, exposure, even vulnerability?"

"There's some truth in that," Fennahar admitted, "but I wouldn't consider it altogether a bad thing. It's not so comforting to be reminded of our real place in the scheme of things, but I suspect it's good for us."

"Then you endure this Surface barrenness for the sake of moral improvement?"

"Moral impro—" Fennahar burst out laughing, and the sound echoed oddly among the hills. Then, noting the other's look of slightly offended incomprehension, he stifled his merriment. "I'm sorry, Terrs. From your point of view, it's a perfectly reasonable question. From mine, the idea of 'enduring' the land and sky is incongruous. I, like most men, find them very beautiful."

"Wherein lies the beauty? The scene is not entirely without interest. But beautiful? I do not see it."

"Look around you. Notice the grandeur of these stark, jagged hills—"

"They are sterile and comfortless beneath the lash of frigid winds."

"To me, these cool, fresh breezes breathe life and freedom, while the atmosphere of the caverns is heavy and oppressive."

"That soft warmth oppressive? It is perfection."

"Then notice the variety, delicacy, and complexity of the vegetation that surrounds us, and know that it's but a very poor, mean sampling of all that Surface has to offer."

"It is true that Surface flora far exceeds the various fungi of the caverns," Terrs admitted. "Yet how can Surface vegetation in its evanescence compare in color, brilliance, perfection, or permanence with our crystal formations that endure throughout the Great Vens?"

"Flowers have one advantage," Lady Verran observed. "They are alive."

"True but irrelevant, Mother. The issue of vitality is beside the point."

"You might think differently if you'd ever *seen* a flower. Or smelled one, especially a rose. But you haven't, so how could you know?"

Terrs was silent.

"Look at the sky," Fennahar suggested. "The stars, that glorious moon—surely they must stir your imagination?"

Terrs looked up and his eyes were drawn irresistibly to the full moon. It seemed he could not look away from it. "They are—not displeasing," he admitted at last, very grudgingly, as if the words were dragged from him by force. "They seem to hold meaning, if one could but decipher the message. Perhaps with High Cognition—" He was silent again for a moment, and then seemed to recollect himself. "But their light is dim and cold, in no way comparable to the rock-light of the caves."

"Then you might prefer lantern light or candlelight, which are bright and warm," Fennahar returned. "And if the open hills of the Nazara Sin hold no appeal, then you might like the walled and roofed edifices of human cities. Or perhaps the canopy of a great forest. The world offers endless variety, Terrs. Words can't begin to convey it. In order to begin to understand, you'd have to see for yourself."

Terrs did not answer at once, and Lady Verran glanced at him in surprise. Ordinarily her son was wont to quash without hesitation and without mercy even the most oblique of encouragements to Surface exploration. But not this time. This time he stood with arms folded and head slightly bowed, sunk in cogitation. Fennahar's words must have affected him. In mounting excitement she awaited his reply.

Terrs looked up at last. "Is there any possibility that—"

The question was never completed. At that moment Nyd, alone upon the nearby hilltop, hissed loudly and uttered a series of urgent croaks. The human conversation ceased. Nyd repeated his signals.

"He's warning us," Verran explained for Fennahar's benefit, and without another word the three of them hurried to the summit of the rise. Nyd stood peering off through the darkness.

Upon the arrival of his companions he lifted his great arm, gestured, and hissed. Verran's eyes followed the gesture and gazing southeast, toward Lanthi Ume, she discerned a faint cluster of orange lights winking among the hills. Her pulses jumped.

The others saw it too.

"Campfires," said Terrs flatly. "They have returned."

"Guardsmen?" asked Fennahar.

"It was only a matter of time," said Verran.

"Verran, you and Terrs and Nyd must get away from here at once. I don't imagine the guardsmen will attack before dawn. We could be halfway to Gard Lammis by then. And when we arrive, I'll buy you passage on a ship bound for Strell—"

"No." Terrs spoke with icy composure. "Mother will do as she pleases, and Nyd will go with her if she leaves. But I will not be driven from my home."

Fennahar stared at him. "That's lunacy. You don't seem to understand the danger—"

"He understands perfectly, Ril." Verran's tone was bleak. "You won't succeed in changing his mind. And as for me, I don't intend to desert my son."

"Then what do you intend? Will you and the Vardruls hide in the depths of the caves? There must be passageways the Guardsmen would never find—"

"No. We will neither hide nor flee," said Terrs.

"You've no other choice."

"One other. We will defend ourselves."

"You don't know what you're saying, lad. You don't seriously imagine you can fight the Ducal Guardsmen, do you? You'll get yourself killed, and quite likely your Vardrul friends will die along with you. Not to mention your mother, who remains on your account. Do you want that on your conscience?"

"Some of us may die," Terrs conceded without emotion "but that is a small price to pay to ensure the lasting safety of our caverns. It is a worthwhile sacrifice and in the greatest sense harmonious. In any event, how should we truly fear to join our Ancestors?"

Fennahar shook his head in frustration. "I can't pretend to understand that attitude. I can only assume you'd rather live. As for protecting the caverns, you're ill-equipped to do so by means of combat, for the Vardruls clearly aren't fighters. They are too soft-natured, too gentle."

"All things are subject to change. The clan members are not unwilling to resist murderous predation," Terrs remarked impassively, and held up his hand to forestall the other's rejoinder. "Fennahar, there is no time to discuss the matter now. The Guardsmen will arrive within a Coloration, and we must hasten to prepare a suitable reception. I have prepared for this moment. Be assured they will find us ready." Without awaiting reply, Terrs turned on his heel and headed down the hill toward the cave entrance.

Nyd, who had understood all, hissed eagerly and trailed in his young master's wake. Excitement had banished all sign of infirmity. Fennahar and Verran exchanged speaking glances. Then Verran shrugged minutely and headed for the cave. After a moment, Fennahar followed.

Chapter Nine

❧❧❧❧❧

The sun was rising when the squadron of Ducal Guardsmen under the leadership of Commander Kronil reached the Mvjri Dazzle. The soldiers were ignorant of the Vardrul title. To them the hole in the side of the hill was simply the cave entrance that had served them so well upon the occasion of their previous visit; more or less familiar territory. The opening had been undefended then, and it appeared deserted now. Still, best to beware of overconfidence. While the White Demons of the Caverns had displayed the most contemptible cowardice in the face of honest human valor, yet they were masters of treachery. The minds within those hideous hairless skulls possessed alien cunning beyond comprehension. Caution was indicated, and therefore Kronil sent a couple of his most reliable subordinates ahead to reconnoiter.

A quick survey of the area revealed no lurking Demons. The mouth of the cave gaped emptily, and Kronil threw his squadron forward at a run. The leaders passed under the archway, pounded along the corridor a few paces, and then, with horrifying abruptness, disappeared—seemingly swallowed alive by the solid stone floor. Cries of pain and panic arose, some of them apparently from beneath the floor. The men at the front of the column attempted to halt, but the pressure of those behind drove them relentlessly on until they too plunged into stone. The shrieks intensified, echoing crazily down the vaulted corridor. Kronil roared orders and some of them were heard. The column slowed, halted, and the pressure on the leaders eased, leaving those in the extreme forefront teetering perilously upon the invisible brink. These men were drawn back to safety by their fellows and order was restored to the squadron. In the midst of that relative calm, the shrieks, groans, and entreaties rising from below were clearly audible.

Kronil commanded silence. Cupping his hands around his mouth, he shouted down at the floor, and was rewarded with answering screams. One voice managed to distinguish itself. "Ten of us down here, sir. One whole, five hurt, two dying, two dead."

"Who's speaking?"

"Sergeant Vhoro, sir."

"Where are you?"

"In a pit right below you. It's a trap filled with sharpened stone stakes. Four of the men came down on them, and they're goners. The hole stretches across the whole corridor."

"How deep?"

"About twelve feet, sir. And maybe ten, twelve feet wide."

"An open hole?"

"Yes, sir. I can see you plain."

"We can't see you. Nothing."

"No, sir. It's Cognition, sir. Must be."

Kronil went cold at the word, then rallied. It was the duty of the Guardsmen to fulfill the will of his Grace, no matter how cruel, dangerous, or imbecilic that will might be. Duty, after all, was Duty—a most reassuring maxim without whose benefit life would prove infinitely more complex. "Too wide to risk jumping," the Commander ruminated. He made his decision. "All right, Vhoro. We're going to come down on ropes, and we'll depend on you for guidance. You keep the men away from the stakes, and we'll see to you. Once down, I'll appoint three or four to safe-lift the wounded, and the rest of us will go forward. Understand?"

"Understood, sir."

Every Guardsman was equipped with a coil of rope. Now two of them affixed their lines to neighboring stalagmites and cautiously descended. It was with wonder that they witnessed their own bodies sink into stone. But they felt nothing. The hot, moist air was unobstructed, and as they sank beneath the apparent surface of the floor, the dim rock-light of the corridor walls did not fail. They found themselves in an open pit, their cohorts above still clearly visible. An exchange of shouts and cries informed them that they could still be heard. Thus reassured, they dared to glance around them, to study the inward-

sloping walls, the murderous stakes, the wounded comrades.
Guardsman Jhorneels was very unpleasantly dead, with a sharpened spear of stone piercing his body from chest to spine.
Equally defunct was the presumptuous Guardsman Fohness,
who had fallen sideways to catch a spike under an arm and
through the neck. Guardsmen Uaitte lay supine of the floor,
his chest and dandified whiskers stained with blood. Uaitte was
still alive, but obviously not for long. Beside him sprawled the
moribund Guardsman Whurose, abdomen ripped wide, entrails
dangling. As for the others, they sported an assortment of
broken bones, cuts, and contusions. A number of them were
weaker and more sluggish than their injuries appeared to warrant, but now was not the time to ponder the cause. Of the
victims, only Sergeant Vhoro had escaped unscathed.

Finding the pit as described, the newcomers shouter confirmation to their fellows, who upon the command of their leader
swiftly descended the ropes, hurried to the far side of the hole,
and proceeded to form a human tower, each man atop the
shoulders of the last. The top Guardsman grasped the edge of the
pit to stabilize the structure, and the remaining soldiers began to
climb. No more than two or three had reached floor level before
the corridor suddenly swarmed with glowng white figures.

They had materialized out of nowhere, those uncanny creatures, and the utter silence of their advance added greatly to
the terror of the attack. Terrible too was their mere appearance—
loathsome travesties of human beings with elongated, emaciated
limbs, fleshless faces, and indescribably alien eyes. They were
armed with rocks and spikes that looked to be formed of sharpened stalactites—no match for good human blades of steel,
yet no doubt lethal enough in skilled hands. At the head of the
White Demons marched a tall young human of subtly peculiar
aspect, and in him the Guardsmen recognized their quarry—Fal
Grizhni's son, whom their master had bade them kill. Amazing
that the youth dared to show himself so openly. The Guardsmen,
however, had little opportunity to marvel. Grizhni's son uttered
a weird, high-pitched cry, and the Demons surged forward.

No need now to complain of the silence—the corridor rang
with the sound of musical, inhuman, strangely beautiful voci-
feration. To the Guardsmen, it was purely horrible—the sight,
the sound, the totally unexpected attack by a mob of the hitherto
timorous Demons. The creatures, evidently wrought to some

incomprehensible pitch of excitement, attacked fearlessly.
Their flesh glowed with ghastly brilliance as they plied their
rocks and sharpened stakes. What they lacked in skill with the
crude weapons was more than balanced by sheer enthusiasm.
The three Guards on the near side of the pit had hardly time
to draw their swords before they found themselves surrounded.
Hideous, shining bodies loomed up on all sides. The blows
rained down furiously upon their bucklers and the soldiers,
overwhelmed by sheer numbers, were swept back to the verge
of the hole. There they made a brief, desperate stand, dispatching a trio of Demons before the thrust of sharpened stalactites
drove them in swift succession backward over the brink. The
three falling bodies landed squarely on the sharpened stakes,
where they wriggled like worms on a fisherman's hook. The
Demons crowded to the edge of the trap. Their leader appeared
to infer the existence of the human tower. Presumably he could
not see it, but correctly guessed its location. At a sign from
the human, the Demons hurled their stones blindly at the invisible soldiers beneath them. In this they had evidently received
some training, for the volley threw with admirable force and
accuracy. At one blow the human tower was shattered, and its
component elements fell upon the stakes below. One man was
left clinging grimly to the lip of the hole. A couple of well-
placed kicks broke his hold to send him hurtling down upon
his luckless companions. Within the hole, the wisest of the
surviving Guardsmen skulked in silence, trusting to the Cognitive illusion above their heads to shield them from the eyes of
their enemies. Those of shorter memory, forgetting the existence of the camouflage, attempted to climb the ropes to safety
on the far side of the hole, and the well-aimed rocks of the
Demons picked them off as soon as their heads broke illusory
surface.

About a quarter of the Ducal Guards were armed with light
javelins—weapons for which little real need had been anticipated. These men were now ordered to the fore. A moment
later the javelins flew to inflict confusion upon the Demons.
Four of the creatures fell mortally wounded, and the light swiftly
faded from their bodies. Those remaining set up melodious
outcry, and the unnatural flickering of their flesh was downright
sickening to behold. A second flight of javelins brought down
three more Demons, putting the rest to flight. The creatures

retreated, despite the strenuous efforts of their human leader to hold them. The youth's voice rose. Depsite the alien language and mannerisms, his extreme frustration was unmistakable. His pleas were ignored, save in one particular. A vew Demons paused long enough to collect the fallen javelins before disappearing in the wake of their brethren. Grizhni's son followed with reluctance.

And a good thing, too, Commander Kronil reflected as he watched the last of the White Demons disappear around a bend in the corridor. Were it not for the cowardice of their foes, the advance of the Guardsmen might have been halted at the outset upon the brink of that cursed invisible trap, which would have constituted an easily defended and almost impassable obstacle had the inhabitants but shown the sense and courage to stand their ground. As it was, however, the way forward was clear.

The Guardsmen navigated the pit, this time without opposition. The ambulatory wounded were lifted to safety and instructed to withdraw. It was noted that a number of the men were unaccountably stupid and somnolent, but the reason for this was not as yet suspected. The dead or obviously dying remained at the bottom of the pit, while all able-bodied soldiers forged ahead in search of Fal Grizhni's son.

The Demons had not commandeered all the javelins. One yet remained, protruding from the body of a lifeless white creature. Perhaps they had not dared to touch it. But Commander Kronil was burdened with no such scruples. Placing one booted foot upon the neck of the corpse, he yanked the javelin free and handed it to Guardsman Wruppo, a recruit of no marked ability and therefore comparatively expendable. Wruppo was ordered forward. He would precede the column by several yards, employing the javelin as a staff in the manner of blind men, to test the floor for other concealed traps.

The Guardsmen advanced. No more traps materialized and as their confidence returned, their pace increased. Presently they were jogging along a corridor that looked deserted as a midnight graveyard. No Demons appeared to block their progress—the mewling monsters hadn't the stomach for honest combat. An ambush was a distinct possibility, however, and vigilance was essential.

That vigilance was soon rewarded. Presently the Guardsmen spied a fleshless white countenance peering out at them from the shelter of a fissure in the wall ahead. Perceiving itself discovered, the face withdrew abruptly and the soldiers thundered in pursuit. Piling pell-mell through the fissure, they entered a tributary tunnel far less spacious than the corridor they had just abandoned. Not far ahead, plainly visible in the feeble glow of the rock-light, fled the White Demon. Kronil wanted that Demon. Once captured, the creature might be induced somehow or other to reveal the whereabouts of Grizhni's son. At the very least, it could serve as a guide through the caverns. The Commander recklessly urged his men forward, but the gap between Guardsmen and quarry did not narrow. The Demon's gait was deceptive, the true speed masked by a certain repulsively smooth fluidity of movement. Without warning the creature changed its course, sliding bonelessly through a narrow split in the lucent rock, and for a moment appeared gone for good. The Guardsmen followed, and found themselves in a low-ceilinged, downward-slanting passage. The Demon had disappeared. Stooping slightly, the men advanced, and as they rounded a sharp bend caught a quick glimpse of the Demon slipping throught an archway not far ahead. For a moment the creature paused, glancing back over its shoulder with an inscrutable expression that Kronil interpreted as mockery, then it was gone. The men gave chase, passing beneath the arch and along a skinny shaft to emerge into a great unimaginably lofty chamber, with vaulted ceiling and glowing walls all richly coated with azure slime. It resembled some nauseous parody of the clean sky above, and Commander Kronil felt his revulsion and contempt rise at the sight of it. The Demon was nowhere to be seen. Directly ahead, only a few feet from the mouth of the shaft, the floor ended in a cliff that fell straight and sheer to a stand of jagged boulders hundreds of feet below. Kronil's lips curved in a grim smile. Had the Demon hoped that the Guardsmen would come boiling out of the tunnel to rush straight over the edge of the cliff? Did the creature actually imagine that men were so easily gulled? It would soon learn otherwise. Kronil glanced swiftly right and left. Wide fissures sundered the walls on either side. Presumably the White Demon had escaped through one, but there was no telling which. Kronil settled on the right-hand exit and took a deep breath, preparatory to bawling orders. An instant before he could open his mouth, a musically alien cry arose, quavered mournfully, and died. This was followed by a piercing, unquestionably human whistle.

Immediately the air was alive with dark, winged forms.

They'd come in response to that summons and there were
hundreds of them, perhaps thousands. They had ember-red
eyes, wicked little fangs, and great leathern wings that buffeted
and blinded the Guardsmen. Their high-pitched cries vibrated
just beyond the range of audibility, but the beating wings
sounded a rataplan.

Kronil felt and heard the claws scrabbing for a hold upon
the crest of his helmet. Wildly flapping wings battered his face.
His vision was obscured and the blows were surprisingly painful. Reaching up, he grabbed his assailant, dragged it down,
and found himself holding a huge brown bat. With an exclamation of disgust, he wrung the beast's neck and tossed the body
aside. No sooner had he done so than another of the bats was
upon him, its wings beating violently at his face. He dispatched
it as he had the first, and then there were two more and he
couldn't see, couldn't breathe. It was deliberate, obviously—
the beasts had been trained to go for the eyes, and the realization
of his enemies' perfidy fueled the Commander's rage. He shook
himself free, and in that moment of unobstructed vision beheld
his men all but enveloped in a swirling live cloud. The
Guardsmen were yelling, cursing, stumbling blindly to and fro
as they beat at the air and at themselves. No great matter. The
bats, while loathsome, could inflict no real damage. Posing
more of a nuisance than a threat, they could not be effectively
countered, and retreat was indicated. Before the appropriate
command could be uttered, a trilling cry was heard and the
White Demons came pouring into the chamber.

Once again they bore stones and stalactites, but this time
many carried the purloined javelins. With them came Grizhni's
son, true heir of his traitorous father, allying himself with the
natural enemies of humanity. Any traces of misgiving that had
troubled Kronil at the prospect of slaughtering a mere boy
vanished at the sight. It would be almost a pleasure to kill him.
But that, the Commander quickly discovered, was a pleasure
not easily achieved.

The Demons had recovered their fortitude, and the
Guardsmen—blinded, distracted, and confused by the bats—
were taken at a serious disadvantage. The melodious attack
quickly pushed the soldiers back to the very edge of the cliff.
That, beyond question, had been young Grizhni's intent all
along. Now that the amateurish thrusts and blows of the white creatures proved deadly as the trained steel of Rhelish mercenaries,

as Guardsman after Guardsman was driven over the brink. The men fell screaming, and it was a curious sight to see the clinging bats abandon the plummeting bodies in midair, right themselves with a flutter of dark wings, and swoop up out of the gulf to batter and harass their masters' remaing foes.

The Guardsmen fought back viciously, and a growing pile of white corpses rewarded their efforts. But mere ferocity was not enough, and one by one Kronil's men went toppling to their doom. Gradually, almost unbelievably, the White Demons and their detestable allies were winning the battle. As each human fell, the confidence of the Demons mounted and the vigor of their attack increased accordingly. Their blows were growing stronger, more aggressive. Some of their thrusts were cunningly placed and disastrously effective. The Demons learned fast, and those employing the steel-headed human javelins were particularly dangerous. And their leader, the human youth, fought with an icy determination worthy of a son of Ert. Commander Kronil recognized all at once that his squadron stood in danger of utter annihilation. No quesiton now of fulfilling the Duke's wishes—the immediate concern was that of self-preservation. If his men did not retreat, they would all die upon the spot.

Kronil struck the clinging bats aside and, in the ensuing instant of unobstructed breath and vision, shouted orders. The Guardsmen able to see and move followed their commander to the left-hand exit. Those unable to do so ended their lives at the base of the cliff.

The soldiers retreated in disorder by way of a featureless tunnel. Only about half of the original attack force was left. Behind them sounded a confused humming punctuated by trills, warbles, and the insistent notes of a lone human voice. Kronil did not need to turn around to interpret the sounds. Grizhni's son was urging his companions to follow up their advantage, and the creatures hesitated. Competent soldiers would certainly have seized the opportunity afforded by the Guardsmen's retreat. Fortunately the White Demons seemed to possess no instinct for such things.

Instinct. What sort of instinct would it take to lead them out of this place? The way back to the gateway by which they had entered the caverns led through the terrible chamber of the cliff. Ahead of them lay a labyrinth in which they might wander lost until they all died of starvation. It would be necessary,

Kronil realized, to locate an alternative exit—of which there
were surely many—or else fight their way back the way they
had come, a prospect that his men would greet without enthusiasm. Difficult, to be sure, but far from hopeless. The
White Demons, for all their guile, remained contemptible opponents. Their clumsiness and inexperience were self-evident.
By means of underhanded tactics they had gained a temporary
advantage, but that could not last long. The natural superiority
of their warlike brethren, the creatures scattered in terror at sight
of the soldiers. Some of them instantly fled the chamber through
an open chamber—persumably devoid of cliff and bats—where
they could turn and engage the Demons freely. Anything resembling a fair fight would settle the Demons once and for all,
and then Fal Grizhni's son could be dealt with at leisure.
Kronil's spirits rose at the thought. The boy would die in
accordance with his Grace's commands, but—not too quickly.
The squadron had suffered and the men deserved compensation;
something to restore confidence and optimism. The protracted
destruction of an enemy would boost the general morale, and
also serve as a warning to surviving Demons. This was strategy
worthy of Kronil's predecessor, the lamented Haik Ulf, and
therefore sure to succeed. All that was needed now was the
space in which to turn and fight.

As if in answer to the Commander's prayers, the tunnel
ended and the Guardsmen emerged into a chamber rich with
crystalline growths interspersed with spectacular fungi. The
presence of a bubbling hot spring doubtless accounted for the
soggy, intolerably sticky warmth of the atmosphere. They had
unknowingly ventured upon the Zmadrc-Lbavbsch gardens.
The room was broad, spacious, and populated. Here and there
stood clusters of unarmed Demons. Evidently lacking the spirit
of their warlike brethren, the creatures scattered in terror at sight
of the soldiers. Some of them instantly fled the chamber through
the great archway that pierced the opposing wall. Others unen-
dowed with such presence of mind cowered on the far side of
the spring. Of far greater interest to Commander Kronil, however, was an anomalous trio already heading for the exit.

Two of the figures were human, one of them recognizable.
The slight, fair-haired woman was Lady Grizhni, a secondary
target but nonetheless marked for death. She was accompanied
by a tall, lean man attired in garments of Lanthian cut. The
man bore a sharpened stalactite. His face was naggingly famil-

iar. Surely he could be glimpsed from time to time upon the
canals of Lanthi Ume—and occasionally even at court? Who-
ever he was, his presence was unanticipated but not entirely
unwelcome. Presumably he possessed some knowledge of the
caverns, and that knowledge, once extracted, would surely
prove useful. The third figure—spiked, hairy, and bizarre—was
unmistakably a demon. Obviously no kin to the White Demons
of the Caverns, this one was a special breed owing allegiance
to Preeminence Terrs Fal Grizhni. It was such creatures as this
that had so fiercely defended Grizhni Palace seventeen years
earlier. Kronil remembered them only too well—remembered
their courage and tenacity. It was thought at the time that all
of the unnatural brutes had been destroyed, but obviously one
had lived on to serve his master's son. No matter. What had
started seventeen years ago could surely be finished today.

"Take the man. Kill the others," Kronil instructed his men.

They needed no urging. With half their number murdered
by Demons, the prospect of vengeance served as a tonic. Weariness and fears forgotten, the Guardsmen charged, shouting
savagely. Pusillanimous as always, the Demons attempted
flight, but justice was not to be evaded. Steel blades flashed
in the rock-light and within seconds the floor was strewn with
slug-white bodies. Some of them were still and dull, others yet
flickered and writhed. The soldiers wasted no time on the
wounded, who could easily be dispatched at leisure. Rather
they chose to direct their energies toward blocking the escape
of the uninjured Demons, and in this their success was gratify-
ing. Guardsmen Lhorno, Dreevid, and Krufaure—three fine
soldiers blessed with quick wits and initiative—instantly sprang
to station themselves before the largest exit. Thanks to this
wise move a major exodus was aborted, and those Demons
attempting to rush the blockade soon learned the folly of their
ways. The three men were fine swordsmen, and Krufaure in
particular was magnificent—the backhanded sweep with which
he severed the neck of a fleeing Demon was splendid to behold.
The creature's head went flying like a bird to land upright upon
a great crystal spar, stuck there neatly as a traitor's noddle
upon a pike—a sight that heartened the men no end. Less
spectacular than Krufaure in their accomplishments, but nearly
as effective in their own way, Lhorno and Dreevid were busy
lopping alien limbs right and left. The colorless blood was
streaming over the floor at their feet.

The skillful blades of Lhorno, Dreevid, and Krufaure sent the Demons scurrying for the smaller exits. There, where the tight, cramped way permitted passage only in single file, the fugitives gathered in panic-stricken clumps—easy prey indeed for the eager Guardsmen who set upon them from behind. The steel bit, the Demons fell, and the strangely lovely melody of their death-cries filled the air.

Backed by a number of his cohorts, Commander Kronil rushed straight for Lady Grizhni, deftly intercepting her retreat before she had covered half the distance to the nearest exit. His sword was lifted, his demeanor wolfish. The woman screamed and fell back. Simultaneously her two companions leaped forward. This stupidity was understandable on the part of the beast; less so for the man—a chuckle-headed numbskull if there ever was one, to employ a ridiculous homemade weapon of stone against trained Ducal Guardsmen!

"Run, Verran!" the man shouted—he was Lanthian beyond doubt—and that was all he had time to say before Guardsman Wruppo was upon him. Wruppo, mindful of his superior's orders, aimed low to incapacitate rather than kill, and this proved his undoing. Despising the crude arms of his opponent, the Guardsman lunged without science, overextending himself a trifle. The other leaped aside, and the next instant Wruppo received the sharpened point of the stalactite full in the face.

Wruppo went down. Instantly relinquishing the stalactite, the anonymous Lanthian stooped to wrest the steel sword from the fallen man's grasp. He was for the moment vulnerable, and Guardsman Tebbo was quick to exploit the brief opening. Tebbo's blade descended like a thunderbolt. The blow would surely have proved fatal had not the Guardsman been shaken in midstroke by the clanging impact of a rock upon his helmet. The sword fell far wide of its mark. Tebbo raised his eyes to behold Lady Grizhni, who had ignored her protector's sensible advice, preparing to launch a second missile. The woman threw with unexpected force and accuracy. Tebbo ducked and the stone whizzed by his ear. In that instant, his opponent rose and engaged blades. The stranger knew how to handle a sword. Tebbo and his companions found their way to Lady Grizhni effectively blocked.

Commander Kronil had scant opportunity to follow the fortunes of his subordinates. The bestial demon with whom he now fought demanded his full attention. It looked to be old.

Its grizzled hair and yellowed fangs suggested feebleness, but
such suggestions were misleading. Devoid of fear, utterly careless of its own life, the creature was dangerous as pestilence.
Half a dozen times within the space of seconds its talons ripped
the air so close to his eyes that Kronil could feel the breeze. In
view of its age, the creature's speed was astonishing. Evading
the thrusts of the Guardman's sword without apparent difficulty,
it ducked in low, claws extended, then out again; and almost
before Kronil felt the first flash of fire, the blood was welling
from a long new gash on his thigh. The Commander cursed
more in rage than pain, and intensified his efforts. He perceived
that the enemy was even more formidable than he had at first
supposed; but he had no inkling of genuine personal peril until
the beast once again managed to spring in close, this time
laying Kronil's face open from cheek to jaw.

Kronil drew back and his enemy followed—a slashing, snarling fury that permitted no respite. A feint, a hiss, another
incredible leap, and the snapping fangs just grazed the Commander's throat. An answering stroke of steel missed by inches.
The creature seemed to float clear, untouchable and invulnerable. And for the first time since the battle began, Kronil
considered the possibility of defeat. For one fleeting instant he
contemplated failure, even death. But fortunately his imagination was not vivid, and he was able to push such conterproduc-
tive thoughts from his mind. The creature before him—demon
or mongrelized beast—whatever it was, could surely be killed.
He knew that well enough, for he himself had participated in
the slaughter of its brethren in the palace of their master. As
he had killed such demons upon that night, so he would kill
the last of them now. Thus reassured, Kronil thrust vigorously.
Perhaps renewed confidence lent him fresh speed, or perhaps
the ancient demon was tiring at last. In any event, the blade
sliced deep into a hirsute upper arm, drawing a gout of blood.

The creature hissed venomously and withdrew a couple of
paces. The path to his quarry momentarily clear, Kronil seized
the opportunity to close in on Lady Grizhni, who stood pitching
rocks at his Guards. Absorbed in her task, she failed to note
his approach. The demon screamed, a terrible hoarse shriek of
fear, rage, and hatred that caught the attention of its mistress.
The Grizhni woman turned to stare. Kronil wheeled quickly,
in time to face the demon as it leaped. The creature rose from
the ground as if borne on invisible wings. Its hideous features

were contorted, fangs bared, and it was snarling ceaselessly, deep in its throat. The Commander, while not an impressionable man, nonetheless experienced a pang of almost superstitious dread. He recovered quickly. Bracing himself, he tightened his grip on his weapon. His perceptions at that moment seemed supernaturally swift. For one instant the demon seemed to hang suspended in the air above, almost frozen at the zenith of its trajectory, and at that exact instant Kronil struck. His blade transfixed the demon's breast. Instinct guided him, and he knew beyond all question that he had killed.

"*Nyd!*" The shriek tore from Lady Grizhni.

The demon's snarls cut off abruptly. Fatally wounded though it was, the momentum of its leap carried it forward. Kronil's sword arm was forced back as the demon crashed down upon him. He felt its talons rake his chest in a deadly stroke that would have rent his heart, but for the protection of his breastplate. With the last of its strength, it struggled to bring its fangs to his throat. Withdrawing his sword with an effort, Kronil thrust the demon violently from him. It tottered backward and fell. The Grizhni woman ran to the creature's side, knelt, and cradled its ghastly head. For some reason, she was crying— probably with fear that she'd be next. Which, of course, she would be.

She was speaking, blathering something that sounded like, "My brave, dear friend—Lord Grizhni would be so proud of you!"

The dmeon's dimming eyes were fixed upon her face. It croaked softly and died.

The bemusement that had held Commander Kronil motionless throughout this inexplicable scene now vanished, and he resumed his advance. The woman raised her tearstained face to glare at him. Her look of hatred changed to alarm as he lifted his blade. She rose and backed away, eyes shifting to and fro in search of a weapon, escape, or rescue. Her second protector, the nameless Lanthian, was hemmed in by Guardsmen and fighting desperately. She might expect no assistance from that quarter. The only weapons at hand were the stones underfoot. Stooping, she seized a rock and hurled it. The missile bounced harmlessly off his chest, and a bark of laughter escaped Commander Kronil. The woman turned to run, and he rushed to block her escape. The gash in his thigh was beginning to make itself felt, and Kronil did not care to pursue his prey about the chamber. Best to end the matter quickly. And so he would have done, but for a stroke of the cruelest misfortune.

The far end of the great chamber was all at once alive with White Demons. They were pouring into the room by way of the tunnel through which the Guardsmen had entered only a few minutes earlier. They were fresh, they were vigorous, and all of them were armed. With them came Grizhni's son, now clearly less quarry than hunter. He had followed the invading humans to this chamber, and the volume of his troops suggested that he had acquired reinforcements en route. Young Grizhni uttered a fluting command. The musical humming of his followers rose in response, and they charged.

All thought of finishing Lady Grizhni was driven from Kronil's mind. Shouting, he strove to marshal his tiring men. Such efforts were in vain. The energy and sheer numbers of the White Demons proved irresistible, and the Guardsmen were swiftly overwhelmed. The creatures plied their rocks, stalactites, and stolen javelins with lunatic zeal. They were everywhere, hordes of them, and the sight of their slain kinsmen piled up in lightless heaps at the various exits clearly increased their ire. The melodies riding the heavy air were dark. The blows of stone and steel were placed to kill, and despite their expertise, the Ducal Guardsmen were as so much cattle. Commander Kronil was forced to witness his squadron destroyed man by man. The soldiers fell, ignominiously battered. Only Guardsmen Lhorno, Dreevid, and Krufaure, in response to the commands of their leader, managed to fight their way out backward by way of the exit they had so gallantly defended; and even then, it was impossible to guess whether they would ultimately reach safety. Commander Kronil had not the leisure to speculate, for his immediate concerns were pressing. Young Grizhni, together with the anonymous Lanthian gentleman, had obviously singled the Commander out as an object of particular detestation. The thrust of Grizhni's stolen javelin, and the strokes of the other's stolen sword came without surcease and without the slightest regard for fair play. In addition, the Grizhni woman was standing off to one side, plaguing the Commander with damnably well-aimed rocks. Despite all this, Kronil might have dealt with his enemies had it not been for the perfidy of the White Demons. Having massacred the underlings, the creatures now turned their attention to the Commander. They clustered around him in a great, luminous mob, and their hateful music scalded his ears. Kronil hacked and slashed to no avail. The creatures crowded close, trilling like giant white crickets. As he lifted his sword to strike, someone—or something—grabbed his arm from behind. Kronil was yanked off balance. The sword was snatched from his grasp and the helmet from his head. Thus unprotected, he was open to the blows of his enemies. A rock grasped in a lucent fist glanced the back of his skull, and internal explosions blasted his mind. Kronil crumpled, descending into darkness.

His oblivion could not have lasted long, but when he awoke, the battle was over. Kronil was lying on his side. He ached all over and his head was splitting. When he attempted to move, he swiftly discovered that his wrists had been pinioned behind his back and his ankles were likewise bound. Nearby he could hear the murmur of conversation. Kronil's mind was in adequate working order, battered pate notwithstanding. No need for his enemies to realize as yet that he had regained consciousness. Their unguarded remarks might prove instructive. Best to maintain pretenses a little while longer.

The Commander raised his lids a fraction and ventured a surreptitious glance. He found that he shared the floor with a host of corpses, both human and demonic. He saw no wounded. Presumably the injured demons had been removed to some other place to undergo their own unnatural medical treatments, if such a term applied. As for his own men—there were no wounded. Here and there throughout the room circulated small parties of White Demons, who seemed to search for signs of life among the fallen. But the pallid forms that they examined were for the most part still and utterly lightless. Only a few feet distant sprawled the body of the hirsute creature whose devotion to its mistress had afforded such inconvenience. A group had gathered about that corpse. Grizhni's son was there, together with his mother and the anonymous Lanthian whose identity Kronil felt himself on the very verge of recollecting. With the humans stood several White Demons. A conversation was in progress, most of it incomprehensible, but some of it conducted in Lanthian. Kronil listened intently and managed to catch the human portion of the exchange.

"What did you say to them, Terrs?" It was the man speaking.

"I told them that the leader of the Guardsmen must be executed," Grizhni's son answered, with no change of expression.

The listening Kronil smiled grimly to himself. He had guessed as much. Now it remained to be seen whether these over-grown maggots would have the nerve to go through with it. Despite the defeat of his squadron, Commander Kronil main-tained the most sovereign contempt for his alien opponents.

"Unnecessary," the man observed. "The Guardsmen have been defeated and destroyed. It would be cruel and pointless to kill the lone survivor."

"He is not the lone survivor," the youth replied. "Three of his followers escaped."

So Lhorno, Dreevid, and Krufaure had made it out, had they? Good. Krufaure could be trusted to persuade his Grace to order another attack. And the next time, with any luck, these accursed caverns would be wiped clean of all life. This thought afforded Kronil considerable comfort.

"He can't harm you now, Terrs."

"Cannot harm us? I do not undestand you, Fennahar. Look around you." The quality of the youth's voice changed. It was no longer cold, composed, or indifferent. Suddenly he sounded as young as he actually was, filled with pain and almost bewil-dered hatred. "Look at the dead kinsmen—how many of them? How many innocent sacrifices to the human lust for blood? How many of the harmless, the harmonious, slaughtered for the sake of one man's idle dreams? And how much more shall we endure if we do not resist, if we do not prove our own strength? *Look at the dead, Fennahar, and tell me these human creatures cannot harm us!*"

Grizhni's widow mumbled something in a low voice, too low for Kronil to make out the words. Stealing a glance at her from under his drooping lids, he saw the tears coursing down her cheeks. He could not understand why. After all, her side had won, hadn't it? For the present.

"We have to do it, Mother," the youth asserted in somewhat softened tones. "And once our home is out of danger, we shall return to the Vardrul ways of peace and kindness."

"If you remember them," replied the woman.

"That man killed Nyd, Mother."

She did not reply. At this point the White Demons, who had conferred quietly among themselves, turned to Grizhni's son. An exchange of musical, incomprehensible remarks followed, at the conclusion of which Lady Grizhni translated, ostensibly for Fennahar's benefit, but actually for Kronil's as well, "The Lesser Patriarchs and Matriarchs of the clans declare themselves unwilling to commit violence upon the person of the captive Guardsmen." She appeared surprised, and perhaps somewhat relieved.

"A little inconsistent, aren't they?" Fennahar inquired. "They just wiped out an entire squadron."

"They were defending themselves, and the Guardsmen were armed. But this is a different matter. They will not raise weapons against a bound and helpless being. They say they will not mark his flesh: They would consider it disharmonious — that is, immoral."

Kronil experienced a surge of fresh hope. It was as he had suspected. These creatures were soft, weak, and stupid. They hadn't the sense or the guts to kill their enemies when they had the chance. Incredible though it was, there was a chance he'd get out of this alive. And if he did so, he'd return one day soon to teach the White Demons the fatal impracticality of their scruples.

"Are they likely to stand firm on that?" Fennahar inquired.

"Beyond doubt," the woman assured him.

Kronil was torn between relief and profound disdain. There was no further need to sham a swoon. Raising himself to a sitting position, he deliberately sought out the eyes of Grizhni's son.

Young Grizhni returned the insolent regard without apparent emotion. Impossible to guess what went on behind those expressionless black eyes of his. "We shall commit no violence," the youth replied at last, and Kronil experienced a prickle of renewed uneasiness. "Fortunately, there is another way."

They bore him along a maze of passageways, carrying him like a sack of meal — no doubt afraid of the havoc a true man might wreak if they went so far as to untie his ankles, the Commander reflected. The touch of those boneless tentacles was abhorrent beyond belief. If he survived this experience, he would spend a few dakkles in one of the bathhouses and scrub himself raw. Only then would he feel free of contamination.

The prospect of bathing seemed less remote than anticipated when they came at last to a subterranean river — a wide, clear stream that raced swiftly over the glowing rocks. Kronil stiffened within his captors' grasp. Did they intend to fling him into the water, bound hand and foot, to watch as he drowned?

Such fears were groundless. A boat waited upon the bank—a crude, flimsy little affair of waterproofed woven covering stretched over a lightweight frame. The craft, obviously designed to carry a single occupant, contained one narrow seat to which the Demons securely bound Commander Kronil. There was no paddle. So they were going to set him adrift, eh? Their mistake, as they would discover—unless of course they planned to punch holes in the bottom of the boat.

They did not. In silence they launched their prisoner. A moment before the boat left the shore, Grizhni's son addressed the Commander succinctly. "Our weaons will not touch you. The river's current will carry you far from us, and you will not return."

"You'd better pray that I don't, boy," was all the reply that Kronil permitted himself. It would not do to incense the creatures now—not when deliverance seemed so close at hand.

When he returned to the caves at the head of an expanded force of Ducal Guards—when the White Demons had been exterminated—that would be the time to discuss this matter at length with Fal Grizhni's son.

The boat slid into the water, and the current took her at once. Kronil could not forbear looking back over his shoulder to shout to the impassive figures upon the shore, "You'll be seeing more of the Guardsmen! That promise is gold!"

If they heard, if they understood, they gave no sign. They were receding swiftly. The current was strong, and soon they were far behind him. Kronil threw back his head, laughing aloud, and the sound echoed at length. He was safe. He was all but free. No doubt the witless Demons imagined that he would drift forever, bound and helpless, to lose himself in the hideous labyrinth of their caverns, ultimately perishing of hunger and terror. The fools! The silly, girlish, weak, sniveling simpletons! Obviously they didn't know men in general, or Commander Kronil in particular. The knots that bound him were good ones, tight and secure. But there were no knots known to Man or Demon that could hold Kronil forever. Before long he would work himself free. There was no means whereby to steer the boat, so he would have to swim to shore, but that was no great obstacle—there was hardly a Lanthian alive who didn't know how to swim. And once ashore, would he manage

to find his way to an exit? Most certainly—he need only follow
the river itself, which undoubtedly issued from the caverns at
some point or other. But the Demons—the mush-minded Demons—hadn't thought of that. Smiling, Kronil applied himself
to the fibrous cords.

It was not easy work. The rough cords, slightly swollen with
moisture, were all but impossible to budge. The knots were
well placed and unreachable. *Almost.* The Demons, obviously
unfamiliar with the niceties involved in binding sentient
enemies, had thoughtlessly fastened one knot just within reach
of the prisoner's questing fingers. By dint of exertion that was
rapidly chafing his wrists bloody, Kronil was able to pull at
the tangled cord. He could feel it starting to loosen. Soon this
knot would be conquered, and then he would proceed to the
next.

So absorbed was the Commander in his task that he scarcely
noted the waning of the rock-light. The tunnel through which
the river flowed was getting dimmer. The current that swept
the boat forward was increasing in strength and speed as the
light failed. So gradual were the changes that Kronil managed
to overlook them. At last, however, the deepening shadows
caught his attention. He raised his head as the boat rounded a
sharp bend, and in that instant the rock-light vanished altogether. The boat leaped forward on the current and a moment
later, Kronil was rushing down the river in total darkness.
There was something about the blackness—the oppressive
heat—and above all the sense of an unspeakably threatening
alien unknown—that was familiar. For a moment Kronil was
confused, and then he remembered. Seventeen years earlier,
when he had accompanied Haik Ulf into that dreadful subterranean chamber in Grizhni Palace—his Preeminence's last refuge—it had felt like this. Very much like this. There had been
darkness, confused terror, and a sense of helplessness that only
killing could alleviate. What was it that Grizhni had threatened
seconds before he died? A night filled with terror, and a night
without end. Like this one? Kronil shuddered within his bonds,
then rallied. Now was not the time to lose his nerve. What's
more, there was no reason. The light had gone, but it would
come back. Even if it didn't, there was nothing to worry about.
He didn't need light to loosen the cords, he didn't need light
to reach the shore.

Kronil reapplied himself to his task. He had succeeded in

untying the first of the knots when a distant rumbling up ahead caught his attention. Thunder? A storm above? Was he nearing an exit? The rumbling increased in volume as the boat advanced, and rapidly grew to a crashing roar that was too constant and unvarying to be mistaken for thunder. And Kronil, stalwart soldier though he was, could not suppress a thrill of terror as he finally identified the source of the noise.

A cataract.

A huge one, by the sound of it. Somewhere not far ahead the river plunged over the edge of a cliff, and the boat was headed straight for perdition. The Commander, now aware of his peril, struggled violently but succeeded only in flaying the skin off his wrists. The cords that bound him remained firmly in place.

The boat, held fast in the grip of the current, was now skimming forward so swiftly that the breeze cooled Kronil's perspiring face—a pleasant sensation, under other circumstances. He could feel the increasing turbulence under the bow, and the roar of the rushing water filled the blind world. A snarl escaped him, and the ferocity of his struggles increased. His hands, and the cords that bound his wrists, were warm and sticky with blood.

Relative calm descended on Commander Kronil a split second before his craft shot over the edge of the cataract known to the Vardruls as the Invisible Falls, that plummeted some hundred and fifty feet in total darkness. As the bow first dipped sickeningly beneath him, one last coherent thought flashed across his mind; the White Demons were not nearly as soft as he'd imagined.

Chapter Ten

❧❧❧❧

In the wake of the news of the squadron's massacre Duke Povon lasped into despondency, for his burdens were great almost beyond bearing. He had lost his finest Guardsmen, including the Commander, and for what? Fal Grizhni's son still lived. So did the young devil's mother. Also alive were most of the grisly White Demons and doubtless they hungered for vengeance, after the insensate malignity of their kind. There were plots afoot, Povon was sure of it, and the knowledge preyed upon his spirits night and day. Already his enemies had attempted his life within the confines of his own bedchamber. Certainly it was to be expected that they would try again, and for that reason the Ducal Palace was guarded like a vault. No stranger was permitted to set foot upon the ducal moorings, much less enter the building. In the past fortnight three trespassers had been apprehended and even now Duke Povon pondered their fate. He was strongly tempted to execute all three despite their collective pleas of innocence, but such a course would surely expose him to the censure of malcontents and enemies of the state, who would seize any opportunity to malign their Duke. It never seemed to occur to such rabble that their much-abused freedom of speech was enjoyed upon ducal sufferance alone. Thus it was, Povon reflected, for the merciful, en-lightened ruler—his patience and tolerance were exploited by his foes! His greatest virtues were turned against him! The Lanthian mob understood nothing but cruelty. A show of force would command the respect of the Commons, but Povon hesi-tated, deterred by the example of his ancestor Duke Braizeiani Dil Shonnet, who had imposed a tax upon the public raftsmen's water-time and been fed to purple crustaceans for his pains.

The Lanthian Commons were a vicious, unpredictable lot. Equally vicious, unpredictable, and restive at the protracted betrothal of his cherished daughter was the Keldhar of Gard Lammis, who now demanded immediate repayment of the loan used to finance construction of the Finzifoyl Folly. Repayment at this time would be more than inconvenient. Implicit within the terms of the Keldhar's correspondence had been the suggestion that settlement of the loan might be postponed indefinitely—perhaps permanently—by means of the intervention of the Duchess of Lanthi Ume upon behalf of her husband. The Keldhaam Gnuxia's cooperation was significant, almost invaluable. Matrimony represented the course of greatest expediency, but for once the Duke hesitated. Keldhaam Gnuxia—forever? With no escape? The prospect was almost unbearable. And yet the alternative—bankruptcy, domestic discontent, public humiliation—was equally unacceptable. The solution to the dilemma was fairly obvious. A successful military strike against the City of Gard Lammis would solve many difficulties once and for all. And Duke Povon, while not a warlike leader, gave some thought to the possibility of busying giddy minds with foreign quarrels. An analysis of the Lanthian financial, political, and military circumstances soon convinced him of the impracticality of this scheme, whereupon Povon considered other means. Quickly he was forced to rule out the possibility of assassination. The elimination of the Keldhar of Gard Lammis would not eliminate the debt of Lanthi Ume. The removal of the Keldhaam was a solution equally ineffectual. Her sudden death would raise certain embarrassing questions. In any event, the Keldhar had another daughter, reputedly as masterful as Gnuxia herself. Bribery of the Keldhar and his ministers was infeasible, and no grounds for blackmail were known to exist.

Wandering off into wilder mental terrain, Duke Povon contemplated self-slaughter as a final solution. It was sweet to dream of the peace, repose, and dignity of the sepulchre, but the means of entry were uniformly unpalatable. The mental images of knives, poison flasks, and hempen nooses that might facilitate transition raised cold sweat upon the ducal brow, bringing horror that could only be alleviated by recourse to the Moon Dream of Uhanna. Povon had a tiny vial of essence, his by courtesy of Beskot Kor Malifon. So far he had managed to conceal the acquisition by attaching the vial to a fine chain worn around his waist under his clothes. For the moment, this subterfuge would serve. After the marriage, of course—Povon shuddered and hastily brought forth the vial. Such a little, insignificant container! What an inadequate quantity it held! Still, he was lucky to have anything at all. What he did possess must be used with great caution, and very sparingly. Following a quick surveillance of the empty lamp-lit chamber—the second best bedchamber in the palace, temporarily graced during the repair and renovation of Povon's own scorched apartment—the Duke unstoppered the vial and treated himself to a tiny sip of the Moon Dream.

The effects of even that minute quantity were almost instantaneous. Povon's nocturnal megrims abated at once. His tensions eased, his spirits rose, the sense of almost tangible oppression lightened, and once again he was able to face the future without dismay. The immediate future, in fact, could be contemplated with positive pleasure, for with the morning came the Parnis Regatta, at whose opening ceremonies his Grace customarily presided. This year, in light of the recent attempt upon his life, Povon had considered eschewing the public exposure that the Regatta entailed. It was clear, however, that the dignity of the House of Dil Shonnet demanded his presence. Moreover, Povon was excessively fond of boat races and had already placed several wagers. Therefore a conference with his closest advisors, in conjunction with a surreptitious swallow of the Moon Dream, had quickly persuaded the Duke that a few simple precautions would ensure his absolute safety. The ornate float from which he would address his ceremonial remarks would not be towed into position at the mouth of Parnis Lagoon until late in the afternoon of the day preceding the Regatta. For the rest of that day and throughout the night, the float would be closely guarded by ducal troops under the leadership of the newly appointed Commander Krufaure. Any Lanthian caught entering the prohibited area would be cut down by Guardsmen, no questions asked. In the early morning, prior to the arrival of the Duke, the float would be rigorously inspected both above and below water for explosives, incendiary devices, infernal machines, and similar undesirable appurtenances. The Duke's own circuitous route to the lagoon was to be held a secret. He would travel in the midst of a contingent of Guardsmen, and once he took his place aboard the float, the soldies would range themselves protectively about the perimeter. In this wise the Duke of Lanthi Ume might demonstrate his courage and patriotism in relative safety. It seemed the best possible solution to the dilemma, and he had the Moon Dream to thank for inspiration. And the generosity of Beskot Kor Malifon to thank for the Moon Dream itself. What an understanding nature had Beskot! How loyally he tended to his ruler's needs! Would he perhaps be willing to do so again in the near future? For Povon's supply of essence was growing very low indeed. He would broach the subject to Beskot upon the morrow. Truly, the Parnis Regatta would be well worth attending!

Povon bestowed a last fond glance upon the tiny vial, stowed it away out of sight, climbed into his second-best bed, and smilingly composed himself for slumber.

The day of the Regatta dawned bright and balmy. The skies overhead were gratifyingly blue and the morning sunlight bounced on the dancing waves of Parnis Lagoon. At the center of the lagoon rose the Victory of Nes, sacrosanct isle of the Select. Mysterious and brooding of aspect, Cognitive in origin, the island customarily eyed askance by the citizens of Lanthi Ume today appeared unwontedly accessible, almost sociable.

The water was crowded with boats. They had been coming in throughout the past three days, for the Parnis Regatta drew contestants from as far away as Hurba. Now a multitude of vessels floated upon the lagoon, assembled there for the Grand Promenade with which the festivities traditionally commenced. During the promenade, the boats would complete three leisurely circuits of the lagoon to the accompaniment of music composed for the occasion; and the owners of those crafts adjudged particularly noteworthy in their respective categories would receive reward at the hands of the Duke. There were of course hundreds of varied sailng vessels, dombuli, sendilli, and knife-prowed racing jistylli, some of them of innovative design. It was noted, for example, that the twelve oars of former champion Gwem Feeno's killer jistyllis *High Cognition* had been lengthened to startling proportions, and the effect of this alteration upon the speed of the craft was the subject of feverish speculation among racing enthusiasts. The small boats were without exception freshly cleaned and painted, polished, sparkling, plentifully bedecked with colored pennants, streamers, and rosettes. Interesting a spectacle though they presented, they were nonetheless eclipsed by the glory of the great glittering venerises,

among which glided the Duke's own *Sublimity,* an all-too-famil-
iar sight to most Lanthians. Impossible to overlook was Kor
Malifon's superb *Golden Exaltation,* notable for her gilded
masts and cloth-of-gold sails. Cru Beffel's macabre *Stroke of
Midnight* with her sable sails sprinkled with silver stars and
crescent moon, skeletal figurehead, and silver fittings was there
as well, together with several others of only slightly lesser
ostentation. In the wake of the looming venerises trailed smaller
vessels nearly as elaborate, and in their own way more remarkable. These belonged to the special category of exhibition boats
known as Caprices, built to embody their creators' wildest
flights of fancy. The Caprices, designed to astonish, vied in
bizarre exaggeration. The resulting confections, while utterly
useless and in some cases just barely buoyant, were nonetheless
marvels of imaginative excess. One of the new ones, Juf
Lohnin's *Nest of Vipers,* was a mind-searing monstrosity carved
all over in the likeness of a vast, writhing, convoluted knot of
a thousand crimson and gold serpents, each creature perfectly
sculpted down to the last detail of tiny scales and lidless glass
eyes. The sails were mottled like snakeskin, and the banners
bore a serpentine device. Almost as noteworthy was Lord Ress
Drenneress's *Enchanted Forest,* whose three twisted masts supported a spreading canopy of limbs and branches, each branch
clothed in beaten copper leaves enameled bright spring-green.
Needless to say, the masts supported no sails. *Enchanted
Forest,* topheavy to the point of danger, was propelled by galley
slaves. Her movements were slow and a stiff wind would probably have capsized her. Such matters were irrelevant, however.
Consideration of mundane utility held no place in Caprice con-
noisseurship, indeed carried the stigma of vulgarity. Artistry
was all.

Spectators jammed the banks of Parnis Lagoon. A few black-
robed figures could be spied patrolling the Victory Pier on the
island. Even the grave savants of the Select were not wholly
immune to the lure of the famous Regatta. Desirable locations
commanding a good view of the course were hotly contested
by the rowdier citizens. Early though it was, several fistfights
had already broken out to be quelled by the civic Watch. The
Ducal Guards, preoccupied with their vigil about the ducal
float, disdained to involve themselves in Commons altercations,
and thus a number of Watchmen were mauled by the volatile
Lanthians.

Most fortunate of citizens were those possessed of property overlooking the lagoon, particularly in the vicinity of the ducal float that marked the starting point and finish line of the various boat races. Such vantage points commanded inordinate short-term rental fees. Curiously enough, the Vezhni Tower, situated at the junction of the Lureis Canal and Parnis Lagoon and directly overlooking the ducal float, was unoccupied. Lord Trune Vezhni, absent from Lanthi Ume upon unspecified business, had not succeeded in finding a tenant prior to his departure. For months the tower had remained locked and empty. And so it would have continued, had not a stranger appeared at dawn the day of the Regatta.

The stranger, a bent and seemingly ancient figure, was swathed in a shabby robe of mud-colored wool. A drooping, bedraggled hat concealed his hair and shaded his visage. In the weak gray light of early morning, his features were nearly invisible. A ragged muffler, carelessly wound, concealed as if by chance the lower portion of his face. From beneath the muffler straggled wisps of a white beard slightly streaked with red. A careful observer might have noticed that the white hair was caked and stiffened as if with flour paste; the red strands were natural. The body hunched beneath the loose brown robe was brawny, and the hands that protruded from the threadbare sleeves were those of a man in his prime. Beside the stranger walked a short, solidly constructed female attired in a kirtle of drab linsey-woolsy. Her hair was bound beneath a knotted kerchief and she carried a bucket filled with rags and scrub brushes. Her appearance was that of an ordinary charwoman. But again, a careful observer might have noted the faint smudges of charcoal beneath eyes and cheekbones, which in the dim light lent a spurious maturity to a very young face.

The area around Vezhni Tower was all but deserted when the two arrived. The crowds had not yet begun to assemble for the Regatta, although they would begin to do so very shortly. Not far away a band of bored, sleepy Guardsmen lounged about the ducal float, where they had been stationed throughout the night. But the bulk of the tower interposed itself between Guardsmen and street. The soldiers did not note the approach of the strangers, did not see the old man hobble to the padlocked back entrance, and could not appreciate the deft authority with which he picked the lock. His companion, however, was more perceptive.

"Nice work, your lordship," she observed with the air of an expert.

"The skill of a locksmith is but one of the essential attributes of the successful bravo, my princess," replied Whurm Didnis fondly. Removing the padlock from its staple, he pushed wide the portal and they walked into Vezhni Tower with the confidence of legitimate inhabitants. Didnis closed the door behind them, dropping the bar into place. They stood in a wide, shadowy, unfurnished foyer. A few stray rays of gray light struggling in through chinks between the closed and barred shutters provided the only illumination, but it was sufficient to guide them to the narrow staircase that spiraled its way to the top of the tower. Didnis abandoned his artificial infirmity, Josky abandoned her bucket, and they began to ascend. The stairs led them past the first five spacious stories to the point at which the building narrowed to a slender, thrusting spike that accommodated but one modest circular chamber per floor. Another several minutes of climbing brought them to the stale-smelling attic. At the center of the attic a ladder reached from floor to a trapdoor in the ceiling. Didnis clambered up the ladder, opened the trap without difficulty, and scrambed out onto the observation platform at the top of Vezhni Tower. Josky followed.

Although Vezhni Tower was surpassed in height and grandeur by many other Lanthian constructions, the view from its summit was nonetheless exhilarating. Father and daughter gazed out over the waist-high guardrail that ringed the platform. Around and beneath them spread the great city, its streets and canals nearly deserted—a quiet aspect of Lanthi Ume glimpsed by few of her inhabitants. To the east the pink light was just beginning to glint off polished domes and tiles, bringing their brilliant colors to life. But most of Lanthi Ume still lay veiled in the mists of dawn. Here and there the lantern light glowed orange at window or anonymous doorway; all else slumbered in vague gray shadow.

At the foot of the tower the Lureis Canal emptied into Parnis Lagoon. Whurm Didnis pointed down at the junction, where a square bulk loomed dark against the silvery water. "There, my sweet Josky, right there below us is moored the ducal float. Do you see it?"

"I'm not blind, your lordship," his daughter replied with an impatient grimace.

"Notice the elevated platform atop the float, crowned with the throne from which his Grace will observe the festivities."

"I'm not a *baby,* your lordship!"

"Consider, my princess. From that vantage point his Grace enjoys an unobstructed view of most of the race course. Conversely, the citizens gathered upon the banks of the lagoon will enjoy an unobstructed view of his Grace. In this wise the Duke demonstrates a tolerable comprehension of the duties and obligations that are the inevitable concomitants of noble rank and privilege—"

"I know, Dad. You've *told* me."

"You will also note, I daresay, the brief expanse of clear and empty air that alone stands between ourselves and the ducal float."

"I *know,* your lordship! I'm not *stupid,* you know!"

"My Josky is the cleverest girl in all the world."

"Then give me some credit. Why are those soldiers poking around the float like that?"

"Ah." Whurm Didnis chuckled warmly. "They search the float for explosives. Perhaps they deem it a wise precaution."

Josky giggled.

"Now, my princess," the bravo continued, "for the sake of your continuing education, you have been entrusted with the care and preparation of our weapon. It is a grave responsibility, but I do not doubt your competence. Now comes my darling's chance to shine, and make her father proud!"

"Pooh, it's too easy." Despite the disclaimer, Josky appeared pleased and consequential. Smiling slightly, she hoisted her kirtle and detached several articles that hung attached to a concealed belt. "I always knew these stupid skirts must be good for something." Swiftly she put the pieces together, fitting small stiff bow to wooden stock; pulling the lever that turned the cogwheel and hooked rod, which in turn caught and pulled the bowstring into a trigger-release notch; and arming the assembled crossbow with a square-headed quarrel. "There. Finished."

Whurm Didnis inspected the weapon. "Perfect, my princess. Swift, efficient, and faultless. As I expected."

"Now what, your lordship?"

"Now we wait. Presently our noble quarry will take his place upon the float directly below us. We observe him at our leisure. We take careful aim. A touch upon the trigger and the bolt flies. The Duke of Lanthi Ume falls, a new Duke takes his place, and the House of Whurm Didnis alters the course of history."

"Will we be famous?"

"In certain circles."

"We should be. We're the best, we are."

"My Josky's heritage manifests itself in her warlike valor. You are courageous as your departed mother, my child, and higher praise than that I cannot bestow."

"What was she like, your lordship?"

"A fiery spirit, my princess. High mettle, dauntless hardihood, a noble heart. Also, the handiest woman with a dagger I've ever known. And you are made in her image."

"Thanks, your lordship." Evidently seeking to disguise her heartfelt filial emotion, Josky gazed down at the ducal float. After a moment she inquired, "How long before his Grace turns up?"

"A couple of hours, perhaps more."

"You mean we just have to sit up here for hours, doing nothing?"

"This platform affords us a splendid view. We shall watch the boats assemble for the Regatta."

"Boats are *boring*, Dad!"

"There are many who would pay dearly for this vantage point."

"Well they can have it for free, as far as I'm concerned. It's boring. Anyway, how can I think of boats when my belly's empty? I've had no breakfast, you know."

Whurm Didnis was smiling as he propped the crossbow against the guardrail. "You do not suppose that I would allow my darling to suffer the pangs of hunger? What kind of a father would I be? Behold, Lady Josky—I have provided for us both." So saying, the bravo reached into one of his capacious pockets to bring forth a napkin-wrapped bundle which he unfolded and spread out on the roof. The napkin contained a small loaf of raisin bread, a slab of cheese, apples, pears, and two small iced cakes. Another pocket yielded a jug of ale and a bunch of grapes.

"Breakfast!"

"A picnic, my child. A picnic at sunrise."

"It's beautiful. What's in those little cake things?"

"Almond paste, I believe."

"Oh, suPREME!"

"Fall to, my lady. Fall to."

They seated themselves and ate their breakfast as the world around them awakened. The chill of night gave way to the mild, humid warmth of a sunlit spring morning. The waters of canal and lagoon shimmered beneath a brilliant sky, the screeching seabirds took wing, and the crowds began to gather upon the banks of Parnis Lagoon. They came slowly at the beginning. The first of them, eager to claim the best sites on the shore, arrived almost upon the heels of Didnis and Lady Josky. A few more came, and their voices rose gaily to the ears of the bravo and his daughter. Within minutes the trickle increased to a steady flow and the Lanthians were pouring in from all directions, thousands of them laden with cloth-covered baskets of food, blankets to sit upon, and wide straw hats to ward off the sun. To the babble of human voices and the cries of the birds was added the plash of oars as the last of the boats came gliding into Parnis Lagoon to take their places for the Grand Promenade. The inevitable hawkers appeared, with their amulets, trinkets, toys, scarves, sweetmeats, and their portable braziers. The fragrance of grilling meat soon mingled with the smells of brackish water, smoke, spices, refuse, and humanity. Close behind the hawkers came the jugglers, acrobats, rat-duckers, beggars, and buskers whose antics lent the proceedings such an air of jollity. And presently the banks of the lagoon were packed solid with spectators. The only space left unoccupied was to be found beneath the great canvas awning, painted and scalloped, that shaded a stand of cushioned bleachers rising to the left of the ducal float.

"There are seats left," Josky noted, pointing. "Why are those fools sitting on the ground when there are seats?"

"Because they know their place, my treasure," replied Whurm Didnis. "Those bleachers are reserved for the use of the quality—members of the great Houses of Lanthi Ume. You observe the colors draped across the various blocks of seats? There's peach and ivory for Dule Parnis, mauve for Wate Basef, amber for Gless Vallage, rose and gray for Rion Vassarion, and so on and so forth. The needs of the quality must be considered. That is only fitting. Someday soon the colors of Didnis shall mingle with all the rest."

"What *are* the colors of Didnis, your lordship?"

"Alas, my child, the colors of our noble House are lost in the mists of time."

Josky's face fell.

"No matter," the bravo consoled her. "Being noble, we are entitled to bear arms and colors. Being Didnis, we are fearless, enterprising, and fit to choose our own emblems. What colors shall be ours, my Josky? It is up to you to decide for all time."

Josky brightened. "Anything I want?"

"Anything."

"Forever?"

"Word of a Lanthian noble."

"Well, then." Josky considered. "I guess—silver. That's the color of a blade. And red is the color of blood. So that's right for us, isn't it? Silver and red for the House of Whurm Didnis."

"Silver and red it is, my darling! And someday those colors will win renown from Lanthi Ume to the shores of the Sea of Ice. Just wait and see."

"I know, your lordship. Someday we'll be rich and famous like we deserve. Especially when we get that idiot Lord Nobody in our pocket once and for all. In the meantime, where's that Duke?"

As if in answer to her query, the musicians stationed below struck up, and the notes of a march wafted to the top of Vezhni Tower.

"He comes, my princess, he comes!"

Josky sprang to the guardrail and leaned far out into space.

"Careful, Lady Josky," Didnis warned. "This tower is supposed to be vacant, remember. Do not call attention to our presence."

"Sorry, your lordship." Josky drew back to hunker down behind the railing, but her excitement precluded professional stillness. She was bouncing gently on her haunches and two spots of color burned on her cheeks. "Look, there he is, getting out of his sedan chair! In plain sight and easy range! Let's take him, Dad!" She grabbed for the crossbow.

Whurm Didnis gently pried the weapon from her grasp. "Not yet, my child. Not quite yet. You've the fire of a true thoroughbred, but you must learn patience. Wait a little."

"But *why,* Dad? There he is! Now's our chance!"

"Ah, the impetuosity of youth! Now listen, my Josky, and learn. It is true that our quarry's in range, and it is possible that a well-aimed shot could bring him down this instant, but there are certain disadvantages to that scheme. In the first place, the Duke walks in the midst of his friends and attendants. They cluster closely around him. The tall, majestic woman at his side nearly shields him from our view, even situated above as we are."

"So what? We could pick him off anyway. I know we could."

"Secondly, he is moving. Observe the briskness with which he advances upon the float. Note the uncharacteristic alertness of his demeanor, the erratic unpredictability and nervousness of his movements. Plainly he is aware of danger, correspondingly unquiet, and therefore by no means the easiest of targets."

"We don't need easy targets, we don't."

"Finally, his Grace is at the moment the cynosure of all eyes— "

"The what?"

"Everybody's looking at him and if we dispatch him now, the source of the shot will be fairly obvious, thus lessening our chances of unhindered departure."

"I don't care, your lordship! I'm not afraid! Let's do it!"

"Child, child." Whurm Didnis shook his head smilingly. "Your courage and elan are superb, but you must learn a little wisdom. Now listen to your father. It never pays to incur unnecessary risk. I know that is hard for you to believe, but when you are older you will find that a modicum of caution is apt to extend your lifespan by decades."

"Caution—pooh! What about fame, Dad? What about glory?"

"One must remain alive in order to enjoy them. Look down, my princess. The Guardsmen now asssist his Grace from Vezhni moorings out onto the ducal float. In but a moment the Duke will ascend to his elevated throne, before which he will stand to address the crowd and signal the start of the Grand Promenade. The music will swell, the boats will move, and the crowd's attention will shift to the vessels. And in that instant, the standing Duke will offer a clear and absolutely unobstructed target for the single shot that circumstances allow us. Moreover,

in the general confusion the origin of the attack will be unclear,
and we shall take unhurried leave. Now tell me, are all these
benefits not worth an instant's delay?"

"Oh, I suppose so," Josky conceded. "But I can hardly sit
still, your lordship!"

"Just a moment longer, my lady. One brief moment."

Down below, the eyes of Lanthi Ume turned to the ducal
float as Duke Povon ascended to his throne. The citizens grew
quiet in anticipation of their ruler's address. The hawkers ceased
their bawling, the buskers their singing, the beggars their
plaints. Conversation died, and the silence that fell over Parnis
Lagoon was broken only by the cries of unregenerate seabirds
overhead. This civic deference was largely a hollow courtesy,
for it was clear that the Duke's speech would be inaudible to
the majority of the spectators massed upon the banks. Experienced a public speaker though he was, Duke Povon could not
hope to project his voice to the far reaches of Parnis Lagoon.
His words would be heard by those in his fairly immediate
vicinity—by his friends, family members, and Guardsmen
grouped about the float; by the velvet-and-brocade aristocracy
lounging at ease beneath the great canvas awning to the left,
and by a group of somewhat lesser distinction for whom some
space had been reserved at the right. He would also be heard
by observers stationed at the windows and upon the roofs of a
few surrounding buildings, including the two at the summit of
Vezhni Tower. Empty courtesy notwithstanding, the silence of
the Lanthians was an encouraging sign, for it suggested the
citizens' continuing regard for their ruler, which in turn
suggested the success of Duke Povon's systematic efforts to
conceal from the Commons the true source of their economic
and social afflictions. Such deceptions had grown more difficult
to maintain of late, but apparently the Commons yet remained
ignorantly loyal.

The Duke stepped out to the edge of the platform. The
cushioned throne with its tasseled canopy stood several paces
behind him. No covering interposed itself between the ducal
head and the sky. Povon stood exposed to the eyes of all Lanthi
Ume. His demeanor, however, was confident. His stance was
firm and his gaze steady. The uneasiness that had plagued him
throughout the perilous journey from Ducal Palace to Parnis
Lagoon had now vanished, for in this place he felt himself well

protected. The float itself had been thoroughly inspected just minutes prior to his arrival. The construction was solid and free of explosives. All those aboard were trustworthy—the favored few included family members, personal friends, a couple of the city's highest dignitaries, and several Guardsmen of famed prowess, including Commander Krufaure. Additional soldiers had ranged themselves across the Vezhni moorings to guard the approach to the float. Armed ducal agents disguised as ordinary spectators circulated through the crowd. The ducal float was totally secure. Here his Grace need not fear the blast of gunpowder or the sudden appearance of the fanatical, knife-wielding assassin. Here Povon was safe.

The Duke commenced his address. His voice, trained and practiced, rolled out over the water an appreciable distance. He spoke at length of Lanthian pride, Lanthian tradition, Lanthian spirit and solidarity. All around the lagoon the spectators fidgeted and waited for the Grand Promenade to begin.

Atop the tower Lady Josky also fidgeted, but for different reasons. Her bright gaze jumped from the target, to her father, to the crossbow with which Didnis now took aim, and back to the target again. Several times she seemed on the verge of speech, but stifled her utterance. At last she could contain herself no longer, and the words burst out, "Your lordship, let *me* do it!"

"Eh?" Didnis turned to stare in amazement.

"Let *me* take the Duke, Dad! *Please!*"

"My Lady Josquinilliu." Didnis shook his head in mild reproof. "You know better than that. Now we have arrived at the ultimate moment. You must not distract me from my task."

"I thought it was *our* task, your lordship! Aren't we partners? Don't we do everything together?"

"Certainly, my child, and yet you must understand—"

"Don't you think I can handle the crossbow? You trained me yourself and you know I never miss. Don't you *trust* me, Dad?"

"I trust you implicitly, my child, and yet—"

"And yet *what*? If we're partners, if you *really* trust me and aren't just saying that, then you'll give me my chance. You have to, if you mean what you say. Besides, I *want* it, Dad!"

"My darling Josky, I have the highest respect for your abilities—"

"You're not acting like it!"

"I've absolute confidence in you, despite your youth and inexperience—"

"Inexperience—hah! Hah, Dad! What about the time I did Cheevo Gubbs with the Living Wire—all by myself? And what about the time Mad Dog Hubid had you backed against the wall, his knife to your throat, and I skewered him from behind? Where would you have been without me then?"

"Finished, no doubt—"

"That's right. Finished. So you *owe* me, Dad!"

"More than words can express, my princess. And yet this is the most important commission of my entire career, and I cannot help but feel—"

"*Your* career! *Your* commission! *Your* glory! Always everything's *yours*! It isn't fair and I'm sick of it! You don't care anything about me!"

"My darling, that isn't true—"

"Then prove it, your lordship! Let me take my shot at the Duke! I *want* it! I can do it, and *I want it!*"

"My Josky, do not ask me—"

"Oh! Now I see what you think of me!" Josky's face flushed beet-red. Her eyes blazed furiously and she beat her fist upon the guardrail. "I hate you!"

"Please, sweet child—"

"I hate you forever and I'll never forgive you! *Never!*" The angry tears gushed down her cheeks.

Whurm Didnis caved in. "No more!" he implored abjectly. "My darling shall have her desire!"

"Oh, suPREME!" The hot blast of Josky's joy dried the tears from her face almost instantaneously. "I love you, Dad! Give me the crossbow."

Didnis relinquished the weapon with reluctance. "One shot is all you have, my treasure. Aim carefully. Use the railing for support."

"I know, I know!" Steadying herself upon the balustrade, she squinted expertly along the stock of the bow.

"Do not fire until the Duke signals the start of the promenade. He will conclude his remarks very shortly now, so be ready."

"I know, I know. Don't talk, you're making me nervous."

Down below, the Duke orated relentlessly. He spoke of Lanthian history, Lanthian boating, Lanthian competitive spirit.

His listeners rustled, squirmed, coughed, fanned themselves, and munched. And up above, the Lady Josky wondered aloud, "Is that old windbag going to go on jabbering forever?" The prolonged delay was evidently telling on her nerves. She was chewing her lower lip, and a slight tremor occasionally shook the finger that rested on the trigger. "Hurry *up!*" she urged irritably.

"Cool and scientific, my princess," Whurm Didnis advised. "As if it were target practice."

"I know. Would you stop talking? You're as bad as the Duke."

"Aim with precision."

"I've *done* that."

"Squeeze the trigger gently—"

"You're ruining my concentration!"

"There, my darling, I think he's nearly—"

"Finally!" Misinterpreting her father's unfinished remark, Josky clamped down almost spasmodically on the trigger. The released bowstring straightened with a solid thunk and the quarrel sped for the ducal float. Father and daughter remained just long enough to observe the results.

"Missed him!" exclaimed Whurm Didnis.

"Well, you startled me into firing early! Let me take another shot!"

"No time, my princess, no time. Leave the bow and come away."

"Just one more quick one—"

"Not now."

With unwonted firmness Whurm Didnis shepherded his daughter back to the trapdoor. As they went, a confused babble of voices arose from the crowd below. The sound spurred them on their way. Swiftly they lowered themselves through the trap, climbed down the ladder, and began the spiraling descent to canal level. A couple of minutes later they were back in the foyer. Pausing only long enough to collect Josky's bucket of rags and brushes, they hurried to the door through which they had entered, lifted the bar, and peeped out. The street outside was entirely deserted, but on the opposite side of the building, the water side, the urgently inquisitive voices and cries resounded. The bravo and his daughter slipped out of the tower. Didnis removed the padlock from his pocket, replaced it on its

staple, and snapped it shut. This done, the two of them—a
common charwoman and her aged, nondescript companion—
skirted the edge of Vezhni Tower, bypassed neighboring Parnis
Dome, plunged into the walkway running between twin pink
marble mansions, and from thence disappeared into the excited
crowd that roiled on the banks of Parnis Lagoon.

As Duke Povon addressed the Lanthian crowd, he did not
see the crossbow quarrel that shot from the summit of Vezhni
Tower to miss his head by inches. He felt a slight, very brief
disturbance in the air. A swift, tiny breeze kissed his cheek
lightly and was gone. He would have paid the matter no heed
save for the scream of pain that followed an instant later.
Povon's oration broke off at the sound and he glanced down
from his platform to behold Beskot Kor Malifon stretched full
length upon the carpeted boards of the float. Beskot's grazed
shoulder was spotted with blood. A short wicked missile stood
upright, its point buried in the wood a few inches behind the
wounded man's head. Povon's reaction was prompt. "Your
Duke has been attacked!" he proclaimed, and with admirable
agility scrambled down from his exposed perch to seek refuge
in the midst of his faithful Guardsmen. Within a heartbeat the
soldiers had surrounded him to establish a solid wall of flesh
and steel between their master and all possible danger. Safe
behind his living ramparts, Povon squatted in teeth-chattering
terror. Around him the Guardsmen deployed themselves, exchanged information and orders, came and went in small swift-
moving parties. Povon paid no mind. The sturdy barriers that
stood between Duke and dissolution were all that mattered.

The sudden disappearance of his Grace confused the spectators, none of whom had witnessed the shot. The Duke had
descended from his platform, yet the signal for the Grand Promenade had not been given. The boats in the lagoon still lay at
anchor, while the ducal float seethed with incomprehensible
activity. Within seconds the rumors were flying. Presently the
plight of the wounded man was noted by those citizens nearest
the float. The news spread like plague, and a hundred different
interpretations vied for public acceptance. It was said that a
fight had broken out aboard the float. It was said that the Ducal
Guardsmen were in revolt. It was said that one of the great
nobles had been killed. Despite the false assurance of many

rumormongers, no one could be certain and therefore the crowd waited in feverish indecision.

The indecision of the crowd did not extend to the Keldhaam Gnuxia. As a member of the ducal party, Gnuxia had steeled herself to endure a sojourn of more-than-ordinarily offensive Lanthian frivolity. As future Duchess to the benighted Commons, it behooved her to countenance if not encourage many of their lamentable self-indulgences. The situation that now presented itself, however, was one with which she was well equipped to deal. Gnuxia cast a quick glance around her, from wounded courtier to upright quarrel, to surrounding buildings. The scene was self-explanatory. When she spoke, she addressed Commander Krufaure, who stood with the Guardsmen ranged about the near-incoherent Duke.

"Where did the shot come from?" demanded Gnuxia.

"Judging by the angle of impact, it must have come from one of those three tall buildings yonder," replied the Commander, pointing.

"And?"

"Search parties have already been dispatched to each, Keldhaam. All citizens encountered within the buildings themselves or their environs will be interrogated and searched."

"His Grace is unharmed?"

"Entirely."

"And the dying swan?" Gnuxia jerked a thumb in Kor Malifon's direction.

Krufaure coughed and lifted his hand, perhaps to stroke his glossy fair moustache, perhaps to conceal a smile. "Sergeant Pohniu, who possesses some knowledge, informs me that the Lord Kor Malifon's wound is very superficial. Nonetheless, a physician has been summoned."

No question but that the man was competent as he was handsome. "That is adequate, Commander. I am pleased. I say I am pleased."

"I am gratified to earn your approbation, for I count the Kildhaam no mean judge."

"I shall expect a report from you when your search parties return."

"All information will be relayed to the Keldhaam without delay. In fact, I shall handle the matter personally."

"Well. Well, then. That is satisfactory, Commander. I commend your efficiency. Now instruct your men to permit me access to my betrothed.''

"All shall be as the Keldhaam desires.'' Krufaure inclined his sleek blond head, turned and issued orders to his men, who parted to clear Gnuxia's way to her cowering Duke. The Commander gazed after her. "That's a fine woman,'' he remarked apropos of nothing, then turned his attention to the yammering courtiers and dignitaries, whose lively distress bid fair to swamp the float.

Gnuxia beat a path to her betrothed's side. The Duke crouched upon the carpeting. His eyes were glazed and his brow was beaded with sweat. Gnuxia wasted no time pandering to his weaknesses. "Well?'' she demanded. "What do you intend to do about this?''

Povon was silent.

"I say what do you intend to do? *Speak up!*''

The Duke perceived that reply was unavoidable. "How fares my friend Beskot?'' he inquired evasively.

"Fearful, sniveling, and womanish, but not in any danger.''

Povon heaved a sigh of relief. Above all things he desired the consolation of the Moon Dream of Uhanna, and it appeared that his last remaining source was not to be cut off after all. The knowledge renewed his courage. "Protect myself,'' he muttered, almost incoherently. "Attack my enemies. Attack. Grizhni. Attack.''

"You fight chimeras, Betrothed,'' the Keldhaam observed impatiently. "I tell you—''

"I will attack,'' the Duke proclaimed with such vehemence that Gnuxia was temporarily silenced. "I will launch the greatest attack ever seen. I shall gather a great force, strike at the Nazara Sin, and eliminate my enemies once and for all.''

"This is foolishness—''

"All of them,'' Duke Povon insisted almost deliriously. "All of them at once. Grizhni's son—the Grizhni widow—the Lanthian traitor assisting them—the White Demons—all of them. Death to all of them. Only then shall I be safe and contented and free of nightmares. Only then.''

"You would do far better to consider—''

"A great force,'' the Duke repeated. "And total destruction. Total.''

In this his Grace proved unusually resolute. It was clear that no rational argument would sway him, for the Keldhaam Gnuxia tried them all to no avail. Povon's hunger for slaughter was not to be denied.

A thorough search by the Ducal Guards did not result in the capture of the would-be assassin. A crossbow and the remains of a meal discovered at the top of the vacant Vezhni Tower yielded no clues as to their owner's whereabouts. No one had been noticed entering or leaving the building. The assassin—or assassins—had gotten clean away.

In light of the morning's regrettable incidents the opening of the Parnis Regatta was postponed. Twenty-four hours later the Grand Promenade commenced without benefit of ducal oration, in the midst of a drenching downpour accompanied by sharp winds that capsized the *Enchanted Forest*.

Chapter Eleven

❦❦❦❦❦

Lady Verran did not start out with the intention of spying on
Rillif Har Fennahar. It was only by chance that she had spotted
him at a distance in one of the corridors, and the sheer peculiarity
of his behavior had arrested her attention. Thereafter curiosity
would not let her rest. She trailed discreetly in his wake, and
the oddity of his actions increased as she watched. Fennahar
was walking slowly, alert gaze sweeping the walls and floor.
The intensity of his regard seemed motivated by something
greater than idle curiosity. His demeanor was studious, his
actions deliberate; his entire aspect, that of a man with a mission. Once again he seemed to be hunting for something. But
what? And why didn't he just come right out and ask for it,
whatever it was, instead of poking around so furtively? Particularly when furtiveness seemed so foreign to his nature? And
above all why was he waving his left hand back and forth in
that extraordinary manner?

Fennahar's arm was extended like a divining rod. Now he
lifted it toward the ceiling, now lowered it toward the floor.
When he came to a fork in the passage, he stretched his left
hand first one way and then the other, as if in search of occult
guidance. After a moment he proceeded along the left-hand
fork, with Verran not far behind. It soon became apparent that
he was heading for the deeply subterranean chamber in which
the great Cognitively fired heating system devised by Terrs Fal
Grizhni was housed, and Verran's uneasiness grew. What could
Fennahar want with the heating system? Was his interest purely
academic, or did he intend harm? The destruction of Fal

218

Grizhni's device would in one stroke deprive the Vardruls of vast tunnel systems whose warm habitability was maintained by Cognition alone. A loud cry, a trilling summons, would have drawn dozens of Vardruls to the spot within moments. Fennahar could easily be stopped. Verran, however, was silent. The man before her had but Small Vens ago risked his life fighting the Ducal Guards in defense of the caverns—scarcely the act of an enemy. Moreover, her strongest instincts assured her that he was trustworthy. And yet—?

What's he up to?

Down the sharp-sloping corridor he went, down to the chamber wherein Vardruls rarely ventured. Grizhni's mechanism, self-sufficient and designed to operate at peak efficiency forever, required no maintenance. A device so perfect was best served by the total neglect of its owners, and therefore the Vardruls for the most part remained respectfully clear of its environs. The chamber was empty when Fennahar arrived. Verran saw him pause at the entrance to finger the silver band on his left wrist, and it occurred to her for the first time that the circle might serve some purpose other than ornamental or sentimental. Handling the metal gingerly with the extreme tips of his fingers, Fennahar slipped the band from his wrist and dropped it into a pocket. Almost as though, Verran thought, the silver burned his bare flesh. Why?

Still rubbing his left wrist, Fennahar walked into the room. From her hiding place behind a stalagmite in the corridor, Verran could see him approach the power source itself, and she tensed. The explorer, however, clearly intended no harm. Although he examined the device with great interest from every angle, he made no attempt to touch it. Presently his attention shifted to other matters and he roamed the chamber, inspecting the crannies and fissures with care. There was not much to investigate, and the search was swiftly concluded. Fennahar stood motionless, lost in frowning abstraction. Once he shook his head, as if to banish some unpleasant or unworthy thought. Then he touched the pocket containing the wristlet, and the frown deepened. Abruptly he turned and headed for the exit. Verran had barely time to draw back out of sight before he emerged. Pausing only long enough to slide the silver circle back onto his wrist, he set off along the corridor, striding very purposefully. For a moment Verran stared after him, then resumed her surreptitious pursuit.

He led her back to the tunnels and excavations she knew
best. He led her back, in fact, to the artificially smooth and
symmetrical arch that marked the entrance to her own personal
chambers, and there he paused to call her name. So he had
come to visit her. Almost Verran answered him then, but lingering doubt and curiosity stilled her tongue. As she watched
he called her name again, then bent his head to listen closely
at the woven curtains that masked the opening. Following a
quick guilty glance up and down the passage, he siipped through
the arch.

Verran caught her breath, torn between bewilderment and
astonished outrage. What did he want, and *how dare he set
foot in her chamber uninvited*? It dimly crossed her mind that
the extremity of her reaction to his intrusion revealed the su-
perficiality of the Vardrul influence upon her habits of
thought—for the Vardruls, burdened with little sense of owner-
ship, possessed no word in their own language to express the
concept of "trespasser." Beyond that, a sense of betrayal fueled
her anger. Verran did not pause to analyze. Quickly she advanced to the archway, nudged a curtain aside, and looked in.
Fennahar was searching the room, riffling lightly through her
few belongings, snooping around behind the stalagmites, running his hands over the tapestries she had woven. Her pulse
jumped at the sight, and she paused a moment to master her
emotion before entering the room.

His back was toward her as she walked in. He was bent
over, inspecting the contents of the small niche wherein she
stored her precious writing supplies—the homemade pens and
ink, the rolls of cloth that served as paper. Verran took a deep
breath. When she spoke her voice was even, and without conscious thought she repeated the simple words that Terrs Fal
Grizhni had chosen when he had surprised her in his workroom
seventeen years earlier. "What are you doing here?"

Fennahar straightened and whirled to face her. For an instant
his face was pale, then reddened deeply. At that moment he
resembled the boy of sixteen she had known in Lanthi Ume,
and the recollection was dangerously disarming. He said nothing.

"Well, Ril?"

Fennahar found his voice. "I am truly sorry, Verran."

She merely looked at him.

"In a way I'm glad this has happened. Now I can tell you why I'm here. I've wanted to all along."

"Then why didn't you? Would it have been so difficult?"

"Yes. I didn't know what your reaction would be. I still don't."

"Reaction to what?" Her face hardened. "Were you sent here by the Duke of Lanthi Ume?"

"No. My uncle Jinzin Farni sent me."

"For what?"

"For your husband's records and notebooks."

"What makes him—or you—think they are here?"

"Uncle Jin has always believed that you hold them. Until recently he had no idea where you might be found."

"Ah. I understand. Then that is what I've seen you searching for so often these past Small Vens?"

"You've seen me?"

"Many times. And now I know your purpose at last. Jinzin Farni wishes to increase his power by availing himself of his predecessor's knowledge and secrets—"

"That isn't his intention—"

"So you have come here under false pretenses, representing yourself as a friend. Rather than asking honestly for what your uncle wants, you have lied, played the hypocrite, and searched through our home on the sly." Her blue eyes were cold with contempt.

"Yes. All of that is true and there is no excuse possible. The only explanation I can offer is that I couldn't risk telling you the truth—not with so much at stake."

"The power and prestige of Jinzin Farni are at stake. Are they worth so much?"

"You don't understand, Verran. There's much more to it than that, so much more that I haven't dared confide in you, despite my inclinations. Unless Fal Grizhni's records are recovered, catastrophe is inevitable. Many will die, all will suffer, and in the end the entire island of Dalyon will be lost to mankind."

Wordlessly she awaited explanation.

"Before he died," Fennahar continued, "Preeminence Grizhni pronounced a curse of darkness, which upon fruition renders all the land unfit for human habitation. This darkness,

which will one day be born at the center of the island and
spread outward to the sea, is poisonous and by all accounts
utterly demoralizing. No human may hope to survive it for
very long, and those who fail to escape Dalyon will die. It is
a malediction that spares no one—spares neither friend nor
enemy, man, woman, or child.''

" 'For I have it within me to visit such destruction upon my
foes and their descendants that this island would bear the scars
for all time','' Verran quoted sotfly, and shuddered as she
recalled her husband's expression that day.

"Verran?"

"It's something he once said to me a long time ago that I've
never forgotten," she told him. "Please go on."

"It can scarcely be argued that the personal wrongs suffered
by Fal Grizhni justify so vast and indiscriminate a stroke of
vengeance. Fal Grizhni lost his life. In exchange, he posthum-
ously takes or destroys the lives of thousands of innocents.
Even Grizhni's supporter and sympathizer Jinzin Farni can't
countenance that. My uncle, having learned of the curse years
ago, believes himself fit to break that Cognition provided he
enjoys access to the information contained in Grizhni's records.
Having recently discovered your whereabouts, he provided me
with a wristlet that warms in proximity to Cognitive influence
and dispatched me to this place to secure the writings. And
that is all of it.''

Verran digested this in silence for a time. Her emotions were
in a turmoil, but dominating all was the profound conviction
that Rillif Har Fennahar spoke the truth. She had never until
this moment suspected that her husband might have found
means of avenging himself. Having been informed, however,
she did not hesitate to believe; nor did she doubt that his vengeance, if effected at all, would be colossal in scope. It was
so exactly like Fal Grizhni.

"But you didn't tell me until you had to," she said at last,
slowly. "If you had managed to find the books, you'd have
taken them and departed in stealth?''

"Ah, then you do have them?''

Her lips tightened as she recognized her slip, but there was
no recalling the words. "They're here," she admitted shortly.
"But you haven't answered my question. You would just have
taken them, without a word? Stolen my son's birthright, the

only memento of his father?"

His eyes fell before her regard. "I don't know. I would have hated myself for it, but it might have been necessary. I couldn't very well ask your permission."

"Why not? Why couldn't you be honest? Why couldn't you have told me what Lord Grizhni did, and asked my help?"

"I didn't know if you'd give it. After all, you lost your husband, lost your home and city, lost everything you had. It wouldn't be surprising if you were bitter. For all I know, in loyalty to your husband's memory you might support his designs."

Do I? Once I would have condoned and supported anything Lord Grizhni did—anything. I thought that was what loyalty meant. And now? The image of her husband's face flashed into her mind. She saw again the rare smile that could so completely transform him, the smile that few mortals other than herself had ever beheld. She saw too the dire, frozen expression with which he had customarily confronted the world, and the recollection chilled her. *You were wrong, my lord,* she told the image. *I don't follow you this time. You chose darkness over light, death over life, as simple and elemental as that. You did as you must, I suppose. You chose as your nature and all the circumstances of your life dictated. But it is not my choice.*

"I do not support his designs," she said. The image of Grizhni faded to resume its place amid the most hallowed memories of a lifetime. She found her present vision occupied by Rillif Har Fennahar. Looking straight into his eyes, she repeated, "I do not support his designs at all."

"Then will you help me?"

"By giving you Lord Grizhni's books to take back to Lanthi Ume?"

He nodded.

"Yes," she replied after only the briefest of hesitations. "You'll have them."

"I wish I'd had the sense to trust you from the beginning. Verran—" He seemed to find it a little difficult to speak. "If I had found and taken those records without your consent—if I'd carried them to Uncle Jin—I'd have come back here afterward. I'd have returned to explain everything to you."

"Right. After the fact."

"Better than nothing."

"Just barely." She couldn't forbear smiling, but the smile swiftly vanished as she observed, "If you stole those records and then showed your face here again, you'd have more to deal with than my resentment. There'd be Terrs to consider. He'd never forgive you, and he's in a position to make you feel his anger. The Vardruls look on him as a leader now. Some of them even call him Grizhni/Zmadrc Patriarch. What's more, he's taught them violence. If he told them to hurt you— even to kill you—I think they'd obey him. And if you stole his father's property, which he treasures, I think he'd do it. The attacks on his home and the slaughter of his friends have brought out everything violent and vengeful in him. I really think he'd have them kill you."

"He'd be deeply angered, and with good cause. But Terrs and I have come to know one another. I believe the boy regards me as a friend. Could he not be moved to forgive—"

"Your friendship would make him feel the betrayal all the more keenly. As for forgiveness—well, he's his father's son."

"Then what if I take the records and he finds out you helped me?"

"That's different. The writings, after all, were given to me. Whether Terrs likes it or not, I have the right to dispose of them as I see fit."

"You're angry with him, aren't you?"

"Yes," she replied in some surprise. "I am."

"Then listen, Verran. When I leave this place, I won't be able to return." Her face fell and he continued quickly, "I'm asking you to come with me. You can't go on living such a life, here in this place. You're dying by inches here. I know you can't go back to Lanthi Ume. But there's a small town with a decent inn on the Hurbanese Road, not so far from here. I could take you to the inn, you could wait for me there while I complete my business in Lanthi Ume, then I could rejoin you and we could go away together, perhaps to Strell or to Szar—"

"But Ril, what about your estates, your family obligations—"

"You forget, I've been seen and doubtless recognized by agents of the Duke. I took the part of the White Demons against the Guardsmen. For that alone, I could easily be condemned as a traitor to Lanthi Ume. It's not so easy for me to go back, either. When I visit my uncle, I'll do so in secret."

"Oh, this is dreadful! Surely it's not too late to make your peace with the Duke! Your uncle's influence—your family's importance—"

"It doesn't matter, I don't care about that. What concerns me now is your decision. Will you come with me? We could marry, have children. Since meeting you again in this place, I've realized why there's never been anyone else I wanted to marry. Come with me—we'd be happy."

Yes, she thought. *We really would be happy. It wouldn't be the same as it was with Lord Grizhni—there will never be another Lord Grizhni. But with Ril, things would be better in some ways. I'd understand Ril. We'd laugh together, there'd be no shadows, and there would be the closeness of equals between us. And there'd be children, growing up in the sunlight— normal, healthy, glad to be alive and human. Happy, loving children, unlike—*

"Terrs," she said aloud. "What about Terrs?"

"He could come with us."

"He'd never leave this place."

"Don't be too sure. He's growing curious about the world. Not only that, but he badly wants more Cognition, and he can't acquire it here."

"I still don't think he'd come with us."

"And what if he doesn't? Terrs is grown, Verran. He's old enough and wise enough to make his own decisions. Those decisions aren't likely to be governed by any consideration of your welfare or preferences."

"I know it. But the thought of just—just *abandoning* my son here—"

"Even if that's what he wants?"

"The only human in all these caverns—hunted by Ducal Guardsmen—"

"You don't feel you could leave him, then?"

"I don't know." She shook her head. "If my son cooperates, then I'll gladly go with you. I want to, very much. But if Terrs won't budge—then I don't know. I can't answer so quickly, I need time to think."

Fennahar nodded, and Verran saw that he was trying to disguise all sign of disappointment, without complete success. Almost then and there she agreed to go with him. The urge was nearly overpowering and the words quivered upon her lips. Rather than speak them, she suggested, "Let's settle the matter of Lord Grizhni's records first. We'll have to find a way of getting them—"

"I thought you said they were yours to dispose of as you see fit."

"True, but I'm not sure we'd be wise to stand on technicalities. Terrs will oppose you if he finds out."

"If the situation is explained to him, as it's been explained to you—"

"Terrs isn't like me, Ril. He doesn't care what happens Surface, at least not much. I believe he'd do what he can to hold his father's writings at any cost, and at this point he can do a great deal."

"You may misjudge the boy."

"I know. The one way of finding out would be simply to tell him the truth. You didn't confide in me until you had no choice. Are you willing at this point to take a chance on my son?"

Fennahar shook his head reluctantly. After a moment's thought he inquired, "Are the records difficult to reach?"

"Well, yes, in a way. They're kept in one of the oldest chambers, called the Stronghold. The room itself is neither locked nor guarded—such precautions don't exist among the Vardruls. However, Terrs himself is in there all the time, especially recently. He has used Lord Grizhni's records to teach himself some Cognition. And now, ever since the last attack by the Guardsmen, he's done nothing but study—trying to learn new ways of defending the caverns, you see. He's there in the Stronghold every Coloration—hasn't come out for Small Vens on end. He wouldn't eat if I didn't nag him, and I don't think he's slept at all. He does nothing but practice, and I don't know which will give way first, his strength or his sanity—" She stopped the rush of words with an effort. "The point is, the records are never left unguarded."

"Can you lead me to the Stronghold?"

"Easily. I'll take you there at Purple Coloration, when nearly everyone sleeps. But Terrs will not be asleep."

"Well, he must be persuaded to rest. There's where maternal influence comes in."

"I have none."

"That can't be true. The boy must be exhausted. Surely you can convince him to return to his own chamber for food and rest?"

"He doesn't have a room of his own, never wanted one. He sleeps in the communal Zmadrc excavations."

"Your chambers, then. Right here. Any place you can keep an eye on him."

"I don't know. It won't be easy. I'll do my best."

"I won't need but a few moments alone in the Stronghold."

"And afterward, you'll be gone for good."

"Yes. When I go, I'd like you to leave with me. There must be several hours left before the turn of Coloration. Will you use that time to think about my proposal?"

She nodded. "I couldn't *not* think about it if I tried. But I haven't even spoken to Terrs yet. What if a miracle occurred— he agreed to go with us—and then discovered you'd gone for the notebooks behind his back? He'd never trust a human being again. Ril, why don't we wait a little? A little more time—"

"I don't dare wait. Fal Grizhni's writings must return to Lanthi Ume—that's the most important thing, which means I must carry them out before the Ducal Guardsmen return to these caves. They *will* be back, as we both know. Beyond that, Fal Grizhni's curse might strike at any time. It may not come for centuries, or it may fall upon our heads tomorrow. We don't know when, and we can't assume we've time to spare. Finally, the savant best qualified to break the curse—my uncle Jin—is deathly ill. I fear he cannot live much longer. When he is gone, there's no Cognizance left of equal power, and none with a similar understanding of the danger that we face. Uncle Jin must have those records without delay. No, Verran. I've waited too long as it is."

She did not attempt argument. "Very well. We go forward at the turn of Coloration. Until then, I'd like to be alone. I need to think."

Hours later, when the walls of certain tunnels and excavations had assumed the indeterminate maroon tint that signaled the shift from the Red to the Purple Coloration, Lady Verran approached the Stronghold. Should she emerge with her son in tow, the watching Fennahar would know that the coast was clear for his thieving.

Not thieving, she reminded herself. *The writings are mine and he takes them with my consent.* Somehow the self-justification failed to reassure her. Her nervousness increased as she neared the chamber and heard the murmur of voices within.

Someone's with him. She paused to listen, and found the words easily distinguishable.

"It is not long before my Future becomes my brother/consort."

Verran recognized the voice of Zmadrc Fourteen.

"Truly. My disharmony lessens from Coloration to Coloration," Terrs hummed in reply.

"Soon the clan ruu will be in phase with Lvjirri."

What could they be talking about? As soon as Verran walked into the Stronghold, she knew. Terrs's advances were self-evident. His hands, altered as she had seen them more than once, shone white and tentacled. So much she could endure with tolerable equanimity. For the first time, however, the youth had progressed beyond mere manual transformation. His arms and legs glowed, the flesh faintly translucent. His bare feet were similarly luminous, the toes elongated and boneless to echo the development of the fingers. Alterations in the body, if any, lay concealed beneath Terrs's robe. His face, head, and hair appeared unchanged and human as always. His eyes were deeply shadowed, the entire visage haggard, gray with sleeplessness and exhaustion. At the same time, his expression reflected extraordinary satisfaction amounting to triumph. Fourteen stood very near him, her tentacles entwined with his.

Verran carefully repressed all sign of astonishment and disgust. Her voice was calm and her expression serene as she extended greetings to her son and his Future. The greetings were returned in courteous Lanthian. Terrs's eyes went hard and challenging, then gradually warmed in the face of his mother's pacifism. In the absence of the overt disapproval he had evidently expected, his look of satisfaction reasserted itself. Verran was glad to see it. It boded well for the success of her mission. She glanced quickly around the small chamber. Off to one side stood a slant that her son had installed for his own use. On the floor at the foot of the slant lay a folio volume, a roll of parchment, a leather binder filled with notes, and a thin plaque of gold incised with words and shapes—Fal Grizhni's treasured relics, filled with secrets of High Cognition. No sense in exhibiting undue interest in the writings—Terrs would surely wonder. Deliberately she averted her eyes.

"It's been many Small Vens since I've seen you," she informed her son quietly. "I've been concerned."

"No need. I have been much occupied, that is all."

"When was the last time you ate? Or slept?"

"I am not certain, I have not noticed."

"Just as I thought. You'll make yourself ill."

"That is unimportant. There is a matter of far greater significance to discuss. Mother, in the past few Small Vens of study and practice, I have achieved successes far beyond anything I have hitherto accomplished—"

"I can see that," Verran replied, with a glance at his luminous flesh. With an effort, she maintained her artificial neutrality of manner.

"Yes, self-transformation is one area in which I have made progress. But there is another, far more important. Mother—" Terrs's impassivity gave way to gladness, and a smile lighted his pallid, tired face. "Mother, I have mastered the Falling Stones at last."

"What does that mean? What are the Falling Stones?"

"Just as it sounds—stones that are Cognitively toppled. Have you any idea what that can mean in terms of the caverns' defense? We shall be proof against invasion. We shall have means of effective self-protection. Mother, I believe the Falling Stones will save us all."

Verran had rarely, if ever, seen him so powerfully affected. Gone was the impenetrable composure, the icy reserve. His eyes were bright and his expression eager. Fourteen, who had understood the Lanthian conversation, brightened in sympathy with her Future's mood and her grip upon his hand tightened.

That's what really matters to him, Verran thought. *Not just Cognition for its own sake, or for personal power—but using it to defend his home, family, and friends. He's not an easy human being any more than his father was, but he has a large and generous nature. I'm proud of him.* It occurred to her then that she was planning to deprive her son of the means whereby to study the Cognition of which he made unselfish use, and she experienced a momentary qualm. *I hate this sneaking deceit! I just want to tell him the truth, and so does Ril. But I'm afraid to. When he finds out, I hope he'll forgive us.* Aloud, she said, "I don't quite understand about these Falling Stones. Are they real, or are they illusory like the covering of the traps you built?"

"They are real, which is the reason this represents such a

great step forward. I have progressed from illusion to reality, and the difference is—well, I will not attempt to explain it. Far better that I demonstrate."

"Perhaps you'd better not attempt Cognition now, Terrs. You've been driving yourself too hard, and you're exhausted—"

"I want you to see this." Gently disengaging himself from Fourteen, Terrs stepped to the slant, stooped, and took up his father's plaque of gold. "Now, Mother. See that group of stalactites over there?" He pointed up at a cluster of slender stone icicles. "Watch them." As Terrs bowed his head to utter chanting syllables, one bright, boneless finger traced the patterns incised on the plaque. Verran's regard shifted uneasily from stalactites to busy tentacle and back again. The improvements in Terrs's Cognitive technique and his corresponding growth in confidence were readily apparent. The youth spoke with low-voiced assurance. He achieved Cognition on his first attempt, with an elegant minimum of utterance and gesture.

If only Lord Grizhni had lived to see his son! Verran thought, and then there was no room left in her mind for regrets as the designated stalactites trembled, rattled like chattering teeth, split off from the ceiling, and crashed to the floor. The fragile stone spikes struck point first, shattering on impact. Verran started violently. Bits of broken stone and dust scattered across the floor, one fragment coming to rest against her foot. She bent to inspect the pebble, and found its edges surgically clean and sharp.

"Well, Mother?" For once there was nothing in the least remote or incomprehensible about Terrs. He looked frankly triumphant, and he had every right.

"That's astounding. You've all your father's natural ability. Oh, if only you could have known him!"

"Do not grieve, Mother. I have every intention of knowing the Grizhni Patriarch, and his Ancestors before him. I am almost there, as you can see."

Disliking the topic, Verran sought to draw her son away from it. "These Falling Stones of yours—does this mean that you can bring down stalactites upon the heads of trespassers?"

"Yes, at any time. And more than these paltry sticks, Mother. My Cognition can topple the greatest rock formations, the most massive boulders. Entire companies of Ducal Guardsmen can be crushed at one blow. They will soon learn not to trouble us. Our future safety is assured. I will show you. See that great rock—''

"Stop, Terrs. No more demonstrations, you're already exhausted. You need to eat and rest, or you'll make yourself ill."

"I am not fatigued," Terrs asserted with patent untruth. His last Cognitive effort had drained him visibly. His shoulders sagged and his movements were unusually indecisive.

"Yes you are. If you don't lie down, you'll soon fall down. And if you don't believe me, just look at your hands and feet."

Terrs obeyed, glancing down in time to see the light fade from his flesh as his extremities resumed their human form. For a moment he stared as if in unpleasant surprise. A vertical line appeared between his brows as he strove without success to restore the Vardrulesque members.

"It's no use, Terrs," said Verran. "You're just too tired. Please come back with me, have a meal and a demi-Coloration's sleep."

"There's no time, I must keep working—"

"You can't work effectively in your present state. You're misusing your precious time if you try. And if you ruin your own health, then you'll not be able to work at all, much less efficiently."

"The Fal Grizhni Matriarch speaks truly," observed Fourteen, her luminosity waxing and waning with a repetitive regularity that conveyed gentle insistence. "The Fal Grizhni Terrs is almost sick with weariness. His Future begs him to heed the Matriarch." Terrs wavered, and she added, "Go rest, and while you are gone, I will visit the death-pool, for it has been Colorations since I have known the Ancestors."

"The Zmadrc Fourteen spends too much time among the dead," Terrs observed in a low voice.

"How shall I abandon my clan? Nearly all the kinsmen have joined the Ancestors. I am part of them."

"Do not forget the living."

"I forget neither the living nor the dead. Do not fear for me, Future. Go sleep, and be at ease."

Terrs rippled his fingers in assent, and with an air of tolerance accompanied his mother from the Stronghold. Now that he had resigned himself to a short suspension of effort, his weariness manifested itself in every dragging footstep. Verran had to slow

her pace to match his. As they passed the niche, half-blocked
by bulbous stalagmites, wherein she knew Har Fennahar
crouched in concealment, Verran cast a nervous glance up at
her son. His expression was tired, preoccupied, unconscious . . .
Terrs obviously suspected nothing. Guilt stirred within her,
and she lowered her eyes.

When they reached her chambers, she set before him a simple
meal that he consumed without interest or appetite. Afterward,
following only the most halfhearted and perfunctory of protests,
he consented to rest. Terrs stretched himself upon a pallet and
lost consciousness within seconds. As the Coloration advanced
and the slime upon the tunnel walls outside the apartment darkened from maroon to purple, the human youth slept on. Verran
watched him as he lay there, studied the white, haggard face
and tried to gauge the mind behind it. As always, her son's
mind and heart were closed to her. Without volition, her
thoughts turned to a subject more comprehensible—Rillif Har
Fennahar.

We never got things settled, she thought. *I never gave him
a straight answer. I couldn't. And now he's leaving. He's
probably on his way back to Lanthi Ume this very minute.
From Lanthi Ume, he'll proceed to the inn on the Hurbanese
Road, and there he'll wait for—a few days. If I don't join him,
he'll know my decision. He'll make his peace with the Duke,
I hope, and resume his life as Lord Fennahar. And I'll never
see him again. Never see the way his forehead crinkles up
when he's puzzled, never hear that funny way his voice breaks
when he laughs. He'll end up married to some Lanthian lady—
someone much younger than I, no doubt—and he'll be happy.
While I am trapped here—* And even as she thought, some
small voice from another part of her mind spoke, *You fool,
you're not trapped. The door of your dungeon is wide open.
You need only walk out. Terrs will do well enough without
you. Walk away.*

Childishly irresponsible. It is not as simple as that.

But yes, my dear. It is exactly as simple as that.

The Coloration advanced, and Lady Verran reached no defi-
nite conclusion. The mental struggle was still in progress when
Terrs's lieutenant, F'tryll'jnr Rdsdr appeared at her door.

"Matriarch—" hummed the Vardrul, and Terrs woke at the
sound. "Fal Grizhni Terrs—I bring news. We are betrayed.

The human Har Fennahar has attempted to carry off the relics of the Fal Grizhni Patriarch, who is neither his Ancestor nor his Connection. We surprised him at the very threshold of the Jnriff Exit, the stolen keepsakes upon his person. He sought to flee, but he has been restrained. All is well and the relics are secure, but what must be done with the thief? Shall he be expelled, to carry his knowledge of our caverns to the enemy? Or''—F'tryll'jnr's next query revealed the extent of Terrs's influence—''shall he proceed alone to the Invisible Falls?''

Chapter Twelve

❧❧❧❧❧

They had detained Fennahar under guard in a small chamber not far from the Jnriff Exit. Verran was momentarily startled at the sight of the four tall F'tryll'jnr kinsmen, armed with captured swords, stationed just outside the room. Sentries, weapons, and all that these things implied were traditionally alien to the Vardrul way of life. But times were changing, Verran reminded herself dryly. Times were changing quickly, because she had elected to raise her son in these caverns.

Terrs paused briefly to confer with one of the sentries. "The Fal Grizhni Patriarch's writings?" he inquired.

"Returned to the Stronghold," replied the Vardrul, with a slight relaxation of the outer ocular ridges accompanied by a slow brightening that suggested successful accomplishment. "Undamaged and currently under guard."

Terrs rippled his fingers and passed on into the chamber, with Verran at his side. F'tryll'jnr Rdsdr—by no means a Connection in this matter—did not seek to impose his presence, but remained outside in the corridor with his own kinsmen.

The room was bare of furnishings. Fennahar sat with his back to the wall, long legs drawn up and chin resting upon his folded arms in an attitude of meditative dejection. He raised his head as the others entered. His expression was unrevealing, and he scarcely glanced at Verran. For a moment she was puzzled, almost hurt, and then realized, *He's protecting me. He doesn't want Terrs to guess that I was helping him.* Instinctively her eyes jumped to her son, whose face was as still as white shadow-sculpture. The stillness, however, did not deceive her. *He's upset, very disturbed,* she thought. *He's doing his best to hide it, but I know that look. He hasn't decided yet what he wants to do about this.*

As the prisoner rose to face him, Terrs remarked quietly, "Fennahar, I am told that you have attempted to carry the Grizhni Patriarch's writings from the caverns. Have I been misinformed?"

"You have not," said Fennahar.

"Appearances are often misleading. I do not wish to judge you wrongly. No doubt you merely sought to examine the writings by Surface daylight?"

"No, Terrs."

"Perhaps, in view of the recent human predations, you thought to remove the relics to a safer place of concealment?"

"No."

"Surely there is a simple explanation that will clear you of all blame."

How very much he wants that to be true, thought Verran. *My poor Terrs!*

Fennahar shook his head.

"And yet I cannot suspect you of theft," Terrs persisted, and Verran heard the mounting distress and anger concealed behind the carefully dispassionate manner. "The thing is impossible. Did we not shake hands?"

Fennahar's face flushed. "Terrs, there is an explanation, but it doesn't clear me of blame. When you've heard everything, I hope you'll be able to forgive me. But before I explain, I must ask you one question. You're fully acquainted with the contents of Preeminence Grizhni's notebooks. Tell me, do those records contain an account of the High Cognitive technique employed to generate a certain intense spreading malignancy of darkness?"

"The contents of my father's records are of no concern to you, Fennahar. It is not a time for you to ask questions, but to answer them."

"Please tell him what he wants to know, Terrs," Verran interjected, and her son glanced at her in surprise. "There's a reason for asking, it's very important. Please, for my sake!"

"Very well, Mother," Terrs conceded half unwillingly. "If you wish it. Yes, the Grizhni Patriarch's notebook contains pages given over to a description of the technique that Fennahar describes. I have never attempted this feat, as it lies very far beyond my powers—beyond the powers of all but the greatest

of savants, I would judge. How did you learn of it?'' he asked
the explorer.

"From my uncle Jinzin Farni. Terrs, you have some knowledge. In your opinion, what would be the effect of such Cognitive darkness if loosed upon the island of Dalyon?''

"Devastating to Surface dwellers," replied Terrs after a
moment's reflection. "Disastrous, and not only for Man. The
animals and the light-loving vegetation as well—all would suffer. Why do you ask?''

"In the moments preceding his death, your father, Preeminence Grizhni, unleashed his darkness. We do not know when
the curse will strike, but every human being upon the island
walks under sentence of death or banishment.''

"I have often read and wondered at the account of the Death
of Light. I marveled at the power of the mind that could conceive
it. But never did I dream that the Grizhni Patriarch had gone
so far as to make use of such dire Cognition. How do you
know that he did so?''

"He spoke of it before he died, well aware that no man
could hinder his designs.''

"How he must have hated the city, and all her inhabitants,''
Terrs mused. "How much he must have loathed humanity in
general. Beyond doubt, he had good cause.''

"He had no cause to inflict his vengeance upon the guiltless.''

"Is there any such thing as a guiltless human? They are
violent and destructive by nature. They killed the Grizhni Patriarch and dispersed his clan. They have come to the caverns
and slaughtered the Vardrul kinsmen. Always they kill without
restraint or pity. Were all the race of Man exterminated, the
world would be a kinder place. Perhaps the Grizhni Patriarch
knew well what he did.''

"Preeminence Grizhni acted without regard for reason or
justice. His final act embodied all the cruel qualities in man
that you deplore. But all men aren't killers, Terrs—there are
some as gentle and peaceable as any Vardrul. We don't deserve
universal condemnation, and that is why the present Selectic
Preeminence dispatched me to these caves to obtain Fal
Grizhni's records, which may be used to break your father's
Cognition.''

"And therefore you attempted to steal the writings.'' Terrs's
anger was rising, but his voice did not do likewise. He spoke,
if anything, more quietly than ever. "You lied, deceived, and

stole from those so misguided as to trust you."

"That is true. I see now that I should have been honest with you from the beginning, but I didn't dare. I was wrong, and I am sorry."

"Your professions of friendship were false," Terrs continued, low voice as bitter as a gale upon the Sea of Ice. "You sought only to set our suspicions to rest. There was never any true friendship. It was all a lie, and the shaking of hands was a mockery."

"No, you're wrong about that. The friendship and respect I feel for you are real and always have been."

"You are a liar, Fennahar, as all humans are. No doubt the charade has amused you. Beyond question you have laughed to witness our foolish credulity, and the ease with which we were hoodwinked."

Oh, this has hurt him, Verran thought, and could not avoid concluding, *and he will strike back.*

"I have never laughed, believe me—" Fennahar protested.

"I have little cause to believe you, as you have already shown yourself treacherous," returned Terrs coldly. "What faith shall I place in the word of a proven liar? I am not in the habit of repeating my errors."

"No doubt I deserve that. I've been guilty of falsehood, but not to the extent you imagine. I haven't counterfeited esteem in order to gain your trust and then betray you. Perhaps it appears so, but I am not such a villain as that. Listen, Terrs. If I had married when most men do"—his eyes turned involuntarily to Verran for an instant, and then away—"then I might well have had a son nearly your age by now. And since I've come to know you, many times it has almost seemed as if you—"

Terrs's face appeared to thaw, crack in places, and refreeze almost faster than the changes in expression could be interpreted by his companions. "Stop there," he commanded harshly, and his arctic anger seemed in part directed against his own momentary weakness. "These maudlin appeals are as vulgar as they are hypocritical, and I despise them. Do not insult my intelligence further."

"Lad, I mean every word."

"You are a liar, Fennahar." The glitter in his eyes recalled a similarly dangerous expression in the eyes of Preeminence Fal Grizhni. "I will not be duped a second time. You are a

human liar, possessing all the dishonesty and vicious deceit of
your kind. The Grizhni Patriarch in his wisdom perceived the
nature of Man and directed his Cognition accordingly. And
who is to say that my father, foreseeing the persecution of the
Vardrul kinsmen, did not stretch forth his hand from beyond
the grave to save us by ridding the island of our human
enemies?''

"Terrs. You desire honesty? You shall have it. The persecution of the Vardruls is the direct result of your presence in their
caverns, nothing more. Your presence endangers all the Vardrul
race. If your regard for them is real, you will eliminate the
threat by leaving these caves and resuming your place in the
world of men, where you belong.''

Terrs's minimal hesitation suggested that he felt the truth of
the other's accusation. "You do not know what you are saying.
You ask me to sever myself from my clan, a separation amounting to death—''

"The separation need not be total or permanent. In any case
you endanger your clan by remaining. Beyond that you endanger the lives of thousands of guiltless human beings unless
you permit me to carry the Lord Fal Grizhni's records back to
Preeminence Jinzin Farni.''

"After all that has passed, you dare demand such a sacrifice?'' For a moment it almost seemed possible that anger
would burst the bonds of Terrs's icy self-control.

"The sacrifice would only be temporary, for Uncle Jin would
return the writings to you as soon as he was done with them.''

"Would he? It is to be assumed that the Preeminence Farni
is no less trustworthy than his kinsmen Fennahar. Your arguments are forceful, and I cannot refuse to consider them. No
less forceful, however, are the arguments of F'tryll'jnr Rdsdr,
who is in favor of dispatching you to the Invisible Falls.''

He'd do it, Verran thought. *He'd actually do it. He's turning
into a monster. He frightens me.*

Fennahar was speechless. Not so Verran, who broke in with
apparent coolness, "You do that, Terrs, and you'd best send
me along with him.''

He turned to her with an air of forbearance. "Mother, this
is not your concern—''

"Isn't it? Think again, my baby dictator. There are a few
things you haven't been told. To begin with, I knew what Ril
was about and I helped him. You're surprised? Perhaps not so

omniscient after all? The fact is, Ril is right, whether you see it or not. So I dragged you out of the Stronghold not long ago, just so he could get in there.''

"You did that for his sake? Not for mine, as you claimed?''

"Both. In any case I actively assisted him, and if he's guilty of some great crime, then so am I. Another point you seem to overlook. Those writings of Lord Grizhni's were given to me. They're my property, not yours.''

"They are worthless in your hands. You cannot use them.''

"But I have the right to dispose of them. I can send them to Preeminence Jinzin Farni if I choose.''

"I do not know if I could permit it.''

"Permit it? Who do you think you are? It's not your decision!''

"Is it not, Mother?''

She chose not to pick up the gauntlet. "One last thing. You speak of your clan, and the hardship of separation. The truth is, I and my Dris Verras kinsmen—and my mother's kin in Gard Lammis—are your only true clan and Connections by blood. And you're not even interested in meeting them. As for the others—the Zmadrcs, for example—despite their kindness, you'll never be part of them, for you'll never succeed in changing your basic nature. Your father could have told you that. Even if you manage to change your appearance by Cognition— even if you meet the Ancestors—even if you alter yourself to such an extent that you can sire children upon Zmadrc Fourteen—you will still be human at heart. Twist and turn as you may, you will never escape it!''

"Mother, I did not guess that you were so much against me. If it is your desire that we shall be enemies—''

"I want no such thing! Oh, Terrs—'' her voice softened, "if you really wish to live as a Vardrul, you will be kind and gentle as they are. No true Vardrul would allow thousands of innocent creatures to die. Vardruls value all life. So do the noblest of men. In saving lives, you combine the best of both races. Let Ril carry Lord Grizhni's writings to Lanthi Ume. When the curse of darkness has been broken, he will bring them back. Despite your anger, you know in your heart that he will keep his promise. Let them go, Terrs. Prove yourself fit to be either Vardrul or Man.''

Terrs did not answer at once. The rage slowly drained from his eyes, the muscles of his face relaxed, and once again he looked his true age. Verran, watching in suspense, found her maternal affections not nearly as diminished as she had imagined. Terrs glanced briefly at Fennahar—a pained, uncertain look. He seemed on the verge of speech. But his decision, whatever it might have been, was interrupted by the entrance of F'tryll'jnr Rdsdr bearing news of a two-pronged human attack. The soldiers, having laid planks across the mouths of the concealed traps, were pouring into the caverns by the hundreds. Two defense forces—one commanded by Lbavbsch Hfu and one by the R'jnrllsch Lesser Patriarch—now moved to repel the invaders, but the leadership of the Fal Grizhni Terrs was essential.

Terrs rippled his fingers curtly. All thoughts of Har Fennahar had clearly been driven from his mind. Without another word he set off for the F'jnruu Batgate, his Vardrul cohorts trailing in his wake.

Verran looked at Fennahar. "You'd best leave now, while you can," she advised breathlessly. "Forget Lord Grizhni's records. Go while you've still got your life."

"And you?"

"I don't know yet. Right now, I'm going after my son."

"He wouldn't want you to expose yourself to danger, Verran. Neither do I."

"I don't give a dakkle what he wants, or you want. I want to know that my son is safe, and there's an end. I'm going," she snapped, and turned on her heel.

"Very well, I'll go with you." Mastering his own impulse to restrain her forcibly, he followed her from the room.

Lbavbsch Hfu was aggressive and courageous for a Vardrul, but by human standards no warrior. He led a semidisciplined, barely trained gang of assorted clan members. Each Vardrul was armed with a sharpened stalactite or a captured human weapon in whose use none was particularly proficient. Each Vardrul was also armed with determination to battle to the death in defense of the caverns, but none possessed more than the most rudimentary fighting skills. Simple determination unaccompanied by experience served them ill. In the absence of the inspired leadership of the young Fal Grizhni Terrs, Lbavbsch Hfu and his followers were severely hampered.

The corridor was clogged with human soldiers—the remnant of the Ducal Guards together with all the Rhelish mercenaries that Duke Povon could afford to hire, eked out with a crew of motley tavern-sweepings. So far the men had been unable to advance beyond the F'jnruu Corridor. But the Guards were engaged in their customary workmanlike slaughter, the Rhelish were equally professional, and the white litter of Vardrul dead was mounting swiftly. An attack by the great brown bats had proved abortive. This time the men were armed with lengths of iron chain which they whirled above their heads to strike the creatures from the air. In the face of such resistance, the bats had retreated in squeaking terror. Only the kinsmen remained to protect the corridor, and their collective hiir was already depressed. They could not hope to hold their position for long.

It was therefore with profound relief and a burst of luminosity that the Vardrul forces greeted the arrival of the Fal Grizhni Terrs, accompanied by a handful of strong-ruu'd F'tryll'jnr kinsmen. The young Fal Grizhni, endowed with warlike instincts beyond the ken of the clan members, could be relied upon to devise some strategic counterattack of startling efficacy. He had done so in the past, and would surely do so again. His ruu was ineffable, his determination absolute, and he did not know the meaning of fear. Lbavbsch Hfu and the others were thus taken by surprise when the Fal Grizhni Terrs fluted the call for a general retreat. The clan members were puzzled but obedient. Back they glided along the F'jnruu Corridor, closely pursued by the shouting soldiers, who had spotted their human quarry. Laggard Vardruls were cut down as they fled, but most of Hfu's group made it to the J'nr Maw, named for the horizontal rows of protruding conical rocks that guarded the entrance to the Long Throat that lay beyond.

Once into the Throat, evasion became easier. The narrow, jagged passageway with its unpredictably uneven floor presented little difficulty to the cave-bred Vardruls. For the humans, however, the way was difficult. Their progress was slow as they stumbled forward, sometimes tripping, sometimes banging themselves painfully against the wall or ceiling projections. By the time they emerged from the Throat into the wide Chamber of Columns, the Vardruls had drawn well ahead of their pursuers.

The Chamber of Columns was curiously formed, comprising a roughly circular open space, a lofty ceiling from which depended stalactites of unusual size, and a number of massive, naturally formed pillars of stone. Spaced at irregular intervals about the perimeter of the chamber were no less than six exits. The Fal Grizhni Terrs motioned his followers to disperse, and the Vardruls disappeared down half a dozen cracks and fissures in the walls. Terrs himself drew back into the fissure approximately opposite the opening of the Throat. Standing there, well out of sight yet possessing a clear view of the entire room, the young human surveyed the area impassively for a moment. Then, withdrawing a thin gold plaque incised with words and shapes from the pocket of his robe, he bowed his head and began to speak. As he spoke, one finger traced the shapes upon the plaque. Those clan members huddled in the fissure next to him looked on without comprehension. Impossible though it was to guess the nature of Fal Grizhni Terrs's occupation, the collective hiir remained high, for the son was proving himself a worthy successor to the legendary Grizhni Patriarch.

As Terrs stood muttering, the Guardsmen came spilling into the Chamber of Columns. More and more men emerged from the Throat to hesitate in confusion at sight of the multiple exits. And as they stood in doubt, young Terrs achieved Cognition.

Floor, walls, and ceiling quaked. Stalactites overhead rattled, and the great pillars of stone rumbled thunderously. The alarmed imprecations of the soldiers mingled with the wondering arpeggios of the Vardrul spectators. The human cries soared to high-pitched screams as the stalactites quivered, cracked from point to base, and tore themselves from the high ceiling to fall like a rain of javelins upon the heads of the invaders. The plummeting stones inflicted considerable damage. Some soldiers, the victims of direct hits, were instantly killed. Others, struck but glancingly, suffered broken bones and dislocations. All were painfully pelted with bits of broken rock. These misfortunes, however, served but as a prelude. Before the deluge of stone had ceased, the great columns that towered from floor to ceiling had begun to shudder visibly. As the stalactites rained down, the pillars quivered, split, and sweated chips of stone. Before the soldiers had fully realized the nature of the force that smote them from above, the chamber was rocked by an explosive roar as the huge columns ripped loose at base and crown, tottered and fell like trees in a hurricane. The columns smashed and shattered as they struck the floor. For a few moments all was chaos as huge chunks of rock bounced and rolled like pebbles, dust billowed chokingly, and stricken men screamed. When the fragments came to rest, the dust cleared to reveal a scene of ghastly carnage. Scores of Guardsmen and mercenaries lay dead, horribly crushed and broken. Many, far less fortunate, still lived—pinned beneath tons of stone. These poor wretches appeared to feel little pain as yet. Their eyes, glazed and shocked, reflected little understanding. One miserable mercenary, legs crushed beneath a rock the size of a double sendillis, was actually trying to shove the stone aside with his bare hands. Another, flat on his stomach with a great spar of stone pinning one ankle, was trying to crawl away and seemed unable to fathom his own lack of progress.

Some of the Guardsmen had escaped final injury. A number lay conscious and groaning softly, their limbs crooked at improbable angles. In some cases the jagged ends of shattered bones protruded through the flesh. A few of the soldiers were still on their feet, but even these relatively lucky ones were liberally splotched with blood.

Even as the men gazed around them, half-stupefied at the suddenness and magnitude of the disaster, a sharp whistle cut the humid air. At the sound of that whistle the Vardruls exploded into the Chamber of Columns. From each of the doorways, from all directions at once they came, a glowing horde of them armed with steel and stone. They attacked without hesitation, and the few remaining Guardsmen were almost instantly overwhelmed. Most of those humans still armed never had time to lift their blades. Dazed, weakened, and badly outnumbered, they were easy prey. Ferocious as never before, the Vardruls killed without mercy, sparing neither the helpless nor the already-dying. Minutes later, not a human soldier remained alive.

Recognition of their newfound savagery might have inspired the Vardruls with horror, had they paused to examine their own actions. Terrs himself paled at the sight of the mangled corpses. No leisure for communal introspection was granted, however. The attack at the F'jnruu Batgate had been spectacularly defeated, but the R'jnrllsch Lesser Patriarch, fighting at the Mvjri Dazzle, still required assistance. Thither the Fal Grizhni Terrs hurried, the Vardruls at his back.

The human squadron at the Mvjri Dazzle was led by Commander Krufaure himself, and it included both the best and the worst elements of the attacking force. Krufaure led the graceless crew of assorted tavern-sweepings hastily recruited for this mission; and to compensate for this, he had also surrounded himself with the finest of the surviving Ducal Guardsmen, and the most battle-hardened of the Rhelish mercenaries. It was to be hoped that this mixture would provide the Commander with a force of at least adequate overall competence. And as the soldiers pounded in fine style across the improvised bridge of planks that spanned the concealed pit at the Mvjri Dazzle, there seemed every reason to believe that such was the case. In perfect formation, the men continued along the Mvjri Corridor as far as the Bright Crossway, at which point they were ambushed by the defending forces of the R'jnrllsch lesser Patriarch. The Vardrul attack was surprisingly effective. The creatures were more than ordinarily aggressive, the element of surprise was on their side, and for a brief period they actually held the upper hand. The ensuing engagement was lively—so much so that nobody noticed the discreet withdrawal of two Lanthian recruits, who, detaching themselves from the rear of Krufaure's squadron, slipped quietly away along the Mvjri Corridor.

One of the men, the aptly titled Frog-face Fouvo, bore the star-shaped brand of the petty thief upon his right hand. His companion, gangling Beebie Jurner, was a harmless ne'er-do-well. Both men numbered among the recruits recently harvested at Snout's Tavern in Lanthi Ume. Both were chronic malcontents, and both detested military discipline. With so much in common, it was not surprising that their friendship had swiftly blossomed. Comradeship established, they had discovered many additional points of similarity, one of which was a shared love of easy money.

"Easy money," remarked Frog-face Fouvo as he and his friend unobtrusively navigated the Mvjri Corridor. Already they had left their comrades a fair distance behind, but the sounds of strife, augmented by the echoes, had not receded in the least. "There's bound to be easy money here, I'd stake my life on it. Keep your eye peeled."

"For what?" inquired Beebie Jurner.

"For anything that looks useful," Fouvo advised. "Look, there's no telling what we might find in this place. Gold. Jewels. Treasure. Anything."

"Where?"

"Where? Why, anywhere! Anywhere at all, my friend! Opportunity seeks strange lodgings, sometimes. Just keep looking."

They kept looking, but encountered nothing beyond rock-lit walls, colored slime, and elaborate mineral formations—things interesting enough in themselves, no doubt, but promising little profit. And presently, growing uneasy at their own temerity in venturing so far from their fellow Guardsmen, Beebie Jurner remarked, "We're like to get ourselves killed, trotting around this place like it was Kripnis Alley. What makes you so sure there's gold to be found here, Frog-face?"

"Why, it only makes sense, doesn't it? Treasure's always underground, isn't it? Anyway, those White Demons have probably killed and robbed and devoured thousands of travelers. And they've got to keep their stolen loot somewhere, don't they? Keep looking."

Down the corridor they sneaked, alert to the presence of enemies or booty. Initially they discovered neither. Upon reaching the end of the passageway, however, they came upon something almost as good.

Fouvo and Jurner stood at the entrance to a broad, high chamber, the most notable feature of which was a glowing, funnel-shaped pool. They had reached the Zmadrc death-pool chamber, whose significance they naturally failed to recognize. The room was not quite empty. Atop a low, flat stone that rose on the bank of the pool, a solitary figure stood absolutely motionless. Its flesh shone bright, almost as bright as fire, and the expression in its huge eyes was uncannily remote, as if it gazed on other worlds.

"What *is* it?" inquired Beebie Jurner, swallowing hard.

"It's one of *them*. Are you blind?"

"I know it's one of them, but there's something funny about this one."

"There's plenty funny about all of them," observed Fouvo sourly.

"No, this one is different. Why isn't it either attacking us or running away, like the others?"

"Who knows? Who cares?" The matter was evidently of greater interest than Fouvo admitted, for after a moment's close scrutiny he observed, "You know, I don't think it sees us."

"Why shouldn't it see us? Its eyes are wide open. *Wide* open—ugh!"

"Open or shut, it doesn't see us. I don't think it hears us either. Watch this." Fouvo snapped his fingers sharply, and the resulting pop echoed at length. The White Demon did not stir. It showed not the slightest sign of consciousness.

"I guess you're right. D'you think it's *dead,* Frog-face?"

"No. Can't you see it breathing? Besides, they don't glow like that when they're dead."

"Then what's wrong with it? Is it asleep? Or sick? Or stupid? What?"

"How should I know? We can't tell much from here. Let's take a closer look."

"Is it safe?"

"You clod-poll, we're two armed men against an unarmed Demon. And one good man is worth a whole spawning of Demons any day."

"That's not what I meant. What if it's sick, Frog-face? What if it's got some Demon-plague? What if we catch the disease and it turns us into White Demons ourselves? What then?"

"Beebie, you haven't the guts of a field mouse, and you will never be worth more than half a dakkle as long as you live. Stay here if you like. I'm going to take a closer look."

Sword in hand, Frog-face Fouvo approached the tranced monster. After a moment Jurner followed. The proximity of the humans exerted no visible effect upon the White Demon, who stood motionless and unconscious as ever. Fouvo and Jurner performed a careful examination, and found much to arouse their interest in a creature so titillatingly like and unlike themselves. Inspection completed, Fouvo stood lost in thought while Jurner amused himself with offensive sallies of wit to which the White Demon took not the slightest exception. Presently the sport grew wearisome, and Jurner took to prodding the creature with the point of his sword. This action produced results. The Demon's skin flickered and the muscular bands around its eyes writhed weirdly. Additional poking produced more marked effects, but soon even this entertainment palled, and Jurner remarked, "This is all very well, but it's getting us nowhere. Let's kill this thing and be on our way."

"Eh? Kill it?" Fouvo was appalled. "Don't even think it! Why man, don't you recognize good fortune when it's staring you in the face? This is what we've been looking for!"

"What, this monster?"

"There you've said it! A monster, our own personal monster to do with as we please. Beebie, if we take this creature back to Lanthi Ume and put it on exhibit in a cage, do you have any idea how much folk would pay to see it? A genuine, living, breathing, baby-eating White Demon?"

"Lots. You've a head on you, Frog-face," Jurner admired.

"I won't deny it. I've had a lot of clever notions in my time, but this here is one of my best. Now the question is, how do we get our Demon out of this place without Big Man Krufaure and the others spotting us? They'd be bound to interfere. Never mind, I've got it. We'll just wait right here a bit. It won't take the Guards long to clear out that tunnel and push on into the caves. As soon as the coast is clear, we'll just scoot on down the tunnel, straight out of this place and back to Lanthi Ume, where we set ourselves up in business. And the dakkles will pour in. More than dakkles—silver shorns. Our luck has turned, Beebie—we're rich men!"

The beauty of this prospect held them enthralled for a time, but at last Beebie Jurner collected his wits so far as to suggest, "We'd better bind the Demon before it wakes up and gets ideas."

"Good thought. Got your rope?"

Jurner nodded. He, like all members of the attack force, had been equipped with a coil of rope whose possible uses were manifold in such a place as the caves of the Nazara Sin. Shaking loose the cord, he now approached the flickering White Demon to loop a coil about the creature's throat. At touch of the rope, the Demon's flesh darkened abruptly. Consciousness returned at last, the great eyes came alive, and they were clouded with terror.

Engaged in deep, strong communion with the Ancestors, Zmadrc Fourteen did not note the arrival of the two Lanthians. Perhaps on some level she was aware of their presence, for the Ancestors seemed to withdraw themselves somewhat and even the powerful, reassuring current of feeling that emanated from her father, the Zmadrc Patriarch, lost some of its immediacy. Instinctively Fourteen sought to strengthen the failing connection, and for a time succeeded in blocking all distraction from her consciousness. The Ancestors were calling to her, and her sense of unity with them intensified with every passing Small Ven. Their thoughts and feelings permeated her, and their voices were stronger than the voices of all save her Future.

Not even the strongest of Ancestral bonds, however, could endure in the face of alien physical contact. Fourteen's consciousness was absent, but her nerves and brain nonetheless registered the highly disharmonious touch of the cord upon her

throat. Dismayed, the Ancestors withdrew themselves and all
Knowledge was lost. Smarting at the pain of the abrupt deser-
tion, Fourteen emerged from her trance to find two human
soldiers at her side. While on of them grasped both her arms,
the other tightened the noose around her neck. The horror of
that transition from the warm oneness of the Ancestors to the
reality of human attack was almost more than Fourteen's mind
could tolerate. Her hiir plunged and her eyes filmed over with
sickening fear. A shrill, discordant cry escaped her.

Evidently startled at this evidence of life on the part of the
hitherto silent, inanimate Vardrul, the human soldiers hastily
retreated a few paces. Fourteen tore the rope away and dropped
it to the floor. Dazed and bewildered though she was, her
movements were swift and fluid as she whirled and dashed for
the nearest exit.

"Quick, it's getting away!"

"Grab 'im, Beebie!"

Fourteen heard and understood the shouts. One of the humans
leaped for her. Dodging lithely, she evaded the outstretched
hands with their cruel, stiff jointed fingers. A feint, a sudden
reversal, and she was past the humans, under the arch, and out
in the Mvjri Corridor.

They were coming after her. Incomprehensibly vindictive,
they meant to run her down. Fourteen fled, but very soon
sensed profound disharmony in the corridor ahead. Human
shouts echoed, together with the fluting music of her own kind
and the clash of weapons. Another battle was in progress,
another of those ghastly paroxysms of blood-letting that had
of late lent such a nightmarish quality to life in the caverns
that Fourteen had been moved more than ever to seek the solace
of the Ancestors. She could not continue along the corridor.
The strife ahead offered greater danger than the humans behind,
and in any event, she could not bear to witness it. Fourteen
ducked into the first tributary tunnel she encountered, but did
not succeed in losing her pursuers. She could hear their
footsteps, heavy but surprisingly swift, and the fear rose in her
until it blotted out every vestige of peace and harmony.

Fourteen quickened her pace, weaving a tangled path through
a maze of tiny passageways. She was growing tired now, confused and correspondingly careless. Often she stumbled, sometimes bruising her nearly lightless flesh upon the stone projections. Terror had fogged her judgment and perceptions. She

no longer knew where she was, nor where she might seek safety. She did not understand why she was pursued by creatures of waking nightmare. She only knew, by some obscure process of subliminal recognition, that capture was worse than death, for her fate at their hands would somehow transcend all horrors of the imagination.

She could no longer hear them now—perhaps she had shaken them from her trail somewhere in the depths of the winding passageways—but Fourteen dared not stop. On she stumbled, heart pounding, breathing distressed, ocular ridges vastly expanded. Often as she went she cast fearful glances back over her shoulder, scarcely heeding the way before her. Even when the ceiling dipped, forcing her down into a crouch, and the air in the tunnel turned suggestively cool, she took no notice of her surroundings. In such a state she emerged from a concealed hole in the hillside some hundreds of yards north of the Mvjri Dazzle into the full glare of Surface sunlight.

The merciless light struck like acid upon the unveiled eyes of Zmadrc Fourteen. A warble of pain escaped her. Flinging one arm across her face she shrank back, instinctively seeking the gentle dimness of the caverns, then paused. She could not go back, for behind her came the men with their blades and cords, their cruel jointed hands, their obscure and indescribably terrifying schemes. She could not face them. Anything was better than that.

Fourteen struggled up the hill. The Surface air was harsh, dry, and unbearably cold upon her unprotected flesh—so bitter that she might almost have welcomed the anesthesia of Cold Stupor. Worse than the cold was the light—the dreadful, overwhelming sunlight that bathed her sensitive eyes in agony. Fourteen was blind. The world around her was lost in whiteness, burning whiteness. She covered her eyes and the white turned to black, which was somewhat less unbearable; but the pain did not recede. Her eyes were aflame, perhaps damaged beyond all recovery. The world around her was alien, and she was alone for the first time, cut off from her clan and indeed from all others of her race. And this last was the most terrible thing of all.

Fourteen wandered in panic and sightless confusion. She dared not linger in hope of rescue by her Future, for the humans might easily find her. She dared not cry aloud to her kinsmen, for the humans might easily hear her. She could only roam the

barren hills in blind quest of a gateway back to the caverns
that she longed for as a lost paradise.

Dazzled as she was, Zmadrc Fourteen had no idea that she
wandered the crest of Spiny Ridge. No six sense warned her of
danger as she approached the verge of Kren's Cliff. Her fall from
the heights of the precipice was as sudden as it was unexpected.
A descent so swift left no time for fear, and when her body struck
the rocks at the foot of the cliff there was no pain, but only joy
and deepest harmony. For in those final moments of life the
Ancestors were with her, she knew them, and their warmth
made her whole as they drew gently unto themselves.

When Fal Grizhni Terrs reached the Bright Crossway at the
head of his relief force, he found the Vardruls under the
R'jnrllsch Lesser Patriarch still stoutly holding their own against
the invading humans. He noted too that his mother was there,
standing behind the Vardrul lines well out of the way of the
combatants. Beside her stood Har Fennahr, armed with nothing
but a miserable short stalactite that he had managed to pick up
somewhere. The frown that creased young Terrs's forehead
revealed his annoyance or perhaps worry at her presence, but
now was not the time to address such concerns. For the second
time that Coloration the youth fluted a call for a general retreat,
and for the second time his army faded away into the depths
of the caves. The humans followed, baying like hounds, and
thus were lured to the deep inner passageways.

There was nothing in the vicinity of the Mvjri Dazzle that
remotely compared with the Chamber of Columns as a vehicle
for the Falling Stones. Terrs was obliged to content himself
with the K'fdrs Excavation, an artificially augmented chamber
boasting an array of very large stalactites and a single, enormous
natural column. This column, the K'fdrs Pillar, was engraved
from top to bottom with glyphs and runes of unknowable antiq-
uity. Historical significance notwithstanding, the column was
in this instance considered expendable. When the Guardsmen
and mercenaries burst into the empty excavation they were met
with a deluge of stone that killed some and left many others
wounded, battered, and reeling. The collapse of the K'fdrs
Pillar squashed several more and filled all survivors with horror.
Despite the terror of the Falling Stones, however, the Guardsmen were not altogether conquered. Casualties here did
not equal those of the Chamber of Columns. Many of the

soldiers were still on their feet, and their commander Krufaure was entirely uninjured. When the combined Vardrul forces of Lbavbsch Hfu and the R'jnrllsch Lesser Patriarch came humming into the excavation, they found their work cut out for them.

The remaining soldiers, now fighting for their lives, desperately sought the exit. What they lacked in numbers they made up in frenzied ferocity, and Vardruls fell to darken by the score. For a time it seemed likely that the remaining humans might win free, but gradually the sheer volume of the massed clan members prevailed. As the rocks, spears, and stolen swords of the Vardruls rose and fell, the Guardsmen were vanquished one by one. And each in turn went down to disappear for a time beneath a cluster of furious glowing forms who rose from their work to leave ravaged corpses behind them. The voices of the Vardruls rose in melodies of sinister beauty that mingled strangely with the hoarse shrieks of dying humans. The enthusiastic slaughter continued until at last only Commander Krufaure and the small party of Guardsmen at his side remained alive. Krufaure fought with a savagery almost more than human. His famous backhanded sweep was much in evidence, and many a Vardrul head had already parted company from its body. The energy and undaunted spirit of the Commander had inspired a band of Krufaure's closest companions, who now fought with a determination almost equal to that of their leader. So violent was the defense of Krufaure and his men that they actually succeeded in fighting their way out of the K'fdrs Excavation. Once clear of the excavation, the men turned tail and frankly fled for their lives, pursued by a number of the most relentless of the clan members. They made it back to the Mvjri Dazzle but a few yards ahead of their enemies. Over the planks that spanned the trap they thundered, pausing only long enough to dismantle the bridge behind them. Immediate pursuit foiled, the pitiful remnant of the Ducal Guardsmen passed from the caverns of the Nazara Sin and thus survived to carry news of the debacle back to Lanthi Ume.

Throughout the seemingly interminable battle, Lady Verran watched from a position of relative safety at the mouth of a fissure in the wall of the K'fdrs Excavation. Har Fennahar, armed with a sharpened stone, remained at her side at all times. The makeshift weapon proved superfluous, however, for no danger approached the two quiet humans. At the conclusion of the fighting, following the final rout of the soldiers, Verran emerged from the fissure to make her way to her son. It was for this purpose that she had come to the Mvjri Dazzle. But now that she stood at Terrs's side, she could not speak.

Terrs had played no part in the dreadful annihilation of the last surviving soldiers trapped in the excavation. The wounded, the dying, the unconscious men—all had been indiscriminately battered and stabbed, and the dead lay everywhere. Terrs had not participated in this, but neither had he attempted to prevent it. He had brought the stones down upon his enemies, fought the survivors, and killed two of them—Verran had watched it all. Now he was filthy with blood and sweat, and his expression— a curious mixture of triumph and horror—so unnerving that she could find no words with which to address him. Instead she watched in silence as the Vardruls tended to their own injured—watched as wounds were bound, feeble living bodies freed of the weight of piled-up corpses, and sightless eyes closed forever. There was little noise there, for uninjured Vardruls went about their work in intent silence, as if by total absorption in the task at hand they might for a little while longer postpone contemplation of their own deeds. Neither did the wounded clan members cry or groan—only a low throbbing hum escaped them, an indescribably piteous sound. Terrs shuddered to hear it, and only then did Verran dare lay a hand upon his arm. He took her hand and held it, something he had not done since earliest childhood. Hands clasped, they stood there watching and did not note the resurrection of a seemingly dead Guardsman who lay in his own blood on the floor just behind them. The soldier, awakening from real or feigned unconsciousness, climbed slowly to his feet. His face was bathed in the blood that streamed from a cut on his forehead and his progress was slow, but fanatic resolve manifested itself in every movement. He made it to his feet with difficulty, swayed and shuffled forward a few paces. His feverish eyes were fixed on the back of Terrs Fal Grizhni. He lifted his blade.

The advance of the Guardsman went unnoted by Verran and by Terrs, but the faltering footfalls reached the ears of Har Fennahar, who stood a few feet distant. Fennahar turned in time to see the blade quivering above young Terrs's unprotected head. Instantly he sprang forward to interpose himself between soldier and target, and with his stone weapon attempted to parry the stroke. The steel blade whistled down and the narrow stalactite shattered under the impact. Flying stone fragments struck Fennahar's head. The blade continued along a somewhat deflected path, opening a wide gash across the explorer's chest. Fennahar cried out, staggered back and fell, bleeding profusely. The noise alerted Verran and Terrs, who spun around to witness the Guardsman transfixed by the javelin of F'tryll'jnr Rdsdr.

Fennahar lay motionless, eyes closed and face colorless under the faded tan. Verran ran to him, called his name, and received no response. He was still alive, but insensible, and losing blood swiftly. The Vardruls in the chamber paid the incident scant heed, so inured were they becoming to the sight of violence. Terrs, however, approached to kneel at the fallen man's side.

Verran tore swatches from her robe, pressing them to the wound to stanch the flow of blood. One by one the rags reddened and she discarded them. The abruptness of her movements reflected increasing nervous agitation. Her hands were starting to shake. "He'll bleed to death," she whispered.

"No, Mother. He will be well, I promise. If the bleeding does not abate naturally, I now have the Cognition with which to ensure his recovery."

"No Cognition! We don't want it! It is a cruel art!"

"Not always. It will save him if other means fail, and I can do no less for one with whom I have shaken hands. He was hurt for my sake."

"Then you recognize his friendship?"

"Yes," said Terrs, after a pause. "I recognize it."

"I am glad of that. If you're his friend, then you'll understand my decision. Ril has asked me to go away with him, and I intend to accept."

"You will leave the caverns? When did you decide this?"

"I'm not sure. At some point I decided without noticing. But I know now. When he recovers I will leave with him, I will return to the Surface and I will be his wife. That is the life that I want, and that is my choice."

"Mother, are you sure?"

"There's more to it than that," she continued, without answering the question. "Ril needs to carry Lord Grizhni's records back to Lanthi Ume. They are my property, and I have given him my permission. The writings will go with us. Not forever, I promise you that, but for now they will go."

Terrs did not reply. He threw her a startled glance, and conflicting emotions warred openly upon his face.

Verran looked into the turbulent black eyes. "I would like you to come with us," she told him. "Not necessarily for long—it needn't be a protracted severing from your Vardrul friends. But you are a human being and you should experience the Surface world. You and the Vardruls alike would benefit by a period of separation, and if you doubt it, only look around you. What's more, you are my son, and fight though we may, I love you as part of myself and I always will. Come with us."

Still he did not reply. Verran busied herself with the ministrations. Fennahar's bleeding had slowed, almost stopped. His wound was less serious than she had feared. The explorer's eyelids were quivering, but he had not yet regained consciousness. All around them the Vardruls tended to wounded and dying, while Verran plied her bandages and Terrs wrestled internally. The youth's deliberations were cut short by the arrival of a group of R'jnrllsch kinsmen bearing the limp and lightless form of Zmadrc Fourteen. Terrs seemed hardly to hear the Vardruls' account of their discovery as the small corpse was placed on the floor before him. His face, as he gazed down at the remains of his erstwhile Future, was utterly still. So long did he maintain his motionless, fixed attitude that Verran forgot her own grief and began to fear for him. In order to break his terrible stillness, she whispered the only inadequate words she knew. "Terrs, I'm so sorry."

"There is no reason to be sorry," he replied very calmly. "She is with her Ancestors. There is no sorrow in that."

"That's—true," she replied with an effort. His frozen demeanor alarmed her. She looked down and pressed the cloth more firmly to Fennahar's wound.

"The ultimate clan-union is an occasion of rejoicing," said Terrs. "The young Zmadrc Fourteen is safe and well."

"Yes. And you?"

"And as for me," Terrs continued, "I will retire in solitude for a time to contemplate her happiness and to ponder my own future course. There is much to consider. During that time I will be alone, entirely alone and harmonious. How should I be otherwise? All is well."

And Verran, catching the faintest tremor in his voice, glanced up quickly to see his face wet with tears, like a block of ice melting in desert heat.

Chapter Thirteen

"Your lordship, we must make an end," remarked the Lady Josky.

Father and daughter sat at their dinner in the room above Grue's Cookshop. Outside the night was dark and wild. Inside the lamps glowed, the fire danced on the grate, all was warmth and comfort. No corresponding comfort, however, reflected itself upon the visage of Yans Whurm Didnis. Didnis appeared despondent. He sat slumped in his chair, eyeing his meal without favor.

"We must finish," Josky insisted.

Didnis sighed. The subject was obviously familiar and unwelcome. He raised his goblet to his lips, made a great show of swishing the execrable vintage around in his mouth before swallowing and answering reluctantly, "My lady, as things stand, there is nothing to be done."

"I can't understrand why you *say* that!"

"Lady Josquinilliu. In the aftermath of the unfortunate incident at Parnis Regatta, the Duke Povon has immured himself within his palace, whither we may not follow. That being the case, we cannot reach him and we are helpless."

"We are *not!* Listen to me, Dad! We've got to finish that Duke. We said we'd do it, we took the payment, and now we've got to deliver. Otherwise we'll never be able to hold up our heads in this town. Everyone will laugh up their sleeves at us, and I won't live that way, I won't. We've got to *do* something—"

"My treasure, you've a tiger's heart wrapped in a girlish hide, but in this case there is nothing to be done. The Duke is beyond our reach for the moment. It is now a time for patience.''

"That's where your lordship's wrong. Dead wrong," the Lady Josky affirmed. "There's plenty we can do, and we're going to start tonight."

"I do not understand you."

"Then listen and I'll explain. The thing is, the Duke doesn't hole up in the palace all the time the way you said. He goes out, all right, but not many people know because the old fart's as rabbit-minded as that son of his, and he goes greasing around in secret—"

"My princess must not forget her dignity—"

"I'm sorry, Dad, but it happens to be true. Anyway, they say the Duke will do just about anything to get away from that Lammish ogress he's got to marry, so he goes sneaking out at night to spend time on his venerise, pickling his brain—"

"They say? Who says?"

"Everybody. You should spend more time talking to folk at the market, your lordship. Be good for you."

"We do not consort with the common herd, my lady. Such associations are beneath us."

"Well, how else are we to learn what's going on? And how can we do our jobs if we don't know what's happening? And if we don't do our job well, if we aren't the best there is, then we're not upholding the honor of the House of Didnis, are we?"

The bravo had no answer.

"Well, then," Josky concluded triumphantly. "There you are. So they tell me that the Duke sometimes spends the nights sailing around the canals, where the Keldhaam Gnuxia can't get at him."

"Indeed? When is the Duke abroad?"

"They didn't say."

"Where does he go when he sails?"

"Here, there, everywhere."

"Sweet child, this information is not uninteresting, but in its present form virtually without use to us."

"Hah! Wrong again, your lordship. I've got a plan. What we do is, we take a good supply of food and we stow away aboard the boat. Then it doesn't matter when the Duke chooses to sail, or where he decides to go. Whenever, wherever, we're right there with him and we pick him off in our own good time."

"Lady Josky, that is an enterprising scheme to be sure, yet wholly impractical."

"*Why* impractical?" Josky demanded, jaw outthrust pugnaciously.

"For one simple reason—we cannot gain access to the Duke's venerise. When not in use, *Sublimity* is moored at the Ducal Palace. As you know, the ducal moorings are guarded day and night. At other times, when his Grace is aboard, a watch is posted. We would be stopped before we ever set foot upon the deck."

Josky's lips twitched impatiently. "Do you think I haven't thought of that? Pooh, I already knew all about the watch. I'm not a child, you know. But I know how to deal with the problem. What's more, tonight's the night to do it. Now listen, your lordship. Right now, this very minute, *Sublimity* lies at the Old Market Pier and there she stays until her carvings have been regilded, her decks freshly varnished, and her hangings cleaned. While the work goes on, the crew's on leave."

"Who has told you this?"

"A dockyard beggar I give crusts to. And Leather Greanah, who goes with the sailors, said the same thing."

"Sweet child, these are not fit companions for a daughter of the House of Didnis."

"Let's not get into that now. We've more important things to think about. Now, your lordship—let's get our gear together, pack up some food, and get on over to that venerise."

"Softly, my child. You are too rash, too hasty. This is a matter that demands much thought and planning."

"No. We've thought and planned enough. Where's it getting us? Now's the time to move, and we're going to do it *now*, before we lose our chance. I'm sick to death of sitting around this place doing nothing. I've had enough of that. I want to *move*, Dad!"

"My treasure, there is such a thing as prudence—"

"I'm sick and tired of prudence all the time! I tell you I want to get this job finished once and for all. If we don't, our reputation's *garbage*. I want to go to the boat tonight, I *want* to and I will. And if you won't come with me, your lordship, then I'll just go alone, I will."

She stared at him challengingly, and Didnis crumpled. "Peace, my own darling. I concede. You shall not venture forth without your father at your side."

"Oh, suPREME! I love you, Dad!" Impulsively she sprang from her chair and circled the table to throw her arms around her father and plant a resounding kiss on the top of his head.

"And I love you, my Josky." Tears of sentiment rose to the bravo's eyes. "Now let us make ready."

As swiftly as possible the two packed food, drink, and assorted weapons. This done, they wrapped themselves warmly against the damp, donned vizards and hats, descended from their lodgings, and made their quiet way along the wynds and down to the Straightwater Canal. There they engaged a public dombulis to carry them as far as Green Jetty, where they disembarked to finish their journey on foot.

Old Market Pier, windswept and rain-drenched, appeared entirely deserted. A couple of lanterns affixed to a nearby building threw forlorn dim light upon wet wooden wharf, pilings slick with algae, stacks of crates shrouded in tarpaulins, and assorted vessels ranging in size from tiny dombulis to great sea-going merchant galley. It was easy to pick out *Sublimity*. One of the largest of the vessels, ponderously castled fore and aft, her eccentric proportions were impossible to mistake.

"There," said Didnis, pointing. "Deserted, by the look of her."

"Then what are we waiting for?" demanded Lady Josky, her clear voice rising above the patter of rain.

"Softly, child. The path is clear and we wait for nothing."

"Good, Dad! That's it! Let's move!"

Together they made their way to the gangplank; and finding the way unguarded, hastily boarded the vessel.

Sublimity was abandoned, or seemed to be. Didnis and Josky stood there in the rain surveying the parquet decks, the golden rigging, and the carven, inlaid masts with wonder. Like most Lanthians, they had hitherto witnessed these wonders only at a distance. Now they could linger, pry, poke, and appraise to their hearts' content.

"Gold, my child. Take note of such things. That wire inlay in the hatch is pure gold. So are those disks inset in the masts."

"Think we might pry 'em loose?"

"My lady Josquinilliu." Whurm Didnis spoke sternly. "We are not bandits; we are not thieves. Would you disgrace our calling?"

"Sorry, your lordship."

"Child, always remember—an act of theft diminishes our honor and debases our nobility. On a more practical level, it calls undesirable attention to our presence.''

"I wasn't thinking," Josky confessed.

"Fear not, Daughter. Your instincts are superlative and experience will refine them. Now come, let us acquaint ourselves with *Sublimity*.''

Together they explored the vessel, which proved less deserted than they had imagined. Far belowdecks, at the end of a narrow passage lined with storage compartments, they came upon a polished portal equipped with a gilded bar of unusual solidity. Didnis lifted the bar, opened the door, and they peered into the chamber beyond. The faint light of a small oil lamp borrowed from the crew's quarters illuminated three great rectangular blocks resembling biers. Upon each bier lay a pitifully emaciated captive bound in place with white, glistening cords. The soft, moist cords slithered like serpents over floor and walls; hung from the ceiling in fantastic designs; and clung avidly to the prisoners' recumbent forms. The men were unconscious. Two lay silent and motionless beneath the weight of clustering cords, and the third moaned piteously in his sleep. The intrusion of the newcomers did not wake them.

"What *is* that?" Josky whispered in awe.

"Those are the the wretches whose life forces are drained to power this vessel," Didnis told her. "See, my Josky, see— *Sublimity* feeds!''

The cords that bound the moaning man pulsed softly, and presently the human outcry died as the victim sank into a more profound swoon.

"Oh, groTESQUE!" opined the Lady Josky.

Didnis shut the door softly. "Not a pretty sight," he admitted, "and yet we may be thankful for it.''

"Thankful? Why, your lordship?"

"The life forces yielded by those prisoners furnish the energy employed by the venerise to perform all functions without benefit of human assistance. That is to say, *Sublimity* requires no crew.''

"Oh, I see what you mean. A fancified hulk of this size"— Josky's expansive gesture took in the entire boat—"might want scores of sailors, otherwise. As it is, the Duke only needs a handful of his pretty servants to look after him. Which means we don't have to worry so much about anyone troubling us.''

"Exactly, my child. With your usual insight, you have penetrated straight to the heart of the matter. But enough of this. Time passes. Let us continue our tour and settle upon a place of concealment.''

They finally chose one of the storage compartments—a dark stuffy hold crowded with barrels, sacks, and crates. It was agreed that they would alternate watch duty, beginning with Didnis. Accordingly they sought what small comfort they could find behind a wall of stacked wooden boxes. The bravo contrived a thin pad of his folded cloak, a lumpy pillow of a sack of meal, and upon this makeshift pallet the Lady Josky stretched herself, with her own cloak as a blanket. It was very late, and even Josky's inexhaustible vitality was a little depleted. Despite the inadequacy of her bed she fell asleep at once, enjoying the untroubled slumber of carefree youth throughout the night, while her father maintained vigil at her side.

The time passed in boredom and discomfort, but fortunately for the bravo and his child, the refurbishing of *Sublimity*, already near completion, went forward apace and was swiftly concluded. On the afternoon of the second day fresh supplies were taken on and the galley restocked. In the evening the helmsman and three attendants came aboard. This tiny group was far smaller than even the minimal crew customarily employed by the Duke Povon. It was to be assumed that his Grace, in seeking to evade the surveillance of the Keldhaam Gnuxia, lessened the risk of discovery by reducing the number of those privy to the secrets of his nocturnal excursions. Gnuxia would soon know all, of course; but that evil day could perhaps be postponed. Whatever the reason, the venerise was nearly empty, a condition that suited Whurm Didnis very well.

That night the great green and gold sails were unfurled beneath clear starry skies. Under impetus of the appropriate Cognitive commands, *Sublimity* slid without fanfare from the Old Market Pier to make her way along the canals as far as the ducal moorings.

The thud of unwonted activity overhead informed the stowaways that something unusual was afoot. Josky, being small and agile, was sent forth to reconnoiter and soon returned bearing news of the Duke's presence.

''One helmsman, three flunkies, and the Duke,'' reported Lady Josky. ''This is going to be a sweetmeat. Let's do it.''

"Not yet, my lady."

"And why not?"

"We lie within shouting distance of the Ducal Palace."

"So *what*?"

"A contingent of Guardsmen is invariably on duty within and about the palace. In the event of disturbance, we do not wish to attract their attention."

"Oh. Yes. I guess that's true. Your lordship—" Josky's eyes shone. "I think you must be about the best father and the best assassin in the whole world."

Didnis blushed with pleasure. "Hush, my child. You will make me vain."

"I hope I'll be like you someday."

"Child, you will be even better. You are well on your way."

Handfasted, they crouched in concealment until the venerise was once more under way. Anywhere in the city they might have gone, anywhere from the Vayno Fortification that guarded the mainland approach, as far as Jherova, outermost of Lanthi Ume's famed Nine Isles—anywhere to escape the vigilance of the Kheldaam Gnuxia. But when they dropped the anchor at last and Lady Josky ventured forth to garner information, she soon returned in a state of high excitement.

"We're home!" she exclaimed in an electric whisper. "They've anchored this tub off the Destula Pier. Can you believe it?"

"With difficulty," Whurm Didnis confessed. "Our neighborhood, quaint and atmospheric though it may be, rarely attracts noble visitors. What can his Grace's purpose be?"

"What difference does it make? There are no Guardsmen here, no one to come if he calls. Let's do it!"

"It would be wiser to wait until they sleep—"

"No more waiting! Now, Dad! *Now!*"

Didnis nodded slowly, and in the feeble light of the oil lamp his shadow bobbed on the wall. "You are right, my treasure. The time has come. We begin by eliminating all possible witnesses to our deed."

"The flunkies?"

"Precisely."

In stealth they emerged from the storage compartment and crept to the galley, where the chef piped the finishing rosettes of cream atop the Duke's chocolate-chestnut dessert. A stroke of the bravo's stiletto, and the cream went pink.

From the galley they proceeded to the forecastle, where Povon's valet sprinkled lavender-water on the silken sheets of his master's berth. Another stroke, and the valet sprawled on the fouled ducal bed.

Amidships the armed sentry slept. His dereliction of duty was punishable by death.

There remained only the helmsman, who was not easily located. Following a fruitless prowl, the Lady Josky spat impatiently, "Enough! We can take care of him later! It's time, Dad! Let's *do* it!"

Didnis nodded dutifully. Without further conversation they ascended to the high poop deck, where they found the Duke Povon polishing off his roasted grouse by candlelight. The ducal pupils were vastly dilated, the ducal demeanor beatific. In honor of his temporary evasion of Gnuxia's vigilance, Povon had toasted his own health in the Moon Dream of Uhanna. Owing to long privation, his tolerance was reduced and the effects of ingestion were unusually pronounced. It had been his Grace's intention to refresh himself at leisure before seeking the counsel of the Sapient Nulliad. Now his plans had been interrupted. At the sight of the intruders, Povon lifted his glass.

"Ah. Company. Delightful," he observed, and giggled.

Didnis and Josky exchanged uneasy glances.

"You may join me. Be so good as to seat yourselves and eat," the Duke commanded with a gracious gesture. "I recommend the fennel custard. It is excellent. No less pariseworthy is the vegetable terrine."

"Oh, groTESQUE!" opined the Lady Josky.

"What do you say, child?" inquired his Grace.

"Vegetables are *garbage*!"

"She says, your Grace, that we are not here to share your dinner," Whurm Didnis explained.

"Indeed?" Povon thrust his lower lip out, appeared to wrestle with a mental problem, gave it up, and inqured, woozily, "Why *are* you here?"

Whurm Didnis wordlessly drew his stiletto.

Duke Povon regarded the weapon in wonder. "What is that for?"

"For your Grace. Prepare yourself."

"Who *are* you?" Povon frowned as if mildly afflicted with

some annoyance he could not quite remember.

"I'll tell you who we are," the Lady Josky broke in before her father could reply. "This is the Lord Yans Whurm Didnis, greatest bravo in all Lanthi Ume. Greatest bravo in all the world, probably. And I'm the Lady Joquinilliu Whurm Didnis, his lordship's only daughter and only assistant. And your son Sneever has paid us to do you, and we're about to earn our commission at last. That's who we are!"

"My lady Josky, there is no need to reveal all this—" Whurm Didnis remonstrated.

"Why not, Dad? I'm proud of it, and I wanted to see the expression on his face."

Duke Povon's expression did not fulfill her expectations. He appeared vaguely unquiet, vaguely perturbed, but nothing more.

"My child, I would urge you to cultivate an austere reticence. There is no need to explain matters to the target."

"Why not, your lordship? Where's the harm? What difference does it make?"

As if in answer to her question, Duke Povon rose from his chair, glassy eyes fixed upon the bravo's weapon. Recognition of danger had at last fought its way through the roseate Moon Dream fog, and the Duke lifted his voice in a tremendous shout, "Helmsman! *Murder!* Helmsman, ho!" Unsteadily he backed away until the taffrail halted his retreat.

"Quick, Dad! Get him!"

Didnis's arm flashed forward and his stiletto flew through the air too fast for the eye to follow. The blade struck home and the force of the blow knocked the Duke backward over the railing. With a scream Povon tumbled headlong from the high poop down into the Straightwater Canal. He struck with a huge splash, and the polluted waters closed over his head. Didnis and Josky ran to the taffrail to peer down into the canal. They saw nothing.

"He's fish-fodder," Josky observed. "You've done it, your lordship! You got the Duke!"

"I'm not so sure." Didnis shook his head. "Where did he go?"

"To the bottom, of course. Where else?"

"There is something not quite right."

"Oh, pooh. You worry too much. If your blade didn't kill

him outright, then he'll bleed to death. If he doesn't bleed to death, then he'll drown. You got him all right."

"I only hope you are right, sweet child. Still, I dislike uncertainty—"

The colloquy was interrupted by the soft thud of a footstep on the deck behind them. Didnis and Josky whirled to face the staring helmsman, who had appeared in response to his master's summons. Their reaction was prompt. With one accord they sprang for him. The helmsman turned and fled, with the stowaways in close pursuit. They managed to corner him on the quarter deck. Josky drew her dagger. Didnis produced his spare blade. Together they advanced.

A strangled squawk of terror escaped the helmsman. His legs gave way beneath him and he sank to his knees. Gazing up into the pitiless faces of the two strangers, he beheld his own death and in desperation cast about for a charm to banish the specter.

"Don't do it!" the helmsman pleaded. "I won't give you away, I swear! I never saw you, I'm blind, I'm deaf."

This appeal exerted little effect, and he tried another approach. "I can help you. Yes, I can! This boat is crammed with valuables. I can show you the secret compartments where they're locked away."

Josky's questioning eyes met her father's. Didnis shook his head minutely.

"It's true!" the helmsman exclaimed, noting the ominous exchange. "I can be useful to you. I can help you escape! This boat, she goes like the wind, you've probably seen it. I know the special commands will make her go. I can have you out of Lanthi Ume and safe away in minutes! You keep the venerise, or sell her abroad for a fortune, but you need me alive to make her go! Trust me, I'll do it!"

Once again the killers traded glances and Josky observed, "The boat's worth a lot more than what Lord Nobody'll pay us. And for such a deed as this, don't we deserve something extra?"

"An unexpected opportunity. A choice. Rich reward and increased danger. Advantages and disadvantages to weigh in the blink of an eye. Why is life never simple?" Whurm Didnis scowled thoughtfully out over the water. What he saw on shore cut his cogitations short. There, plain in the moonlight, a familiar chubby figure was dragging itself from the canal. The dripping figure collapsed face down on the Destula Pier, rested a moment, then climbed to its feet, cupped hands to mouth, and shouted, *"Help! Murder!"*

Didnis and Josky froze, their blades pressed to the helmsman's throat.

Duke Povon cast a terrified glance back over his shoulder at the boat, then took to his heels, still screaming. For a moment his receding cries echoed, then faded away into silence.

Josky came abruptly to life. "If we're going to catch him, we'll have to swim for it. Come on, your lordship!" She ran to the deck railing and began to climb over.

Didnis halted her with a despairing gesture. "Useless, my child, useless. Do not attempt it."

"What d'you mean? We'll run that sniveling lump to ground in five minutes flat. Come *on*, Dad!"

"Alas, impossible. Impossible." Didnis shook his head so vehemently that the beard-beads clacked. "My lady, you know the complexity and intricacy of the Destula. The neighborhood offers a thousand escape routes, ten thousand hiding places. Once vanished therein, the quarry is not to be found."

"I don't believe it! Somehow we'll find a way!"

"The Duke has disappeared. Once ashore, where do you propose to begin the search?"

"I don't know. I guess there are a lot of places," Josky conceded, after a moment's thought. "But we've got to try, at least!"

"Child, child. As you grow older you will learn the folly of squandering your energies upon hopeless enterprises. The mature intellect recognizes futility."

"Then what are you saying?" Josky looked more than a little crestfallen. "Do you mean we have to just go back home and sit around waiting until another chance to get him comes along? That might take weeks!"

"It is not quite as simple as that, my lady. We can't go home to wait for another chance. As a matter of fact, we can't go home at all."

"What do you mean? Why not?"

"Because, my impetuous princess, in your enthusiasm you revealed our identities to his Grace. The Duke now knows our names, our faces, our patron's identity, and when he reaches safety he will undoubtedly rouse the entire city against us all.''

"You mean then—even if we got him after this, we wouldn't be paid for it?''

"In all probability, there will be nobody to pay us. Lord Sneever's circumstances tremble on the verge of sudden alteration, I fear. Poor fellow!''

"Oh. Yes. I guess I shouldn't have done that.''

"It was imprudent. My lady's youthful high spirits sometimes lead her into mischief.''

"I'm sorry, your lordship.''

"We learn by our mistakes, sweet child.''

"I suppose so. Well, what do we do now? We're paupers, we are.''

"Lady Josquinilliu, no self-respecting bravo possessed of a blade shall remain a pauper for long. Victims abound and our services are everywhere in demand. Fortunately we need no longer rely upon the whims of our patrons to maintain comfortable livelihood. Out of seeming misfortune, great good may arise.''

"What do you—?" Josky's eyes fastened on the quaking helmsman still kneeling at their feet, and she took her father's meaning. "Oh. I see. The *boat*. Yes, I see!''

"The boat. Just so. In view of the dangers to which we have subjected ourselves, we are surely entitled. And with this venerise upon which to build our fortunes, the House of Didnis shall once again be numbered among the great.''

"SuPREME, Dad! Where'll we go, then?''

"Anywhere we choose. Perhaps I'll carry my Josky to the shining cities over the sea. We might visit Szar or Strell, or we might marvel at the cloud-capped towers of glorius Ny Yuivawn. Or perhaps we might journey to the interior of Dalyon itself, where we'll rule our own kingdom, and my Josky shall be a true princess indeed. What would my Josky like best?''

"They all sound good, your lordship. But it is really grotesque that we have to leave Lanthi Ume without finishing the job we took on. I don't like to lose, I don't. And running away like this—it's like we were banished or something.''

"My lady, no venture culminating in the acquisition of a vessel such as this one may be counted a failure. In the truest sense we may consider ourselves victorious. As for running away, we do no such thing. We spurn the city. Disenchanted with the crassness of all Lanthians, we withdraw in displeasure.

We banish *them*. We bestow our presence upon another place. Be of good cheer, my treasure. There is a world elsewhere.''

Josky nodded, her eyes alight. For a moment the two stood, hands clasped, lost in their vision of a golden future. Then reality reasserted itself, and Whurm Didnis turned to the helmsman. "Stand, fellow," he commanded.

The helmsman obeyed with alacrity.

"You will convey us from the city without delay. If you wish to preserve your life, you will obey all my commands and all commands of the Lady Josquinilliu without argument, reserve, or hesitation. You will steer the venerise, maintain order, and attend to our personal comforts. Is that understood?''

The hapless hostage nodded.

"Good. Then take us hence, at your best speed!"

Under the eyes of his captors, the helmsman descended from the quarterdeck to take the tiller. The appropriate Cognitive commands were uttered, the venerise lifted her bow from the water and flew forward like a hawk released from bondage.

"Oh, suPREEEEEEEEEME!" the Lady Josky exclaimed ecstatically, the words torn from her lips to trail upon the wind.

Past sleeping palaces and mansions they flashed, along the canal past parks, gardens, towers and monuments, market squares, slums, and follies glittering under the moon. At length they reached Jherova, swinging northwest around that outermost island to hug the irregular coastline. With the fairy lights of Jherova twinkling at their back, they sped into outer darkness, And thus *Sublimity* passed from Lanthi Ume, her final destination a mystery.

Through the Destula fled Duke Povon, nearly delirious with terror. He found himself alone and lost in a strange and terrible place. He was wet clear through and the knife wound in his shoulder burned unbearbly. He might or might not be pursued by killers, set upon him, so they claimed, by his son Sneever. *Sneever!* The warm tranquility of the Moon Dream had vanished, and nothing now served to shield his mind from the disagreeable reality. Povon was unused to fear and pain. Tears mingled with the canal water that dripped from the ducal visage.

On he went, short legs churning as they carried him deeper into the slum, but he was growing winded quickly. Soon his breath was coming in gasps, and his footsteps faltered. He did not dare to stop, but his pace slowed and the nature of his surroundings began to impress itself upon his reluctant senses. He trotted along a narrow alley of excremental atmosphere. On either side rose the decaying tenements whose projecting faces, nearly meeting overhead, blackly shadowed all but a narrow strip down the middle of the street, where an open kennel ran loathsome in the moonlight. Upon the ubiquitous heaps of refuse the rats ranged openly. The creatures did not bother to flee at his approach, and he endured the full beady battery of their insolent eyes as he passed. But Povon suspected that eyes were more sentient than those of the rats observed his progress. The alley was deserted, every window in sight close-shuttered, but who could guess what sinister sentinels those darkened sockets might conceal? Poven sensed, with sudden and horrible certainty, that he was watched by more than rats and that the regard was far from benevolent. And the icy fear crept like a glacier along his veins, raising the gooseflesh as it went, stirring the hair at the back of his neck and freezing him by inches. Only the hot trickle of blood from his wounded shoulder remained untouched by cold. A thin, keening whimper of anguish escaped him and he shrank back into the shadows, paralyzed with terror but for the moment surely hidden from view. There in the fetid darkness crouched his Grace, helpless and racked with fits of trembling. But in the midst of all his agony and bewilderment, one thought rose above all others, rose so strong and certain that it found voice:

"This is wrong. I am Duke and never meant to suffer. Someone should tend to me."

His whispering voice hissed along the silent alley, to be answered by the chitter of rats. So deep a chord of truth was struck that Povon repeated himself.

"Someone should tend to me."

But who? Who would succor the Duke?

Into his mind flashed the image of a face—a waxen, high-browed, basilisk-eyed countenance marked with eccentric furrows.

"Nulliad," muttered his Grace.

He recalled that he had come to this place in search of Nulliad's counsel. He recalled too that the very mention of the Expulsion's name had tamed the ferocity of the Destulan hooligans. Nulliad, a force to be reckoned with, could surely offer aid if not comfort. With Nulliad he would be safe. But where in this detestable warren was the Expulsion to be found? Dimly

Povon recalled an alley whose entrance was marked with a carven salamander, and from thence a short passage to a stygian cul-de-sac. He frowned, trying to remember. To reach the alley, it was necessary to walk alongside the water for a way. Of that he was nearly certain. He needed to return to the water.

It was only with an effort that Duke Povon could bring himself to emerge from the sheltering shadows. Reluctantly he rose to retrace his steps. His progress was stumbling and cautious. Periodically he paused, hand pressed tight to his reddened shoulder, to strain his ears for the sound of pursuit. He never heard it, and presently he emerged from between two ghostly abandoned storehouses to behold the moonlight dancing upon the ripples of the Straightwater Canal. Povon surveyed the water. *Sublimity* was gone. His beloved venerise had vanished with all aboard. His crew, whose chiefest concern should have been his welfare, had abandoned him in this dreadful spot. They were faithless, untrustworthy, and utterly selfish, as all of his subjects were. Perhaps—the Duke swallowed hard at the thought—perhaps they were actually traitors. Had they conspired against him? If so, he would be revenged. There were many pleasing forms that retribution might take, but now was not the time to address such matters, consoling though they were. Povon turned to the left, stumbling along the embankment. The pain in his shoulder was growing worse, pain far greater than he had ever known, hot and throbbing like a living thing. Such agony was bewildering, almost overwhelming. He sobbed quietly and his tears blurred the moonlit world. On he stumbled, past dark squalid dwellings, deserted piers, and past a cloaked trio of such quietly threatening aspect that he dared not pause to beg assistance.

On he went, so preoccupied with his own misery that he scarcely noted the path before him until a sharp hiss halted him in his tracks. Dashing the tears from his eyes, Duke Povon looked down to find the ground at his feet alive with slinking forms. They were too large for rats. For a moment he stared uncomprehending, then glanced up to find he had come to the Bridge of Spiteful Cats. There it rose, its scarred old span crowded with hundreds upon hundreds of feral felines, an entire self-sufficient population of them. They crouched there motionless, watching him with their strange violet eyes, and Povon experienced a momentary qualm. Was there not some talk that the creatures were vicious? Had there not been some project afoot years earlier to exterminate the dangerous vermin? Povon himself had opposed the needlessly expensive undertaking.

It would almost seem that they were warning him, even threatening him. His presence, the message seemed to be, would not be tolerated upon or near the Bridge of Spiteful Cats. But that was clearly ridiculous. He was Duke of Lanthi Ume and hardly apt to alter his course for sake of a tribe of stray tabbies.

Nulliad and safety lay beyond the bridge. Povon resumed his advance, and the affronted cats converged around him. They blocked the path ahead, and now they were in back of him as well. He couldn't walk forward without striking them. His silk-shod foot encountered a lithe body. He heard a yowl of rage, and the creature spun to drive its claws and needle fangs into his calf. Povon yelped and kicked, but the cat clung grimly. At last he bent, seized the animal by the scruff of the neck, jerked it loose, and flung it aside into the Straightwater Canal.

At this a symphony of sinister hisses arose, so malevolent that Povon flinched at the sound of it, paused and attempted to back away. He backed into a couple of cats, who instantly attached their hissing selves to his ankles. Povon kicked violently, and one of the felines went flying. Its place was immediately taken by two others that could not be dislodged. Small and light though they were, their ferocity was inordinate and their little fangs sank deep. A howl of pain and fear escaped Duke Povon, and the bridge cats' savage chorus rose in response. One of the creatures launched itself in a prodigious leap that landed it upon the trespasser's shoulder, to which it clung screeching and clawing. Its talons raked Duke Povon's face and its teeth jabbed the side of his neck. Blood flowed freely. The Duke screamed, flailed, and kicked wildly. Other cats leaped and Povon staggered beneath the assault, tottering backward until a cunning sinuous form managed to wind itself between his legs. The Duke tripped and went down to sprawl full length upon the embankment. Instantly he disappeared beneath a writhing, screeching, clawing mound of cats. They were all over him, scores of them, clinging with particular avidity to his throat and face. He could not draw a breath to scream for help. He was blinded, deafened, overwhelmed. The oddly sweet odor of their fur filled his nostrils, and with it mixed the scent of his own blood. Blood was pouring from a hundred bites and scratches, blood filled his eyes, and his strength was leaving him. His struggles were almost halfhearted as he felt them begin to drag his body away. The transport was slow, progressing in a series of starts and stops, but it was inexorable.

They found the Duke's suggestively diminished carcass two days later in the wynd behind the abandoned warehouse a short distance from the bridge. So great was the transformation that another three days passed before his Grace could be identified.

Following the death of his father, Lord Sneever Dil Shonnet assumed the title of Duke. His investiture was greeted by the public with the dutiful resignation appropriate to the exit of a distrusted ruler and the succession of an equally unpromising heir. If the spirits of the Lanthians were lukewarm, however, Lord Sneever's were white-hot.

To be Duke! To rule at last! To be the master of all he surveyed! Thus ran Duke Sneever's thoughts as he supervised the transfer of his belongings from his own chambers to the suite of rooms formerly occupied by his father. To be sure, life was not altogether devoid of puzzles and problems—life never was. Certain unsolved mysteries yet remained to trouble Sneever's mind. What, for example, had been Duke Povon's purpose the night of his death in strolling the Destula unattended? What had become of the great Cognitive venerise *Sublimity* and all aboard? And above all, what had become of the hired assassin who might or might not have fulfilled his commission? In view of his evident success, why did not Whurm Didnis step forward to demand payment? But then, *had* he been successful? The Duke Povon was dead, certainly, but not by stroke of axe or knife—rather, by the claws and fangs of spiteful cats. Could the bravo rightfully claim credit for the deed? Should he appear, was he entitled to recompense? Was Didnis responsible for the disappearance of *Sublimity*? In short, what had actually transpired?

Duke Sneever pondered at length, but reached no satisfactory conclusion. There was no point in dwelling upon insoluble mysteries, particularly with so many more pleasant matters to occupy his attention. The obligations of sovereignty were more than balanced by its pleasures, or so it seemed to Sneever. The respect, deference, and adulation he now received were balm to his ancient wounds. Thus his spirits were high upon the evening two weeks subsequent to Duke Povon's obsequies that the Keldhaam Gnuxia presented herself at the door of his new apartment. Gnuxia was overwhelming as ever, but this time she held no terror. He was prepared for the interview and able to greet her with composure, even assurance.

Sneever conferred with her in his private audience chamber, while her women remained in the antechamber. The magnificence of the surroundings together with his own newfound greatness lent him unwonted confidence. His nervous tics were under control, his manner dignified as never before. For the first time he felt competent to deal with the Keldhaam Gnuxia. Leaning back in his great chair and assuming an expression of perceptibly patronizing kindness, he launched into his carefully rehearsed speech. "My dear Keldhaam, misfortune unites us. As I have lost a beloved father, so you have lost an equally revered betrothed. We share each other's sorrows and yet I fear your woes transcend my own, for you now find yourself alone, a helpless woman and a foreigner in our midst. The warm affection you have inspired in the hearts of all Lanthians during the term of your visit may perhaps provide some comfort, but—alas!—cannot alter the sad realities of your situation. Therefore it is fitting that I, as Duke, shall do aught in my power to ease the lot of one who was so nearly—my mother. Rest assured that you will enjoy my protection until such time as you choose to satisfy a doubtless fervent longing for your Lammish home and your own kinsmen. Despite our own deep attachments, we shall not attempt to deprive you of such solace. Therefore, dear lady, until the very morn of your departure, our common grief shall make us one."

"More than grief shall make us one," Gnuxia informed him, and something in her tone caused him to glance at her in sudden uneasiness.

"Keldhaam?"

"I have this very day received a letter from my father, his Splendor the Keldhar of Gard Lammis," Gnuxia announced grimly. "You yourself will undoubtedly receive a communication of similar nature, relayed by means of official envoy within the near future. In view of the Lanthian tendency toward carelessness and procrastination, the news is apt to be delayed, and therefore I myself have undertaken to notify you of my father's wishes. His Splendor has expressed the desire, or rather the *resolve*, that we two shall be wed. As you have correctly surmised, I long for Gard Lammis. However, his Splendor is best served by my presence here in Lanthi Ume, and therefore I must resign myself to marriage. Sir, I consent to be your wife.''

Sneever stared at her, aghast. For a moment he gasped for air, then managed to reply, ''Keldhaam, I do not see how that can be.''

''It shall be. His Splendor wishes it.''

''It—it cannot be right. You were affianced to my father—''

''Sir, you have inherited your father's responsibilities as well as his privileges. I, the Keldhaam Gnuxia, daughter to his Splendor the Keldhar, was the greatest of your father's responsibilities.''

''I—I am n-not certain it is legal.''

''If it is not, then the trifling law will be changed.''

''But—t-that is to say—''

''We must do something about that stammer of yours, Betrothed. It is not fitting that the ruler of even such a place as Lanthi Ume shall exhibit vocal deformity. It may be that a course of physic is endicated. I will set about devising one. Your father, well acquainted with my decoctions, valued them according to their merits. You shall do likewise.''

For the first time since Duke Povon's death, Sneever's right eyelid began to twitch. Gnuxia studied the motion with alarming attentiveness.

''It—it isn't possible for me to think of marriage now,'' Duke Sneever muttered at last. ''Not yet. Not—not until the war is over.''

''War? What war? What nonsense is this?''

''My father's war against the White Demons of the Caverns. My brave father's war must be carried to a successful conclusion.''

''War? How like a Lanthian to term that grubby little exchange a *war*. In Gard Lammis we would call it a skirmish. And how like your fatuous father to send his mortal Guardsmen against demons armed with supernatural power! Commander Krufaure, with whom I have enjoyed several illuminating discussions, has described the entire affair.''

''Nevertheless, the war must be finished,'' Sneever insisted feebly.

''The war *is* finished,'' Gnuxia informed him. ''*I say it is finished!* That foolish endeavor, so pointless and ill-conceived from the very beginning, was a product of your father's despic-

able vices, the rotten fruit of his delirious dreams. It was a
waste of money, men, weapons, and time. In life, your father
was deaf to reason. But now that he is dead, his folly shall not
continue. There will be no further attacks upon the caverns of
the Nazara Sin. It is over. His Splendor, concerned for the
state of the Lanthian economy, will doubtless support me in
this. The war is finished. Do you understand me, Betrothed?''

Sneever nodded wordlessly.

"*I say, do you understand me?* Answer, sir!''

"Yes, Keldhaam. Yes.''

"That is satisfactory. I will leave you now, but presently I
shall return bearing a potion of my own creation, designed to
remedy the obvious deficiencies of your vocal cords. From
there we will proceed to your other deficiencies, on which I
hereby declare war, for I am the sworn enemy of all physical
and moral imperfections. Rest assured, sir, you have fallen
into capable hands. And so I will bid you adieu—for now.''

The Keldhaam Gnuxia turned on her heel and strode from
the audience chamber. Sneever sat quite still, watching her go.
Both his eyelids were jerking violently.

A few days later the Keldhar's letter arrived, its contents
exactly as Gnuxia had predicted. His Splendor, urging the
innumerable benefits of so brilliant a match, earnestly besought
the new Duke's signature upon a formal contract of betrothal.
At first his Grace was inclined to demur. However, following
a conference with his treasurer and various bookkeepers, during
which the extent and terms of the Lammish debt were revealed
to him for the first time, Duke Sneever found it expedient to
agree.

Chapter Fourteen

The great brown bat swooped into the chamber and alighted before Lady Verran. Stooping, she detached the tiny pouch from the animal's collar, loosened the strings, and shook forth a collection of colored pebbles. She stared at the stones in surprise.

"What is it?" inquired Har Fennahar.

"A summons," she told him. "From Terrs."

"Finally. Are you going to him now?"

She nodded. "I almost feel nervous about seeing him again, after all that's happened. He's been through so much, and changed so that it seems I hardly know him anymore. And now, after this long silence, I don't know how to approach him."

"Would you like me to come with you?"

"Very much," she replied at once, then added hesitantly, "if you're well enough."

"Of course I'm well enough," he replied, and she did not argue a point whose truth was self-evident.

Fennahar's wound, stitched shut with lengths of boiled fiber, was all but healed. He was strong again, healthy, and undoubtedly eager to leave the caverns. She could see it in his face, in his eyes, in every gesture—he wanted fresh air and sunlight. He wanted to go, and he wanted her beside him. Throughout the slow Small Vens of Terrs's solitary retreat, however, the explorer had not once pressed her for a decision, for which she was grateful. While her son wrestled with his personal demons, she could hardly abandon him. Unlikely though it seemed, Terrs might want or even need the comfort of his mother's presence. On the other hand, Fennahar's tact was admirable and his patience great, but not inexhaustible. How long could she expect him to wait?

But now the suspense was about to end, and Verran found herself prey to curious anxiety. In what state of mind would Terrs emerge from his solitude? The possibilities were varied, but one thing was certain—the effects of his long isolation would be profound. Of that she had no doubt.

Together they walked the corridors, soon arriving at the mouth of the narrow tunnel that led to the Stronghold wherein Terrs had spent the solitary Small Vens. There they found F'tryll'jnr Rdsdr and a couple of his armed F'tryll'jnr kinsmen standing guard at the entrance. Verran was taken aback—the sentries were a new and unpleasant manifestation of the changes overtaking the caverns. Briefly she wondered if Fennahar would be challenged. The F'tryll'jnrs, however, made no attempt to detain the humans, merely uttering courteous trills as the two edged sideways through the pinched opening.

At the end of the passage, curtains masked the entrance to the Stronghold. Verran paused there. Her heartbeat quickened and instinctively she reached for Fennahar's hand, found it and held on tight. Only then did she call aloud, "Terrs? Are you there?"

"Come in, Mother."

Surely his voice had altered? Or had it always been so beautifully musical? Verran and Fennahar slipped through the curtains and froze, staring.

Terrs was unclothed. Even in the absence of natural rocklight, the new luminosity of his flesh would have illumined his metamorphosis. Arms, legs, torso—all were startlingly transformed. But it was upon his head rather than his body that his mother's gaze rested longest. Terrs's thick black hair, eyebrows, and lashes were gone. The contours of the skull beneath the glowing scalp were subtly alien. The features had acquired a new, intense angularity and the lips had all but disappeared. Concentric ridges of muscle ringed the eyes, wherein Terrs's single failure revealed itself. For in contrast to the foam-pale eyes of the true clan members, the convert retained intensely black irises. Failure notwithstanding, those strange hybrid eyes reflected a new—peace? Tranquility?

Harmony. The word is harmony, Verran thought, and wondered at her own composure. Fennahar was clutching her hand so hard that it hurt, and he had gone white. But she herself was calm. She realized then how long she had steeled herself to withstand this moment. What she had feared so much had come at last, it was here, and her heart was not breaking. Rather she was filled with calm acceptance, even something akin to relief that the waiting was over. Aloud she could only ask quietly, "And are you content at last, Terrs?"

"More than content, Mother." No question but his voice possessed an alien resonance never there before. "For the first time, I am no longer alone—no longer locked in the solitary prison of self."

"What do you mean?"

"Mother, I have touched others at last. I have known the Ancestors. I have known the Fal Grizhni Patriarch. I have known his power and his anger and all that he was. It is clear now." His luminosity mounted as he spoke, triumph manifesting itself in the level of his newly acquired hiir.

"You were close to Lord Grizhni?"

"I felt his ruu. I have a clan."

He took her hand, twining his tenacles about her fingers, and she saw his flesh lighten to a white, impossible brilliance as he experienced the clan-warmth—the current of oneness and understanding that surged only at the touch of a kinsman—for the first time.

Verran thought she sensed a faint response thrilling along her own nerves. Imagination? She was not certain. For a moment there was silence as she watched his flickering flesh and the undulations of his ocular ridges reflect his reactions to experiences she could never share, never understand. At last she said, "I am happy for your—your new harmony. I am glad that you have what you wanted so much. But I don't know what to say to you."

"That is because there is little left to say." Terrs's flesh dimmed and he released her hand abruptly. "Not long ago, you told me that you and Fennahar intend to leave the caverns together. It is a wise decision, for this is not a place for humans. You urged me then to accompany you. My transformation answers you. I belong here now, and I cannot leave. You are unselfish to rejoice in my success, Mother, for you are well aware that it must separate us."

Verran bowed her head wordlessly, but Fennahar observed, "Terrs, it isn't impossible for you to come with us, even now.

You have the Cognition to reverse the change, if you wish.''

Terrs curled his tentacles backward in the Vardrul gesture of negation. ''The thought of assuming my old deformities fills me with such horror that I do not believe I could achieve the Cognition to do it. Cognition does not visit the reluctant, unfocused mind.''

''Won't you consider trying it, even briefly, for your mother's sake?''

''Fennahar, you are one with whom I have shaken hands, but I must refuse you. My place is here and I wish no other home. I will employ my powers, such as they are, in defense of the clans. I will seal the great dazzles, and camouflage the small entrances by Cognition, and then perhaps we shall be safe from human invasion forever. I shall choose a sister/consort and my clan will grow.''

Verran was startled into speech. ''Zmadrc Fourteen—?''

''—Will always live in my memory. But I must choose a new consort, and the clan of Fal Grizhni will continue in this place. So the Grizhni Ancestors would wish.'' The two humans were silent, and after a brief pause, Terrs inquired, ''Where will you go?''

''To Szar or Strell, perhaps,'' Fennahar told him. ''We can't go back to Lanthi Ume, but we won't want. My brother Frev will see to our welfare.''

While he spoke, Verran's eyes ranged the Stronghold, coming to rest on a niche wherein lay a folio volume, a roll of parchment, a leather binder, and a thin plaque of gold. ''The records,'' she said. ''Lord Grizhni's records. We must take them.''

''No, Mother.'' Terrs spoke with quiet finality.

''They'll be returned to you, I promise. You know how desperately they're needed.''

''No. I have instructed the various kinsmen not to permit the writings from the caverns.''

''How dare you? Those records were given to me!''

''But not to use contrary to the Grizhni Patriarch's desires and intentions. You act as his adversary now. You attempt to thwart his plans, but I will defend them.''

''What do you know of Lord Grizhni's plans?''

''Much. I have known the Fal Grizhni Patriarch, Mother. I have *known* him. His anger was bitter and endless as death. It was his desire to inflict vengeance upon his murderers. It was his intention to smite Lanthi Ume, to bury her in darkness forever, and to deprive humanity of the island of Dalyon. I will not oppose the Patriarch's designs, and I will not allow you to do so. The Patriarch's intentions will be fulfilled."

"Terrs, he acted in great anger, at the height of his fury. Your father was by no means devoid of kindness and mercy. If he had had more time, time to reflect—"

"We cannot assume he would have reconsidered. The Knowledge of Ancestors has taught me much. My father's Cognition presages the emergence of the Vardruls from our caverns. Our clan prophecies foretell the coming of a great ruler who will lead us back to the Surface that is rightfully ours. Perhaps I am that ruler, or perhaps it is one of my descendants. Certainly that hope inspired the Grizhni Patriarch, whose Cognition will prepare the Surface for our coming. We do not know when the change will occur, but the Patriarch may sleep secure in the knowledge that we shall be ready."

"Have you no sense of justice? Or pity?"

"Yes, for the clan members persecuted by men. But come, Mother. Must we quarrel to the very end? We are soon to part. Let us make our peace."

"That's what I want, too, Terrs! Only—don't you see? Can't you understand how many will suffer? Haven't you any concern for the innocent of your own kind?"

"They are no longer my own kind."

"You think not?" She faced him squarely. "There's a very great deal of the humam left in you, and it will always be there, Terrs. Always."

"If so, I will surely overcome it. I am a Vardrul."

The curse of Fal Grizhni descends on Lanthi Ume in *King of Darkness*, coming in 1989 from Ace Books.

CAPTIVATING TALES OF FANTASY WORLDS BY TODAY'S BRIGHTEST YOUNG AUTHORS

PATRICIA McKILLIP

___ 0-425-09452-9	The Forgotten Beasts of Eld	$2.95
___ 0-425-09206-2	The Moon and the Face	$2.95
___ 0-425-08457-4	Moon-Flash	$2.75

ROBIN McKINLEY

___ 0-425-08840-5	The Blue Sword	$2.95
___ 0-441-10149-5	The Hero and The Crown	$2.95

PATRICIA C. WREDE

___ 0-441-13897-7	Daughter of Witches	$2.95
___ 0-441-31759-6	The Harp of Imach Thyssel	$2.95
___ 0-441-75976-9	The Seven Towers	$2.95
___ 0-441-76014-7	Shadow Magic	$2.95
___ 0-441-79591-9	Talking to Dragons	$2.25
___ 0-441-76006-6	Caught in Crystal	$2.95

JANE YOLEN

___ 0-441-09167-9	Cards of Grief	$2.75
